How the Scoundrel Seduces

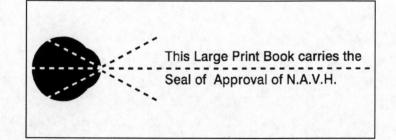

This Large Print Book carries the
Seal of Approval of N.A.V.H.

HOW THE SCOUNDREL SEDUCES

SABRINA JEFFRIES

THORNDIKE PRESS

A part of Gale, Cengage Learning

GALE
CENGAGE Learning·

Farmington Hills, Mich • San Francisco • New York • Waterville, Maine
Meriden, Conn • Mason, Ohio • Chicago

GALE
CENGAGE Learning·

Copyright © 2014 by Deborah Gonzales.
Thorndike Press, a part of Gale, Cengage Learning.

Thorndike Press® Large Print Romance.
The text of this Large Print edition is unabridged.
Other aspects of the book may vary from the original edition.
Set in 16 pt. Plantin.

LIBRARY OF CONGRESS CATALOGING-IN-PUBLICATION DATA

Jeffries, Sabrina.
   How the scoundrel seduces / Sabrina Jeffries. — Large print edition.
      pages cm. — (Thorndike Press large print romance)
   ISBN 978-1-4104-7306-6 (hardcover) — ISBN 1-4104-7306-6 (hardcover)
   1. Nobility—England—Fiction. 2. Romanies—Fiction. 3. Family secrets—Fiction. 4. Large type books. I. Title.
PS3610.E39H687 2014
813'.6—dc23   2014028753

Published in 2014 by arrangement with Pocket Books, a division of Simon & Schuster, Inc.

Printed in Mexico
1 2 3 4 5 6 7 18 17 16 15 14

To the wonderful staff at Creative Living
—
thanks for everything you do.

THE DUKE'S MEN SERIES
FAMILY TREE

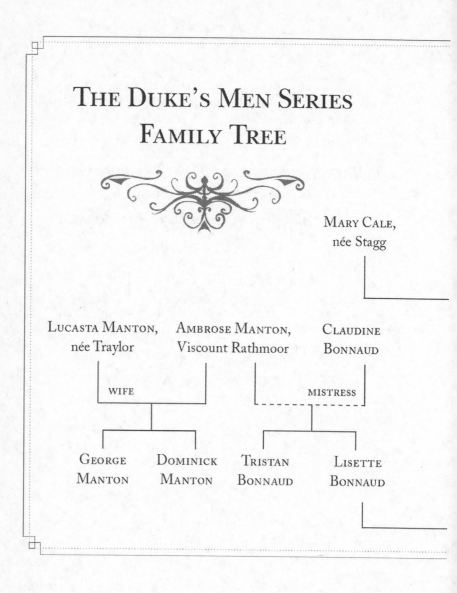

Mary Cale,
née Stagg

Lucasta Manton,
née Traylor   Ambrose Manton,
Viscount Rathmoor   Claudine
Bonnaud

WIFE   MISTRESS

George
Manton   Dominick
Manton   Tristan
Bonnaud   Lisette
Bonnaud

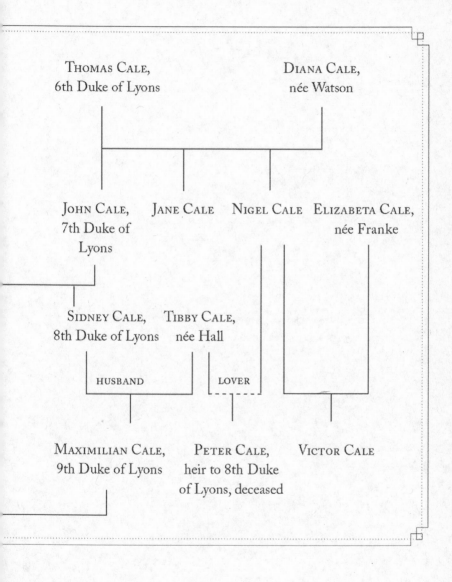

Thomas Cale,
6th Duke of Lyons

Diana Cale,
née Watson

John Cale,
7th Duke of
Lyons

Jane Cale

Nigel Cale

Elizabeta Cale,
née Franke

Sidney Cale,
8th Duke of Lyons

Tibby Cale,
née Hall

HUSBAND

LOVER

Maximilian Cale,
9th Duke of Lyons

Peter Cale,
heir to 8th Duke
of Lyons, deceased

Victor Cale

PROLOGUE

Yorkshire
1816

With daylight fading in the Viscount Rathmoor's bedchamber, seventeen-year-old Tristan fought to free his hand from his father's grip. He should go light a candle and stoke the fire, perhaps even see if the doctor had arrived.

But Father was having none of that. "Don't leave me."

"I just thought I should —"

"Stay with me." He clutched Tristan's hand hard enough to hurt.

Tristan avoided looking at the red stain soaking the hasty dressing that he and the groom had inexpertly applied to the viscount's wound. Father had gone through worse. He'd once faced down native pirates in Borneo and lived to tell the tale. He was good at having adventures. And telling tales.

Tristan's throat tightened. Father was

good at everything . . . except caring for his family. Or rather, his *families.*

Using Tristan's hand for leverage, Father tried to pull himself into a sitting position.

"Don't!" Tristan cried. "You have to conserve your strength until the doctor arrives."

Father shivered. "No point, lad. I'm dying. Up to you . . . to take care of . . . your mother and sister. You're . . . the man of the house now."

Panic seized Tristan. "You mustn't say that. You'll be fine."

Father *had* to be fine. If he died, Mother and Lisette would never survive it.

He swallowed his tears, determined not to shame himself, then drew the cover up to his father's chin in an attempt to stop the trembling. Father was just cold. Someone really should stoke the fire.

"Get away from him!" ordered a voice from the door. "You have no right to touch him."

He bristled at the sight of George Manton, his loathed half brother, nine years his senior. George was heir to the Rathmoor title and estate because he'd been born on the right side of the blanket.

Tristan had not. Which was why everyone in town called him "the French bastard," even though he was only half-French and had been born and raised right here at Rathmoor Park.

"Leave the lad . . . alone," Father managed. "I want him with me."

George entered, his eyes glittering in the candlelight. "Your damned by-blow is probably responsible for getting you shot in the first place."

"That's a lie!" Tristan cried, half rising in his chair.

"Enough." Father's breath came in staccato gasps, like that of a prime goer in the final lengths of a race. "No one's fault. Gun misfired. It . . . was an accident."

"We'll see about that," George said. "You can be sure I'll speak to the groom and whoever else was present."

"Where's Dom?" Father asked. "I need . . . Dom."

When George grimaced, Tristan prepared himself for anything. George resented Dominick, his legitimate younger brother, almost as much as he resented his half siblings, probably because Dom's birth had caused the death of Lady Rathmoor when George was only seven.

Perhaps that was why Dom and Tristan had taken to each other like collies to cattle — the fact that George wanted nothing to do with either of them. Besides, in the eyes of the law, a second son was only slightly superior to a natural son, since the future of either still depended on their father's whim. That alone cemented their brotherly friendship.

"Dom's still in York," Tristan told his father. "He should return tonight."

"Can't wait," Father ground out. "Must do this . . . now. Fetch . . . my writing desk."

Father's fractured speech sparked Tristan's alarm. When George didn't immediately act, Tristan jumped up and pushed past the burly arse to get to the portable writing desk their father had carried through Egypt, France, Siam, and whatever other place had seized his fancy in the past two and a half decades.

As he brought it back, Father dragged in a laboring breath. "Write this down, lad."

With a wary glance at the fuming George, Tristan took out the quill and inkpot to record the words his father dictated in halting speech: "I, Ambrose Manton . . . Viscount Rathmoor, being of sound . . . mind, make this addition . . . to my will and testament." Father paused to catch his breath. "To my natural son Tristan Bonnaud, I bequeath my gelding . . . Blue Blazes —"

"Father!" George said sharply. "Blue

12

Blazes should go to Dom or me."

Father's gaze grew steely. "I promised him to . . . your half brother last year. Tristan picked the Thoroughbred for me, so the lad should . . . have him."

George flushed as Tristan hastily wrote the words. Tristan loved Blue Blazes, who'd earned top prizes ever since Father had bought him at an auction in York. No surprise that George wanted the gelding, but honestly, George would inherit every-thing else. He didn't have to have Blue Blazes, too.

And did this mean that Father hadn't put them in his will at *all*? How could that be?

When Father went on to make provisions for Dom, Tristan bent his head to hide his dismay. Bad enough for Father to be hap-hazard about his natural children, but about Dom? It wasn't right.

Then Father left several trinkets from his travels to Lisette, and the cottage and an annuity of two hundred pounds to Mother, his mistress for the past twenty-some years. Whom he'd kept promising to marry, but never had, because of the possible scandal. And now there would never be a chance of it.

Father would survive. He must!

"One more thing, lad," Father rasped.

13

"Put down that Fowler will . . . train you as his . . . assistant."

As George swore under his breath, Tristan hastily scribbled the words. Father had talked for years about Tristan's learning to be a land agent under the present one, but Tristan had never dared hope for that. He couldn't imagine anything more wonderful than working with Fowler, and perhaps replacing the older man one day.

When he was done, Father reviewed the paper, then thrust it at George. "Sign it . . . and put 'witness' beneath your name. No one will . . . question the codicil . . . if *you* sign. It goes against your . . . interests."

George crossed his arms over his chest. "Aye, it does. Which is precisely why I *won't* sign."

A shrewd expression crossed Father's face. "I may yet . . . live, boy. The doctor is . . . on his way. If I survive . . . I'll make you regret . . . defying me."

Father could do it, too. If he chose to sell off unentailed portions or mortgage the lot, George would spend the rest of his life digging out from under the debts. Besides which, George depended on Father for money until he inherited.

Tristan held his breath. As long as George couldn't see the rapidly spreading red stain hidden beneath the heavy covers, he might acquiesce.

The sound of hoofbeats outside apparently decided him. George grabbed the codicil and the quill from Tristan and signed. But then he just stood there staring at the paper.

Father held out a trembling hand. "Give it to me."

George hesitated.

"Give . . . it . . . to . . . me . . ." Father choked out, but his voice was clearly weakening.

Tristan leaned forward to raise Father's head and plump his pillow. "Hold on, Father." His stomach lurched. "Help is nigh. You can't leave us. You can't!"

Father's eyes clouded over. "Get . . . the . . . paper, Tristan. Promise me . . . you'll give it . . . to Dom."

"Quiet now." A chill wracked Tristan at seeing Father's struggle to speak.

"Promise me!" his father said through clenched teeth.

"I promise. Now be still." Tristan held his hand out to George. "Give it to me, all right? Can't you see it's upsetting him?"

But George stood frozen, his eyes fixed on the damned piece of paper. Then they both heard a gurgling sound, and George jerked

15

his gaze up. "Father?" He went to stand on the viscount's other side. "Father!"

Blood trickled from Father's mouth, and Tristan's pulse faltered. "No, this can't be happening! No, no, no . . . Father!"

He cradled Father's head in his hands, but Father's eyes were fixed now, and his chest didn't move.

"We have to help him," Tristan told George. "We have to do *something*!"

"Move away!"

Tristan backed off. George set down the codicil, then bent to shake Father's shoulders. "Father," he said firmly. "Damn it, wake up!"

When the glassy stare didn't alter, George grabbed a hand mirror from the dressing table and held it over Father's mouth. Then he let out a low curse.

"Well?" Tristan asked fearfully.

George's face looked carved in stone. "There's no breath. He's dead."

"That's a lie!" In a frenzy, Tristan tried to revive his father, chafing his hands and rubbing his chest, but that eerie stare never altered. For once, George was telling the truth.

Tristan's blood ran like sludge through his veins. Father was gone. They would never again attend races together, never go hunting grouse or deer. There would be no more lazy evenings at the cottage while Father regaled them with wild tales of his travels.

Ruthlessly, Tristan fought back tears. His half brother would mock him, especially since George wasn't crying himself — though he stared fixedly at Father as if to glower the man into reviving.

"What do we do?" Tristan whispered.

"*We* do nothing. I'll mourn my father's passing and see to his burial. *You* will leave this house. Now."

Shock gripped Tristan. "You wouldn't . . . Surely you can't mean to banish me from —"

George reached over to close Father's eyes and pull the cover over his face. "I mean to do whatever I please from this day on. I own this house and everything in it." He fixed Tristan with a look of pure vitriol. "So you are to get out and never darken these doors again."

The command wasn't entirely unexpected. Tristan had only ever been welcomed inside by Father and Dom, and now even Dom would hesitate to go against George.

Thinking of Dom reminded Tristan of his promise. Dom was studying to be a barrister and thus knew about legal matters. That was

17

why Father wanted *him* to have the codicil.

Tristan rounded the bed, heading for the side table where George had set the paper down, but George blocked his path.

"Let me pass," Tristan said.

"Not on your life."

Fear froze Tristan's spine. If George didn't honor the document . . .

No, surely even George wasn't *that* awful. "I promised Father I'd give Dom the codicil. Surely you won't prevent me from keeping my promise."

Like a crow feeding on carrion, George pecked at his hopes. "If you think I'll let you and your whoring mother cheat me out of one penny of my inheritance, you're mad."

Whoring mother. Damn it, Tristan had heard those words far too often from George. He thrust his face into his brother's. "If you ever dare to call my mother a whore again, I'll beat you to a bloody pulp."

George snorted. "You can try. But I was always able to trounce you. That hasn't changed."

The hell it hadn't. Tristan lunged for the document, hoping to take George off guard, but George anticipated the move and tossed the codicil into the fire.

"No!" Tristan cried, turning for the hearth.

George caught him from behind, hanging on no matter how Tristan fought to get free. "You'll never see Blue Blazes again, you hear me?" George hissed. "And you'll damned well never be trained as a land agent, if I have anything to say about it."

Tristan's heart constricted as he watched his hopes burn. "Father wanted me to have a future." It was proof of his love, and God knew Tristan had few enough of those. "You would go against his dying wish?"

Now that the document was ashes, George shoved Tristan aside. "He wasn't in his right mind. And I'm not going to put up with you hanging about Rathmoor Park for the rest of my life, fomenting scandal everywhere we go."

Scandal. Tristan was sick to death of it. Thanks to the Manton fear of scandal, Mother had never had a chance at a decent life. He couldn't let George do this!

"So why not give me Blue Blazes?" At least then Tristan could race the animal and perhaps support his family that way. "You have plenty of other fine horses. You don't need Blue Blazes, too!"

"You wouldn't know what to do with the beast even if you did own it," George spat.

"It's not as if you'll have the money to take care of it."

"I could race him —"

"Where?" George's cold gaze flicked dismissively over Tristan. "Do you actually think racing gentlemen will allow a Frenchy bastard like you to move in their circles? They only tolerated you because of Father."

"That's not true!" Tristan cried, though he feared it was. "Everyone says I know a lot about horses. Father told me his friends were impressed."

"By your ability to pull the wool over his eyes, perhaps. But even if I *did* allow you to have the gelding, you have nothing else to impress them with." George sneered at him. "Why do you think Father never had you educated beyond the Ashcroft dame school? He knew there was no point. You're too stupid to do anything but live off his generosity, and I'm putting a stop to that."

Bile rose in Tristan's throat. Without the annuity or even the horse, how would they survive? What would happen to Mother and Lisette? "I'll tell everyone what you've done." Might as well use the family hatred of scandal against George. "You won't get away with it!"

George laughed. "Who will you tell? The servants? The villagers? It's your word

20

against mine, and you're naught but a bastard. Even if they did believe you, they know whose money pays for their very lives, so they won't dare act on it."

"Dom would." Tristan balled his hands into fists. "He'll never stand for this. You burned up his inheritance, too."

"I'll take care of my legitimate brother," George said icily. "I would have fought the codicil legally anyway, and you would never have seen the money."

"Then there was no need for you to burn it," Tristan shot back.

George shrugged. "It saves me from waiting months for a court proceeding. That's why Dom will side with me — because he needs my fortune to live. He certainly won't defy me over the likes of you and yours."

"Forget the legalities! I'm still your blood. So is Lisette."

George went rigid. "Only because of an accident of birth. You are nothing to me. And I want you out of this house *now*!"

When Tristan just stood there, George strode past him into the hall. "Hucker!"

Tristan tensed. The brutish man of affairs was always at George's beck and call, and John Hucker appeared in the doorway within moments.

"The doctor ain't arrived yet, master —"

21

"It's 'my lord' now, if you please," George clipped out.

That seemed to shake even Hucker. He glanced beyond Tristan to the bed and paled. "I see."

"Take this bastard," George went on, "and get him out of my sight. I don't want him within a mile of this place."

"Yes, m'lord." Hucker squared his shoulders, then approached Tristan with a frightening deadness in his features. "Come along now, boy. You heard the master . . . I mean, his lordship."

Tristan glared at George. "You haven't seen the last of me. I'll make you pay for this if it takes the rest of my life."

"Get him out of here, damn it!" George ordered Hucker.

When Hucker took Tristan's arm, Tristan wrenched free. "I'm going." Then he marched into the hall.

As he strode downstairs, each echoing step further fueling his anger, he could hear Hucker following him. To hell with George and Hucker! And to hell with Father, too, who'd neglected his duty to his children until it was too late.

Instantly, guilt seized Tristan. What was wrong with him to be thinking ill of Father, who wasn't even cold in the grave? None of this was Father's fault. It was George's, all George's.

Once outside, Tristan expected Hucker to let him go on alone, but the infernal arse fell into step beside him, swinging a lantern at his side.

"You don't have to dog my steps back to the cottage," Tristan grumbled. "I can find my own way in the moonlight. Leave me be, damn it."

"If his lordship says he wants you a mile off, then I'm making sure you're a mile off."

"Shall we hunt up a yardstick so you can measure?" Tristan snapped.

Hucker said nothing, just kept stubbornly beside Tristan the whole way across the lawn.

Hucker had once been a halfway decent fellow, back when he'd worked for Father as house steward. George was already in school and Dom was still at home, so Hucker used to sneak treats to Tristan and Dom whenever they set out for their adventures in the cave near Flamborough Head. It was Hucker who'd taught Tristan the rudiments of accounting, Hucker who'd given Tristan his first cigarillo at the tender age of eight.

Then George had come home after finishing at Harrow. While Father had been on one of his trips, leaving George in charge, George had promoted Hucker to his personal man of affairs and everything had changed.

Now Hucker was as mean as George. Dom liked to say Hucker had been infected with the George and wasn't likely to recover.

"I don't know how you can work for him," Tristan said. "He's a cheat and a liar."

"He's the master. I do as I'm told." Hucker slanted a glance at him. "If you was wise, you'd do as you're told, too. There's naught to be gained from going against him. You ought to have learnt that by now."

"So I'm supposed to forget that he stole my inheritance from me, that he means to destroy my family?"

Hucker didn't even ask him to explain. "You're a bastard. There weren't much chance for you anyway. It's just how things are."

Tristan was well used to being called a bastard, but the fact that Hucker could be so cold stoked his temper. They were passing the stables now, and Tristan tensed. Blue Blazes was in there. *His* Blue Blazes. It wasn't fair. None of this was fair, damn it!

They were halfway to the cottage when Hucker finally left him. Tristan walked only far enough to be out of the wretch's sight.

Perhaps he should wait for Dom to arrive, in order to warn him about what George had done.

Then what? George was right about Dom siding with his legitimate brother. Dom had no choice; as long as he stood with George, he'd be safe. And it wasn't as if Dom could do anything to help them. He had no property of his own.

Which meant that Tristan and *his* family would starve. The cottage belonged to the Rathmoor Park estate, as did most everything in it. Bloody hell, if George wanted to, he could throw them out tomorrow.

How were they to live? Where could they go?

The sound of violins drifted to him through the forest, jerking him from his dark thoughts. It was the Gypsies — or as they preferred to call themselves, the Romany people. Having a nomadic spirit himself, Father had always allowed them to camp on the land, but that would no doubt change once George was in charge. They, too, would be kicked out, if not tomorrow, then soon. Perhaps he should warn them.

He headed through the forest toward their campfires. At least his friend Milosh Corrie, the horse trader, would understand the injustice of his losing Blue Blazes. Milosh appreciated the beauty and spirit of such a beast.

Damn George. All right, so perhaps Tristan could never have afforded to keep Blue Blazes, but he still could have sold the horse to Milosh for a good price, and then . . .

That stopped Tristan in his tracks. Milosh would be eager to buy such a fine gelding. He'd have the money for it, too, perhaps enough to enable them all to live until Tristan could find work. And the horse *was* Tristan's by right, no matter what George said. If Tristan took it, he'd only be honoring Father's wishes.

He could do it without being suspected. The grooms would be having supper. He could be in and out with Blue Blazes while they were still above the stables. If he left the stall door open, they'd think the gelding had wandered out.

It could be done . . . but only if he went now. And only if he convinced Milosh to buy what the world would consider a stolen horse.

I promised him to . . . your half brother last year. Tristan picked the Thoroughbred for me, so the lad should . . . have him.

Father's words decided him. To hell with the world and its unfair laws. Blue Blazes was *his,* damn it. So only he had the right to decide the horse's fate.

An hour later, Tristan watched as Milosh evaluated the gelding. The Gypsy had seen Blue Blazes before, but never up close and never long enough to make an assessment.

Milosh leveled Tristan with a wary gaze. "He's yours. Your father gave him to you."

Time to own up to what he'd done. He refused to risk his friend's life — Milosh would have to go into this knowing everything.

Swiftly he recounted the evening's events. When he was done, Milosh muttered a few words in Romany. Tristan had picked up some from spending time with the Gypsies, so he recognized the meaning as "reckless idiot."

Tristan gazed steadily at the man who, though only a couple of years older than he, was as accomplished at buying, trading, and training horses as any chap Tristan had ever seen. "I can take Blue Blazes back if you want. Leave him near the stables for the grooms to find."

That seemed to give Milosh pause. He obviously wanted the Thoroughbred. "Your half brother will have anyone hanged who's found with the beast."

"Then make sure you're not. Decamp at

27

first light. You're going to have to leave anyway — George will never let you stay. By the time he realizes that Blue Blazes is gone, you and your people will be long gone, too, and no one will think anything of it, given George's dislike of Gypsies."

"They'll think we stole the horse."

"They'll think *I* stole him, but they won't be able to prove it. Because Blue Blazes will have vanished."

Rubbing his bearded chin, Milosh examined the horse again. "You're sure no one saw you take him."

Tristan thought of the noise he'd heard near the stable as he'd left, then dismissed it. It had just been a dog. "Yes. I'm sure. There would have been a hue and cry. Besides, Hucker escorted me off the grounds himself. If something happens, he'll be the first person George blames."

Milosh's lips tightened into a line. "He'll simply lie about it."

"To George, you mean?"

"To George, *for* George. Either way, Hucker can't be trusted."

The conviction in his voice gave Tristan pause. "Why do you say that?"

Milosh's gaze grew shuttered. "You know it's true."

"Yes, but it sounds as if you've had firsthand experience with it." Tristan searched Milosh's face. "If you know of a time when Hucker lied for George over something important, especially if it's something I could use against George —"

"What do you want for the horse?" Milosh asked bluntly.

Tristan stared hard at him, but Milosh clearly wasn't going to explain. The Gypsies could be a secretive lot, even with someone they liked. After all, Tristan was still a *gadjo* — a non-Gypsy.

Tristan muttered an oath. "Two hundred and fifty pounds. He's worth five hundred, so you'll make a tidy profit."

"Only if people know his bloodlines, but I can't sell him as Blue Blazes. Then there's the risk I take by keeping him until we're far enough away to be sure no potential buyer knows of his disappearance." He shot Tristan a canny glance. "I'll pay you a hundred and fifty and not a penny more. And only because it's you."

"And because it will be a slap in the face to George. *And* to Hucker."

Milosh conceded the point with a tight nod.

A hundred and fifty pounds would support his family in York for a couple of years and give him time to find work.

He took one last longing glance at the horse he would dearly have loved to keep, then held out his hand. "Done."

Milosh shook it. "I hope you don't live to regret this, my friend."

"I won't. I have to take care of Mother and Lisette somehow. Because as soon as George is declared the heir, we'll have nothing and nowhere to go. And I can't let that happen."

The next night, a sober Tristan stood on the beach at Flamborough Head with his mother and sister. He'd gambled and lost. He still had the money Milosh had given him, but now he was running for his life, his family with him. Because it had not been a dog he'd heard outside the stables — it had been some man who'd identified Tristan as having stolen the horse.

George was scouring the countryside for him and Blue Blazes, Mother and Lisette had been kicked out of the cottage, and they'd had to use part of the money to purchase secret passage to Biarritz, France, so they could go by land from there to Toulon, where Mother's family lived. Because George was already trying to get him hanged.

Staring over at his mother's grief-stricken

expression, he swallowed hard. She'd lost her home and her true love all in one day, and he was responsible for at least half of that.

Lisette slipped her hand into his and squeezed. "It'll be all right, Tristan," she whispered. "Dom says he'll write to us faithfully to let us know what's going on. And surely one day we'll be able to return."

Tristan winced. That was the worst of it. Dom had *not* sided with George. Dom had sided with *them,* and it had cost him everything. And all because of Tristan's rash theft.

No, damn it! Because their negligent father hadn't bothered to update his will after Dom was born, which was why George had been able to burn the codicil and leave Dom and the rest of them penniless. Even if Tristan hadn't stolen the horse, George would have kicked them out. They'd still have ended up having to leave the cottage with nothing, just not so soon.

And though they could have stayed in England, what good would that have done them? George would never allow Dom to give them one penny, so they would have lost everything anyway.

Father's words came to him: *Up to you . . . to take care of . . . your mother and sister. You're . . . the man of the house now.*

Yes, he was. And he'd done what he must to make sure they could survive until he found work. The true villain in this was George.

Squaring his shoulders, Tristan stared out over the waters that would soon separate him from the only home he knew. It didn't matter. He would endure. They would all endure, even if he had to work like an ox to manage it.

But no one was ever getting the better of him or his family again. He would learn how to maneuver in this stupid, treacherous world however he could. He would learn how to fight, and he would learn how to win.

Then one day he would return to Yorkshire with all his newfound knowledge. And when he did, George had best watch out. Because Tristan would make his half brother pay for his villainy if it was the last thing he ever did.

1

London
February 1829
When the hackney halted, Lady Zoe Keane drew her veil aside and peered out the murky window to survey the building standing opposite the Theatre Royal, Covent Garden.

This couldn't be Manton's Investigations. It was too plain and ordinary for the famous Duke's Men, for pity's sake! No horses standing at the ready to dash off to danger? No imposing sign with gilt lettering?

"Are you sure these are their offices?" she asked Ralph, her footman, as he helped her out.

"Aye, milady. It's the address you gave me: 29 Bow Street."

When the brittle cold needled her cheeks, she adjusted her veil over her face. She mustn't be recognized entering an office full of men, and certainly not *this* office. "It

33

doesn't look right, somehow."

"Or safe." He glanced warily at the rough neighborhood. "If your father knew I'd brought you to such a low part of town he'd kick me out the door, he would."

"No, indeed. I would *never* allow that." As Mama used to say, a lady got what she wanted by speaking with authority . . . even if her knees were knocking beneath her wool gown. "Besides, how will he find out? You accompanied me on my walk in St. James Park, that's all. He'll never learn any different."

He mustn't, because he would almost certainly guess *why* she'd sought an investigator. Then, like the former army major he was, he would institute draconian measures to keep her close.

"I shan't be here long," she told Ralph. "We'll easily arrive home in time for dinner, and no one will be the wiser."

"If you say so, milady."

"I do appreciate this, you know. I'd never wish for you to get into trouble."

He sighed. "I know, milady."

She meant it, too. She liked Ralph, who'd served as her personal footman ever since Mama's death last winter. From the beginning, he'd felt sorry for Zoe, "the poor motherless lass." And if sometimes she

34

shamelessly used that to her advantage, it was only because she had no choice. Time was running out. She'd already had to wait *months* for Papa to bring her and Aunt Flo to London so she could maneuver this secret meeting.

They mounted the steps, and Ralph knocked on the door. Then they waited. And waited. She adjusted her cloak, shifted her reticule to her other hand, stamped snow off her boots.

At last the door opened to reveal a gaunt fellow, wearing an antiquated suit of cobalt-blue silk and a puce waistcoat, who appeared to be headed out.

"Mr. Shaw!" she cried, both startled and delighted to see him again so soon.

He peered at her veiled face. "Do I know you, madam?"

"It's 'your ladyship,' if you please," Ralph corrected him.

As Mr. Shaw bristled, Zoe jumped in. "We haven't been introduced, sir, but I saw you in *Much Ado about Nothing* last night and thought you were *marvelous.* I've never witnessed an actor play Dogberry so feelingly."

His demeanor softened. "And who might you be?"

"I'm Lady Zoe Keane, and I'm scheduled

35

to meet with the Duke's Men at three P.M."

It wasn't *too* much of a lie. A few months ago she'd caught the well-known investigators orchestrating a fake theft in order to capture a kidnapper. In exchange for her silence, they'd agreed to do her a favor at some future date.

That date was now.

She only hoped they remembered. Mr. Dominick Manton, the owner, and Mr. Victor Cale, one of his men, both seemed responsible fellows who would honor their promises.

Mr. Tristan Bonnaud, however . . .

She tensed. That bullying scoundrel had caught her by surprise, and she *hated* that. Why, he hadn't even wanted to agree to the bargain! No telling what he would do if things were left to him.

"Have you just been here to see the investigators?" she asked Mr. Shaw, who continued to block their way in.

He grimaced. "Alas, no. Since 'all the world is a stage,' I am employed here as well as in the theater. I serve as butler and sometime clerk to Mr. Manton."

Oh, dear. She only hoped he wasn't privy to his employer's meeting schedule. "In that case, perhaps you should announce me." When he stiffened, she added hastily, "I would be most honored. What a pity that I didn't expect you to be here, for then I could have brought my playbill for you to autograph."

Given how he arched his eyebrows, that was probably laying it on a bit thick. "What a pity indeed," he said, but ushered them inside.

Removing her cloak and veiled hat, she surveyed the foyer. This was more like what she'd expected: simple but elegant mahogany furniture, a beautiful if inexpensive Spanish rug, and nice damask draperies of a pale yellow. The décor could use a bit of dash — perhaps some ancient daggers on the walls for effect — but then, she always liked more dash than other people.

Besides, the newspapers told enough daring tales about the Duke's Men to make up for any lack of dash in their offices. Supposedly they could find anyone anywhere. She dearly hoped that was true.

"I don't believe the gentlemen are present at the moment." Mr. Shaw kept eyeing the front door with a peculiar expression of longing. "They must have forgotten your appointment. Perhaps you should return later."

"Oh, but that's impossible!" she burst out. When his suspicious gaze swung to hers, she cringed. Why must she always speak the first thing that came into her head? No matter how she tried to behave as Mama had taught her, sometimes her mouth just said what it pleased, and to hell with the consequences.

She winced. Not *hell.* Ladies didn't so much as think the word *hell,* not even ladies whose papas used the word regularly while teaching their daughters how to manage the estates they would one day inherit.

Sucking in a breath, she added sweetly, "I can't imagine that the famous Duke's Men would forget an appointment. Perhaps they came in the back."

After the risks she'd taken to meet with them, the thought of being thwarted because they were all out investigating made her want to scream.

He sighed. "Wait here. I'll see if anyone's in." He darted up the stairs like a spider up a web.

As soon as he was out of earshot, Ralph grumbled, "Still don't see why you want to consult with investigators. Your father would gladly find out whatever you wish to know."

Oh, no, he wouldn't. She'd already determined that. "Don't worry. It's nothing that will get you into any trouble."

It was only the entirety of her future, but

she couldn't tell Ralph that. None of the servants could ever know of this.

The door opened behind her. "Well, well, what have we here?"

She froze. She would recognize that voice anywhere. Oh, botheration, why did it have to be *him*?

Steadying herself for battle, she faced Mr. Bonnaud . . . only to be struck speechless.

This wasn't the Mr. Bonnaud she'd encountered in the woods near Kinlaw Castle, when she'd extracted her promise from the Duke's Men. That fellow had been barrel-chested, thick-waisted, and rough-looking, with a floppy hat and a beard that hid most of his face.

Oh, right, supposedly he'd been wearing a disguise.

It had been most effective. Because the man before her now wasn't remotely burly or bearded or badly dressed. He was lean and handsome and garbed almost fashionably, if one could call a sober riding coat of dark gray wool, a plain black waistcoat, tight buff trousers, and scuffed boots fashionable.

Not that any woman would care about his clothes, when his broad shoulders and his muscular thighs filled them out so well. Heaven save her.

Then he removed his top hat of gray beaver to reveal a profusion of thick black curls worthy of a Greek god, and she stifled a sigh. The combination of his aristocratic nose and finely crafted jaw with that hair was stunning. Absolutely stunning.

No wonder his name was so often linked to beautiful actresses and dancers. With those fierce blue eyes and that seducer's shapely mouth, he probably spent half his time in bed with willing females.

The images that rose in her mind made her curse her wild imagination. Ladies weren't supposed to think about *that* either.

He looked closely at her, and recognition leapt in those splendid eyes. "Lady Zoe," he said, bowing.

"Good afternoon, Mr. Bonnaud."

He crooked up one eyebrow. "Finally decided to call in your favor, did you?"

With a furtive glance at Ralph, who avidly watched the exchange, she said, "I wish to consult with you and your companions, yes."

Just then Mr. Shaw returned. "Ah, there you are, Mr. Bonnaud. Is Mr. Manton with you?"

"He's tying up some loose ends, but he said he'd be along shortly."

"I understand. As usual, 'Time shall

unfold what plighted cunning hides.' " Mr. Shaw nodded to her. "This lady claims to have an appointment with the . . . er . . . Duke's Men."

The Shakespeare quote threw Zoe off guard. Had Mr. Shaw guessed that she was hiding something?

She watched Mr. Bonnaud warily, preparing herself for anything. So when he had the audacity to wink at her, it surprised her — and sent a little thrill along her spine that was too annoying for words.

"She does indeed," he said, eyes agleam, "a rather long-standing one. Don't worry, Shaw — I can see you're impatient to be off to rehearsal. I'll take care of her ladyship."

"Thank you, sir," Mr. Shaw said, then rushed out the door.

"I take it that Mr. Shaw isn't as fond of his butler duties as his acting ones," she said.

"Precisely. A point illustrated by the fact that his real surname is Skrimshaw, but he insists upon being called by his stage name."

"Oh! That's a little strange. Though I can't say I blame him. He's an excellent actor. He's wasted in this position."

"As he is very fond of telling us, I assure you." Mr. Bonnaud gestured to the stairs. "Shall we adjourn to the office?"

Ralph jumped up, and Zoe said hastily,

"Wait down here for me, Ralph."

"But milady —"

She handed him her hat and cloak. "I've already met Mr. Bonnaud and his fellow investigators, and I promise they can be trusted."

Some of them could, though it looked as if she was stuck with the one she wasn't sure about. Not that it mattered. She was desperate enough to settle for Mr. Bonnaud.

Lifting her skirts, she headed for the stairs, feeling the man fall into step behind her. Only when they were past the landing and well out of Ralph's hearing did she say in a low voice, "I prefer to wait until the head of the Duke's Men is also present before proceeding."

"Do you?" he drawled. "Then let me give you a piece of advice. If you want to get on Dom's good side, stop calling us 'the Duke's Men.' He hates when people refer to the business he built himself as if it were an extension of His Grace's empire."

How odd. "One would think he'd relish his connection to a duke."

Mr. Bonnaud snorted. "Not everyone is as enamored of your sort as you might think, my lady."

The contempt in his voice irritated her, especially given her reasons for being here.

"Is that why you tried to shoot me the last time we met?" It still rankled that he'd not only managed to rattle her, but had kept rattling her even after it had become clear he was no threat.

"I didn't try to shoot you. I only *threatened* to shoot you."

"Three times. And the first time, you waved your pistol in my face."

"It wasn't loaded."

She paused on the stairs to glare down at him. "So you *deliberately* put me in fear for my life?"

He smirked at her. "Served you right. You shouldn't have been galloping after men who were reputedly in pursuit of a thief."

The heat rising in her cheeks made her scowl. She had nothing to be embarrassed about, curse it! "I had good reason."

He took another step up, coming far too close. "Do tell."

Staring into his eyes was only marginally less alarming than staring down the barrel of his pistol months ago. Good heavens, but he was tall. Even standing two steps below her, he met her gaze easily. It did something rather startling to her insides.

She tipped up her chin. "I'm not saying anything until your brother is here. In case you threaten to shoot me again."

Amusement leapt in his gaze. "I only do that when you're interfering in matters beyond your concern."

"You don't understand. I had to —"

"Quiet," he ordered, cocking his head to one side.

Just as she was about to protest his arrogance, she heard sounds of conversation below.

"Dom is here." Mr. Bonnaud nodded toward the top of the stairs. "So unless you want him to think we're dallying in the staircase, I suggest we continue up."

She blinked. "Dallying? *Dallying,* mind you?" She marched up the last few steps. "As if I would ever in a million years dally with you." She wouldn't. Really, she wouldn't!

His low chuckle behind her put the lie to her words. "Never say never, my lady. A vow like that is sure to come back to bite you in the arse. Which would be a shame, given that you have such a fine one."

Oh, Lord, he was staring at her bottom.

How *dare* he stare at her bottom? Not to mention, refer to it as an . . . an *arse.*

The second they moved into a long hallway, she turned to give him a firm set-down. Then she froze at the sight of his smug expression. He was deliberately trying to

44

provoke her, the sly devil, just as when he'd threatened to shoot her.

This time he wouldn't succeed. She cast him a pitying smile. "And here I'd heard that you were so witty and charming toward the fair sex, Mr. Bonnaud. How disappointing to discover you have only the coarsest notion of how to compliment a lady."

Though his mouth hardened a fraction, he still skimmed her with a blatantly impudent look. "The operative word is *lady*. And since you seem to be a lady in name only, given your penchant for sticking your nose where it doesn't belong —"

"Lady Zoe?" Mr. Manton appeared at the top of the stairs.

Oh, thank goodness he was here, and she didn't have to deal with his infuriating half brother anymore. She offered him her hand. "Mr. Manton. How good to see you again."

Sparing a veiled glance for Mr. Bonnaud, he shook her hand. "Under much better circumstances than last time, fortunately."

All too aware of Mr. Bonnaud's gaze on her, she smiled brightly. "I was delighted to hear that you and your fellow investigators routed the true villains eventually." There, that sounded perfectly cordial and ladylike and all the things Mr. Bonnaud said she wasn't. "I was also pleased to learn that they received the justice they deserved."

"Indeed they did. We appreciate your discretion in that matter, I assure you."

Her pulse pounded. "So you remember your promise."

"Of course. What's more, I'm pleased to honor it." He gestured toward an open doorway. "Why don't we discuss the matter in my study?"

"Thank you." As he led her into the room, she felt his brother fall into step behind her, no doubt staring at her "fine" arse again.

Let him stare. Now that she knew he only did it to provoke her, she refused to let it annoy her. It wasn't as if he meant anything by it. He *did,* after all, have a string of beauties trailing after him throughout London, and she wasn't widely acclaimed a beauty herself.

Oh, men flirted with her, but that was to be expected. She was rich, after all, with a substantial inheritance to come. She would much rather they flirted with her because they found her interesting, but barring that, she wouldn't mind being admired for her feminine attributes.

Unfortunately, English gentlemen weren't generally attracted to olive-skinned women with foreign-looking features, no matter how much Mama had always praised her "exotic" appearance. And her aunt, Mama's sister, despaired of her clothing choices, claiming that they had a bit *too* much dash for good society.

Zoe sighed. Even if by some chance Mr. Bonnaud didn't mind any of that and actually found her attractive, it made no difference. He hardly seemed the marrying sort. And she had too much at stake to be interested in the other sort — scoundrels and rakes and rogues. No matter *how* handsome and daring they were.

"So," Mr. Manton said as he gestured to a chair and took his own seat behind the desk, "what do you require of Manton's Investigations?"

Having circled around to lean against the wall nearest the desk, Mr. Bonnaud leveled an enigmatic stare on her.

She looked at Mr. Manton, and the enormity of what she was about to reveal hit her. For half a second, she reconsidered her decision. If the Duke's Men ever let slip even a tenth of what she was about to tell them, her future would be over, and her family's estate, Winborough, would be lost forever.

"My lady?" Mr. Manton prodded. "Why are you here?"

Then again, it might be lost forever if she

47

didn't involve them. Truly, she had no choice.

Gripping her reticule in her hands, she fought for calm. "I need you to find my real parents."

2

Tristan gaped at the woman, then burst into laughter. When Dom and Lady Zoe glared at him, he quipped, "Oh, you were serious, were you?"

She looked down her pretty little nose at him like the pampered aristocrat she was. "Perfectly serious, I assure you."

Dom shot him a quelling glance. "Perhaps you should explain, my lady."

Tristan crossed his arms over his chest. "If you can. Last I heard, your 'real' mother was dead, and your 'real' father lived at his Yorkshire estate. Though I suppose he's at his London town house now, given that you're here plaguing us with your nonsense."

God save him from silly young ladies of rank. With nothing better to do than attend balls and flirt, they created dramatic tragedies in their lives to make up for the fact that they were bored.

When she bristled, Dom murmured, "Tristan, do *attempt* not to be rude."

"I'm merely stating facts. Thanks to her ladyship's recklessness, we now have to waste our time satisfying her ridiculous favor."

He could ill afford the time, too. Ever since Dom and the duke had engineered his safe return to England, Tristan had been itching to wreak his vengeance on George by finding something to ruin the arse. Having discovered nothing in London, he needed to investigate near Ashcroft and Rathmoor Park. And perhaps search for Milosh, since the horse trader had hinted years ago of some secret about George.

"We promised Lady Zoe that we'd help her," Dom pointed out.

"On an obviously frivolous wild-goose chase," Tristan said in a hard voice. "What she wants will tie us up when we already have more cases than we can handle. Well-paying cases, I might add."

"If this is about money," she put in, "I do mean to pay you."

That arrested them both.

"Then . . . er . . . how exactly is this a favor?" Dom asked.

She arched one silky brown eyebrow. "Do you generally do investigations for unmarried young ladies, paid or otherwise, without the knowledge or consent of their families?"

"Not usually," Dom admitted.

"*That's* the favor."

Tristan exchanged a glance with his brother. That altered matters, making this both more palatable and infinitely riskier.

"Still," Dom said, "my brother does have a point. Have you any *legitimate* reason to believe that your parents are other than Lord Olivier and his late wife?"

She sighed. "Sadly, I do. It's a bit complicated, and I hardly know where I should start."

"At the beginning, Lady Zoe," Dom said gently.

"Good idea," Tristan said, less gently.

Dom was generally the one to handle clients, because he considered Tristan's approach to be . . . problematic. Since men of rank were invariably hiding something and Tristan had no patience for liars, he liked to provoke them until they revealed the truth. It had always worked for him as an agent for the secret police in France.

But aristocrats had little power there. Here, they were petty tyrants. Which was why Dom's more circumspect approach was infinitely more politic.

With Lady Zoe, however, Tristan didn't

care about being politic. She'd played a dangerous game by blackmailing them, and she was damned lucky that they were gentlemen. It had been madness for a fetching filly like her to make demands of a group of armed men.

And God help her, she *was* fetching, despite the unusually busy pattern of her red wool gown. Nipped in at the waist to accentuate her lush figure, it fit her very well — too well for his sanity.

Then there was her generous red mouth that made him think of raspberries, juicy and sweet to the taste. Not to mention her thick coil of chestnut hair garnished with a fringe of ringlets about the face. He had an errant urge to unwind that coil just to see how far it would fall.

He scowled. What was wrong with him? So what if she was pretty? She was also an innocent. An annoying, incredibly reckless innocent, to be sure, but he drew the line at ruining innocents, no matter how reckless.

Eyeing him warily, she drew in a deep breath. "A few years ago, before Mama first fell ill, Mama's sister — my aunt Floria — and Papa took it into their heads that I should marry my cousin Jeremy Keane."

"The American artist?" Dom asked.

"You've heard of him?"

"Who hasn't? My new brother-in-law, the duke, can't stop talking about Keane's upcoming exhibition at the Society of British Artists in Suffolk Street. I understand that the king himself has acquired two of his historical paintings for the palace, and Max is determined to buy one himself."

"Yes," she said irritably, "apparently my cousin is very good at what he does. But that doesn't mean I wish to marry him. I've never even met him, for pity's sake! Besides, what could he possibly know about running an estate or serving as my representative in the House of Lords or —"

"Wait a minute," Tristan interrupted. "You're a woman. What have you to do with the House of Lords?"

"Ah yes, old boy," Dom put in, "I don't suppose that's something you'd be familiar with. Lady Zoe is that rare thing in England — heiress to a title in her own right. When her father dies, she will become the Countess of Olivier no matter whom she marries. Or even *if* she marries."

That stunned him. He'd never heard of such a thing. But perhaps he'd misunderstood. "If she gets her own title, why can't she sit in Parliament like the other lords?"

"You said it yourself," she cut in. "I'm a woman. And even women with titles aren't allowed to sit in Parliament. I would need a representative."

"Like a husband." Dom stared at the young woman. "You are *first* in line for the title and the estate, I take it?"

She nodded. "Mr. Keane is my second cousin; he would be next if something happened to me."

"It's not unusual for a father to want his daughter to marry the male heir if he has no sons," Dom said. "But in your case —"

"There's no need," she finished. "Since I inherit regardless of my choice of husband, I ought to be able to marry whomever I please." A frown knit her brow. "That is, assuming there's no challenge to my bloodline."

"Ah. I begin to see your concern," Dom said. "The fact that your father is pushing this cousin on you has made you curious about his reasons. Is that it?"

"Unfortunately, it's more than that." She clutched her reticule tightly. "Shortly after I turned nineteen and was presented at court, Mama fell ill. That put a halt to my season before I even had time to receive offers of marriage. Aunt Flo and I were too engrossed in taking care of Mama to worry about balls and such."

She rose, clearly agitated, and began to

pace before the desk. "After she died, her loss was too new for me to endure another season, so we put it off a year. It was only last autumn, a few weeks before the house party at Kinlaw Castle, that we started preparing for me to have a full season this spring. And that's when Aunt Flo made her revelation."

"That your parents aren't really your parents," Tristan said, unable to keep the skepticism from his voice.

"Exactly. My aunt and I were discussing my cousin's impending trip to London, and she started instructing me in how to behave around him." She looked suddenly self-conscious. "She thinks I'm too . . . impulsive."

"Can't imagine why," Tristan muttered, "when you do things like ride off into the woods after gentlemen in pursuit of a thief."

"Now see here," she retorted, rounding on him, "I did that because I was hoping I could *help* somehow, and then you gentlemen would be so grateful that you would agree to take on my case."

That brought him up short. It put a slightly different slant on her actions, made them seem more calculated than reckless.

If he could believe her. "That's not what you said when you confronted us. You said you wanted to see 'the great Duke's Men in action.' Those were your exact words."

Dom shot him a bemused glance. "How odd that you remember them after all this time."

What the hell was that supposed to mean? "Don't you?"

"Yes, but I always do," Dom said with a shrug. "You're generally better at ferreting out the meaning *behind* the words."

"Is he really?" she broke in. "Then he ought to realize that I couldn't have revealed my real purpose at the time. You three were in the midst of some scheme, and I didn't want to muck with your plans."

"No, just get something out of them for yourself," Tristan said.

"Can you blame me?" She met his gaze with rank belligerence. "Sometimes a woman must resort to subterfuge to get things done."

Dom chuckled. "You must admit, old boy, that she has a point. Our sister has been saying the same thing for years."

"That's different," he said grimly. "Lisette wasn't born a fine lady. She knows how to take care of herself in a pinch."

"As I recall," Dom countered, "that's not what you claimed when you asked me to bring her back to England last year and get

56

her a husband."

"It worked, didn't it? She snagged herself a duke."

"Yes, no thanks to either of us," Dom said. "And Lady Zoe's plan worked, too. In fact, it took rather quick thinking to come up with it."

Much as Tristan hated to admit it, his brother was right. Once Lady Zoe had realized the situation, she'd handled matters admirably. Any other fine lady would have fainted or some such rot. Lady Zoe had faced them all down and used the circumstances to get what she wanted.

Just as a man might. But then, she'd been born to a title and an estate like a man; that had to have shaped her character. And if she proved not to be the heir after all . . .

He shook off that thought. He doubted that her parents could have hidden such a monumental secret from the world. "So, when exactly did your aunt make her grand revelation?" he asked, determined to get on with this nonsense.

Her withering stare amused him. She was so easy to provoke. Which meant he might actually get the truth out of her.

"It was after I lost my temper and told Aunt Flo I would never marry Mr. Keane. I pointed out that an American couldn't possibly appreciate Winborough and all it stood for, so she could just forget any union between us."

Dropping abruptly into the chair, she folded her hands in her lap. "That's when she said I *had* to marry my cousin. Because if anyone ever found out that I wasn't really my parents' daughter, I would lose all claim to the title and the estate. But if I married Mr. Keane, Winborough would be protected for our children even if my cousin learned the truth, since our son or daughter would inherit either way."

"Ah," Dom said. "Did your aunt explain *why* she thought you weren't your parents' daughter?"

"That's the complicated part." She fiddled nervously with her reticule. "Several months before my birth, my parents took a long trip to America to visit my cousin's branch of the family and then tour the rest of the country. I was born on their voyage home. At least that's what Mama wrote to Aunt Flo upon their return."

"But your aunt found that suspicious," Dom said.

Lady Zoe nodded. "Mama and Papa had been married for six years by then, so Aunt Flo couldn't believe Mama would have waited until after I was born to share the joyous news that she was finally with child."

That gave Tristan pause. There was a certain logic to her aunt's assumptions.

Her jaw tightened. "When Aunt Flo came to visit, she badgered my mother into admitting the truth — that Mama had never been with child at all. Instead, Papa had bought me from a Gypsy woman on the road home from the coast."

A stunned silence fell on the room.

Then Tristan shoved away from the wall. "Oh, for God's sake, a Gypsy would never sell her babe."

To think he'd actually begun to be swayed by her tale! But her claptrap about the Romany indicated the same narrow-minded ignorance drummed into her sort from birth. George used to spout it himself to justify his mistreatment of Milosh and his friends.

The memory lent an edge to Tristan's voice. "She certainly wouldn't sell her baby to a *gadjo.* The Romany prefer their own way of living to ours. There's no way in hell a Gypsy would offer her child to an Englishwoman under any circumstances. It simply wouldn't happen."

Lady Zoe looked taken aback by his vitriol. Then her manner grew defensive. "Mama told Aunt Flo that the Gypsy

59

woman had been badly beaten. The woman's husband hadn't wanted the child and had knocked her about, so she'd decided to get rid of the baby to avoid further beatings."

"More nonsense," he growled. "The Romany don't generally beat their women. Rot like that is spread by landowners who don't understand Gypsies."

"Aunt Flo said —"

"Your aunt Flo is clearly a fool!" He strode up to loom over her. "Or a liar. She probably invented the whole thing just to get you to marry that artist fellow."

Paling, the young woman rose. "I considered that, actually. Especially after she begged me not to mention it to Papa. But of course I could not let it rest."

"Why does that not surprise me?" Tristan muttered.

She ignored him. "I demanded the truth from Papa. He was clearly shaken, but insisted there was no truth to tell." A shuddering breath escaped her. "That's when I knew something wasn't right. And when I asked for details of my birth, he abruptly ended the conversation. He said there was nothing more to discuss, and that I must never mention the matter again."

Damn. That did sound odd.

"A few hours later," Lady Zoe went on, "Papa brought Aunt Flo to me and urged her to speak the truth. She said she shouldn't have told me what she had. That she'd only meant to convince me to marry Mr. Keane."

"You see?" Tristan said, a trifle snidely. "Yet you chose not to believe her, just as you chose not to believe your father."

When Lady Zoe's eyes met his, their fathomless sorrow caught him entirely off guard. "Oh, but I did believe her. Because Aunt Flo never lies. And nothing she said contradicted her earlier revelation. She expressed regret at having told me, which I'm sure was the case. And she explained that she'd only meant to further her aim to see me married to my cousin, which is undoubtedly true, too. The one thing she *didn't* do was take back her story."

He stared her down. "You're playing with words now."

"As was my aunt. She wanted to preserve Papa's secrets, while also impressing upon me how much is at stake if I don't marry my cousin. Of that, I am sure."

"But naught else?" Dom interrupted. "Because you're here asking for our help. And if you were sure of the truth, you would marry your cousin and be done with it."

The pink flush that stole over her cheeks made Tristan's breath sharpen. Lady Zoe might be trouble, but she was a very pretty trouble. How irritating that he kept noticing it.

She edged away from Tristan to face Dom. "You've captured my dilemma exactly, Mr. Manton. If my aunt is telling the truth, then I should definitely marry my cousin. It's the only sure way to save Winborough."

"From what?" Tristan asked pointedly.

"From an American who knows nothing about running an English estate. Who can predict what he would do to it? I have a duty to my tenants and servants to make sure that Winborough is preserved, even if he inherits it."

"And the fact that you'd be left in poverty has naught to do with it, I suppose," Tristan drawled.

She stared him down. "Papa would take care of me regardless. My dowry alone is enough to support me all my days." Her eyes got a faraway look. "Though I suspect that if the truth came out before I married, I would have trouble finding a husband."

"Perhaps among the *ton,*" Dom said kindly, "but not necessarily among more sensible gentlemen."

Her grateful smile was tinged with sadness. "Yet if I marry a man of my choosing and the truth comes out later, who knows how my husband would handle it?"

"Excellent point," Tristan snapped. "You wouldn't want any scandal tainting your husband's reputation." Because of course she would marry someone rich and important and appropriate to be consort to the prospective Countess of Olivier. Someone just like Father.

Though she stiffened, she conceded the point with a nod. "I wouldn't want him to be affected by any of it — scandal, or the loss of the title for our children, or the loss of my wealth. It wouldn't be fair to spring that on a man after he'd married me with certain expectations."

That certainly put him in his place. He grudgingly admitted that no man deserved to be taken by surprise in his choice of wife.

She went on. "And I'd still have the problem of my cousin's inheriting a property he couldn't handle. I can't risk that, even if it means marrying a stranger."

"But you prefer *not* to marry a stranger, I take it," Dom said. "You hope that your aunt *is* lying about the Gypsy woman, so you can marry whom you please."

She smiled at him. "Absolutely. And even if she's telling the truth, but you and your fellow investigators learn that this Gypsy woman and her husband have taken my secret to their graves, I'm still safe. Because if our servants had known of it, they certainly would have revealed it by now. Aunt Flo only told me under duress." Her expression turned haunted. "Either way, I have to be sure, don't you see?"

Dom steepled his fingers. "I suppose the matter is even more urgent now that your cousin is coming to London."

The grateful smile she bestowed on him scraped Tristan's nerves. "You understand me perfectly. In a few days, Mr. Keane will be here, and I must know how to proceed. I'd hoped for more time to prepare, but we only learned of his impending visit a month ago. Then I had to convince Papa to bring us here well in advance of it, so I could find a way to consult with you and your men. It wasn't a matter I dared broach in a letter."

"Certainly not." Dom tapped his fingers on his desk. "Let me make sure I understand you correctly — you wish to hire us to find out if your mother really bore a child on that voyage from America. If we learn that she didn't, you want us to hunt down the Gypsy woman who actually bore you. And possibly her husband as well."

"You've summed it up brilliantly," she said.

Perfectly. Brilliantly. His brother got the gushing compliments, while she raked Tristan over the coals. He wasn't used to that, even from her sort.

Women like her did sometimes turn up their noses at him on the few occasions when he frequented "good society." But when no one of their class was around, they were perfectly eager to smile and bat their eyelashes. Many a married lady of rank had tried to seduce him, and even the unmarried ones flirted with him, practicing for their more serious pursuit of lords.

But, ever conscious of their reputations, they only showed their true colors privately, in the dark. Give him an honest actress or opera dancer in his bed any day over some bored baroness. They knew what they wanted, and they went after it with gusto. They didn't hide their desires behind hypocrisy.

Lady Zoe knows what she wants and is going after it. She just doesn't want you. *And she's being perfectly honest about it.*

True. Damn her. It shouldn't annoy him that she was apparently the one female immune to his flirtations. But it did.

"Have you any information that will help

us with the search?" Tristan demanded. "Do you even know what ship your parents traveled on?"

Drawing a sheet of paper from her reticule, she placed it on the desk. "I wrote down everything about my birth that I could glean from talking to servants, tenants, and villagers over the past few months. I had to be careful, though. I dared not risk rousing suspicions in anyone."

"That must have been difficult," Tristan quipped. "Clearly subtlety isn't your strong suit."

To his surprise, a rueful smile crossed her lips. "It certainly isn't. Still, I did my best because I also couldn't take the chance of my questions getting back to Papa. He tends to be overprotective."

"Which makes sense, when you consider that you're his only heir." Dom picked up the paper to look it over.

"True," she murmured. "Not to mention that he keeps forgetting he's no longer in the army."

"The army?" Tristan echoed, taken aback.

Dom glanced up from the sheet of paper. "Don't you remember hearing about the Keanes of Winborough? The estate is near the town of Highthorpe, only a couple of hours away from home."

Home. Tristan hadn't thought of Rathmoor Park as home in a very long time. It reminded him too powerfully of what he'd lost. "Might as well have been a couple of *days* away if her family wasn't keen on racing."

"Good point. Father's friends did tend to be exclusively from that set. In any case, Lady Zoe's father was Major Keane before his elder brother died, leaving him to inherit the title."

"And Mama and Aunt Flo were the daughters of a colonel," the young woman put in. "Father runs our family the way he used to run his regiment. Or so I would guess, since I wasn't even born then."

A certain vulnerability flashed over her face, and Tristan realized how young she must be. Based on what she'd said about her coming-out and her mother's death, she couldn't be more than twenty-one, barely into her majority.

The thought of a woman that age facing a fight for what was rightfully hers unsettled him. It reminded him of how easily he and Lisette had been deprived of their own inheritance. Dom, too, because of the vagaries of English law. In France, Dom would have inherited a portion no matter what George did to prevent it.

Still, *Lady* Zoe had a father who cared about her and meant to give her a tidy inheritance, regardless of whom she married. It was why she felt free to act recklessly. Unlike Tristan, she'd never had to risk paying for her reckless behavior with her life.

"Unfortunately," she went on, "when Papa is being the Major, he saddles me with one of our fiercer servants as a gaoler, who dogs my every step. I could never have come here today if Papa had realized what I've been up to."

Instead, she'd coerced her pup of a footman into doing her bidding. No wonder her father felt compelled to give her "fiercer" servants as gaolers.

Dom held up her paper. "I see no information here about the Gypsy woman. Can you tell us anything else about that?"

"I do have a name for her," she said with a sideways glance at Tristan. "She called herself Drina. Apparently she didn't mention a surname."

Drina was actually a popular Romany name. Perhaps her aunt's tale wasn't entirely spurious. Still, it wasn't much to go on. It would require several forays into the different Gypsy camps, and there were quite a number.

As it finally dawned on him what this

could mean for *him,* his blood raced. Lady Zoe wanted someone to talk to the Romany; he wanted to find Milosh. He might actually get paid for doing what he'd been itching to do for months.

"Did your parents know where Drina's people had camped?" Dom asked.

She furrowed her brow. "Mama told Aunt Flo that Drina was headed west for York when they encountered her. Perhaps she was going to join her family."

This was getting better and better. With both Winborough and Rathmoor Park near the road to York, Tristan could easily investigate them both.

But he was getting ahead of himself. "What time of year was this?"

"January. Mama and Papa disembarked the ship in Liverpool, then traveled by coach to York. They were headed home to Highthorpe when they met up with Drina. That's all I know."

Tristan glanced at Dom. "Many of the Romany winter in major cities like York or Edinburgh or London. Some even take houses for those months."

Lady Zoe began to tremble so violently that she had to sit down again. "My aunt's tale might be true, then." Her gaze, oddly unfocused, met Tristan's. "I might indeed

69

be a Gypsy by birth."

"Not necessarily," he said, inexplicably alarmed by her distress. "There are things about the tale that don't make sense. Why would this Drina have been on the road in January? The Gypsies who used to camp on my father's land left for town in early November, not two or three months later, when there was more likelihood of snow."

She swallowed hard. "Still, you must admit that I *look* like a Gypsy, with my coloring and my hair —"

"Nonsense," he said.

Granted, she looked unusual, rather like a Russian princess he'd once met. But not so unusual as to provoke suspicion about her heritage. Her skin was the creamy hue of marzipan, and her hair wasn't dark enough. Though she did have a Gypsy's high cheek-bones, her eyes were pure English — green as the wolds of York in summer.

"You look half-Gypsy at most." As something occurred to him, Tristan searched her features again. "Perhaps the Gypsy story is only partly true. Perhaps you really aren't your mother's child. But you could still be your father's."

Her eyes got huge in her face. "What are you saying?"

"Nothing," Dom put in with a look of

caution.

Tristan ignored him. "Perhaps Drina was your father's mistress."

3

For half a second, all Zoe could do was gape at the wretch. Then she leapt from her chair. "That's impossible. Papa would never have shamed Mama so. They were in love!"

Mr. Bonnaud cocked his head. "So were Dom's parents, yet his father — *our* father — took my mother as a mistress fairly early in their marriage. He claimed to love her as well. That sort of thing happens in England more than you think."

"Don't drag our family into this, Tristan," Mr. Manton warned.

Paying him no mind, the dratted devil began to pace before her. "It would explain all the inconsistencies — why a Romany woman was alone on the road to York without her people. Why your father took you in so readily, even though your mother could still have borne him children. Drina might have been waiting for him when your family arrived at Winborough. Perhaps he

72

was just hiding the truth from your mother when he said that he'd bought you."

Zoe glowered at him. "And the fact that Drina was beaten, what of that? I suppose you're going to blame my father for that, too."

"Certainly not," he said.

Her pulse steadied a little.

"But Gypsies have a stricter morality than Englishmen realize. All rumors about them to the contrary, they don't allow adultery or fornication. If Drina had shared a bed with your father, then her husband — or her own father — might have beaten her for it."

"You claimed that Gypsies don't abuse their women," she pointed out.

He shrugged. "They don't generally, but it's hard to know what a husband might do when faced with his wife's adultery." He paused in his pacing to shoot her a meaningful glance. "Or what an English husband might do to cover up his own."

Heat rose in her cheeks. She'd had quite enough of this. "You are a vile, *vile* man. To cast aspersions on my family with nothing more than a few facts —"

"I'm merely trying to get at the truth." His eyes glittered at her. "That *is* what you want, isn't it?"

"Not from you." Turning on her heel, she

approached the desk. "Mr. Manton, I want you to promise that your brother won't be involved in this investigation. He's clearly biased against my family, for no reason that I can see, and I don't want his bias to affect his judgment."

Mr. Manton glanced from her to Mr. Bonnaud, then sighed. "I'm afraid I can't promise you that, Lady Zoe."

"Why not?"

Mr. Bonnaud was the one to answer, in his typically self-satisfied manner. "Because I know more about the Romany people than Dom and Victor put together. I speak their language, I'm familiar with their customs, and I'll have no trouble learning the where-abouts of all the major Gypsy families."

Botheration.

"He's right," Mr. Manton added. "Tristan spent far more time with them than I did. I was either at school or going about in society with our father. And Victor has had no dealings with them at all."

The words had scarcely left Mr. Manton's lips when a knocking sounded from down-stairs.

He rose. "That's probably the records I've been waiting for. So if you'll excuse me . . ."

Surely he wasn't going to rush out of here and leave this matter unresolved! "But . . .

74

but I don't want Mr. Bonnaud to be part of this!" she cried as Mr. Manton headed for the door.

Mr. Bonnaud gave a harsh laugh. "I think my brother has made it clear that you don't have a choice." When she whirled on him, he added with a smirk, "Not if you want Drina found. Assuming that she even exists."

Heaven save her, this was not to be borne! "I could always tell the world that you're a thief," she hissed, unable to govern her temper any longer. "*You* were the one seen running from Kinlaw Castle that day. And I'm the one who can testify to that."

That didn't seem to faze him one jot. "Go ahead, my lady, tell the world." Mr. Bonnaud marched up to lower his voice to a threatening rasp. "Then *I'll* tell the world that you might not really be heir to the Earl of Olivier."

She gasped. "You wouldn't dare!"

"Not unless he has to," Mr. Manton broke in. His tone turned forbidding. "I promised you our discretion, but that was contingent upon yours. If you choose to engage my brother in a fight that could ruin him, then you'll have to engage me as well. And I assure you, I'll defend us both by any means necessary."

The warning gave her pause. She hadn't meant to take this to such an extreme. It was just that Mr. Bonnaud had the most abominable ability to shatter her control. Now, thanks to him, she would have to regain lost ground . . . which meant choking down great gobs of her pride.

"I understand." She forced a smile. "And I . . . apologize for my rash words. Manton's Investigations *is* doing me a favor, after all. I didn't mean to be ungracious."

When Mr. Manton acknowledged her words with a tight nod, she went on hastily, "But I still think that Mr. Bonnaud —"

"You have no choice," Mr. Manton cut in. "And for more reasons than my brother's knowledge of the Romany. You see, I'm in the middle of a case involving a marquess's missing valet, and Victor is tied up in a case at court. Tristan happens to be the only one free to pursue this matter just now." He eyed her steadily. "Unless, of course, you wish to wait longer to have it taken care of."

She let out a frustrated breath. "You know perfectly well I can't."

"Then Tristan will be handling your case." As the knocker sounded downstairs again, he added, "I really must tend to that. I'll leave you and my brother to work out the details."

76

Then he was gone, and she was alone with her nemesis.

How mortifying. She couldn't even bear to look at him after she'd let her temper get the better of her. When would she learn that just because she *felt* something didn't mean she had to let it fly? As Mama always said, *If you keep your true feelings private, you'll never feel regret.*

Regret was a bitter pill indeed.

After a moment, Mr. Bonnaud murmured, "Was that really so hard?"

"What?"

"Apologizing."

"You have no idea," she muttered.

When he remained silent, she ventured to look at him and was astonished to find his smirk gone and his eyes surveying her thoughtfully. "Pax," he said. "I didn't mean to provoke you."

"Oh, yes, you did! You've been provoking me since the moment we met."

"True. Nonetheless, I shouldn't have carried it quite so far."

She eyed him uncertainly. "Is that your idea of an apology?"

A ghost of a smile crossed his lips. "Take it however you like, princess."

Princess? Knowing him, he probably meant that as an insult. "Last I checked, I was never heir to a royal title."

His eyes gleamed. "A Gypsy princess, then," he amended in a slow, silky drawl that made her stomach flip over.

"We're not even sure that I *am* a Gypsy."

"No. But by the time I'm done, we'll know the truth one way or the other, I promise."

"Don't make promises you can't keep."

Leaning back against the desk, he stared hard at her. "I happen to be very good at what I do. I worked for La Sûreté Nationale in France for years, you know."

"I didn't know, actually." But she did know about the French secret police, who had supposedly cut crime in Paris by nearly half. There'd been articles about them, now that the home secretary, Robert Peel, was attempting to start a police force in London. "Details of your former life haven't appeared in the newspapers."

"Yes, well, there are many things that don't appear in the papers. That doesn't make them any less true."

He had a point. And now her curiosity was roused. "What exactly did you do for La Sûreté Nationale?"

"I was an agent. So was Victor. We caught criminals by pretending to *be* criminals."

"That certainly explains why you were so successful at playing the thief the day we first met," she said testily. "You make a very convincing criminal."

One eyebrow quirked up. "You really don't like me much, do you?"

Torn between telling the truth and being circumspect, she settled for something in the middle. "I don't like having pistols pointed at me." Her voice hardened. "Or mud slung on my father's good name."

"Ah." He drummed his fingers against the desk, then said softly, "Still, you can't ignore the possibility that you could be your father's by-blow."

She winced. She had never met anyone like him — so blunt, so rude, so . . . honest. She'd find it refreshing, if not for the fact that he was insulting Papa. "You'd really enjoy it if I proved to be so, wouldn't you? It would make me the same as you."

"Hardly." Eyes of arctic blue pinned her in place. "Unlike you, I don't get to choose between being the pampered heir to an estate or merely *marrying* the pampered heir to an estate. So no, we aren't remotely the same."

"In one respect we are." She regarded him with a faint smile. "It seems you really don't like me much, either."

He blinked. Then his lips twitched as if he fought a smile of his own. "Actually, I haven't decided that yet." He raked her with a slow, sensual glance that sent a thrill skittering through her. "I daresay I could like you a great deal . . . under the right circumstances."

There was no mistaking his meaning. Or its effect on her. And she would die before she let him guess it. "Does that sort of blatantly lascivious glance generally sway women to jump into your bed?" she asked tartly.

"Often enough to make it worth the attempt." He grinned. "Besides, it need only work occasionally. A man must sleep *sometime.*"

She rolled her eyes. "At least now I understand why you're convinced that Drina was my father's mistress. You judge him by your own low standards."

The insult slid off him like rain off an oak leaf. "Have you a better explanation for why Drina's people left her to bear a child among strangers in the dead of winter?"

"No," she admitted reluctantly. "But there *is* one hole in your lovely theory. When I asked around in Highthorpe, I was told of a local proscription against Gypsies dating back for decades. So how could Papa have taken a Gypsy mistress when there were never any Gypsies around Winborough?"

"Can you really be sure of that, princess?"

"Stop calling me that." She knew he meant to mock her for being the "pampered heir to an estate," something he clearly neither understood nor approved of. "And I'm telling you, I never so much as saw a Gypsy growing up."

He eyed her skeptically. "No tinkers, no itinerant musicians, no soothsayers of any kind?"

"Not in Highthorpe." A long-ago memory drifted into her mind. "I did meet a fortune-teller once, but that was in London. One of my good friends had a Gypsy soothsayer at her birthday party when I was a girl. I remember because Papa got so angry when I told —"

Pain ripped through her. "Oh, Lord, I'd forgotten that. He went on and on about the foolishness of hiring Gypsies to spout nonsense in the ears of young, respectable girls. I thought he was just being overly cautious, as usual." Her voice dropped to a whisper. "But what if it was more than that?"

"You mean, what if she was your father's mistress?"

"No, of course not," she said dismissively. "What if Papa didn't like Gypsies because he bought me from one of them?"

81

His face clouded over. "I told you — the Romany don't sell their children."

"But it *could* happen."

"It's highly unlikely." He crossed his arms over his chest. "It makes far more sense that the former mistress of your father would have shown up at the party because she wanted to find out if you were all right. Did the woman show any special interest in you? Ask you any probing questions?"

"Not really. She just read my palm along with all the other girls'."

"What did she say?"

"A great many things." As the memories rose, she walked over to the window to stare out at the waiting hackney. "That I was born of secrets and sadness. That it would either destroy my future or lead me to greatness. And she said something about a person becoming the hand of my vengeance. Whatever that means."

"It could mean anything," he said with surprising gentleness. "A good fortune-teller leaves the predictions vague or mysterious on purpose so that you can make what you wish of them. Most of what they tell people is rot anyway."

She dearly hoped so, considering something else the woman had said: *A handsome gentleman with eyes like the sky and hair like a raven's wing will come into your life.*

Oh, Lord. She could well imagine what Mr. Bonnaud would make of that. Then again, perhaps Jeremy Keane also had blue eyes and dark hair. Or perhaps fortune-telling *was* all rot.

She drew a deep breath. "So, I suppose you mean to focus your investigation around proving my father to be an adulterer."

"Actually, I should first determine if your aunt's tale is even true. I'll head for Liverpool in the morning to examine the Customs records for the year of your birth."

"That sounds time-consuming."

"It will take a few days, yes."

"But I don't *have* a few days!"

"You do want to be sure that she's not lying before we pursue the Gypsy connection, don't you?"

She bit her lower lip. "I suppose."

"Then you must let me do this my own way. I'll work as swiftly as I can." He glanced at the window. "But keep in mind that if the Customs records prove your aunt's story to be true, it will take me quite a bit longer to explore your past. All of this occurred years ago, which makes it hard enough, but with the Romany keeping to themselves as they do . . ." He shook his head.

"I know," she said. "But at least I'll have some idea of how to proceed with my cousin while you're looking for the mother who actually bore me."

Silence fell between them, thick as fog and twice as impenetrable. She could feel his eyes examining her, as if he were looking for cracks in her armor. He wouldn't have to look hard. Lately, her armor was flimsier than muslin.

Then he shoved away from the desk. "You do realize you don't have to pursue this at all. You could just go on with your life and hope no one ever learns of this."

"But what if someone did? If I *am* a Gypsy, then my Gypsy mother, at the very least, knows where I am and who I am. What's to stop her — or someone in her family — from trying to blackmail me once I inherit the title and my fortune? And if word got back to my cousin, he would surely fight to gain the title and the estate and disinherit me. That would be disastrous."

"Because of the scandal?" he said cynically. "Or because you'd lose all that lovely money and high rank?"

"Neither, you dratted —" She caught herself when she saw the glint of satisfaction in his eyes. He was deliberately provoking her. Again. She moderated her tone. "Hundreds of people depend upon Winborough for their livelihood, and I take my responsibilities to them very seriously. But you wouldn't understand that, would you? You live for yourself alone."

"Yes, thank God," he said, though a telltale tightening about his lips belied his seeming nonchalance. "I wouldn't have your meddlesome duties for all the money in England."

"My cousin might very well feel the same. He's an artist, accustomed to catering only to his muse, not to the needs of tenants and servants. And Winborough can ill afford an owner who will let it fall into disrepair while he's off painting pictures of trees."

"You're not an art lover, I take it," he said sarcastically.

"I like art well enough in its place, but there are more important matters to deal with on a large estate. That's why it's imperative that I marry Mr. Keane if I prove *not* to be the legitimate heir. Papa isn't exactly young, so I can't take the chance of my cousin inheriting everything in his own right before we can make sure he could handle it."

"Fine. Then marry him." His expression was impassive. "Even if you *do* turn out to be your parents' daughter, you still have to marry in order to produce the requisite heir. Personally, I think you ought to do as you please and take your chances, but if you insist on saving the family estate, you might as well marry him as anyone else. Assuming that you can stomach him, that is."

Men could be so obtuse. "There's more to love than that."

He snorted. "Who said anything about love? Marriage, especially in your world, is about two things: gaining or securing property, and satisfying one's desires. You already know what you have to do to secure your property. Now you need only determine whether you can desire your cousin and he desire you."

"Yes, and what if he doesn't? What then?"

He swept her with a long, heated glance. "Then he's blind and stupid, and you won't wish to marry him anyway."

When the offhand compliment sent her silly pulse into a scamper, she chided it silently. Mr. Bonnaud was well known for his blithe flatteries. He didn't mean anything by them. "All right, what if he desires me but I don't like *him*?"

"Liking has nothing to do with desire." He walked to the door. "Trust me, you'll know within seconds of meeting him whether you desire him. Although if your cousin has any talent at all with women, he can *make* you desire him."

"How ludicrous." She couldn't believe they were even having this conversation. It was most . . . inappropriate. Yet she didn't want to stop it, either. "I could never desire someone I just met, no matter what he did to coax me into it. And I certainly could never desire someone I didn't like."

"You think not, do you?" He shut the door, then came toward her.

"What are you doing?" she squeaked, alarmed by the determination in his eyes.

He stopped mere inches away, his gaze dropping to her mouth. When she swallowed beneath the force of his penetrating stare, a sudden heat flared in his face. "Since we've already established that you don't like *me,* I'm giving you a little demonstration of what I mean."

And before she could react, he bent his head to kiss her.

She was stunned. Then appalled. Then horribly, awfully intrigued. Because Mr. Bonnaud didn't kiss like the two fellows who'd given her dutiful pecks on the lips during the early days of her debut. He kissed like a man who knew exactly what he was doing.

Impossibly, though his lips were soft, his kiss was hard. Bold. All-consuming. It demanded a response, and she gave it willingly.

She told herself it was out of simple curiosity. Mr. Bonnaud had women trailing after him everywhere, and she was dying to know why.

Then his hand slid about her waist to pull her close, and the tenor of the kiss changed, and she forgot all about her curiosity. She forgot her name and where she was and why she was even here. She forgot everything but the feel of his firm body plastered to hers, his muscular arm wrapped about her waist, his hot mouth coaxing hers open so he could slip his tongue inside.

Something wild and wanton uncurled in her belly. So this was how a scoundrel kissed a woman, with long, heated strokes of his tongue. She couldn't breathe, couldn't think. And strange, *wonderful* things were happening to her in places a lady didn't even acknowledge existed. Lord save her.

In a flash, she understood how he'd gained his reputation with women — by doing *this* to them. That thought brought her to her senses enough to drag her mouth from his. "Mr. Bonnaud, we shouldn't —"

"No, we shouldn't, princess," he agreed,

then perversely kissed her again.

Now her pulse beat at a positively giddy pace, and her belly warmed. Or something down there warmed anyway. Which most assuredly shouldn't happen.

She didn't care. Because he was giving her such raw, heady kisses that her head spun. She couldn't catch her breath, but what need had she for breath when he was giving her his? Their breaths mingled, their mouths mingled, everything mingled until she feared her knees might actually buckle.

Unbidden, the fortune-teller's last remark concerning the "gentleman with eyes like the sky" burst into her memory: *If you let him, he will shatter your heart.*

Not if she had anything to say about it.

She shoved him away. "Enough," she murmured, fighting for breath. And sanity. "That's quite enough, sir. This demonstration is over."

4

Tristan could only stare blindly at her, his blood running fast and his heart beating even faster.

Demonstration? What demonstration?

Oh, right. He'd been making a point before it had turned into . . . whatever the hell *that* had just been.

He'd kissed plenty of women and seduced at least half of those he kissed, so he knew what kisses felt like. And they had never once felt like *that.*

A good kiss was pleasurable, a better kiss was erotic, and the best ones were often the prelude to a seduction. They damned well weren't like being turned inside out and upside down.

They weren't supposed to be, anyway. They were *supposed* to be under his control. He was always the one leading the kiss, not following it like a hound scenting blood . . . or perfume as sweet as Yorkshire's violets.

Thank God she looked as flummoxed as he was. Her eyes were fathomless, like the waters off Flamborough Head, and she gulped breath after breath.

He followed the convulsive motion of her throat, wishing he'd thought to plant a kiss in the hollow just there, where the skin was softest and the pulse beat —

"I'm afraid your demonstration proved nothing," she said.

He had to sift through his addled brain to figure out what he'd been trying to prove. Ah yes. That a woman could desire a man even if she didn't like him. And that a man could *make* a woman desire him.

"Seems to me I proved a great deal," he rasped.

Of course he had. And now that he didn't have her lush body in his arms, with her soft mouth opening beneath his and her delicate moans turning his blood to fire, his good sense was reasserting itself.

He probably just needed sleep or food or . . . a knock in the head. That was why he was being an idiot, imagining he'd felt anything but the usual lust for a pretty woman. That was why he'd been fool enough to touch the sort of woman he usually avoided.

That was why he was standing here letting her pretend to be unaffected by their kisses. "Admit it," he growled, "despite not liking me, you desired me."

He headed for her once more, and she backed away.

"It wasn't desire," she said. "It was curiosity, nothing more."

He bore down on her. "Tell me, princess, do you often lie to yourself?"

"Don't call me princess."

"Then speak the truth, damn it! And perhaps I'll stop."

She came up against a table and halted. So did he, though a few inches more would put him well within reach of her again. But he didn't want to be that close. Not when all he wanted to do right now was provide her with another "demonstration," over and over, until she admitted that she wanted him.

That wouldn't be wise. If he had any sense at all, he would never attempt such a demonstration again.

But it chafed him that she was *still* denying their attraction, even to herself. Any other chit like her would be enjoying the chance at a private flirtation where she needn't be careful.

Instead, she looked panicked. "Please, Mr. Bonnaud . . ."

"Tristan," he ground out, irritated that she behaved as if he might ravish her on the spot. "After what we just did, you can damned well call me by my Christian name in private."

Hell and thunder, what was wrong with him? He was behaving like an arse, and God only knew why. Still, he refused to take the words back.

She curled her fingers into her skirts as if to keep from reaching for him . . . or, more likely, slapping the tar out of him. He was probably lucky she hadn't already done so, given her mercurial nature. He was traveling so far beyond the bounds of propriety that he'd soon be in another county.

"Have it your way . . . Tristan," she said in a frosty tone. "I concede that you may have shed a certain new light on my impression of relations between men and women, but —"

"Don't pretty it up with fancy words. There's nothing to be ashamed of, no matter what you've been taught. For a few moments, you enjoyed our kisses. Admit it."

"All right, perhaps I . . . found them intriguing." She drew herself up stiffly. "But that doesn't change the fact that I want

93

more from marriage than mere physical attraction. I happen to believe in marrying for love. My parents were wildly happy together, and I'm determined to find a match like theirs if I can."

"*Love?*" he said with a roll of his eyes. "Oh, for God's sake —"

"What? You think it impossible that I might marry for love?"

"Not you specifically. Anyone. It's naïve to plan one's future around an unattainable dream. You're begging to be disappointed." Though at least she would have her money to soothe her disappointment. Mother had gained nothing but heartache and loss from *her* unattainable dream of love. It was why he'd put his heart on ice long ago.

"I'd rather find that out for myself, thank you very much."

He managed a shrug. "If some fantasy of love is what you're after, then you'd better pray that you *are* the true heir to Winborough. Or be prepared to take your chances on hiding the truth about your past from your cousin."

She frowned. "It's possible that I could fall in love with *him.* Unlikely, I should think, but possible. That would certainly solve everything."

The fact that she could speak so nonchalantly of another man after practically swooning in his arms irritated him, and then his *irritation* irritated him. The woman was a plague, damn her.

A perverse urge to plague *her* rose up in him. "You know what they say: It's just as easy to fall in love with a rich man as a poor one."

Instead of taking the bait, she cast him a smooth smile. "Interesting words, coming from the man who considers love 'an unattainable dream.' Forgive me if I don't take advice on marriage from a bachelor more famous for seducing women than courting them."

Sliding from between him and the table, she headed for the door. "In any case, since you seem to have a plan for investigating my family's past, I believe we're finished here." Reaching for the door handle, she added, "I'll expect a report from you as soon as you return from Liverpool."

"Of course." Bristling at being so summarily dismissed — and in his own bloody office, too — he snapped, "Shall I come to the Keane town house to present my report? Or send it to you by the mails?"

Ah. *That* got a reaction at last.

Two spots of color appeared high on her cheeks. "That won't do, and you know it.

We'll have to find some discreet way to communicate."

"*Discreet.* Your sort's polite word for hiding the truth."

She leveled a dark glance on him. "Manton's Investigations does offer discretion. Your brother insisted that it would be provided."

Damn. He really was losing his mind, to even hint otherwise to a client. "I will be perfectly discreet. *If* you'll tell me how to accomplish that feat."

After a long pause, she said, "I could invite you to the soiree my aunt intends to throw for my cousin when he arrives, but I hope to have this settled long before then. And, well —"

"I'm not exactly acceptable in polite society," he said silkily. At heart, she was just another fine lady with her nose in the air.

Her gaze flashed to his. "Acceptability has naught to do with it. I'm not supposed to have met you, remember? You weren't officially at that house party. You were sneaking around pretending to be a thief, and since Aunt Flo *was* at that house party, she'll know you weren't there. So she'll find it highly suspicious if I insist upon inviting a stranger to a soiree. I can get away with inviting Mr. Manton, the Cales, and the duke and duchess —"

"You've never met the duke and duchess," he smugly pointed out.

She rolled her eyes. "He's a *duke.* My aunt would think it mad *not* to invite any duke with whom I can presume to have some connection by virtue of his relation, Mr. Cale. Besides, Mr. Manton said that the duke is interested in my cousin's paintings, so I need only claim to have heard that somewhere."

God, he hated it when she was sensible and logical, making him appear biased and obnoxious. Which he apparently was, at least regarding anything that concerned *her.*

"The soiree is out, then." He forced himself to behave like an investigator rather than a slavering hound thirsting for another taste of her mouth. "Do you plan to go anywhere else I might be permitted to roam? The theater, Bond Street . . . Vauxhall —"

"Oh! I know what we can do. When I'm in London, I ride on Rotten Row every afternoon during the fashionable hour. You could meet me there. No one will think anything of a gentleman accompanying me for a few circuits."

"Riding in Hyde Park. Of course. What

else would an heiress do for fun?"

"Rotten Row is the perfect hunting ground for ladies seeking husbands. Or didn't you know?"

Why did he get the feeling she was trying to provoke *him* now? And why, by all that was holy, was it working? "Husband-hunting. Always a rousing sport. I suppose you go there dressed to kill."

"No, indeed. What good is a dead husband?" She smiled airily. "I go dressed to maim only."

"Why does that not surprise me, princess?"

Her smile vanished. "I thought you were going to stop calling me that."

"I said 'perhaps.' " He strolled up to the door, where she stood poised for flight. "But I've changed my mind. It suits you."

She looked suddenly defensive. "You mean, it suits *you* to mock me."

The uncertainty in her voice gave him a twinge of guilt. "I'm not mocking you, I swear. Truth is, you remind me of a Russian princess I knew in Paris." He managed a teasing tone. "She dressed to maim, too."

She wouldn't look at him. "One of your many conquests, I take it?"

"Hell and thunder," he said irritably, "it's not as if I go about seducing every fetching female I see. And princesses don't generally consort with men like me anyway." Although the Russian chit *had* flirted outrageously with him, something he didn't see any point in mentioning.

Her hands worried the reticule attached to one of her slender wrists. "About that . . . er . . . kiss of ours, you will keep it . . . I mean, if my cousin were to hear of it, let alone Papa —"

"I'm not going to tell anyone, if that's what worries you."

Her gaze shot to his. "And you won't . . . attempt another one."

"I can't promise any such thing." What was wrong with him? Hadn't he just been telling himself that he shouldn't repeat it? "However, since we're unlikely to be alone again, it shouldn't be a problem."

The relief on her face spiked his temper higher, and it was all he could do not to grab her and kiss her again, just to provoke her.

"Well, then." She donned the ladylike reserve she seemed to put on and off like a cloak. "I'll see you in a few days at Rotten Row."

Then she was gone, leaving him with his blood in high riot and his hands clenched at his sides.

God, he really hoped that his jaunt to Liverpool turned up clear evidence that she was her father's heir. Because if he had to deal with her for weeks on end, he might end up strangling her.

Or doing something far more dangerous.

No, what was he thinking? It was to his advantage to have her be part Gypsy, and he dared not jeopardize the investigation by being an arse. He needed this chance to locate Milosh. He would just have to keep his distance, and communicate with her as little as necessary.

That shouldn't be too hard; she was soon going to be gadding about with her American cousin. Though that thought oddly didn't sit well with him, either.

The door opened and he tensed, thinking she'd returned. But it was only Dom, with a pile of papers in his hands.

"I caught Hucker outside, watching the place," Dom said grimly as he set the pile on the desk.

That instantly put Tristan on alert. "Bloody hell. George must really be desperate to find some way to ruin us, if he can spare Hucker for days at a time."

"Either that or George can't afford to pay the man his salary, so Hucker's hoping that if he can find something on us, George will give him money for it. My spies in Ashcroft tell me that our brother falls deeper into debt every year."

"Which only makes him more dangerous," Tristan pointed out. "A cornered animal will attack with particular savagery."

"True. That's why I made sure to run Hucker off for good. I told him that if I saw him around here again, I would charge him with breaking and entering, and get my close friend the chief magistrate to lock him up."

Tristan tensed. "Do you think he believed you?"

"Hucker's a coward at heart. He won't risk his neck on the off chance that George will save it for him."

"I hope you're right. Because our brother is determined to see me in shackles, one way or another, and he'll do whatever is necessary to make that happen."

But Tristan wouldn't be the only one to suffer for it. Dom would almost certainly lose the business if Tristan was dragged to gaol over some trumped-up charge. So it wasn't just for himself that Tristan wanted George brought down; it was for Dom, too.

Dom had never once chastised Tristan for the chaos set in motion by the theft of Blue Blazes, but that didn't alter Tristan's guilt.

He hated that he'd given George a reason to deprive Dom of his rightful inheritance. He hated that he'd sentenced Dom to a life outside of the society where he belonged. And most of all, he hated that there wasn't a damned thing he could do about it.

"Fortunately," Dom said, "I managed to send Hucker packing before Lady Zoe came downstairs."

"But he saw her enter?"

"Almost certainly, but she came in a hackney, so he won't know who she is, and he definitely won't know why she was here."

"I damned well hope not. That would be sticky for her as well as for us."

Dom slanted a glance at him. "Speaking of sticky matters, her ladyship seemed awfully flustered when she left."

"Can't imagine why," Tristan lied. Dom would probably *not* approve of how Tristan had handled the woman.

Not that it mattered. They were equal partners in the business, which meant they had equal say in everything. Tristan had put plenty of his own money into Manton's Investigations once he'd returned from France, so Dom had added his name to all the legal documents.

"What do you think of Lady Zoe's tale?" Dom asked him.

"I think it highly unlikely that her father acquired her from a Gypsy."

"Though if he did, she has a reason for concern," Dom pointed out.

"I suppose."

Dom leaned against the desk to eye him with rank curiosity. "Lady Zoe irritates you, doesn't she?"

To avoid his brother's too-probing gaze, Tristan headed for the decanter stashed in a cabinet near the window. "No more than the average lady of rank."

"That's nonsense. I've never seen you be anything but perfectly charming to pretty women, no matter what their rank. If anything, the ladies of rank rouse you to exert yourself even further. You flirt and you flatter, and in so doing dismiss them as anything but potential bed partners. It's your peculiar way of keeping them at arm's length."

Sometimes he hated how perceptive his blasted half brother was. "So perhaps I've changed my tactics," Tristan said as he poured himself a generous glass of brandy. "Perhaps I've given up on hiding how much ladies of rank irritate me."

"And you made this profound change for Lady Zoe?" Dom lowered his voice. "Take care, Tristan. That particular young lady is not yours for the picking."

Tristan downed a slug of brandy. "I don't recall saying that she was."

"You didn't have to. I saw how disheveled she looked when she left here, with her lips reddened and her —"

"Are you implying I did something inappropriate while you were gone?"

"Did you?"

Tristan scowled. "If you didn't trust me, you shouldn't have given me the case," he said, avoiding the question. "But now that you have, I'll handle it however I see fit."

"That's what I'm afraid of."

"I'm not as bad as rumor has it, you know," he grumbled. At Dom's snort, he added, "All right, so I'm almost as bad. But that doesn't mean I can't behave myself around Lady Zoe."

"I hope you will. Because she's the marrying sort — not the tumble-in-the-hay sort."

"I'm quite aware of that, believe me," he bit out.

"Although I suppose if your intentions are honorable —"

"Oh, for God's sake, you know I'm not looking to marry."

Dom blinked. *"Ever?"*

"I suppose I will one day, after the business is on a firmer footing." He swirled the brandy in his glass. "But only when I find a pretty woman who doesn't bore me, with a keen mind and a solid character."

"That's unlikely to happen, when you only associate with featherheaded actresses and giggling opera dancers." Dom's gaze narrowed on him. "And might I point out that Lady Zoe fits your description."

Tristan glowered at him. "First you tell me that the woman isn't mine for the picking, and now you suggest I marry her."

"I'm merely saying —"

"I don't see *you* rushing to marry, either," he went on, tired of Dom's poking at him. Time to go on the offensive. "Even though Jane Vernon has been waiting fruitlessly for you all these years."

The temperature in the room instantly dropped. The minute Dom clenched his jaw hard enough to shatter teeth, Tristan regretted baiting him. But he *did* want to know why his idiot brother remained stubborn about the woman he'd been engaged to thirteen years ago. It was clear to everyone on God's green earth that his former fiancée would still marry him if Dom would only renew his offer.

"Leave Jane out of this," Dom snapped. "Lady Zoe is our client, and I deserve to know whether you can handle her properly."

"Trust me, I can handle Lady Zoe perfectly well." Properly, improperly, and every way in between. As long as she didn't get too close. "I can certainly handle her better than you handled Jane."

"Damn it, Tristan —"

"I suppose you've heard that she's engaged to the Earl of Blakeborough."

Judging from the warning glitter in Dom's eyes, he had indeed heard. "I don't want to talk about Jane."

"Right. Because God forbid you'd admit that you shouldn't have let her go after George threw us all out."

"I didn't let her . . . Blast it, this is none of your affair!" Shoving away from the desk, he headed for the door. "I wish you and Lisette would stop plaguing me about Jane. You don't know the situation."

"We would if you told us."

Dom glared at him. "Go to hell." Then he headed out the door.

Tristan stared after him, sipping his brandy. Getting Dom to leave him be afforded him little satisfaction. Dom still clearly had feelings for Jane, but that wouldn't do him a bit of good if Jane meant to marry some other fellow.

Perhaps it was Jane's connection to

George that put Dom off. As the cousin of George's wife, Jane spent a great deal of time with the arse. It might have changed her. George might even have convinced Jane to see matters from his side — though if he had, Dom was better off without her.

Tristan set his glass down. That gave him just one more reason to find out George's dirty secrets. Because he had no doubt that George was at the root of why Jane had jilted Dom. And Tristan would make the bloody devil pay for *that,* too.

He glanced out the window. It wasn't dark yet, and the mail coach didn't leave London for Liverpool until 7:00 P.M. If he traveled tonight he could be in the Customs offices first thing in the morning, which might shorten his trip.

Good. Because the sooner he found out the truth about Lady Zoe's birth, the sooner he could either move on to the next phase of his investigation . . . or be free to pursue his other leads.

Either way, he *would* figure out how to hoist George by his own petard.

5

Three days after her visit to Manton's Investigations, Zoe paced the drawing room of her family's town house, which spanned most of one end of Berkeley Square. Aunt Flo sat perfectly straight on the only half-way comfortable chair available, awaiting Mr. Jeremy Keane with complete composure.

Meanwhile, Zoe was a bundle of nerves. After landing in Liverpool, her cousin had sent a note ahead that he'd be arriving sometime midafternoon. It was already well past noon, so he should be here any moment. Two days early, thanks to favorable winds.

Botheration. Mr. Bonnaud was almost certainly still in Liverpool himself.

His voice sounded in her head. *After what we just did, you can damned well call me by my Christian name in private.*

Her cheeks heated. She refused to think

of that scoundrel as Tristan . . . except at night, when reliving their foolish, impulsive, *intoxicating* kisses. He shouldn't have kissed her.

She shouldn't have let him. Because now she thought of it all the time. Which was ridiculous. *And* annoying. Truly, men as smooth-tongued and handsome as Mr. Tristan Bonnaud shouldn't even be allowed out in public until they were at least forty.

When an image of a prison full of rakes, rogues, and scoundrels waiting for their hair to go gray sprang into her mind, she giggled.

"No giggling," Aunt Flo chided as she set down her embroidery. "You sound like a chit fresh out of the schoolroom. You are heir to the Earl of Olivier, for heaven's sake! Behave like it. Gentlemen do not like silly girls."

"No, they do not," Papa said as he entered the room. "And what in God's name are you wearing, girl?"

She gazed down at her perfectly presentable gown. "A day dress. Why?"

"It's yellow. It should be white. Girls your age are supposed to wear white."

"But —" Zoe began.

"She's hardly a girl anymore, Roderick," Aunt Flo said, patting her perfectly coifed salt-and-pepper hair. "Besides, white hasn't been the fashionable color for day dresses for some time."

"Fashion be damned, she ought to be wearing white." He tugged at his modestly tied white cravat as he went to gaze out the window. "Mr. Keane is not coming here to see a circus show."

Zoe winced. "I hardly think that a yellow —"

"And what about those purple gloves?" he asked, directing the question to Aunt Flo. "And the black things about her wrists?"

"The color is lilac, not purple, and the lace bracelets are —" Zoe began.

"Well, I agree with you there," Aunt Flo said, taking small, even stitches in the fabric. "Yellow and black and lilac. A vile combination, but one she got straight out of some ladies' magazine. And you know your daughter. She must have a bit of 'dash' in her clothes . . . and in the furniture and draperies and her curricle."

Zoe sighed. "I don't see what's wrong with —"

"Gentlemen don't like 'dash,' " Papa muttered. "They like sensible girls with sensible ideas."

"I have sensible ideas," Zoe protested. "It's just that —"

"It's not the clothing that worries me,

flashy though it may be," Aunt Flo went on. "It's the way she carries herself. She walks too fast for a lady."

Papa turned to scowl at Aunt Flo. "Don't be absurd. She walks perfectly fine."

"Says the Major, who would have us all marching about like soldiers if he could." Aunt Flo stabbed a needle into her embroidery. "That's the trouble. She spends too much time rambling about Winborough with you. I don't know what Agnes was thinking, to let you drag her everywhere from the time she was five."

"I always liked —" Zoe began.

"She had to learn how to manage the place," Papa said stiffly. "It'll be hers one day. And I'll have you know . . ."

At that point, Zoe gave up. This had been going on for three days, a constant battle between Papa and Aunt Flo about how she should act and dress and walk, and who was at fault for the things she did badly. Though she was used to the criticism and knew it came from good intentions, today it unnerved her.

Did they say such things because they were sure that she wasn't of their blood? Or was it just because they wanted the best for her? Or both?

Oh, Lord, what if she *wasn't* really Papa's

daughter?

Fighting to put that horrible possibility from her mind, she took Papa's place at the window while he and Aunt Flo argued. They were still arguing ten minutes later when a coach pulled up in front.

Zoe froze. He was here. It was time. Heaven save her.

Holding her breath, she watched as the steps were set down and the carriage door opened. A booted foot emerged, followed by a second. When they proved to be connected to a very tall, lean man with hair the color of ripening wheat, she sagged against the window frame in abject relief.

He wasn't ugly. He wasn't short or fat or — her greatest fear — half-bald like Papa. And when he turned to speak to the footman, and she saw his attire in full, she broke into a smile. Watching him meet Papa might actually be fun.

Turning from the window, she said cheerily, "It looks like Mr. Keane has arrived, Papa."

Aunt Flo settled her skirts. "Come away from the window, for pity's sake! We can't have him see you gawking like some urchin at the fair."

Meanwhile, Papa was smoothing his coat and straightening his posture. Zoe bit back a smile. One of the many things Papa had taken away from his years in the army was the necessity of dressing sharply, which, to him, meant precision creases, dull colors, and nothing remotely remarkable.

Their butler appeared in the doorway. "Mr. Jeremy Keane, my lord."

When the man walked in she watched her father, whose expression became so carefully fixed in a smile that she knew at once he was screaming inside. Because Mr. Keane wore attire that was the very essence of remarkable — a green and gold striped waistcoat beneath a bottle-green coat, with a matching striped cravat casually tied about his neck.

Papa thrust out his hand to the fellow. "Welcome to our home, cousin."

With a genial smile, Mr. Keane shook it. "Thank you, sir. I'm pleased to meet you all at last."

Swiftly, Papa made introductions. Zoe noticed that her cousin seemed distracted. He kept surveying his surroundings as if taking inventory of the furnishings. Only when Papa introduced her did Mr. Keane give anyone his full attention.

Zoe offered him her hand. "We're delighted to have you here."

"Glad to be here, coz," he said most

informally as he took her hand. To her surprise, he brought it to his lips and pressed a kiss to it.

Papa snorted beside her. She well knew his opinion of hand kissing — it was "Frenchified" and excessive.

As Mr. Keane released her, his eyes, almost the same blue as Tristan's, gleamed. Yet somehow when she looked into them, naughty images didn't immediately spring to mind as they had with Tristan.

You'll know within seconds of meeting him whether you desire him.

Balderdash. Why was she listening to anything that devil had said, anyway? For that matter, why was she even comparing her cousin to the man?

When he straightened, Mr. Keane swept her with an interested glance, much as Tristan had, from the lilac ribbons in her coiffure to her black kid slippers. But though his smile broadened as if he liked what he saw, it didn't rouse any heat in her belly.

Should she be alarmed by that? Or pleased?

Definitely alarmed. She might have to marry him, after all.

"How pretty you look, Lady Zoe," he said smoothly. "I was afraid that English ladies might prove duller than our bold American ones, but clearly I was wrong."

At least he knew how to flatter a lady properly, unlike a certain dark-haired gentleman. "Thank you, sir. Coming from an artist as accomplished as you, that is quite a compliment."

He shrugged. "I confess I see things differently from most. It's contrasts that fascinate me, not similarities. So sometimes I enjoy clothes with a bit more . . . shall we say . . ."

"Dash?" she put in, deliberately not looking at Papa and Aunt Flo.

"That's the word." A smile tugged at his lips. "Dash."

When Papa stiffened, Aunt Flo jumped in. "You must be hungry after your long journey, Mr. Keane. Cook has prepared a bit of tea and some cakes, if you are so inclined."

"I don't drink tea, but if you have coffee . . ."

"We do," Zoe said hastily before Papa could launch into his lecture about the evil effects of coffee on the constitution. She gestured to the door. "This way, Mr. Keane."

The next two hours passed pleasantly enough, despite Papa's reserve. As her cousin drank coffee and downed ginger biscuits at an alarming rate, Aunt Flo consulted him on her plans for the soiree she intended to throw tomorrow to celebrate his visit to London. He seemed oddly reticent to discuss it and soon turned the conversation to wild tales of his voyage. Before long, he had them laughing at his deft characterizations.

Even Papa unbent enough to add a few anecdotes about his days in the army. She'd heard them all more than once, but Mr. Keane seemed to find them interesting enough. So it was nearly four o'clock before she noticed the time.

She turned to her cousin. "I know you must be exhausted from your journey, so if you'd like to retire to your room for a bit before dinner . . ."

"Actually, after being cooped up on a ship for days and then for hours more in that carriage, I have plenty of restless energy to work off. I'd rather take a walk, or even ride, if that's possible."

"Zoe goes riding nearly every day, sir," Aunt Flo put in eagerly before Zoe could prevent it. "I'm sure she'd be delighted to have you join her."

Oh, dear, she hadn't planned on taking her cousin with her on her daily rides. But the likelihood of Tristan's having already returned was small, so she ought to be safe.

"And you, Lord Olivier?" Mr. Keane asked. "Will you be joining us, too?"

"Not if I can help it," Papa retorted. "Even in the winter, Rotten Row has far too many people to suit my taste."

Papa's sciatica always acted up in damp, cold weather, though he wasn't about to say that to their cousin. The Major never liked to be seen as weak.

Mr. Keane's eyes met hers, twinkling. "Any place called Rotten Row has to be entertaining."

"It is indeed, sir. And if you'll give me a moment to change into my riding habit, I'd be happy to accompany you there."

A short while later she and her cousin set off on horseback down Curzon Street for Stanhope Gate, with Ralph lagging far behind. Clearly Papa had ordered Ralph to give them some privacy.

Her cousin apparently noticed, for he glanced back at the footman, then winked at her. "I'm happy your family didn't come along."

"Oh? Why?"

"Because now you can tell me all the things I really want to know. Where can I find a good cigar? I have completely run

117

out. And where do the most interesting folk congregate — the most reckless ladies and the boldest gentlemen? Am I likely to see many at this Rotten Row place?"

She gaped at him, hardly sure where to begin answering. "Papa has cigars, I think," she said. "But he would never smoke them around me."

"Ah."

"As for where *interesting* people congregate, you will get to meet some tomorrow night at Aunt Flo's soiree."

As predicted, she'd had no trouble convincing Aunt Flo to invite the rest of the Duke's Men, though she'd made no attempt to invite Tristan. She only hoped that if she didn't see Tristan by tomorrow night, she could find out from Mr. Manton what Tristan had discovered.

Slanting a glance at her cousin, she noticed a decided chill in his expression. He hadn't seemed too happy about the soiree when Aunt Flo had first mentioned it, either. "I hope you don't mind that my aunt has arranged a party so soon after your arrival."

"I confess that I tire of being trotted out to be admired as the great Jeremy Keane," he said in a clipped tone. But when he caught her frown, he sighed. "Forgive me, I don't mean to be ungrateful for your family's kindness. My mother has always spoken highly of yours, from when your parents visited America shortly before your birth."

Her breath quickened. "Do you remember it? You would have been old enough."

"I was eight . . . but I wasn't home when your parents came. I was visiting my American grandmother at the time."

"So you didn't meet them," she said, trying to keep the disappointment out of her voice.

"No. Why?"

"I was just curious to know what they were like back then."

She could hardly tell him that she wanted to know if there'd been any mention of Mama's impending child when her parents were visiting there. But surely if his family had suspected that Mama hadn't actually borne Zoe, they would have said something before now to *someone,* and almost certainly to him.

They rode past one of the bigger mansions, and his expression turned pensive. "This seems a very nice part of town."

The abrupt shift in subject threw her off. "It's generally considered to be so, yes."

"It must cost a great deal to live here."

She bristled at the statement. "I wouldn't

know, sir," she said, though that was a lie. "Well-bred English ladies — and gentlemen, for that matter — don't discuss such matters."

He cast her a sidelong glance. "I've offended you. Forgive me."

"Not at all."

"I want us to be friends," he said, in that too-familiar manner he'd used ever since his arrival.

She softened. "We're cousins, so of course we'll be friends."

He arched one eyebrow. "I have a few American cousins who might disagree," he said dryly. "I'm considered something of an outlier even by family."

"Why?"

His expression hardened. "Because of my blunt speech. I don't suffer fools easily."

"Believe it or not," she admitted, "I'm considered blunt by English standards myself."

"Aha, I *knew* it! I was sure from the first that we were kindred spirits. Any lady who wears yellow and lilac together has to share my well-developed sense of adventure."

He kept using that word *friends*. Perhaps Papa had been too quick to assume that her cousin would be interested in marrying an Englishwoman.

They rode through Stanhope Gate, and her cousin frowned at her. "We're in a park."

"Yes. Hyde Park. That's where Rotten Row is."

His frown deepened. "I imagined something more . . . 'rotten.' A street of gaming hells or theaters or even brothels."

"Mr. Keane! You must not speak of 'brothels' in polite society. Goodness gracious. Do you say such things in front of American ladies?"

"Of course not." He was staring straight ahead down the path. "But everyone in America knows that you English lords and ladies are licentious. That's why my ancestors fled to the colonies in the first place."

She was about to give him a piece of her mind when he glanced over and she saw the glint in his eyes. Oh, Lord, another one. He was teasing her.

Two could play that game. "And everyone in England knows that you colonials all eat bear and fight off Indians regularly. So where are your bear-hide boots? And where did you stow your hunting knife in your dashing clothes?"

He laughed. "All right, coz, you have me there."

They'd reached Rotten Row, so she turned onto the wide path. There weren't nearly as

121

many people riding as in the height of the season, but it was busy enough to require that they keep to one side.

"We're here," she told him.

He stared about him in confusion. "Why is a dirt track under the trees called Rotten Row?"

"Truthfully? Because certain of the English could not pronounce 'route du Roi' properly."

"So it was once a road for kings?"

The man continued to surprise her. "You speak French?" She couldn't resist teasing him again. "I thought you Americans spoke nothing but Indian."

He eyed her askance. "Firstly, Indian isn't a language — each tribe has its own. Secondly, I know all the appropriate languages. I did have a proper education." His tone turned acid. "Even by English standards."

"Now it's my turn to beg forgiveness for offending," she said softly.

"No offense taken." He stared out over the crowd, his expression pensive. "As I told you before, I wish us to be friends. Because I will need a friend in the coming weeks."

"Why?"

"You have no idea how cutthroat artists and critics can be. And they are almost certainly going to be disappointed by the work I've chosen to exhibit. They're expecting a young Benjamin West."

She had heard a little about the American artist who'd visited England more than half a century ago and ended up staying. "Wasn't he a portrait painter?"

"And a painter of grand historical scenes." His voice tightened. "That's what they want, especially since my earlier work was exactly that." He got that distracted look on his face again. "But I mean to give them something more natural . . . and more savage — scenes of death in dark forests and drunken, bloody fights in taverns. What happens when man encounters his own mortality."

She swallowed hard. "That sounds . . . um . . ."

"Depressing?"

"Perhaps a bit." She'd already witnessed Mama's death firsthand; she didn't need to see death in paintings, too. "But then, I don't know much about art."

He snorted. "That's the problem. The fine academies of London and Paris and even my native Philadelphia have convinced people that only certain lofty persons can truly appreciate art. But everyone ought to be able to find works that resonate with them, whether ordinary or fantastical. And decent artists ought to be able to mine drama from even the mundane."

She brightened. "You mean, like the drama of an owl swooping down upon a mouse?"

"Something like that. Though I prefer that people be part of the drama." He glanced around. "I was hoping to see some drama at your Rotten Row, but there's not much drama in *this* crowd to paint. I suppose that cavalry officer flirting with a maid has potential. Or that child entangling himself in a rosebush in his attempt to escape his nurse."

His gaze wandered farther, then fixed on something off the path ahead. "Better yet, there's that mysterious rider under the oak tree ahead who's been watching us for the past ten minutes."

"Watching us?" She followed the direction of his gaze, then caught her breath.

Lord save her. Tristan was here.

6

Tristan wasn't sure why it annoyed him to see Zoe riding with a gentleman who looked so blond, well formed, and respectable, if a bit raffish.

Perhaps it was because the man was also clearly eligible, given his age and the way he edged his horse closer to her protectively as he spotted Tristan staring. Apparently the sight of a road-weary fellow wearing a serviceable greatcoat stained by mud and rain put Zoe's blasted gentleman friend on guard.

Good. Let him worry.

Still, with Zoe's gaze assessing him, Tristan regretted riding over here in such haste. He should have waited until tomorrow, when he could look more presentable. But given his news, he'd thought he should tell her as soon as possible.

Ballocks, you arse. You just wanted to see her.

He scowled. All right, so perhaps she *was* a sight for sore eyes in that fur-trimmed riding habit that skimmed her figure so well. And perhaps he'd been looking forward to baiting her and making her blush. To annoying her by calling her "princess."

It meant nothing. *She* meant nothing. No matter how entertaining he found her, in the end she was only a client and an excuse for searching for Milosh.

Right. And he was only an investigator. Who itched to kiss her throat just where the fur brushed the skin. To feel that delicate mouth open beneath —

Damn it, he was *not* here for that.

She murmured something to the gentleman, then rode toward Tristan with her companion at her side.

He gritted his teeth. Why hadn't she dispensed with the fellow so he could give her the news in private?

"Mr. Bonnaud!" she said as they reached the shade of the oak. "How good to see you again."

"Good day, Lady Zoe. You're looking very well."

Tristan watched her companion's reaction, but if the man knew who Tristan was by name, he showed no sign of it. Behind him, however, Footman Ralph glowered at

Tristan in a way that gave him pause. Had Zoe confided to the pup what had happened in the office earlier in the week?

That seemed unlikely. Even he would surely have reported that to her father if he'd known.

"Mr. Bonnaud," she said in the lyrical voice that made his every muscle flex, "may I present my cousin Mr. Jeremy Keane?"

Bloody hell. Leave it to the man to show up when and where he wasn't wanted.

Keane acknowledged him with a nod, but his gaze grew calculating as he glanced from Tristan to Zoe. "Any friend of my cousin's is a friend of mine, sir. How exactly *do* you know Lady Zoe?"

Before Tristan could answer, Zoe jumped in. "We met at some party, did we not, Mr. Bonnaud?"

"Yes." Tristan forced a smile. "Clearly a very dull one, since neither of us can remember which one it was."

Her cousin gave a hearty laugh. Damn. The chap had a sense of humor. Not to mention extraordinary good looks for an American. Tristan had secretly hoped that Keane would be less . . . Adonis-like. Especially after what Tristan had learned on his trip.

"In any case," Zoe hastened to say, "my

127

cousin has just arrived from America." She cast Tristan a meaningful glance. "He disembarked in Liverpool."

It took Tristan a second to catch on to why she'd mentioned it. "I was just in Liverpool myself, Mr. Keane."

"Were you? How odd. What were you doing there?"

Fortunately, Tristan was accustomed to thinking on his feet. "I was meeting a friend of mine and his wife, who'd come here from Canada. I'd heard gossip that his wife had recently borne a child, but the rumors turned out to be false. She set foot on shore without a babe in arms. And her husband confirmed that she was not, nor had ever been, *enceinte.*"

He dared not look at Zoe, but her sharp intake of breath told him that she'd taken his meaning. She would want to hear details later, of course, want to know exactly what he'd found out at the Customs office, but at least she now had a definitive answer as to whether she'd been born on her parents' voyage.

She had not.

But clearly she didn't quite wish to believe it. "Are you talking about our mutual friend . . . Mrs. Major?" she asked shakily.

Mrs. Major? Oh, right, she called her

father "the Major." "Yes, that's her. Came on shore and went through Customs with only her husband for company."

The color drained from her pretty cheeks. When she almost seemed to sway in the saddle, he wished to God he didn't have to do this with an audience.

Swallowing convulsively, she searched his face. "I was so hopeful . . ."

"Yes, we all were." Well, that was a lie — he'd been hoping to be able to pursue the Gypsy angle further, and now he could. But knowing what it meant for her, he hated having to give her such news. "Unfortunately, the Majors hadn't added a child to their nursery after all."

Twisting the reins round in her hand, she gave a jerky bob of her head. "It's sad, but such is life. I suppose it can't be helped."

"No." Taking pity on her, Tristan changed the subject. "So, Mr. Keane, what brings you to London?"

"Business." Keane slid a knowing look at Zoe. "And a bit of pleasure, too, I hope."

Damn it all. Now that Zoe knew she wasn't her mother's daughter, she would be angling to *marry* this fellow. He shouldn't be bothered by that; why did he care whom the chit married?

But he was. And he did.

129

"You may actually have heard of Mr. Keane," Zoe said in that carefully precise tone that betrayed her agitation to Tristan. "He's a well-known American artist."

With a clear penchant for fetching females. "How interesting. I've never met an American. Or, for that matter, an artist." Some devil seized him, and he added, "In my line of work artists are scarce, although I suppose I could include that forger I caught last year in Antwerp. It takes a certain amount of artistry to forge a banknote, don't you think, Mr. Keane?"

To his surprise, Keane burst into laughter. "More artistry than I would dare use, sir. I understand that they hang forgers in England. And since I prefer to keep my neck its usual length, I don't intend to practice any artistry of *that* kind."

Zoe looked annoyed. "I'm sure Mr. Bonnaud wasn't implying that you might be a criminal."

"Of course not," Tristan said. "Anyone can tell that your cousin is a respectable man."

"I wouldn't go that far," Keane drawled. "But I do try to uphold the law, if only out of a sense of self-preservation. And can I assume, from your activities catching forgers, that you try to enforce it?"

Zoe shot Tristan a warning glance.

He ignored it. "You could say that. I work for an investigative agency in London."

"A working man, eh?" Keane looked speculative. "It's good to hear that English aristocrats aren't as insular as we Americans have been led to believe. Clearly they do respect a useful sort of man, if they're willing to invite him to society parties where he can meet young ladies like my cousin."

"Oh, yes," Tristan said with a smirk for Zoe, "the English aristocracy is quite enlightened. We all ramble about together, don't we, my lady?"

She stared daggers at him. She did that a lot. He rather liked it. Her temper was what lent her kisses all their fiery intensity, and he was definitely fond of her kisses.

Shifting her attention to her cousin, she said loftily, "You seem to be laboring under a misapprehension about English aristocrats, Mr. Keane. We, too, are useful sorts, as Mr. Bonnaud knows perfectly well. Lords run their estates and serve in Parliament, both of which duties they take quite seriously."

"Really?" Keane said. "Sounds dull to me."

"It's not dull at all!" she said fervently. "I can't speak firsthand of serving in Parliament, but running an estate . . ." Her face lit up. "You have no idea how wonderful it is to be a steward of the land, to know that your efforts bring food to hundreds, supply farmers with work, transform rough lawns into glorious gardens. Watching it all take shape before one's very eyes is magical."

Keane gave a cynical laugh and turned to Tristan with a raised eyebrow. "What do you think, Bonnaud? Does that sound magical to you?"

Envy pierced him unexpectedly . . . of her life, her manner of existence . . . the land she got to oversee.

He scowled at himself. Envy? Absurd. He didn't envy her one jot. He might have considered such work rewarding years ago, when Father had dangled in front of him the possibility of doing some of it. But after years of crisscrossing the Continent and England, he probably wouldn't care for it.

He'd much rather spend his time poring over birth records, watching a house for hours while waiting for his quarry to emerge . . . trudging through the human muck of London looking for needles in haystacks.

Sharing a house with his brother that was less a home than a convenient place to sleep.

"That doesn't sound remotely magical,"

he forced himself to answer. *Liar.*

Zoe gave him a sad look. "I understand why you would not wish for such a life, Mr. Bonnaud — you've never known what it's like, so it must sound very tedious to you." She turned to her cousin. "But you, with your liking for seeing the drama in the mundane, ought to appreciate it."

"I appreciate it, coz," Keane said. "I just prefer to observe it, to paint it. I have no desire to be part of it. Can't imagine anything more soul-destroying than going over endless account books and arranging planting schedules."

Mangling her reins, she leaned forward in the saddle. "But you're Papa's heir if something should happen to me! Surely you wish to know a little —"

"A very little," her cousin quipped. "Let us therefore pray that nothing *does* happen to you." He waggled his eyebrows. "And if you're worried that I've come here to murder you and your father in your sleep so I can inherit, you can put that idea to rest. The idea of running Winborough doesn't appeal to me."

When she looked stricken, Keane said in a teasing tone, "Unless, of course, I get to do more of what I've always heard that English lords *really* spend their time doing:

133

gambling, wenching, and watching cock-fights. That sort of life I might enjoy . . . when I'm not painting."

"Haven't I already made it clear that English lords don't live that sort of life at all?" Zoe cried.

Tristan suppressed a snort. Even after learning she was a lady in name only, she was still defending their kind.

Keane exchanged a knowing glance with Tristan. "So *none* of them are spending their time at gaming hells and hunting lodges? All that gossip about English gentlemen that we hear in America is invented?"

"A complete fabrication," Tristan said before Zoe could answer. "And the mistresses they hide in little cottages are imaginary, too, along with the money sunk into bad investments, and the time spent drinking until all hours at fine gentlemen's clubs."

Zoe's eyes sparked green in the fading light. "I'll grant you that there *are* gentlemen who are irresponsible gamblers and rakehells, but I know none personally. My father divides his time between sitting in Parliament and running Winborough, or teaching *me* to run it. My aunt spends her days in charitable works or in teaching me valuable skills as well, and her friends do the same."

Suitably chastened, Keane said, "Forgive me, coz. I get carried away in tweaking your English nose. But I am well aware of your father's fine character, I swear."

"It isn't entirely your fault." Straightening in her sidesaddle, she shot Tristan a veiled glance. "Mr. Bonnaud enjoys egging you on, I'm afraid. But of course, his perspective of the aristocracy is a bit different since he spends all his time with criminals."

"Not *all* my time, my lady," Tristan said dryly. "I'm here at Rotten Row, after all, observing the many fine ladies and gentlemen from London's upper echelons." He swept his glance over the crowd. "And they do appear to be very busy with their estates, indeed." When she bristled, he added, "But then, everyone must have some relaxation, eh, Keane?"

"Absolutely. And since my cousin is clearly unwilling to tell me — or, more likely, is unaware of — where to find them, perhaps *you* could reveal the location of the famous gaming hells and brothels of London."

Zoe's rigid stance gave Tristan a twinge of guilt. He and Keane really were taxing her composure. Brothels, indeed.

He should rebuke Keane for speaking of that in front of a lady. But it might be better to fall in with the man's request instead, just to show Zoe that Keane would *not* make her a good husband, in case she hadn't already figured that out on her own. "Say the word, Mr. Keane, and I'll give you a tour of the most wicked spots."

"Why does it not surprise me that you know where they are?" Zoe muttered.

Tristan bit back a smile. "You should expect that of a man who 'spends all his time with criminals,' my lady."

"Speaking of that, Bonnaud, perhaps you could give me a tour of the places where criminals congregate, too," Keane said. "I'd like to paint them. The seedier, the better. I believe in showing man's natural savagery."

The American was turning out to be not at all what Tristan had expected. And probably not what Zoe had expected, either. "I can show you all the natural savagery you crave, sir," Tristan said. "If you have the time."

"He doesn't," Zoe said firmly. "I have it on good authority that the Society of British Artists has a number of activities planned for him in connection with his exhibit." She lifted her chin at her cousin. "And don't forget Aunt Flo's soiree tomorrow night, sir. You must attend that, or she will be very hurt."

Keane groaned. "Right." Then he glanced

at Tristan. "Are you attending? That might liven it up."

It damned well would. Zoe's family would pitch an apoplectic fit if a half-French bastard who worked in 'trade' darkened the hallowed doors of their fine Mayfair town house. "I'm afraid I'm not invited."

"Aren't you?" Keane glanced from Tristan to Zoe with decided speculation in his eyes. "Well, then *I* invite you. The soiree is for me, after all, so I ought to be able to invite a friend, eh?"

Panic showed in Zoe's face. "I'm sure Mr. Bonnaud is far too busy with his cases to come to a soiree. Aren't you, Mr. Bonnaud?"

Not on his life. He wasn't about to pass up a chance to see Keane's effect on the unsuspecting English public. He couldn't wait to watch the fellow prove himself to be exactly the wrong sort of husband for her. To see her family's shock firsthand.

Besides, he still had to give her a report on what he'd found. How better to do that than at a soiree where her family would be preoccupied with their guests? Indeed, getting to know her family more directly would help his investigation.

You know bloody well that's not why you want to go. You want to thumb your nose at

137

them all. And dance with her.

Ignoring that truth, he said, "I'm sure I can make time for one soiree, princess."

When her gaze widened in alarm and Keane eyed him with interest, Tristan realized what he'd called her. Damn. He was usually more circumspect.

Zoe tried to smooth it over. "Well then, sir, we'll be happy to have you attend. Since your brother is invited, it should be an easy matter for you to accompany him."

"Then afterward we can take that tour of gaming hells and brothels, eh, Bonnaud?" Keane said, though the gleam in his eyes showed that she hadn't distracted him from Tristan's slip in the least. If anything, the man had made note of it. "Perhaps your brother can join us."

"Perhaps," Tristan said noncommittally, although Dom would rather eat rocks than visit a brothel. He was practically a monk in his habits.

"We should go, cousin," Zoe cut in with a glance at the darkening sky. "It's getting late, and Papa will be expecting us home soon." Turning her mare determinedly back toward the path, she added with a note of false cheer, "Good evening, Mr. Bonnaud. We shall see you tomorrow night."

"I'll be there . . . Lady Zoe." He'd nearly

said "princess" again just to "tweak her nose" as Keane put it, but something in her vulnerable stance had kept him from it.

Still, he couldn't regret his earlier slip. Keane was clearly not for her, so if thinking that Tristan had a close friendship with Zoe would put the man off, so be it.

Tristan had lived daily in the shadow of his father, who'd married out of a sense of duty. It had cost Father's wife and family dearly. It had cost Mother and Lisette and him even more.

Being the wife of a man whose tastes ran to brothels and gaming hells was no life for Zoe, no matter what it meant for her precious Winborough. Somehow Tristan had to force her to see that, to consider other alternatives.

Because no estate on earth was worth making a bad marriage.

7

Zoe stood in the receiving line at the soiree, wanting desperately to cry. All these people treating her like Lady Zoe, when she was nothing more than someone's castoff. And why did it haunt her so? She'd known Papa might not be her father and Aunt Flo not her aunt. Still, after Tristan's surreptitious revelation yesterday had confirmed it . . .

Swallowing her tears ruthlessly, she forced a smile for the next couple in the line, who just happened to be Victor Cale and his wife, Isabella. Did they know her situation now? Could they tell her heart was breaking? Were they secretly thinking that she looked nothing like her family and really didn't belong . . .

"Thank you for coming," she said in as normal a tone as she could muster.

"It's good to see you again, Lady Zoe," Mr. Cale said. There was no irony in those last two words, thank heaven. So perhaps he didn't know.

"The decorations are just lovely," Mrs. Cale added.

"Oh, thank you," she said, and they moved on.

The Keane town house was decked from stem to stern in cherry blossoms, without a bit of dash anywhere, which had bothered her when Aunt Flo had dictated the décor last week. Zoe had argued for lilacs or painted paper lanterns or anything that might make the place sing. But Papa and Aunt Flo had been determined to serve her up to her cousin like a sacrificial virgin, and only white would do for that — both the décor and her gown.

She'd fought over that, too, but lost, so her red shawl had been her tiny rebellion against marriage to her cousin.

Which was pointless now — she *had* to marry him. He held the key to saving Winborough; she couldn't risk the repercussions if the truth got out. He might say he had no interest in inheriting, but he also kept making veiled comments about the money. Besides, his family might force the issue even if he did not.

A shiver wracked her. She wasn't the true heir. She wasn't even a Keane. She was Romany.

Which meant she must wrangle a marriage proposal out of her cousin. But how? He didn't seem remotely interested in settling down with a wife. Or, for that matter, settling down with an estate in England and a seat in Parliament.

She glanced at Mr. Keane, standing between her and Papa in the receiving line, dressed in fine evening wear. Tonight, his only bit of dash was his trousers of a brilliant yellow, though they were certainly enough to give Papa heart failure.

She saw Mr. Keane's expression, and her stomach knotted. He was clearly uncomfortable. His lips were drawn into a tight line and he kept watching the door, probably wondering how soon he could make his escape.

She was watching the door, too, but for Tristan. His reference to her as "princess" had roused her cousin's curiosity enough to force her into fielding his sly questions about their "friendship" all the way home yesterday.

Fortunately, Mr. Keane had possessed the good sense not to continue the discussion in front of Papa. And he'd spent most of today on Suffolk Street directing the hanging of his paintings, while she and Aunt Flo prepared for the soiree.

A couple stepped up to Papa — no matter what, he would always be "Papa" to her — and he enthusiastically greeted them as the Duke and Duchess of Lyons. He had apparently met the duke at Parliament, but when the duke introduced Papa to his wife, Zoe didn't need a copy of *Debrett's* to remember exactly who the woman was. Tristan's sister.

The two were practically twins. Though younger than he, Lisette Bonnaud Cale was as lovely as her brother was handsome, with the same inky hair and the same riveting blue eyes.

Zoe's heart began to pound. If Tristan's sister was here, could he be far behind? She resisted the urge to lean forward for a glimpse of him. Instead, she smiled politely while Papa introduced the couple to the other members of his family.

The minute the duke heard Mr. Keane's name, a smile broke over his face. "I'm honored to meet you, sir. I probably shouldn't admit this, but my good friend at the Society of British Artists sneaked me in to view some of your works right before Lisette and I headed here. Unfortunately he wouldn't let me purchase any, or I would now be the proud owner of *Asylum*."

Her cousin's eyes lit up. "You didn't find

143

the subject too dark and oppressive? That's what the American critics said of it."

"No, but then I have reasons for that," the duke answered enigmatically. "I liked that the viewer had to look closely to detect the difference between the insane and their keepers."

"So you spotted the manacle on the youth."

"Half-hidden by his trousers? Yes! I spotted it straightaway!" The duke became so animated in his speech that the duchess laid a hand on his arm as if to steady him.

Seeming to rein himself in, Lyons covered her hand with his. "I found it clever how you use light and shadow. How you suggest that the asylum's keepers are as mad as the inhabitants. And I quite admired the irony of the title — that the asylum *should* be a refuge for the mad, but isn't."

"No one ever grasps that," Mr. Keane said. "For that alone, I will *give* you the painting, sir."

"Nonsense, let him purchase it," drawled a voice behind the duke. "Max can certainly afford it."

She froze. Tristan was here and speaking most familiarly with the duke, who merely laughed.

Aunt Flo, who stood on her other side,

gave a shocked gasp. "Who is *that* impudent fellow?" she whispered.

"Bonnaud!" Mr. Keane exclaimed. "You came. Excellent."

"Is that Rathmoor's French by-blow?" Aunt Flo hissed in Zoe's ear. Thank heaven the room was too loud for anyone else to hear.

Zoe bristled. If the truth ever got out, this was the sort of nasty thing people would say about *her*. Did her aunt even realize that?

"Yes," Zoe hissed back. "He's a by-blow. So is his sister, yet you don't seem to mind *her* being here."

"Of course not. She's a duchess," Aunt Flo said matter-of-factly, as if that blotted out the circumstances of the woman's birth. As Zoe despaired at making her aunt understand how very *wrong* that all was, Aunt Flo surveyed Tristan critically. "I must say, he's dressed very well for a by-blow. Simple but smart. I wouldn't have expected it."

That brought Zoe up short. He was, wasn't he?

He wore a splendid suit of black superfine with touches of velvet. There wasn't an ounce of dash in his matching black velvet waistcoat or his white shirt and simply tied cravat, yet the overall effect was, as Aunt

Flo called it, "smart." So smart it made her mouth water.

A pox on her love of a well-dressed man.

Aunt Flo's fingers dug into her arm like claws. "Nicely attired or no, I did *not* invite him. What's he doing here?"

Judging by Papa's expression, he was wondering the same thing. But he clearly wasn't about to remark on it in front of the duke. The fact that Lyons seemed perfectly comfortable with Tristan set the course for how everyone else was expected to treat him. Since the duke accepted him, Papa and Aunt Flo would be forced to do the same, thank heaven.

Besides, they couldn't ignore the fact that Mr. Keane was clearly pleased by his arrival. Her cousin shook Tristan's hand vigorously.

"Good to see you again, sir," Tristan said.

The duke gaped at him. "How on earth did you meet Mr. Keane before even I had a chance to do so?"

When everyone turned an expectant eye on Tristan, she groaned. Her family would wonder that, too. And if they learned the truth, she was sunk.

Tristan's gaze locked with hers. "We met at the park yesterday. I was with a group of young gallants who knew Lady Zoe, and they introduced me to her and her cousin. Eh, Keane?"

She could have kissed him. Now, if only her cousin would support the lie . . .

"Exactly," Mr. Keane said with a sardonic smile. "Though I must confess I instantly forgot the names of the other gentlemen after hearing your trenchant observations about the English, Bonnaud. You are still going to give me that tour of London sometime, aren't you?"

"As I said yesterday, I'm at your disposal." With a glance back at the line lengthening behind the duke and his family, Tristan added, "Come, Max, let's go find Victor. I believe he and Isa have already arrived."

"We'll talk later, sir," the duke told Mr. Keane before allowing himself to be drawn off.

As the next person moved up to Papa, Mr. Keane bent to whisper, "You said you met Bonnaud at a party. I take it there's more to the story?"

With her heart clamoring in her chest, she smiled up at him. "You must allow a girl to have *some* secrets, cousin."

Something glinted in his eyes before Papa introduced the next person, and Mr. Keane's attention was diverted. As she turned to see where Tristan had gone, she caught him frowning at her.

Why should *he* have cause to frown? She was the one having trouble keeping all her secrets straight. Though she couldn't really blame Tristan for showing up at Hyde Park. He'd only done what she'd asked him to do, after all.

With any luck, Papa and Aunt Flo would believe Tristan's explanation of how they'd met. Her cousin, however, was another matter. His suspicions were thoroughly roused now.

She ought to give Tristan a wide berth tonight, for the sake of fostering a closer friendship with Mr. Keane, but how could she? She had to gain the full report on what he'd discovered in Liverpool.

By the time she was done in the receiving line and went on to the ballroom, the dancing had begun and Tristan was already twirling his sister about the room. Thankfully the duke accosted Mr. Keane before he could claim Zoe for a dance, and the two men fell into a deep and intense discussion, so she didn't have to worry about her cousin just yet.

Papa came up beside her to stare out over the swirling guests. "I don't like that rogue being here."

"Which one?" she asked lightly.

She could see at least five gentlemen whom she would deem rogues. Perhaps Aunt Flo's strategy was to invite scoundrels in order to provoke Mr. Keane into offering to save her by marrying her. Or perhaps Aunt Flo simply couldn't distinguish between rogues and other gentlemen as long as they had titles and fortunes.

"I'm speaking of Bonnaud, of course." Papa clasped his hands behind his back in a military stance. "I can't believe Keane invited him. Didn't you try to stop him?"

"I could hardly be impolite. Besides, you wouldn't wish to look high in the instep around our American cousin, would you? I doubt that Mr. Keane has the same issues with bastardy that —"

"It's not Bonnaud's bastardy that concerns me, dear girl," Papa said. "It's his past."

"You mean, his . . . er . . . wild reputation with women." When Papa looked at her with a question in his eyes, she added hastily, "It's common knowledge. Everyone gossips about it. Is that what worries you?"

"Among other things." The Major's heavily lined brow beetled into a frown. "If he asks you to dance, be sure you refuse."

"Papa! That would be beyond rude."

"Rude or no, if I see him dancing with

149

you, I swear I will call him out."

"Over a dance? Don't be ridiculous."

"I will not have a man like him dancing with my daughter — not after what he did as a youth in Yorkshire."

"Oh? What did he do?"

"Well, I only have the information second-hand, but I was told —"

"Roderick!" Aunt Flo cried as she came hurrying up. "Can't you get Mr. Keane away from Lyons? He ought to be dancing with Zoe, not discussing art. I don't care if Lyons *is* a duke. This may be one of our few chances for Mr. Keane to see what a fine dancer Zoe is!"

Papa sighed. "I can't *make* the fellow ask her to dance, Flo."

"Of course you can. Just use that stentorian voice you regularly inflict upon the rest of us." Aunt Flo turned her matron's eye on Zoe. "And you, young lady. Why aren't you dancing? If your cousin sees how well you pirouette, he might be inspired to do his duty."

"I hardly think that my pirouette is impressive enough to —"

"Go, go!" Aunt Flo said, shooing her off. "If you keep standing here in the corner away from the young gentlemen, *no* one will ask you to dance!"

"Yes, Aunt Flo," she mumbled.

This idea that she was just another debutante on the marriage mart, and not a complete fraud, vexed her. It wouldn't be so hard if she could talk to Aunt Flo and Papa about it, but neither of them would even acknowledge the truth!

Meanwhile, Aunt Flo kept throwing her at men. But sadly, the man Zoe wanted to dance with was unacceptable, and the man she *should* dance with seemed to have no interest.

She skirted the dance floor, picking her way among the guests. She was so intent on scanning the dancers for Tristan that she nearly ran into him.

"My lady," he said, bowing.

She acknowledged him with a nod. "Mr. Bonnaud."

Lord, but he did look spectacular in evening clothes. Those tight trousers encasing muscular calves . . . that wealth of black curls she wanted to tame with her hands. Had it suddenly grown amazingly warm in the ballroom?

A furtive glance behind her revealed Papa still arguing with Aunt Flo, but that wouldn't last long. Aunt Flo generally won. Zoe had to cut this short.

"Mr. Bonnaud, I'm afraid I must —"

"Would you do me the honor of dancing with me, Lady Zoe?"

She blinked at him. "No!" When he raised an eyebrow, she stammered, "I-I mean, much as I would like to, I —" She noticed those standing nearby listening in. "I told Aunt Flo I would make sure everything is ready for the champagne toast coming up."

A speculative expression crossed his face. "I understand. Later, then."

"Yes, perhaps." How she wished all these dratted people weren't around them!

He glanced down at the floor. "Beg pardon, my lady, but I believe you dropped something. Perhaps from your reticule?"

She started to protest that her reticule was sitting on a chair somewhere when she looked down and saw a folded piece of paper. "Oh! Yes, I must have . . . that is . . . Thank you, sir."

As she bent to pick it up, he tipped his head at her and was gone. She unfolded the slip of paper to find the scrawled words, *The east terrace. Fifteen minutes.* He'd been prepared in case she refused him, thank goodness.

Sliding the paper inside her glove, she headed off toward the kitchen in case anyone was watching who'd heard their exchange. But just as she reached the other end of the ballroom she glanced back to see Papa now speaking to her cousin.

She groaned. Clearly Aunt Flo had won the battle, and Mr. Keane was being ordered to dance with her. She'd better escape while she could.

Out in the hall, she paused for breath. Did she dare meet Tristan alone? Might Papa stumble across them?

It seemed unlikely. Papa would find it too cold to go outside, and Tristan had chosen his rendezvous spot well. The east terrace couldn't be seen from the street and had to be accessed from the library rather than the ballroom. So it was unlikely that anyone would stumble across them by accident.

And thanks to her white lie about the champagne, she had an excuse for being absent from the ballroom — as long as no one mentioned it to Aunt Flo. Now she merely had to pray that Tristan could disappear without comment, too.

Unfortunately, someone stopped her in the hall to ask about the musicians, so by the time she sneaked through the library and out onto the terrace, it was twenty minutes later, not fifteen.

Oh, Lord, he wasn't here. He'd gone.

But wait — was that tobacco she smelled?

"You're late. I began to think you weren't

coming."

The husky words, spoken from out of the darkness, sent a frisson of anticipation coursing along her skin. Drat him. The last thing she needed with her life in a shambles was to feel frissons of anything for the scoundrel, yet they seemed to happen with astonishing regularity.

"I had some trouble getting away," she said to the glowing tip of his cigar, all that she could see of him. "We don't have much time, so you'd best get right to it. It wouldn't do to be caught out here together."

He emerged from the shadows, and the gas lamp from inside bathed his serious expression in a soft light. "I suppose your 'papa' warned you off. Is that why you refused to dance with me?" When she didn't answer at once, he waved the cigar, painting a swirl of smoke between them. "Let me guess — he told you I was a big bad wolf who ate sweet young virgins like you for breakfast."

The apt description rankled. "He's not as narrow-minded as you think."

"So that's a yes."

"You can be very annoying sometimes, do you know that?" She pulled her shawl about her thinly clad shoulders. "It's freezing out

154

here. Tell me what you learned in Liver-pool."

"Fine." Dropping the cigar onto the ter-race, he crushed it with his heel. "I assume you understood what I was trying to convey yesterday at the park."

"Yes. That I wasn't listed in the Customs records as having entered the country with Mama and Papa."

"Actually, you *were* listed."

"What? But I thought —"

"Unfortunately, when I saw the entry I re-alized that the original had been altered and an addition made. So I looked up the fellow who'd worked for Customs at the time, and he confessed the truth."

When he hesitated, she prodded, "Which was what?"

"Your parents came through Customs without a babe in arms. But a month later, your father returned to Liverpool and paid the gentleman a substantial sum to alter the record. The Customs officer only admitted to it when I told him I was there seeking the truth on your behalf."

Her head swam. She must have swayed a little, because Tristan stepped up to steady her with a hand beneath her elbow.

"Are you all right?" he murmured.

Somehow she managed a nod.

155

His eyes bored into her. "You already suspected this. It shouldn't come as a shock."

"It's just that . . . until now, it all seemed rather abstract. Like some fantastical story from a fairy tale about children discovering that their parents were really kings or something." She met his gaze. "But when you speak of bribes of officials and Customs records . . . it becomes so much more real. True."

"Ah. I can understand that."

He stood so close that she could feel his warm breath float across her cheek. But when she saw the sympathy in his eyes, it was suddenly too much for her. *He* was too much for her.

Feeling exposed, she tugged her arm free and moved away from his perceptive gaze to the railing, where it was easier for her to think. "None of this proves that my parents were Gypsies."

"No. I won't know that until I do more investigating."

Staring down into the garden, she clutched the rail for support. "When? How soon can you start?"

"I already have. I asked around town today and learned that there's an encampment of Northern Romany clans near Chelsea. Since most of the Gypsies from particular shires know others in their area, I'm hoping that they can tell me about those from Yorkshire. Or that they may *be* from Yorkshire. You never know."

She faced him. "I want to go with you when you visit them."

"Not a chance." His eyes glittered like stars in the semidarkness. Or ice crystals that no amount of female persuasion would melt.

"Why?" she demanded. "I'm paying you. So if I say I want to go —"

"I take it that you don't trust me," he said, his tone harsh.

"No . . . I mean . . . yes, I trust you." She rubbed her chilled arms. "That's not the reason I want to go."

Leaning one shoulder against a pillar, he scrutinized her with the sort of intense look she supposed was necessary in his profession. "Then what *is* the reason?" One side of his mouth crooked upward. "Tiring of your cousin already, are you?"

She huffed out a frosty breath. "That's not it, either. I just . . . I need to hear every word for myself. What if the Gypsies' account sparks a memory of something I overheard as a girl? Or what if they reveal details that only I can make sense of in light

157

of my childhood?"

He stared at her. "You don't understand. I may have to go to several encampments before I glean anything of substance. And how the devil will you get away from this town house to go gadding about town with me?"

"I could do what I did last time. Tell Papa that Ralph and I are going for a walk."

He snorted. "If your Ralph knows one iota of this, he will go straight to your father. He was clearly conflicted yesterday in the park. If you continue much longer to abuse his confidence, he *will* betray it. He knows who pays him."

She sighed. "You're probably right. But there must be some way we can manage it."

"Sorry, but I'm fresh out of ideas for how to sneak a young lady out of her home without her parents . . . her *guardians* noticing."

This situation was slipping from her fingers moment by moment. She hated that feeling. She was used to being in control. "Well," she said peevishly, "I daresay you could think of some way to let me come along if it meant not having your activities of last summer exposed."

He chuckled. "Is that a threat? Because you may recall what happened the last time you attempted that with me."

She knotted her shawl in her fist. "I swear, sometimes you can be very —"

"Annoying," he finished with his usual smirk. "You already said that." Then his smirk vanished, and he pushed away from the pillar. "But I might be willing to come up with a scheme for taking you with me. *If* I were given the proper incentive."

"Incentive?" Given the flare of heat in his gaze, she doubted he meant money.

As he came toward her, the terrace seemed to shrink to encompass just the two of them. She gulped down air, trying to calm her agitation.

Trying to still the excitement unfurling in her chest.

Then he held out his hand. "Dance with me, princess."

8

Tristan wanted, just once, to feel their bodies moving in tandem. To have her in his arms again. It was a foolish whim, but he wanted it all the same. And he could swear she did, too.

"Dance with me," he said, this time making it a demand.

"That's all?" she asked, her eyes luminous in the gaslight. "Just a dance?"

He couldn't suppress his grin. "You were hoping for more, were you?"

"No! I mean . . . I merely assumed, given your reputation . . ."

"What exactly did your father tell you about me?" he asked, his eyes narrowing.

She twisted the ends of her shawl in one hand. "Leave Papa out of this. He's merely being cautious and looking out for me."

"By throwing you at Keane, a man you barely know."

"A man I have to marry, if Aunt Flo's tale

160

of my past turns out to be as true as it's beginning to seem."

That inflamed his temper. "All the more reason you should dance with *me* while you still can." When she didn't take his hand, just continued to stare at it, he added, "Come, Zoe, it's just a dance."

She glanced beyond him to the French doors leading out onto the terrace. "Someone might see."

Obviously she meant Keane, damn it. And the image of her and Keane laughing and whispering together in the receiving line earlier rubbed him raw.

Stepping within a breath of her, he hardened his tone. "No one will see anything — we're alone out here. My price for letting you go with me tomorrow is a dance, so you either pay it or I go alone. Simple as that."

Fire flared in her face. "Do you always have to blackmail women to get them to dance with you?"

"Not usually. Most of the time I merely have to ask."

He lifted his hand to brush her cheek, and she swallowed. The motion of her throat enthralled him. God, she was beautiful, a fairy princess in this light. It made him ache to touch her all the more.

But when he reached for her waist and

she stepped back, he went on in a bitter voice, "Are you refusing me because you despise me? Or because you're afraid you might actually enjoy dancing with a low fellow like me?"

"I'm afraid of Papa shooting you!" When he lifted an eyebrow at that, she said, "Or your shooting Papa. He said he would call you out if I danced with you."

"Did he, now?" At least her refusal wasn't because of Keane. "I don't care what your father threatened. I want my dance." He held out his hand again. "The risk makes the reward all the sweeter."

Desperation lit her face. "There's no music." Seconds later, the muted sounds of a waltz being struck up drifted to them from the ballroom, and she groaned.

He laughed. "Fate is conspiring against you. And who are we to resist Fate?"

She mumbled an exasperated oath. "Oh, all right." She took his hand. "But only one, or Papa will get suspicious and come looking for me."

"One dance will suffice," he said, laying his other hand on her waist to pull her as close as he dared. Which was far closer than would be proper in a ballroom.

Good thing. He wasn't feeling particularly proper at the moment. Just the way she followed his lead as he fell into the intimate steps of the waltz sent his blood soaring.

He had her in his arms again. For a while, anyway, before she ran off to try to tempt Keane into offering for her.

With a scowl, he dragged her up against him until she was practically anchored to him at the waist. Keane could go to hell.

Her gaze shot to his, soft and searching, and he met it brazenly, his heart thundering in his ears. For the first time, he wished she was *not* heir to an earl. That she was not determined to save her father's estate for future generations. That she really was a Gypsy princess he'd met in a forest some- where, and he could offer —

What? Marriage? He must be daft. He didn't need or want a wife right now. For the moment, he preferred his rootless exis- tence.

Liar.

"You . . . dance well," she ventured, her cinnamon-scented breath driving him to dis- traction.

"You sound surprised."

"I wouldn't have thought you'd have many chances to dance, given your profession."

And your station.

At least she'd left that unsaid. "I used to live in Paris, remember? Dancing well is

163

practically a national requirement." They took a few more steps together before he added, "You waltz pretty well yourself, princess."

"You must stop calling me that," she murmured. "Yesterday I had to evade several questions from my cousin because you let it slip."

Good. "I suppose that was foolish of me." He bent his head to her ear. "But surely when we're alone, I can be forgiven for it."

He was far too close for propriety, but he didn't care. If she wanted him to put some distance between them, she could push him back, and the fact that she didn't roused such fierceness in him that he could no longer resist his urges. Still waltzing her about the terrace, he began to kiss her delicate ear, then her satin-skinned cheek.

She gripped his hand painfully tight . . . but didn't push him away. "So . . . so what is your plan?" she breathed into his hair.

"For what?" He traced her jaw with his mouth.

"You said . . . if I danced with you, you'd come up with a scheme for getting me out . . . of our town house."

"Ah, *that*." He nuzzled her neck. "Well, we need a tactic that gets rid of your Ralph."

"Most assuredly. He would tell Papa for

certain if I met you somewhere to go to a Gypsy camp."

He tongued the sweet silk of her throat that had been tempting him all evening, and she let out a gasp, then persisted in continuing her blasted conversation. "B-but the only way for me to go anywhere without him is . . . is for me to go with Aunt Flo or some other suitable . . . female."

What the devil was she talking about? Oh, right. How he was to extricate her from the town house without Ralph. He'd better figure that out right quick if he wanted to keep kissing her.

"Would my sister be considered a suitable escort?" he asked.

"Your sister?" She pulled back, a smile breaking over her face. "Of course! That's brilliant! If the duchess came here to take me shopping, no one would think anything amiss." Her smile abruptly faded. "But then you'll have to tell her the whole story about my past, and I can't risk that."

"I don't have to tell her a damned thing. She'll get you out of the house, I'll meet you to take you off her hands, and then we'll arrange a place for you to join her once we're done."

She eyed him skeptically. "Will she agree to that?"

"Lisette will agree to anything I ask, trust me." Indeed, she'd be happy to see him with a respectable female for once and not his usual run of light-skirts. "All I require is a few moments alone with her tonight to explain the situation. Then she can request permission from your guardians before we leave."

As they kept dancing, she glanced away, her brow furrowed. He hoped she was being sensible, considering all the ways this could go wrong. And realizing how foolish she was to insist on going with him.

"My cousin is spending all day again tomorrow arranging the paintings for his exhibit," she finally said, "so as long as Papa doesn't guess that you're involved, he'll probably allow me to go shopping with your sister. She *is* a duchess, after all."

So much for Zoe being sensible. "Having a duchess for a sister does have certain advantages." A thought occurred to him. "But won't your aunt wish to join us?"

"Leave Aunt Flo to me. She hates shopping, so I'm sure it won't take much to talk her out of the excursion."

"Then shopping it is."

She'd met her side of the bargain, so he had to meet his. And it might be good for her to experience a Romany camp firsthand.

It might prove to her that they weren't the sort of people she'd assumed. He still believed that her father must have taken a Gypsy mistress. It was the only explanation that made sense.

Unfortunately, it didn't change anything about her situation. She would still feel compelled to marry her cousin.

The thought roused his temper. He would simply have to convince her that marrying Keane was a mistake. That she'd be better off trying to keep the past hidden.

Or he would find her Gypsy mother and buy her silence. That might work.

For what? Making sure some other fellow feels free to marry her? What good does that do you? If you're not willing to marry her yourself, then why do you care if she marries Keane?

Determined to ignore the logic of that, he released her hand so he could manacle her waist with both arms and tug her flush against him. When she lifted her hands to his neck, he exulted. For the moment, she was *his,* damn it. Only his.

The fragrance of violets, *her* fragrance, engulfed him, and he buried his face in her hair once more. With a groan, she arched her head back, giving him access to her tender throat, and he kissed and tongued the hollow there until he thought he'd burst into flame.

Her throat moved convulsively. "Th-the music has stopped."

They were barely dancing now anyway, sketching rapidly shrinking circles on the terrace. "Has it? A pity. I guess we'll have to do something else to entertain ourselves."

"Like what?"

"This," he rasped, and kissed her cheek. "Or this." He kissed her nose. "Or even this." And he brought his mouth down on hers.

She let him, too.

At last.

As she opened to him, he couldn't believe he'd resisted kissing her lips *this* long. God help him, she had a miracle of a mouth, soft and warm and silky. And the feel of her arching into him, rising to the kiss like bread beneath a master baker's hands . . . *His* hands. For the moment at least, she was his to enjoy, his to savor . . . his to kiss. Not Keane's or anyone else's.

The unexpectedly possessive thought knocked him back on his heels. He was losing his mind. This was a flirtation, nothing more.

Yet it felt like more. She clung to his neck with a need that roused his hunger . . . and met an answering need in him as he plundered her mouth and fought not to stroke the body that would beggar a king. That would beggar *him* if he attempted to claim it.

So why couldn't he let her go?

Because . . . because . . .

He had no clue. All he knew was that he'd been itching to taste and smell and touch her ever since the last time. And this . . . flirtation wasn't scratching that itch.

A moan sounded deep in her throat that spiked his itch to an ache, and then to a dark craving he couldn't seem to satisfy. He kissed her harder, deeper, hoping to assuage the hunger, but it only made him more reckless. With a groan of defeat, he let his hands roam her body — down over her hips, up the length of her slender waist . . . higher and higher, until they rested right beneath the breasts he ached to caress.

That must have alarmed her, for she tore her mouth from his. "I gave you a dance. I met the terms of our agreement."

At least she wasn't shoving him away. "This has naught to do with our agreement."

He dragged openmouthed kisses down her jaw to her neck. She had the softest skin. Was she this soft underneath her clothes?

Or even softer? The very idea of exploring all that delicate, creamy skin with his mouth and hands stiffened his cock painfully.

"Then why are you —"

"Because I want to." He sucked at the place where her pulse throbbed in her throat. "Because you want to."

Her heart beat a wild tattoo against his mouth. "For a man who doesn't like me, you certainly seem to like *kissing* me."

"I could say the same for you, princess," he murmured against her throat.

"You're the one who blackmailed me into dancing with you," she said peevishly.

He dropped a kiss on the upper swell of her breast. "And you're the one who's still here, even though the music has ended."

Stiffening, she started to pull away, but he caught her head in his hands and stared down into her gorgeous eyes. "Stop lying to yourself, for God's sake. You danced with me because you wanted to. Because you don't really want to sacrifice yourself to Keane for the sake of an estate that isn't even yours."

Her lips tightened into a mutinous line. "Perhaps I don't see it as a sacrifice." She arched one perfect eyebrow. "My cousin is a handsome artist, after all. And *he* regards me as something more than a mere conquest."

The very real possibility of that hit Tristan with an unfamiliar jolt of an emotion he'd never expected to experience. Jealousy. "Then why aren't you in the ballroom with *him,* instead of out here with me?" he asked with a possessive edge to his voice.

She paled, then shoved free of him. "An excellent point. I shall remedy that situation at once." Whirling on her heel, she marched off toward the French doors.

"Hell and thunder, he's not right for you, and you know it!" When that halted her, he added in a low voice, "You deserve a man who wants you for yourself. Who doesn't give a damn about your bloodlines and your estate and your title."

She faced him with an unreadable expression. "And do you have a likely candidate to offer?"

He went rigid, then muttered a curse under his breath.

"That's what I thought," she said. "Thank you once again for the utterly useless advice."

"Zoe —"

"I don't have a choice! Can't you see that? Every other possibility has serious risks. Marrying my cousin is the responsible thing

171

to do, the *prudent* thing to do."

"Since when are you prudent?" He walked up to her. "Being prudent didn't get you a chance at hiring us. Being prudent didn't send you looking for the truth. Don't be prudent about this."

"Why? So you can add another conquest to your list, just for the pleasure of thumbing your nose at men like Papa and my cousin?"

"Certainly not," he bit out, even though he feared there was a sliver of truth in that barb.

"This is just an amusing entertainment for you." She wrapped her trailing shawl about her like armor. "But for me, it's my *life.* I'm going to be hard-pressed as it is to coax my cousin into marrying and staying in England. So I would appreciate your not trying to make this any harder, merely so you can have a bit of fun."

He stood there, stunned. He wanted to protest her accusation, but how could he? This *was* just an interlude for him. Because the only other choice was something more serious, and that was definitely not what he intended.

Was it?

She forced a smile that scarcely covered the sadness in her eyes. "Thank you for agreeing to take me with you tomorrow, and thank you for the dance. But I have to go. And if you care for me at all, don't follow me. The last thing I need is my cousin seeing us come in together."

Then she opened the French doors and went into the library.

He wanted to go after her, but she was right. He was mucking with her life. Though it wasn't for the reasons she thought, that hardly mattered. Nothing could come of this but a mild flirtation.

So he should just do what she was paying him to do, and keep his distance. That would be the "prudent" thing. And it would be easy enough with Lisette probably joining them tomorrow. He'd have no time alone with Zoe anyway.

Besides, he had more important matters to concern him. Let her marry whom she pleased. If she didn't care that her cousin was obviously wrong for her, then why should he?

He'd fairly well convinced himself that he didn't care one whit by the time he thought it safe enough to enter the library. But that all went to hell when he found Keane standing near the door into the hall.

Damn. How long had he been there? Surely if he had run into Zoe, she would have coaxed him from the room to keep him from spotting Tristan outside.

Keane caught sight of him, and a half smile twisted his lips. "I see I was right."

"About what?"

"I figured something must have drawn my cousin out of the ballroom into here, and now I see it was you."

Playing dumb, Tristan glanced about the room. "Lady Zoe is here?"

"She was, as I'm sure you know. She was too agitated to notice me coming out of the ballroom down the hall. But I certainly noticed *her*." He cocked his head. "She's a hard woman to miss. Wouldn't you agree?"

"I would. Which is why it's surprising I didn't see her. But then, I've been outside on the terrace smoking." He pulled out his cigar case. "Care for a cigar?"

With a quick glance at the open French doors, Keane took one. "Don't mind if I do." He lit the cigar off a nearby candle and puffed on it a moment before dropping into a chair. "These taste like shit."

Tristan shrugged as he took one out for himself and lit it. "The good ones are too costly for my purse. You can blame the duty on American tobacco for that." He sat down, too, and began to smoke, wondering where this was leading.

"Now I know what to send Lord Olivier for Christmas next year," Keane quipped. He drew on the cigar again, then blew out smoke. "So, what exactly is the nature of your friendship with Lady Zoe?"

Tristan nearly choked on his cigar. He'd thought he'd dodged that bullet. "I don't know what you mean."

"Of course you do." Keane knocked some ash off into a nearby salver. "I don't for one second believe that she was in here and you were out there, separate and alone all this time."

Tristan blew out smoke, weighing how to approach this. Lying seemed unwise, since it would lend weight to Keane's suspicions. "It's that obvious, is it?"

"She's a pretty woman. And you don't strike me as the sort of man to ignore pretty women." He smoked a moment. "In any case, the two of you can't seem to get your stories straight about how you met. Or where. Or when."

Cursing the man for his perceptiveness, Tristan shrugged and opted for a version of the truth. "Her prettiness aside, our association isn't personal. I am . . . er . . . investigating a small matter for her. But her father would never approve, so we have to meet privately to consult."

175

"Why wouldn't her father approve?"

"Everything you've heard about the English aristocracy is mostly true, no matter what her ladyship claims. They tend to be insular and hidebound. If you hadn't invited me here yourself, I could never have attended."

"And that's the only reason he wouldn't approve?"

Peculiar question. "As far as I know."

"Interesting."

Tristan wasn't sure why, and that worried him. Keane had this alarming ability to be virtually unreadable. Perhaps it was a peculiar talent of Americans.

After a long moment during which smoke wreathed them both, Tristan said, "I hope you understand that my friendship with her ladyship must be kept secret from her family."

"Trust me, I am not a tattler." Keane searched his face. "So it's nothing romantic then?"

He managed a pained smile. "Lady Zoe is . . . shall we say . . . inaccessible to the likes of me."

"A cat can look at a king," Keane pointed out.

"Yes, but he can't marry one, can he?"

Keane lifted an eyebrow. "Who said any-

176

thing about marriage?"

A vise tightened around Tristan's chest. "I hope you're not suggesting that I would dishonor the lady. Or that the lady would allow me to dishonor her."

"I'm not suggesting anything. Merely asking questions."

"To what purpose?" Tristan snapped. "Have you a 'romantic' interest in Lady Zoe yourself?"

"Would you care if I did?"

This conversation was growing more frustrating by the moment. "As I told you, the lady is inaccessible to me. In every possible way. So I would be foolish to care."

It was the truth. But it was also not an answer.

Keane wasn't stupid enough to miss that. "Well then," he said with a smooth smile as he stubbed out the cigar in the salver, "since the lady is accessible to *me,* I believe I shall go beg a dance of her." He rose and headed for the door, but halted there to look back at Tristan. "Are you coming?"

The gleam in his eyes revealed his decided interest in witnessing Tristan's reaction. The man was baiting him. Tristan just wasn't sure why. "What's your game, Keane?"

"What's yours?" the American countered.

Abandoning his cigar, Tristan stood. "I've

already told you."

"Yes. I'm still trying to decide if I believe you."

Tristan sauntered toward him. "I don't know how things work in America, but in England, a man who calls another man a liar to his face risks being challenged to a duel."

"It's pretty much the same where I'm from." Keane slanted a glance at him. "But only hotheaded fools fight duels. And you don't seem *that* sort, either."

"Depends on the provocation." He preceded the man into the hall. "Because if you breathe one word of this to her father and her aunt, or in any way make trouble for her, I might well consider meeting you on the field."

Keane stared at him soberly a moment. "Duly noted." Then, as if someone had turned off a switch, he smiled broadly and clapped Tristan on the shoulder. "Now that we've settled that, old chap, let's go join the party. The sooner I can fulfill my obligations to the family this evening, the sooner we can go on that tour of London debauchery that you've promised me."

"Tonight?" Tristan said.

"Why not tonight?"

Good question. Perhaps a jaunt about

London's stewpots would remind him that he had no business kissing Zoe. Caressing Zoe.

Wanting Zoe.

"Yes — why not tonight, indeed?" he said.

9

When Zoe's cousin finally asked her to dance, she was so relieved that she didn't notice it was a waltz until he was taking her hand on the floor. Not that she minded waltzing. But the waltz would forever be imprinted on her memory as the only dance she'd shared with Tristan.

In private. On the terrace. Under the moonlight.

Waltzing would never be the same for her again.

"You seem distracted, coz," Mr. Keane said as he began the dance.

She forced a smile. "I have a great deal on my mind."

He digested that in silence. Thank goodness the music was loud enough that she didn't feel honor-bound to talk. And thank goodness he wasn't a bad dancer. For an American, anyway.

His gaze bored into her. "So your father

tells me I shouldn't have invited your friend Bonnaud to this affair."

Botheration. She couldn't believe Papa had discussed that with Mr. Keane. "Papa can be a stickler for propriety. And Mr. Bonnaud, with his work as an investigator, isn't what we call 'good *ton.*' It means —"

"I know what it means, coz," he said with the barest smile. "I read British papers and books. But that's not the reason your father gave for his alarm."

As she realized what he meant, she colored. "Oh, and since Mr. Bonnaud is . . . well . . . illegitimate —"

"That wasn't the reason, either." He swung her into a turn. "Apparently your Mr. Bonnaud has a tawdry past."

"He's not *my* Mr. Bonnaud." Then the rest of his words sank in. "Tawdry past? You mean, because of his reputation with women?"

"No. Because of his reputation for thieving."

Her breath stuck in her throat. Had Papa somehow heard about the subterfuge played by the Duke's Men at Kinlaw Castle months ago? That made no sense. They'd covered it up very well. And surely if he'd heard, others would have, too, but there hadn't been a peep of it among the gossips.

"I don't know what you're talking about," she said.

"Don't you?" His hand tightened on hers. "I assumed that you knew quite a bit about Mr. Bonnaud."

"No, I — I only recently met him." It was true, even if it did leave out a great deal. "So what is this about thieving?"

"Your father said that Bonnaud was rumored to have stolen a horse from his half brother years ago."

Ohhhh. So that was what Papa had meant when he'd spoken of something Tristan had done in Yorkshire in his youth. "If that's true, it was clearly some misunderstanding, since Mr. Manton obviously has no problem with him now."

Mr. Keane's gaze was steady on her. "Not *that* half brother. I gather Bonnaud has another one who happens to be a viscount?"

She missed a step. Fortunately, he caught her, guiding her effortlessly until she was back in rhythm.

"Yes," she admitted, "the Viscount Rathmoor. But I . . . never heard anything about a stolen horse."

"Your father says it was widely rumored in York that the Thoroughbred was never recovered. That Bonnaud fled to France to escape being hanged for the theft." Mr.

Keane watched her as if to gauge her reaction. "And that he only returned to England last year when the Duke of Lyons married his sister."

She frowned. Tristan *had* lived in France for years, but since his mother was French he might have gone there because of her. He *was* estranged from his viscount half brother, but so was Mr. Manton, by all reports, and no one was accusing *him* of theft.

"Surely if he were guilty of such a thing they would have apprehended him once he came to England," she pointed out.

"Perhaps. Or perhaps the viscount is wary of the duke's wrath. I don't know how these things work in England, but I imagine the influence of a man so highly placed would be as far-reaching as in America."

That much was true. Though if Tristan were a criminal, why would the secret police in Paris have hired him as an agent? And why would Mr. Manton risk his reputation to include Tristan in his investigative business?

No, the rumor made no sense. Papa was just listening to old gossip and jumping to conclusions. Tristan was no criminal.

We caught criminals by pretending to be *criminals.*

183

She brightened. That was it! Tristan had pretended to be a criminal in Scotland just last year, so perhaps he'd been pretending to be a criminal years ago, too. Though she could hardly see how pretending to be a horse thief helped a person catch anyone. And if he'd been young . . .

"Did Papa say how old Mr. Bonnaud was when all this happened?"

Her cousin moved her smoothly about the floor. He really did excel at dancing. It was a mark in his favor. A small mark, but still . . .

"I believe he mentioned that Bonnaud was a youth at the time."

She thrust out her chin. "Well, it sounds like idle rumor to me." Determined to get him off the subject of Tristan, she added, "You'll find there's a great deal of that in London society. It can be very disturbing."

"There's not much gossip about you and your father and aunt," he pointed out.

That arrested her. "Did you . . . expect to find some?"

A dark look crossed his face. "People are almost never what they seem."

"Well, *we* are!" she said petulantly.

But the truth was, they were not. Papa had either had an affair with a Romany woman or bought Mama a baby. So Zoe

184

was either part or all Gypsy, and nothing in her upbringing had prepared her for that.

They danced a few moments before he said, "I must admit — you and your family aren't what I expected."

Her heart began to pound. "I beg your pardon, Mr. Keane?"

"You really ought to call me Jeremy." He cast her the unreadable smile that had begun to grate on her nerves. "We're friends now, are we not?"

"I don't know. You tell me." She sounded snippy, but she couldn't help it. "You're the one who said we're not what you expected. Is that good or bad?"

"The unexpected is never good or bad. It's just the unexpected, Zoe." He searched her face. "I *may* call you Zoe, may I not?"

"Of course." She might have to marry him, after all. "I just . . . hope we don't disappoint you." Or at least not enough to run him off.

"Now *that,* I assure you, could never be the case." When he followed that statement with a heated glance worthy of London's best rakehells, she wondered if he meant it. Or was just trying it on for size.

Because the whole time they'd been dancing, she'd felt none of the fluttering excitement, the thrilling anticipation, that five

185

minutes in Tristan's arms had inspired. Unfortunately, she wasn't sure if that was due to her or her cousin.

Or both.

Thrusting that unsettling thought from her mind, she said, "So, how exactly are we not what you expected?"

"Your father used to be a soldier, right? And I was unaware that soldiers lived so . . . extravagantly."

"They generally don't, unless they inherit great lands and property."

"Ah, but great lands cost a great deal to maintain."

He kept harping on money. Why? Was he trying to figure out if he could inherit Winborough free of obligation so he could sell it? Or run it into the ground while he enjoyed what "English lords *really* spend their time doing: gambling, wenching, and watching cockfights"?

That possibility chilled her blood.

"This house alone," he went on, "looks like something far beyond an army major's means."

He'd said he was blunt, but goodness, this was *very* blunt indeed. "Clearly, you don't understand how things work here. Didn't your father ever explain any of this to you? Winborough leases the land to tenants, and

186

that provides the income for everything: this house, our way of life —" She slanted a glance at him. "My dowry."

"My father was too busy bemoaning my interest in art and trying to force me into running his mills to explain the English way of life to me," he said, completely ignoring her reference to a dowry. His jaw tightened. "Fortunately, my sister became the willing recipient of his vast wisdom and took over the running of his mills after his death, so I no longer have to worry about it."

"Your sister! Do Americans approve of women managing businesses?"

"Not usually." He smiled. "But that doesn't generally stop the women from doing it." The music was coming to an end. "You shouldn't be surprised, however. *You* help your father run your estate."

"That's different. It's built into the inheritance that way."

"You really have to meet my sister," he said amiably as he led her from the floor. "She would like you."

"Would she?"

"Though I have to warn you" — he bent his head to whisper — "she has no idea of how to dress with dash. Her idea of a suitable gown is one that won't show dirt when she goes to the mills. My mother despairs.

She can't stop hoping I will one day be a captain of industry."

That statement gave her pause. Perhaps she'd been looking at this situation the wrong way. If her cousin had no plans to run his late father's businesses and preferred to live the debauched life of the idle nobility, she ought to offer him just that — a life of ease, painting whatever he pleased. As long as *she* handled the part he hated, perhaps they could get on well together. He could paint in England as easily as he could in America.

Though he'd still have to sit in Parliament. That probably wouldn't appeal to him. And there was the pesky problem of her not desiring him, handsome as he was.

You don't really want to sacrifice yourself to Keane for the sake of an estate that isn't even yours.

She scowled. Curse Tristan for putting such ideas in her head. She was *not* going to shirk her duty to Winborough! She might not be Papa's blood but she was still his daughter.

Tristan and his heated kisses and caresses couldn't change that. All he did was try to wreak havoc on her plans! And make her want things she couldn't have.

Well, no more. She would keep things

strictly business with him. Because unless he determined that there was absolutely no reason for her to fear her Gypsy background rising up to destroy her life, she was going to have to marry Mr. Keane . . . Jeremy. She might as well resign herself to it.

"Looks like she and her cousin are getting on well enough," said a voice at Tristan's side.

Dom. With his gut clenching, Tristan turned deliberately away from the disturbing sight of Zoe with Keane. "Yes, it appears that matters are proceeding according to her damned plan."

"How did she take the news about her parents?"

It's just that . . . until now it all seemed rather abstract. Like some fantastical story from a fairy tale about children discovering that their parents were really kings or something.

Her reaction had shaken something loose in him, reminded him of the terror he'd felt when he'd realized that Father hadn't made provisions for any of them.

"She took it as well as can be expected under the circumstances," he evaded. "She'd already been halfway to believing her aunt anyway. I just confirmed it for her." And in so doing, pushed her toward marrying Keane. Who didn't seem averse to the idea.

Tristan gritted his teeth. He didn't care. Not. One. Whit.

"So I suppose your next step is to —"

"Dom!"

Tristan and Dom turned to find their sister headed toward them with a woman at her side. When Dom muttered an oath, Tristan realized with a shock who it was, even though he hadn't seen her in almost thirteen years.

Jane Vernon.

Now nearing thirty, with the same lush red curls, brown eyes, and freckled nose as before, she had blossomed from a slender, bookish creature into a shapely woman. Possessed of a grace and poise Tristan wouldn't have expected, she managed to cover whatever distress she must be feeling at the sight of Dom.

Tristan resisted the urge to laugh. Their minx of a sister had turned into quite the little matchmaker lately, having recently been triumphant in pairing her doctor with her husband's widowed cousin. But this was going beyond the pale, a fact made painfully obvious by Dom's rigid jaw.

"Look who I found in the retiring room," Lisette said lightly. "It turns out that Jane's mother went to school with our hostess. And I knew that you would both be annoyed if you didn't get to see her."

Jane looked everywhere but at Dom. Dom, meanwhile, couldn't seem to look anywhere but at her. If a man could be said to swallow a woman whole with his gaze, that was what Dom was doing.

Though the idiot still hadn't spoken a word.

"It *is* good to see you, Jane," Tristan said into the painful silence. Some demon possessed him, and he added, with a wink, "I would have braved even George's ire to call on you if I'd had any idea how very lovely you've grown."

Jane's grateful smile brought a warmth to her eyes that any man would find engaging. So he wasn't surprised when Dom turned stiff as a poker beside him.

"Oh," she said, "but I am still the same 'Freckles' you dubbed me when we were young." With a furtive glance at Dom, she added, "And you've turned out rather well yourself, Tristan. Though I'd already assumed as much, given the rumors about you and your women."

"All lies," he said in mock protest. "It's not like you to listen to lies, Jane." When his fool of a brother *still* remained silent, he

191

added, "And speaking of rumors, I hear congratulations are in order. You're engaged to marry the Earl of Blakeborough, right?"

"Yes." This time she looked directly at Dom. "I got tired of waiting for my life to begin."

Dom flinched as if struck. Then he shifted a hard gaze to their sister. "I know that Max lets you run wild as his duchess, but even you should realize that this is highly inappropriate."

When Lisette paled, Tristan turned on Dom, ready to defend her. But Jane didn't give him the chance.

"Well, well," she said bitterly, "Saint Dominick rears his lofty head at last, always ready to instruct people on how to behave. Careful, Dom. One day that church you're building around yourself shall become your crypt."

Dom's demeanor softened a fraction. "And will you come to my funeral when it does, Jane?"

Color rose in her cheeks. "No. It has become painfully apparent that the dead never rise again. Not even saints." Turning pointedly away from him, she smiled at Tristan. "It was good to see you." She broadened her smile to include Lisette. "To see both of you. But my mother will be wondering where I am, so I'd best go find her."

Then, with a little bow, she walked off.

As soon as she was out of hearing, Lisette turned on Dom. "You are such an arse sometimes, Dominick Manton! Honestly, I don't know what she ever saw in you." With a sniff, she headed off toward her husband on the other side of the ballroom.

"She's right, you know," Tristan muttered to Dom. "When it comes to Jane, you *are* an arse."

Leaving his brother to stew in his own juices, he stalked after Lisette. "Hold up, sis!" he called out. "I need to discuss something with you."

She halted as Tristan came alongside her. With a glance back at Dom, she frowned. "Why does he behave like that? It drives me mad!"

"You mean, because he doesn't fall in with your matchmaking?" When Lisette glared at him, he added, "You ought to know by now that you can't spring things on Dom. He needs time to assess and evaluate and . . . whatever it is he does when he's examining all the facts. Throwing Jane at him out of the blue is bound to rattle him."

"That doesn't mean he has to be cruel to her. Why, until she provoked him, he refused even to speak to her!"

"With words, anyway," Tristan said dryly.

"You have to talk some sense into him. Otherwise, she's going to marry that Blakeborough fellow." Lisette seized him by the arm. "She and Dom *belong* together. Surely you can see that."

"If they belonged together they'd *be* together, dear heart. Perhaps it's time you let that dream go." At her exasperated look, he said hastily, "But that's not what I wanted to talk to you about."

She was back to watching Dom. "Oh?" she said absently.

"I need a favor from you. It involves a case."

Shifting her attention to him, she laid her free hand on her protruding belly barely disguised by her clever gown. "Max doesn't want me doing too much with the agency, now that the time for the birth is drawing near."

"It's nothing taxing. Just shopping. You do still shop, don't you?"

"I do. But what could shopping possibly have to do with a case?"

"You'd be surprised. It's like this . . ."

10

The morning after the soiree, the duchess showed up right on time to fetch Zoe. Although Aunt Flo was there to welcome her with great enthusiasm, Papa and Jeremy were still abed. They must have played cards into the wee hours or something.

Zoe didn't mind that her cousin was absent. She'd been dreading his questions about her outing with the duchess. The man was awfully nosy.

But Papa . . . She still hadn't had a chance to speak to him about the rumors concerning Tristan and the horse theft. Was there more to it than Jeremy had said? Did she dare ask Tristan about it today?

Probably not. She needed Tristan to do his job well, and he'd hardly be eager to work for her if she accused him of being a thief. It had been difficult enough to wrangle his agreement to include her on his trip to the Gypsy camp.

Zoe and the duchess headed out into the cold, their half boots crunching on the snow that had fallen earlier in the week. Once they were handed into the Lyons carriage, the duchess turned to Zoe with a broad smile. "What a delightful redingote you're wearing! I love pink and green stripes. Indeed, I have a gown with a similar pattern, though not in wool. And your bonnet is just adorable. Are those really seashells worked into it with ribbons?"

"They are. I bought the bonnet in Highthorpe, the town near our estate. The milliner there knows I prefer unusual clothes, so she made it just for me." Zoe patted it fondly. "I've never seen one like it."

"Nor I." The duchess leaned forward to examine it more closely. "I'm fond of doing ribbon embroidery myself, but it never occurred to me to include seashells. I shall have to try that."

"I can give you the name of my milliner," Zoe said, "although I think it's probably a long way to go for a hat."

The woman turned pensive. "And it's in Yorkshire, besides. We don't go to Yorkshire."

She said it as if it were a rule. "I thought you and your brothers were *from* Yorkshire?"

"Yes. Precisely why we don't go there."

Because of the thieving? Zoe nearly asked. But she wasn't sure that was anything but vicious rumor. Besides, it would be unwise to offend the duchess.

In any case, Her Grace changed the subject. "Tristan tells me that this jaunt is about a case. That you have hired him to investigate something?"

That put Zoe on her guard. "Yes."

Zoe's expression must have shown her concern, for the duchess added hastily, "He didn't explain what it was; he's always discreet. I only know that it involves visiting a Romany encampment."

"He *told* you where we're going?" she asked, her heart in her throat. She'd assumed he would keep that discreet, too.

"He didn't have a choice." The duchess favored her with a small smile. "I wasn't about to allow my rogue of a brother to go off alone all day with an unmarried young woman as pretty as yourself. So I'm going with you to chaperone. It was the only way I would agree to do this."

Botheration. How could Tristan ask questions at the camp with the duchess around? Granted, the woman could be considered one of the Duke's Men, given her marriage to the duke himself, but it wouldn't do to have her guessing their purpose. The more people who knew Zoe's dilemma, the more likely it was that someone would let the truth slip.

The duchess settled back against her seat. "We're meeting my rapscallion brother there. Last night he told my coachman where to go."

"So he's already at the encampment?" Zoe gritted her teeth. "He *knew* I wanted to be with him the whole time he was questioning the Gypsies. But he just *had* to go there early, even though he promised —"

"I'll be surprised if he even makes it there before us," the duchess said mildly. "When we were leaving your lovely house after the soiree, he was heading off with your cousin for some . . . tour of London debauchery. That's what he called it, anyway. And if it was anything like my brother's usual shenanigans, then he's cropsick this morning."

Lord, Zoe had forgotten all about his promise to Jeremy. Leave it to Tristan to corrupt her cousin. Although Jeremy had seemed awfully eager to be corrupted.

She glanced out the window as they drove past Hyde Park. Might it be a good thing that Tristan and her cousin were becoming chummy? Perhaps Tristan could learn something of use to her in her campaign to gain a marriage proposal from Jeremy.

Then again, after the way Tristan had protested that scheme, would he even tell her if he *did* learn anything?

"I hope it doesn't distress you," the duchess added. "That my brother and your cousin were . . . well . . . going to unsavory places half the night."

Zoe forced a smile. "Why ever would it distress me?"

"Just now you looked upset."

"Only because I need your brother to be fully competent to do his job today," Zoe lied, trying not to think of Tristan sporting with whores in a brothel. "And if he's cropsick —"

"Oh, trust me, he could still fight three men with one hand tied behind his back. He was a very successful agent in France."

"So he said."

The duchess regarded her with an odd look. "He told you about that?"

"Of course. He used to work with La Sûreté Nationale, right?" When the woman nodded, Zoe added, "He was trying to convince me that he could handle my investigation."

"How strange." The duchess looked her over as if seeing her in a new light. "He never speaks of his work in France to anyone, not even clients, because of how

199

the English distrust the French."

"Well, perhaps he thought I wouldn't mind."

"Perhaps," the woman said, sounding skeptical.

"He was trying to convince me to take him on. I was rather . . . well . . . reluctant."

"Were you?"

Why did the duchess keep eyeing her as if she were a new bauble being pondered for purchase?

"Yes. He and I got off to a bit of a rocky start. That's all."

"What sort of a rocky start?"

Oh, dear. She shouldn't have mentioned that. "Nothing of any consequence, Your Grace. Truly."

The duchess regarded her a long moment, then cast her a calculating smile. "Call me Lisette," she said, leaning forward to pat Zoe's knee. "You and I are going to be great friends, I expect."

Zoe couldn't imagine why. Though it couldn't hurt to have another of the Duke's Men — or women, in this case — on her side. "Then you must call me Zoe."

Lisette nodded. "Now, you simply must tell me of this 'rocky start' that is of no consequence. How else am I to keep up with my rascal of a brother?"

Zoe did her best to prevaricate. But as they journeyed to the Romany camp, the duchess persisted in quizzing Zoe about her association with Tristan. Short of lying or remaining stubbornly silent, Zoe wasn't sure what to say.

And after Zoe let slip that she'd initially met the Duke's Men in Scotland, Lisette, who'd apparently heard the whole tale about Tristan disguising himself as a thief, managed to drag that part of the story from her. Zoe soon found herself telling Lisette of the bargain she'd forced the brothers into, although not *why* she'd wanted the bargain in the first place.

Fortunately, Lisette didn't pry too much into the nature of Zoe's investigation. The reason for that became clear when Lisette admitted that Tristan had agreed to let her come along only if she didn't badger Zoe about it.

Zoe's heart fluttered a little over that. Clearly he'd known how persistent his sister could be. And if he could keep Zoe's secrets even from his obviously demanding sister, then surely he would keep them from just about anyone.

By the time they arrived at the camp, Lisette had begun to treat Zoe like an old friend, relating her fears about the upcoming birth of her child and waxing poetic about her apparently wonderful and generous husband.

Envy stabbed Zoe. If she went through with her plans to marry Jeremy, could she ever hope for such a warm partnership? It seemed unlikely, if her cousin preferred debauchery to social events.

Then again, that would make him like half of the other husbands among the *ton*. The thought was lowering indeed.

The carriage halted. A ramshackle row of houses stood near the road, skirting an ice-crusted field crowded with tents that didn't even reach as high as Zoe's chin. The smoke of many fires filled the air as Gypsies and Londoners alike wandered the paths trodden into the ground between the tents.

The minute she and the duchess got out, they were swarmed by bronze-skinned children dressed in colorful rags, who seemed oblivious to the cold. And to their poverty as well. Unlike the poor sullen urchins she sometimes saw begging on Bond Street when she shopped, these little ones were laughing and gabbing in some unfamiliar tongue, probably Romany.

Zoe could have sworn they were talking about her clothes, for they kept gesturing at her bonnet and muttering the word *staddi*.

"Please, miss," one bold boy finally said in accented English, "where did you buy such a fine hat?"

A voice from beyond them answered, "Somewhere you could never afford, *chavvi.*"

Tristan strode up to the children and spoke a few words. When he then tossed a handful of coins onto a nearby frozen patch of ground, the children screamed with laughter and ran after them, deserting the coach.

Zoe gaped at them. "What did you say?"

"That the fine lady was a princess, and that whichever of them could produce the most beautiful neckerchief for her before we left would get another handful of coins."

"That's incredibly generous of you," Zoe said softly.

"Hardly," he said with a shrug. "The best way to keep a lot of children out of your hair when you're trying to get something done in a Romany camp is to give them money and a purpose. Now they'll spend their time plaguing their mothers for neckerchiefs for the lovely lady. And they'll leave us be."

As he walked over to speak to the duchess's coachman and footmen, Lisette leaned close to whisper, "Don't let him fool you.

He's trying to impress you."

"I doubt that," Zoe said. Yet her heart gave another of those annoying little flutters that he seemed to incite whenever he was around.

Especially when he was dressed like an adventurer, in a rugged greatcoat and mud-spattered top boots, with a battered beaver hat that made her wonder how many wild excursions it had seen. How many *he* had seen. For it was clear that he was daring enough to brave any terrain on a mission.

It gave her an odd sort of thrill to think that he'd taken on *her* mission.

Upon his return, he stared pointedly at his sister. "I know you'll want to buy some goods while you're here." He gestured toward a path that twisted through one end of the camp. "Your best bet is down there. That path leads to an excellent ribbon merchant."

Crossing her arms over her chest, Lisette glared at him. "I can't go gallivanting about a Romany camp alone."

He raised an eyebrow. "Oh? Grown too lofty for that now that you're a duchess?"

Zoe caught her breath at the barb, but the duchess merely laughed. "Yes. I believe that I have. So you're stuck with me."

"Not a chance, little Miss Meddler. We're

going another way, and you're not invited."
He snapped his finger, and one of the
duchess's footmen approached. "Besides,
you won't be alone."

She looked as if she might protest further.
Then she let out a dramatic sigh. "Oh, very
well. I do enjoy a good ribbon merchant."
And she stalked away, with the footman at
her side.

Tristan offered Zoe his arm, and as she
took it he murmured, "Sorry about having
to bring her along. I had hoped to meet you
at the Bond Street shops and take you off
with me, but she flat-out refused to help
me, as she put it, 'seduce a lady of quality.' "
His voice tightened. "She seems to think I
have no scruples."

Zoe let him lead her down the main path
between the tents. "I can't imagine where
she would get such a notion. Perhaps from
your willingness to take visitors on 'tours of
London debauchery'?" When his eyes narrowed on her, she cursed herself for bringing that up and added, "Have you learned
anything about Drina?"

He let her change the subject. "Not yet,
I'm afraid. I didn't arrive here much before
you. I've asked around, but without a family name it's difficult to learn anything.
Someone did mention that I should talk to

the folks camped on the far end, so that's where we're headed."

For the next hour, they went among the tents, speaking to anyone who would talk to them. With some, a mere word or two in their language turned them effusive. With others, it took a few coins.

As it turned out, everyone they consulted knew a Drina somewhere, but inevitably the female turned out to be too old or too young, or to not have been pregnant at the time specified, or to have some other problem that excluded her.

In the course of their questioning, Zoe learned that Gypsies tended to keep to certain counties, so a Drina who was part of a Surrey clan, for example, wasn't likely to have ever been in Yorkshire. And the lack of a family name was a bigger issue than she would have guessed. Each clan comprised only a few families, so knowing that name would have vastly helped Tristan find the woman.

As they left a tent after encountering yet another dead end, she murmured, "The Romany are not what I expected."

"In what way?"

She glanced over to where a young woman was scrubbing sheets furiously behind a tent. "For one thing, they're much cleaner than I'd always heard. And the women are not . . . well . . ."

"Little whores?"

"Sly," she said with an arch glance.

"It must come as quite a shock to you to find that Gypsies aren't all dirty and wild thieves," he said, with an edge to his voice.

She colored. "One does occasionally hear of those who are."

"Right." A muscle clenched in his jaw. "One hears an astonishing amount of information about the Romany, when you consider that few people have ever had any firsthand dealings with them."

"Perhaps if Gypsies weren't so clannish and wary of strangers, people wouldn't make those assumptions."

"The people we've been dealing with today haven't been like that," he pointed out. "It's only when they're bullied and driven from pillar to post that they grow wary of strangers. But they can tell that we're respectful of their customs." He stared ahead, more somber than before. "And in winter, they're desperate enough to talk to anyone who might give them a chance of making some money."

"Yes, I noticed some of the men asking if you know where they can find work. I always heard that Gypsy men were lazy."

"It's easy to apply that word to a people one doesn't understand, with unusual customs and strange beliefs. They're nomadic, so they like to roam, and they believe in living for the moment, so amassing a fortune isn't important to them. We English are the opposite, so we assume that their rootlessness and lack of ambition translates to a hatred of work, when really it's just . . . rootlessness and a lack of ambition."

Something suddenly occurred to her. "You defend them because you're like them. You have no roots and you like to roam."

"I defend them because they're generally good people. Or at least as good as anyone else you run across. That's the only reason."

They walked a moment in silence, with him stiff and stony-faced beside her.

"Did I insult you somehow?" she finally ventured.

"Certainly not."

She had. She was almost sure of it. But uncertain of how, she figured it was better not to press him.

A young woman standing near a tent smiled hesitantly at Zoe, and Tristan halted to question her in Romany. With an apologetic smile, she shook her head. They moved on.

"I take it she knew no Drinas?" Zoe asked.

"I'm afraid not."

Wanting to banish this tight-lipped, wary Tristan, she said, "I have to admit, your being able to speak their language has been very helpful." When he cast her a veiled glance, she teased, "Go ahead and gloat. You were right. You were obviously the appropriate choice for this assignment."

His stiffness finally melted, and he said lightly, "I do so love it when you eat crow, princess."

"Don't —"

"Call you that. I know." He gestured down another winding, muddy path. "I can't help myself." He raked her with a sidelong glance that took in every inch of her. "Especially when you're dressed like a princess."

"I didn't have a choice, you know. Aunt Flo would have been suspicious if I'd gone out shopping with a duchess wearing my roughest clothes."

"Believe me, it's fine. More than fine." For a moment his gaze held hers, smoldering with just enough heat to singe her. Then he jerked it back to the path. "Because this actually works out better. They're in such awe of you that they're eager to say whatever will please the elegant lady."

She burst into laughter. "No one has ever called me elegant."

"Why not?" He seemed genuinely surprised.

"Because I'm about as elegant as a lamppost. Aunt Flo says I am too sturdily built for elegance."

He shook his head. "We've already established that your aunt is a fool."

"Oh, she doesn't mean it to be unkind. She also says I have excellent teeth and a pretty nose."

"Rather like a fine horse," he quipped.

"Exactly. My aunt would probably prefer putting me up for auction at Tattersall's to gain me a husband. It would be so much easier than squiring me around to parties."

"Trust me, if she did that, you'd have enough bids to put the lie to her claims about your lacking elegance."

The compliment warmed her. "Would you bid on me?" she said lightly.

"In a heartbeat." This time his heated glance did more than singe. It inflamed her senses.

She forced herself to look away. "Yes, well, you're used to buying women. Just how many brothels *did* you and my cousin visit last night?" The words were out before she could stop them.

He eyed her consideringly. "That was not my idea, and you know it."

"Yet you happily went along with it."

Oh, Lord, stop talking about it, you fool!

But as usual, she ignored all sense when it came to him. "My cousin was still abed when I left, so I daresay the two of you had quite the night."

His eyes gleamed at her. "You'll have to ask *him* about that. When I last saw him, he was being welcomed into a brothel with open arms. I figured he could handle the women on his own, so I went home."

She snorted. "You honestly expect me to believe that."

"Which part? The part about your cousin? Or the part about me?"

"The part about you, of course. I know my cousin must have been doing *something* to come in so late."

"He did it alone, I swear. I knew I had to be on my toes for today's jaunt, so I retired at a decent hour." With one of his irritating smirks, he laid his hand on the small of her back and leaned in close. "How intriguing that you care. You don't seem the least concerned that I left your cousin at a brothel, yet you're determined to find out if *I* was there with him. Jealous, are you?"

Pulling away, she walked a little ahead. "Don't be ridiculous. I don't care what you do with your evenings."

211

"If you say so, princess," he drawled in that self-satisfied tone that so provoked her.

She could feel his gaze on her; he was probably looking at her arse again. "I already know what sort of man you are."

"Do you really? And what sort is that?"

"A rogue."

"Yes, indeed." He said it as if it were a badge of honor!

"And a . . . a seducer," she snapped.

He laughed outright. "That, too, when I get a chance of it."

His smug amusement and utter lack of shame were suddenly too much to bear. She halted to look at him. "And a horse thief."

The blood drained from his face, and his smile vanished.

Her pleasure at having unsettled him fled. Hadn't she already decided that he was *not* a horse thief? And even if he were, hadn't she decided not to question him about it until he'd done his job for her?

"Or so I was told," she added hastily. "Though I'm sure it was only —"

"By whom?" His voice was sharp, distant.

"What?"

"*Who* told you I was a horse thief?"

Botheration. "Well . . . I, um, heard it sort of secondhand, actually —"

"Mr. Bonnaud!" A boy came running up

212

to them. "Mr. Bonnaud! You must come talk to my father's aunt!"

Still staring at her expectantly, he said to the boy, "About what?"

The boy was breathing hard. "About the man you asked about this morning. Milosh Corrie."

Tristan's attention instantly shifted to the boy. "Does this aunt know where Milosh is?"

"Where he works at night. Yes. She was sleeping when you asked about Milosh before." He tugged on Tristan's arm. "Come, you must talk to her now. Before she naps again."

"Of course." Tristan glanced at Zoe. "Why don't you stay here while I —"

"No," she said firmly. "I'm coming with you."

With an exasperated look, he threaded his fingers through his hair. But he must have realized he couldn't leave her there alone while he wandered Lord only knew where, for he muttered an oath, then gestured to her to accompany him.

The boy was already rushing off, back in the direction from which they'd just come. As they hurried to keep up, she murmured, "Who's Milosh?"

His jaw went taut. "A man I grew up with.

213

I told you, the Romany used to camp on my father's land."

"And will he help us find Drina?"

"He might," he said noncommittally. "The Yorkshire Romany probably all know each other, and he is of that clan."

"Oh, that's good." But how odd that he hadn't mentioned this Milosh fellow before.

She prepared herself for a renewal of their conversation about the horse thieving, but he looked distracted now.

He wasn't the only one. Her mind whirled with all the information she'd learned today. Seeing how meanly the Gypsies lived made her realize just how lucky she'd been that her parents had bought her. *If* they even had. She began to understand why Tristan had scoffed at the notion.

Despite the children's poor attire, she'd seen not one instance of cruelty to them. They roamed the camp freely and happily. Everywhere, there were babies — being nursed, being dandled on knees, being sung to. It was hard to imagine those doting mothers selling any of their children.

Within a short while, they had returned to the row of tumbledown houses near the road. When it became clear they were headed for one, Zoe looked over at Tristan.

"Why do some reside in tents if there are these?"

"Taking a house in the city, even a mean one, is expensive. Only a few of the Romany can afford it, and usually those who can belong to large families, with lots of able-bodied men able to contribute to the rent."

They entered to find themselves in a barren room furnished only with bedrolls, cushions, and a fireplace. Several women milled about, preparing food, dealing with children, and cleaning.

The boy drew them over to a wizened old woman huddled before the low-burning fire. She was swathed in shawls of exotic colors, one of them wrapped about her gray head. Her gap-toothed smile included them as well as the boy, who spoke a few words to her in Romany. She gestured to Tristan to come closer, and they began to converse in her language.

Until now, Tristan had always begun the conversation in Romany to gain the person's trust but had quickly changed to English for Zoe's benefit. Not this time. And the longer the conversation went on, the more annoyed she became. She heard the name Milosh several times, but not Drina.

When at last there was a pause, she said, "What does she say about Drina?"

A shadow crossed Tristan's face. "I haven't asked yet. I was easing into it."

He spoke to the woman in Romany again. Her face darkened, and she shook her head no, then muttered a few words and put her head down on her chest. It was not the reaction they'd been getting from others.

Apparently Tristan thought so, too, for he asked her something else, but now she wouldn't speak to him at all, just kept shaking her head.

The boy faced them, his expression apologetic. "You must go now. Auntie is tired."

Zoe's heart dropped into her stomach. "But —"

"Go!" the boy said, with a worried look at his aunt. "She will say no more."

Taking her by the arm, Tristan began walking toward the door.

"Tristan!" she cried. "She knows something."

"She says she doesn't. And badgering her won't get us anywhere." When Zoe dragged her feet, he added under his breath, "I'll speak to Milosh. If he hasn't heard of Drina, perhaps he'll help us convince the old woman to tell us what she knows. But for now, we're done here."

Only then did Zoe let him lead her outside.

As they hurried down the path, she glanced at him. "So she *did* reveal where Milosh is."

"Not where he is now, but where he'll be tonight. Apparently his whole family — and other Yorkshire Romany — flock to booths in Lambeth every evening, where they tell fortunes and sell gimcracks to the crowds in attendance at the theaters and taverns thereabouts."

"So Drina herself might be with them. If she's Yorkshire Romany, that is."

"She might. Hard to be sure."

Just then someone called out to them, and they turned to find Lisette heading their way.

"I do hope you two are done," she said as she approached, "because I have perused as many ribbons as I can bear, and I can bear a great deal of ribbon shopping." Given that she carried a basket full nearly to overflowing with paper packets and loose ribbons, she didn't exaggerate.

"I'll wager we've learned as much as we can here," Tristan said.

The duchess looked up at the sky. "Even if you haven't, it's clouding over, and I refuse to get caught out in the rain. Or worse yet, the snow. Besides, I'm famished. There's a wonderful cookshop in this part of town, so I was thinking we could go there for a spot of tea and some pigeon pie before I bring Zoe home and you go back to Manton's Investigations."

"Well?" he asked Zoe.

She shrugged. "We've been all over the camp, and so far we've found out nothing. We might as well leave. We can always come back if you can't learn anything from your friend Milosh."

When the duchess dragged in a sharp breath and Tristan winced, Zoe knew she had stumbled somehow.

"Milosh Corrie?" Lisette asked, her voice rising to a squeak.

"Yes," Zoe said. "You know him, too?"

"I did in my youth, though only a little. But Tristan knew him *very* well." Lisette glared at him. "And clearly, big brother, you have finally lost your mind."

11

Bloody, bloody hell.

Tristan wasn't sure who was driving him the most insane right now — Zoe for letting slip Milosh's name, Lisette for remembering who the man was, or the boy who'd brought up Milosh in front of Zoe in the first place.

Now Zoe regarded him with confusion, Lisette looked fit to be tied, and he would clearly have to make explanations to one, if not both.

Assuming Lisette even gave him the chance. She blocked his path, her hands on her hips in her best imitation of Mother at her most infuriating. "I can't believe you'd risk getting mixed up with Milosh again! What are you *thinking*? You know Hucker has been sniffing around London, hoping to find something on you for George. If he discovers you're consorting with Milosh —"

"He won't discover anything, damn it.

Surely you know I can elude Hucker when necessary."

"You didn't elude him last year, and you nearly ended up in Newg—"

"Lisette!" he said sharply. "I am still with a client."

His sister blinked. Then her cheeks turned scarlet as she apparently realized the imprudence of mentioning that he'd been headed for prison last year, before the duke had bullied George into dropping the charge of horse theft.

"And I need to talk to Milosh," he went on, "because of Lady Zoe's case." Actually, he wasn't sure that Milosh would know a bloody thing about that, but he hadn't found anything here, and it was worth the attempt.

"Who is Hucker?" said Zoe into the strained silence.

"No one." He shot his sister a warning glance.

With a sniff, Lisette turned on her heel and continued heading for the road and their waiting coach. Tristan fell into step behind her, as did Zoe. God, he didn't need this right now, when he was so close to finding Milosh.

"Clearly, Hucker is *not* no one," Zoe ventured.

"It's a family matter," he snapped. "Nothing to concern you."

When Lisette muttered an oath under her breath, he gritted his teeth. Thank God they'd come separately, and he would be shed of his sister shortly.

Zoe glared at him. "Fine, no talking about Hucker. But obviously Milosh concerns me. You said he has something to do with this case."

"I said he might be able to tell us something. That's all."

"So why haven't you mentioned him before?"

Lisette threw a smug glance at him over her shoulder. "She asks excellent questions, doesn't she, Tristan?"

"If you don't shut up, sister, I swear I will gag you with those ribbons."

"You wouldn't dare." Lisette flashed him a minxish smile. "If you even attempted such a thing, Max would string you up by your toes. I'm having his child, you know."

"Yes, and driving us all to distraction in the process," Tristan grumbled. "He might actually thank me for gagging you."

"Careful now," his sister said archly. "This child will be your niece or nephew, so you should be nicer to me."

That practically knocked his feet out from

under him. He'd been thinking of the baby as Lisette's child, not as *his* niece or nephew. This would be the first baby born to the three siblings. Hell, the first baby born to all four of them, since George hadn't managed to spawn any children with his wife, either.

Why did the thought of having a niece or nephew bother him? He liked children well enough when he had dealings with them, which wasn't often. But a baby who looked up to him as an uncle, who might turn to him for advice or comfort or . . . or anything . . . That was another matter entirely.

"Well?" Zoe asked, breaking into his thoughts.

He glanced over at her, still wrestling with the idea that he would soon be an uncle. "Well what?"

She huffed out an exasperated breath. "Why haven't you mentioned Milosh before? Why didn't you say you had a friend who was a Yorkshire Romany who might shed light on my case?"

Damn, but the woman never let anything go. "Because I didn't know he was in London, all right? I didn't know *where* he was." That was true, at least.

"But that Gypsy boy said that you'd asked about Milosh before we even arrived, so you clearly came here intending to look for him."

They'd nearly reached the coach. Just a few more feet. "Honestly, you're making far too much of this."

"Am I? Your sister mentioned George. Does this have anything to do with the rumors that you stole a horse from your half brother years ago?"

Christ in heaven. How had he managed to forget her mentioning that earlier? And what the hell was he supposed to tell her? He had to tell her something.

Both women looked expectantly at him. Meanwhile, a pack of boys and girls were descending on them, waving neckerchiefs and clamoring to be heard. He'd forgotten about his bargain with them, too.

That tore it.

"Quiet!" he shouted, cowing even the Romany children. He scowled at his sister. "Since you're 'famished,' I suggest you go to that cookshop nearby and get something to assuage your hunger. Stay as long as you please. Zoe and I have a few things to discuss, and we need time alone to do so."

"But —" Lisette began.

"I'm not arguing this with you, damn it! Give us an hour to talk, and I swear you can have her back."

"It's fine, Lisette," Zoe put in. "And he's

right — I do need to talk to him in private, if you don't mind."

Lisette looked wary. "Well, if you're sure . . ."

"I'm sure. Come back in an hour, all right?" Zoe's gaze dropped to Lisette's belly, and a wistful look crossed her face. "Go feed that child."

With a nod, Lisette headed for the coach. As soon as it drove off, the children began waving strips of fabric at Zoe.

Tristan growled, "Choose a damn neckerchief, so we can be done with them."

"You don't have to curse at me." After scanning the array, she picked one with pink spots. "For Lisette's baby," she explained as the ruby-cheeked girl on the other end of it beamed at her and chattered madly to Tristan.

Mention of the baby made his gut knot, and he wasn't even sure why. Ignoring that disturbing reaction, he gave the girl a large handful of coins. The others started clamoring again, but he told them he had no more money. That did the trick and they wandered off.

Except for the boy who'd sent them packing from the old Gypsy woman's house. Tristan hadn't seen him join the group. "Have you got any more news for us?"

Tristan asked. "Did your aunt tell you anything about Drina?"

"Forgive me, no. But about Milosh, I found this . . ." The lad handed over a crumpled piece of paper. Tristan opened it to find a sketch of a tilted cart much like one Milosh's family used to travel in.

The boy pointed to a stylized picture of a saddle painted on one side. "This is for the Corrie family. If you go to Lambeth, look for this, and you will find Milosh."

"Thank you," Tristan said. "That will help immensely."

"Yes, thank you," Zoe said. A cold wind swept them, and she shivered.

"One more thing, lad," Tristan said. "Is there somewhere my lady and I can go to warm up? A place with a fire, and perhaps some food?"

The boy cast Zoe an uncertain glance, then nodded. "This way." He began walking back to the row of houses.

"Whose house is this?" Tristan asked as the lad opened the door and ushered them into an empty parlor of sorts, furnished much the same as the other one. "And where are the residents?"

"It's my family's. Father leased it from the owner of this field for three months. All the women are next door just now, and the men went to another town for work, so you and your lady may use it if you please."

The lad pointed to a basket near the hearth, then held out his hand. "For a shilling, you may have bread and cheese."

"We'll take it, thank you," Tristan said, handing him the coin.

While the boy made up the fire in the hearth, Tristan removed his hat and gloves and tossed them onto a cushion. Following his lead, Zoe did the same, but with the prim little motions of any princess.

As soon as the fire was roaring, the lad headed for the door. "I must see to my auntie."

"Thank you," Tristan said.

The boy paused in the doorway. "You and your wife may stay as long as you need."

"Oh, but I'm —" Zoe began.

"We won't be long," Tristan said hastily. "Thank you again."

With a nod, the lad left. As soon as he was gone, Tristan said, "You mustn't tell him we aren't married. The Romany are stricter than the English when it comes to men and women. They would never allow us to be alone together if they knew you were unmarried. Understood?"

She sighed. "Yes."

Fetching the basket of food, he fished out

226

hunks of bread and cheese and handed them to her. She began to devour them as if she hadn't seen food in days.

Tristan had never watched her eat before, and she did it with such lusty enjoyment that he couldn't tear his gaze from the surprisingly erotic sight. God only knew what else she would do lustily.

When that errant thought made him harden, he stifled an oath. That was *not* why they'd come in here.

He got right to the point. "I need to know where you heard the rumor about my being a horse thief."

She concentrated on tearing more bread off the loaf. "Why does it matter?"

"Because it's not widely known, and certainly not in London. I'd prefer to keep it that way."

"So it's true, then?"

Hell and thunder. "It's not that simple. And it has naught to do with you. Or this case."

Her face clouded over. Walking to the fire, she threw the remainder of her bread and cheese into it. "That's not entirely accurate, is it?" She dusted off her hands. "It has to do with Milosh, and you keep saying Milosh is part of this case."

He could cheerfully have throttled his

sister for making the connection between Milosh and Blue Blazes. "Who told you about the horse, Zoe?"

"I'm not even sure that —"

"*Who told you,* damn it?"

She turned from the fire to stare at him. "My cousin." When Tristan let out a low oath, she added hastily, "He got it from Papa, who said he heard it years ago. Winborough and Rathmoor Park aren't that far apart, after all."

True, but Dom had said there was no indication that Tristan's desperate act was bandied about in Yorkshire. Supposedly George had used his influence to keep the theft quiet to avoid a family scandal. But the arse had damned well kept the arrest warrant in place, until Max had forced him to relinquish it.

And he probably hadn't bothered to squelch the servant gossip, which might explain how her father had learned of it.

"What *exactly* did your father say?"

"I don't know." When Tristan snorted, she said, "Honestly, I don't! I haven't had a chance to talk to Papa about it yet. He was still sleeping when I left this morning. So I only know what Jeremy related while we were dancing last night."

"Jeremy?" The unfamiliar tightness in his

228

chest fired his temper. "Now you're calling your cousin *Jeremy*? How cozy."

She crossed her arms over her chest defensively. "He's my cousin. We're allowed to be cozy."

"Yes, indeed you are." Dropping the basket, he came toward her. "Has it occurred to you that he has good reason to be saying nasty things about me?" And why the devil hadn't the man mentioned it to *him* in all their drunken wanderings last night?

"It wasn't like that," she protested. "My cousin merely said that Papa had warned him not to be chummy with you because of your . . . past."

"Which included stealing a horse."

"Yes." She stared him down.

"And you, of course, weren't a bit surprised to hear tales of my career as a thief," he snapped, his stomach roiling.

"Actually, I *was* surprised. I found it highly unlikely that either the French secret police or your brother would have hired a thief to do investigations."

He breathed a little easier. A very little easier. "So why mention it?"

"Because I wanted to know the truth, of course. After seeing you pretend to be a thief for a case once before, I assumed

229

that . . . perhaps this was the same."

The fact that she'd given him the benefit of the doubt set him back on his heels. Until something occurred to him.

Coming up to her, he said, "I would almost believe that, if not for how you threw the words at me so accusingly."

"What do you expect, when you provoke me at every turn?" Her eyes glittered at him. "When I call you a rogue, you take it as a compliment, and when I call you a seducer, you freely acknowledge it. It's . . . It's . . ."

"Annoying?"

"Unseemly."

Startled, he let out a laugh. "*Unseemly?* I don't believe I've ever been insulted with such a milksop word before. It's a bit like the opposite of 'damning with faint praise' — you're praising with faint damnation."

He circled her slowly. "And I notice that you have no such damning words for your cousin, who talks freely of brothels and gaming hells before a lady and who is still abed after his exertions last night. While *I*, the 'unseemly' rogue and seducer, am here, trying to help you."

His temper was starting to ebb, replaced by a fierce awareness of the fact that they were alone. That she was darting uncertain looks at him even as her cheeks grew pink beneath his stare.

Something decidedly wicked roared to life inside him.

She must have sensed it, for she rubbed her arms nervously. "It's not the same with Jeremy. He's American. He doesn't know any better." Her gaze met his. "You do. And you're the one who took him to the brothel in the first place."

"Because he asked me to." He halted mere inches from her. All the air seemed to have been sucked from the room, for he could hardly breathe with her this close. "But I didn't stay."

Rank suspicion showed in her lovely features. "Of course not." Turning away, she headed for the door. "You would never go to a brothel, never consort with whores —"

"I swear I didn't last night." When she reached for the door handle, he strode up behind her to draw her back against him until her fine arse was anchored against his rapidly thickening flesh. "Do you want to know why?"

"No," she whispered, though she didn't pull away when he started kissing her neck.

"Because when I saw the women ranged in the windows, when I saw their calculating looks, assessing my purse . . . and other things, I realized I didn't want any of them

231

in my bed."

Her breath quickened, and suddenly he couldn't be cautious anymore. Not with her. Not when her violet scent swamped him and her soft body was curving into his, hardening him to stone.

"That's why I left, princess," he rasped. "Because I realized it was you I wanted in my bed. Only you."

12

Zoe's pulse jumped into a gallop. He wanted "only her" — in his bed. Not in his life, or as his wife, or anything acceptable. Oh no. In his *bed.*

As if to emphasize that, he pulled her back against him, let her feel the thick rod between his legs, and she gasped. She knew how men joined with women, because she'd seen the beasts in heat on her estate — the rams with their ewes and the stallions mounting their mares.

But this was different. Feeling his flesh harden against her fed her vanity, oddly enough. All those beautiful women he'd been with . . . yet he wanted this with her?

No matter how much she reminded herself he was only satisfying a physical need, she still exulted that he wanted to satisfy it with *her.* At least he was honest about it. He wasn't pretending to want marriage.

What else could she expect from an unrepentant rogue, anyway? "It doesn't matter what you want," she lied. "It doesn't even matter what *I* want."

"It matters to me." He splayed his hand over her belly, startling a hot rush of need through her, and she thought she would evaporate into steam right there. "Don't," she whispered, the word more a desperate request than a command. "Please, Tristan, don't . . ."

"Don't what?" His fingers stroked her through her gown. "Desire you? Need you?"

"Yes . . . no . . ." She frantically tried to grab her wits before they fled entirely. "You're just doing this to keep me from asking you about the theft."

"Not a bit." He nipped her ear, making her gasp. "I don't care what you ask, because I won't talk about what happened in Yorkshire."

Lisette's earlier words about avoiding their home county leapt into her mind. "But the rumors are true, aren't they? You did steal a horse. Otherwise you wouldn't refuse to speak of it." Or avoid Yorkshire.

"As I said before, it's not that simple. And it's *not your concern.*"

"But it is," she choked out as his hand moved in ever-widening circles, making her wobbly inside and out. "What if you get ar-

234

rested?"

"Are you worried about me?"

"Yes! Your sister was concerned enough to caution you about involving Milosh. How could I *not* worry about you?"

"You needn't." His breath grew heavy on her neck, and his hand was roaming now, inching up to her bosom. "I can take care of myself." His hand covered her breast. "And you."

Pure shock kept her frozen. But when he kneaded her there, where she hadn't even known she wanted his touch, the sensations bursting through her drove out the shock and replaced it with a wild, ungoverned thrill that was better even than riding neck-or-nothing through Winborough's fields.

"Ohhh, Tristan . . ." she moaned.

Deftly, he unfastened her redingote just enough to slip his hand inside, and then down beneath her corset and her shift to her naked flesh.

Her *naked flesh.* Good Lord in heaven.

When his thumb thrummed her nipple with delicate strokes, she nearly came out of her skin. Anything that felt *that* amazing had to be wrong.

"You shouldn't . . . we shouldn't . . ."

"Why not?" His other hand roamed now, inching down her belly.

235

"Because . . . because . . ." It was hard to think in the wake of such astonishing caresses.

"Romany or not, you were raised an heir to a kingdom . . . a princess, if you will. And princesses can have whatever — whomever — they damned well please." His voice lowered to a fierce rasp. "So have *me.*"

Her heart did a little somersault. She chided it ruthlessly. "As what?" she whispered. "My paramour?"

He was inching up her skirts now, dragging them up her thighs. She ought to run away.

She couldn't.

"Keane isn't right for you," he said hoarsely.

"That's not an answer." And still she didn't run away.

"But it's true, all the same." He gently pinched her nipple, and her soft cry echoed in the empty room. "Tell me, Zoe, does he make you yearn? Make you feel like this?"

"How would I know? He's never . . . touched me this way."

He fondled her breast shamelessly. "And do you *want* him to? Do you imagine it, think of it, wish for it?"

"He's . . . he's a respectable gentleman."

"Some gentleman, going off to brothels

for his pleasure," he growled. "And what does that have to do with anything?"

"A respectable gentleman wouldn't make me . . . want this."

"Ballocks."

The coarse curse should have brought her out of her senseless fever to have him touch her. Instead, it added to the delicious wickedness of it.

He laved her ear with his tongue. "Any man you plan to marry should do precisely that, respectable or no. And the fact that Keane doesn't —"

"I didn't say that."

That seemed to unleash some reckless-ness in him, for with a muttered oath, he dropped his hand from her breast to where his other hand now lifted her skirts above her thighs. Then he cupped her between the legs. Right over the part of her that felt hot and achy and damp.

She groaned.

"Are you telling me you want *him* to touch you like this?" He branded her neck with rough, needy kisses. "That you want him to excite you the way I am?"

She made a last effort to fight the languor-ous enjoyment stealing her will. "Who says . . . you excite me?"

With a muttered curse, he combed his

fingers through her curls down there until he was stroking the slick flesh. "Your lush, wet heat does. You want me."

"No," she lied.

"Yes." He delved deeply with one finger, and she nearly went out of her mind.

"Oh my . . . Tristan. *Tristan.*" She dug her fingers into his thighs as she arched up against his hand. "What . . . are you *doing* to me?"

"Arousing you," he said in a guttural murmur. "Showing you how it should be between a man and a woman who desire each other."

"So now you . . . mean to give me lessons? The sort of lessons I ought to be learning from my future husband?"

"While he's off spending his time in and out of brothels?" He was rubbing himself against her now, his thickened flesh like a brand against her bottom.

"That's hypocritical . . . coming from you."

He stroked her hard between her legs, making her gasp. Making her *want.* "Tell me the truth, Zoe. Do you desire Keane?"

His sensual caresses made it impossible for her to think. For her to do anything but feel. And yearn. And *need.* "Why does it matter?"

238

"Because if you desire him, I swear I'll let you be from now on. I'll let you pursue him to your heart's content."

She ought to lie. She couldn't. "It doesn't matter if I desire him. I still have to . . . pursue him."

"That doesn't answer my question, and you know it."

Abruptly, he turned her in his arms to press her against the door. He still held her skirts bunched up in one hand, exposing her from the waist down, but now he leaned into her as he resumed his fondling below.

With ruthless intent, he kissed his way down the opening in her redingote to the swells showing above her corset. As her breath quickened, he released her skirts so he could pull down her corset cup to expose one linen-clad breast. Then he seized it in his mouth through the fabric and sucked it. Hard. Thrillingly.

A groan of pure pleasure escaped her, and she caught him by the shoulders to hold him close. He tongued her nipple as his finger continued its cursed caress until she was shimmying beneath him and wanting things she couldn't begin to understand.

Abruptly he halted everything. When she uttered an inarticulate cry, he ground out, "Tell me, damn you! Do you want him?"

"No!" When his eyes searched her face, she admitted, "Not like this. No."

An intense satisfaction lit his face. "Thank God."

Then he was kissing her hard, his hands inflaming her senses above and below. It was too much at once. With a deep moan of surrender, she gave herself up to the delicious excitement. Oh, to have him like this with her always . . .

No, she wouldn't torture herself. He was with her now, giving her a taste of what it could be like . . . if he weren't such a rootless rogue.

"How you make me burn," he murmured against her mouth. Leaving off caressing her breast, he caught her hand and pushed it down to cover the bulge in his trousers. "You see what you do to me? You see how you drive me mad?"

She exulted at the idea of holding *him* enraptured, and rubbed the long length of him through his trousers.

With a guttural moan, he thrust into her hand. "Hell and thunder, yes. Like that, princess. I didn't sleep last night because of this . . . this ache for you."

"Me neither," she admitted, reveling in how his flesh seemed to leap beneath her fingers. "You're more accomplished at roguery than I realized."

"This isn't roguery."

Her heart soared. She hated herself for it. "Then what is it?"

"I don't know. But I've never done this with a woman like you before. Never wanted to." The uncertainty in his face told her that he spoke the truth. "I only know . . . I don't want it to end."

He thumbed her between the legs in a blatantly carnal caress that jolted her. And made her press herself into his hand in a wordless demand for more.

In answer, he undid his trousers enough to slide her hand inside. "Stroke me while I give you pleasure, sweetheart."

Sweetheart? He'd never called her that.

His gaze burned into her as he closed her hand around his rigid staff. "Let us find our pleasure together."

"I don't even know what that means," she whispered, but she let him guide her into pulling on his . . . his thing, up and down, over and over.

"It means I won't ruin you," he hissed through clenched teeth. "But I do intend to make my mark on you, to keep you from hurtling headlong into an ill-considered marriage to . . . Keane."

The flush in his face, the responsiveness

of his flesh to her touch, fascinated her. But he gave her no time to dwell on it or question his motives, before he was kissing and fondling her again.

This time his strokes were steady, calculated to set a fire in her. He ignited the blaze with his fiery touch, fed it and stoked it and fed it some more, until her very skin felt aflame, and she was panting and moaning.

He tore his mouth from hers. "Yes, sweetheart, like that. Let it take you." His eyes were unfocused. "Come for me. I want to see you . . . shatter." As he quickened the motion of his thumb below, he urged her hand to increase its pace as well. "I want to . . . shatter with you."

Lord, that was exactly how his strokes against that pulsing place between her legs felt, a persistent drumming like the . . . rap of a hammer against glass. Tapping . . . tapping . . . tapping . . . until the glass . . . chipped . . . then cracked . . . then shattered!

She cried out, and he swallowed the cry with his mouth as his flesh jerked in her hand and he shattered, too.

They stood there a moment, joined at the mouth, joined by the shared intimacy of their hands down there. It was lovely and sweet and the most wonderful moment of her life.

Until out of nowhere, the words of the fortune-teller leapt into her mind: *If you let him, he will shatter your heart.*

Lord save her. It might already be too late to prevent that.

With a moan, she jerked her hand from his trousers. It was damp, and she stared down at it uncomprehendingly for a moment, before the truth hit her. "No. No, no, no . . ."

Panic rising in her chest, she wiped her hand on her petticoat, then slid from between him and the door. As her skirts fell once more to cover her shameless body, she worked frantically at fastening her redingote buttons.

She refused to fall in love with him. She couldn't. *Mustn't.*

"Zoe . . ."

"Enough, Tristan. You made your point."

Scowling, he buttoned his trousers. "And what point was that?"

She could scarcely breathe, much less think. She must have lost her mind to let him . . . to do what they had just . . . Heaven save her. "That you're a master at seduction."

"That wasn't the point I was making," he

said hoarsely as he came toward her.

"No?" She scooped up her gloves and bonnet. "You weren't trying to prove that I find you more appealing than I do my cousin?"

"All right, that was part of it, but —" He fixed her with a bleak stare. "You shouldn't marry a man you don't desire."

"But I can't marry the man whom I *do* desire, can I? He doesn't want a wife — and even if he did, it wouldn't help my situation." She hurried for the door. "So now I get to know what I'll be missing, and be even more miserable marrying the only choice of husband open to me. Thank you."

He blocked her path. "Damn it, Zoe, that wasn't what I was trying to do."

"But that's what you achieved." She scowled at him. "And all because you wanted to distract me from asking questions about your checkered past."

"That is *not* why!"

"Isn't it?" Fighting back tears, she tied her bonnet on and donned her gloves. "Every time I mention Milosh, you say he's connected to my case, but when you spoke to that old woman you didn't even ask about Drina until I prodded you."

His face grew grayer by the moment.

Though she knew she was partly chafing

at the fact that he wanted her only in his bed, she couldn't prevent the bitter accusations from pouring out. "Did you ever even intend to find Drina? Or was that just a ruse to settle your own affairs?"

He bore down on her, forcing her away from the door. "I didn't travel to Liverpool to find Milosh, that's for damned sure. And today, when you were with me, you watched me spend an entire day hunting for the elusive Drina."

"Yet all we gained was directions to *your* childhood friend." Her voice shook. "Who might get you arrested somehow for horse thieving."

"Hell and thunder, he's not going to get me arrested!" He looked around for his hat and gloves. "Is that what this is about? You're worried I won't get your bloody information for you?"

"Perhaps," she lied. "What good will you do me if you end up in gaol?"

A muscle jerked in his jaw. "That's what this comes down to. You still don't trust me." As he clapped his hat on his head, his gaze drifted down her with an insolence that made her bristle. "You're perfectly happy to let me kiss you and put my hands on you, but God forbid you trust me with anything *important.*" He whirled toward the door.

She followed him, a sickening feeling in the pit of her stomach. "That's not fair! You hide the truth and follow your own plan and refuse to tell me how your friend and your half brother George and my case are connected. Yet you think I should just believe whatever —"

"I don't give a damn what you believe." He reached the door and yanked on his gloves. "My past is my concern. I have a right to keep it to myself. You paid me to investigate *your* past, not mine."

Grabbing the door handle, he gave her a cold glance that chilled her to the bone. "So now you have a decision to make. Tonight I will speak to Milosh and learn what I can about *your mother.* Meanwhile, you need to figure out if you still trust me to handle this. If not, just say the word when I give you my report at Rotten Row tomorrow afternoon, and I'll hand the whole thing over to Dom."

"Tomorrow afternoon! But you have to take me with you when you go tonight."

"Are you mad? It was hard enough to arrange this jaunt today; there's no way in hell to sneak you out of your father's house at night just so you can —"

"How do I know you'll even ask about Drina?" She was still smarting from his refusal to give her the facts about his past.

"You won't tell me how you're connected to Milosh. For all I know, you have your own plans for him."

His eyes blazed at her. "So that's what you think of me. I'm always going to be the dirty bastard to you, the coarse, unmannerly oaf in gentleman's clothing."

"I didn't say that," she whispered.

"You didn't have to." He yanked open the door. "And since you obviously think me a liar and a thief, I will let Dom handle the matter from now on."

He stalked out onto the frozen path and headed for the road, the tail of his greatcoat flapping in the wind.

Lifting her skirts, she ran after him in a fury. "How dare you blame me for your . . . your pigheaded refusal to tell me what's going on? I have a right to know!"

Like the cursed *man* that he was, he just kept walking.

Up ahead, the duchess's coach pulled up and the footman helped Lisette out. She came toward them with a smile. "I hope I didn't take too long," she said as she approached. "But the cookshop was farther than I thought."

"It's fine," Tristan clipped out. "We're fine. She's all yours. I'm going on." He paused to glance back at Zoe as she reached them. "I'll give my report to Dom in the morning. He can pass it on to you." He tipped his hat. "Good day to you, my lady."

He continued resolutely toward a horse tied to a tree farther down the street.

"Drat you, Tristan!" Zoe cried, and hurried after him.

The duchess caught her by the arm before she could even pass. "Let him go for now. When he's in a temper, there's no reasoning with him."

"But you don't understand."

"I understand you'll get nowhere with him if you don't let him cool down." Lisette gazed over to where he'd already untied his mount and was swinging into the saddle. "Come. Let's head back to your father's. You can tell me all about it on the way. Then if you still want to face down a bear, I'll make sure to get him trapped up a tree for you, all right?"

He was already riding off. She couldn't exactly run after a cantering horse. With a nod, she let the duchess lead her back to the Lyons carriage.

They climbed in and set off toward Mayfair. Zoe was a seething mass of emotion — one minute furious, the next despairing, blaming herself for pressing the issue, then blaming Tristan for taking her halfway to

seduction while still refusing to tell her anything.

He claimed *she* didn't trust *him*? He
didn't trust her one whit!

"So tell me," Lisette said, "what has my
brother done now?"

Perhaps the duchess would reveal what
Tristan wouldn't. "He claims that Milosh
has something to do with my case, but he
won't say how. What the devil does Milosh
have to do with Tristan?"

Lisette winced. "I gather that my brother
really doesn't want you —"

"To know that he stole a horse from your
half brother? That he fled to France because
of it?"

"He *told* you?"

She debated whether to lie. But it hardly
seemed fair to gain information by deception when what she wanted was an end to
the deception. "No. I heard rumors from
my father, and I need to know how much is
true. And how much is foolish society gossip." Her voice grew choked. "Tristan won't
tell me. Will you?"

The duchess looked troubled. "What's so
important about your case that you ask me
to reveal something about my family history
that very few people have ever heard? Can
you tell me *why* you want to know?"

Zoe swallowed. "I wish I could. But my case isn't just my own. Too much is at stake for me to unveil my secrets." Reaching forward, she seized Lisette's hands. "But I *can* tell you I need to know for more than just reasons of this case. Your brother is . . . not merely an investigator to me."

Heaven save her, it was true. How terrifying. Because he clearly didn't feel the same. Or not as deeply, anyway. "I doubt that it matters, but —"

"You want to know if you've misplaced your affections," Lisette said softly. "If you're being a terrible judge of character."

With tears clogging her throat, she nodded.

Lisette gazed out the carriage window. For a long, agonizing moment, she appeared to be considering something. But just when Zoe was sure the woman would refuse, she turned back to Zoe and set her shoulders.

"Very well," Lisette said with a hint of defiance. "I'll tell you."

13

The clatter of hooves on cobblestones, the grind of scissors being sharpened, the lilting cries of sellers hawking primroses and matches and milk — all of it penetrated the duchess's carriage, and none of it drowned out the chilling tale of Tristan's break with George Manton.

Zoe listened with her fists clenched and her blood rising. "How did your half brother get away with it? Didn't anybody protest?"

"No one was about to stand up to the newly minted Viscount Rathmoor." Bitterness crept into Lisette's voice. "Not the townspeople who called Tristan 'the French whore's bastard,' or the servants who knew better than to cut off their own noses to spite their faces."

"But Dom stood up to him."

"Dom tried," Lisette corrected her, "and George cut him off completely. Without money, Dom had no choice but to quit his studies as a barrister. He was forced to rely on his own resources, and his best one proved to be his friendship with Jackson Pinter."

"*Sir* Jackson Pinter?"

The duchess nodded. "They met when Dom was studying a legal case that Sir Jackson was involved in. So when George destroyed Dom's hope for a future, Dom asked Sir Jackson for a position as a Bow Street runner. He made his living that way until only a few years ago, when he established Manton's Investigations."

"And you and your mother and brother went to France."

"*Fled* is more like it." Lisette stared out the window. "Dom sneaked us off the estate to Flamborough Head. From there, we boarded a smuggler's skiff for the Continent."

A sudden lurch in the pit of her stomach made Zoe clutch the squabs. "You crossed the English Channel in a *skiff*? It's a miracle you even survived!"

"It was a sailing skiff, so not as tiny as you might think, but the journey *was* rather harrowing." Lisette smiled faintly. "From that day on, Maman refused to set foot on anything that traversed water. She said she'd rather drown than spend hours repeatedly losing the contents of her stomach."

"What about Tristan?"

"He was so angry at himself for putting us in that position that he stopped at nothing to protect us, took any number of reckless chances on our behalf. He nearly beat one of the smugglers to a bloody pulp for attempting to steal a kiss from me."

"Of course he did," Zoe said. "You were only fourteen, right?"

The duchess nodded. "When we neared the shore off Biarritz and the smugglers threatened to toss us out unless we gave them the rest of our money, Tristan held the captain at knifepoint until his men pulled the skiff in to the beach and let us off safely."

Her eyes grew misty. "He was outnumbered four to one, and they were armed. So after they allowed Maman and me to get off, he made them go back out to sea well away from us before he jumped into the water and swam for shore in the midst of a tempest."

"Good heavens."

"The dratted fool was banged up so badly by the rocks that he could scarcely run when the smugglers made for land again, still eager to steal the remainder of our funds." Lisette shook her head. "Fortunately, the storm was still going on, so we eluded them, though it was a narrow escape."

Tears stung Zoe's eyes over what all of them had suffered, but most especially Tristan. Her dear, tormented Tristan. No wonder he hated "her kind." No wonder he thought her half-mad for trying to unearth her Gypsy family. She'd gained the world despite her ignominious birth; he'd lost everything because of *his*.

And because of a foolish theft of a horse. "So if Tristan really stole that Thoroughbred, why is he here and not in gaol?"

"It's a long story, but the gist of it is that in exchange for Tristan's having found my husband's cousin, Max made sure that George withdrew the charges. Of course, that won't stop our blasted half brother from trying to destroy Tristan some other way. For example, by using Milosh."

Now that Lisette had explained who Milosh was to Tristan, Zoe was torn between anger that Tristan had used *her* situation to find Milosh, and worry over why he had chosen to do so. What could he possibly be planning?

"Does George know that Milosh is the one who bought the horse all those years ago?" Zoe asked.

"There's no way to be sure. Milosh and his family left the same night we did. That wouldn't have seemed odd — everyone knew that Papa was the only one allowing them to camp on the land and that George would kick them off as soon as he could. But with Milosh being a horse trader, George might have put it all together."

"Still, if there's no more theft warrant, how could your half brother use Milosh to hurt Tristan?"

Worry lit Lisette's features, so much like Tristan's. "If George has guessed that Tristan sold the horse to Milosh, then he could have *Milosh* arrested, especially if he sees Tristan taking up with the man again. George could claim he dropped the charges because he'd figured out that Milosh, not Tristan, did the stealing."

"But there's no evidence, nothing concrete to tie Milosh to the horse. Or surely his lordship would have had the Gypsy arrested years ago."

"George doesn't need evidence. He's got Hucker to lie for him, and any number of servants. What's more, he knows that Tristan would never stand for Milosh taking the blame for his crime. Tristan feels bad enough that Dom suffered for it. He would do whatever he must to save Milosh."

Zoe dragged in a sharp breath. "Like what?"

"Who knows? Probably admit to the theft. Or . . . I don't know, challenge George to a duel or something. They truly despise each other."

She was beginning to get that impression. "Then surely Tristan realizes all of what you're telling me. So why is he taking such risks to see Milosh?"

Lisette shrugged. "Because of your case, I assume."

"I don't think so. I think he has some reason he's not telling either of us. Before you and I even reached the camp this morning, he was looking for the man." Zoe stared out the window for a long moment, her heart in her throat. "It's far more likely that he used my case as an excuse to hunt up Milosh for his own purposes."

The duchess smoothed her skirts. "Perhaps at first. But I watched him with you today. The way he acted, the way he looked at you —"

"I'm sure he looks at all women the same. He *is* a rogue, after all."

"Yes, sometimes." Lisette searched her face. "But don't let my big brother's blustering fool you. There's more to Tristan than he lets on."

"Oh, trust me, I know." Zoe hardly saw the buildings they hurtled past on their way through town. "Still, when it comes to women . . ."

"He's never taken up with a lady, you know. His . . . er . . . preference has always been experienced women who are using him as much as he's using them. And I have never seen him look at a mere client — at *any* female — as if the world might stop spinning if he couldn't have her."

I've never done this with a woman like you before. Never wanted to. I only know . . . I don't want it to end.

Curse the man. Why must he crawl under her skin at every turn?

"Not even in France?" she asked, thinking of all the lovely Frenchwomen he must have met.

Lisette snorted. "Especially not in France. Good Lord, he had no time for women there."

Zoe's gaze shot to her. "Why not?"

"He spent it working." The duchess's lips thinned into a tight line. "When we first arrived, we all did. I took in piecework, Maman trod the boards, and he worked at the Toulon shipyards during the day and took a job as a watchman at night. He scarcely slept for days on end."

An unsettling image of Tristan wielding a hammer at a shipyard half-asleep flashed in her mind. "Toulon? I thought he was in Paris."

"Not until a few years later, after La Sûreté Nationale hired him. We stayed in Toulon with Maman's family to save money." Lisette's voice tightened. "He took every case they threw his way, determined to earn enough so that Maman and I wouldn't have to work anymore, especially once she fell ill. It was only after she died and I moved in with him that he stopped his frenzy."

Zoe glanced out the window to keep Lisette from glimpsing her agitation. The duchess painted a picture of Tristan that differed vastly from the one Zoe had been clinging to.

He fought for his family like her. He sacrificed for his family like her. And no doubt he hurt when someone refused to trust him.

Like her.

Somehow she must find a way to talk to him again. She couldn't let him go on thinking she distrusted him because of his bastardy or anything else.

"Are you all right, my dear?" Lisette patted Zoe's hand.

"I will be." As soon as she could speak to Tristan.

There must be a way to sneak out of the house and get to Tristan before he went off to see Milosh. She didn't know what his purpose was in meeting up with his old cohort, but it couldn't be good. She had to warn him about everything Lisette had said.

And she had to tell him that she understood. That she didn't blame him for any of it. That she trusted him.

Until she did, she couldn't rest easy.

"Are you sure you won't need me for anything this evening, Mr. Bonnaud?"

Taking the kettle off the hob, Tristan carried it over to the kitchen table and sat down to dismantle his pistol. "I'll be fine, Shaw, thank you."

Skrimshaw cast the pistol a pointed look. "When Mr. Manton left this evening, he did not tell me you were on a case."

"I'm not. This is personal."

"Ah. And dangerous, I take it?"

Tristan began to clean the gun's parts with boiling water. "Didn't Shakespeare say, 'To be prepared for war is one of the most effectual means of preserving peace'?"

Skrimshaw's already florid features turned positively scarlet. "No, sir, he did not. That

259

was said by that American colonial named George Washington."

Tristan barely smothered his laugh. Tormenting the man was such great fun. "How odd. I could have sworn it was Shakespeare. Are you sure?"

"Quite sure." Shaw rolled his eyes. "The only reference to war from the Bard that I remember is 'He is come to open / The purple testament of bleeding war.' " Skrimshaw watched as Tristan poured sand in the pistol barrel and shook it. "I hope that you do not intend to open any such thing while your brother is away."

"Me? Never."

That wasn't entirely true. If Tristan found out anything from Milosh tonight about George, he would happily open a "bleeding war" with his damned half brother. Because he meant to make George rue the day he'd burned that codicil and cast them out of their homes.

Tristan rinsed sand from the barrel with hot water, then set about rubbing dry all the cleaned parts.

Skrimshaw eyed him uncertainly. "Perhaps I should not go to rehearsal."

"Nonsense." Tristan glanced at the butler's worried expression and forced a laugh. "I am merely preparing myself to venture into

260

Lambeth. You know how rough it can be in that part of town. Truly, it's nothing more than that."

Skrimshaw's face cleared. "Ah. Well, in that case, I shall be off. If you have need of me, I'll be at the theater."

With a nod, Tristan waved him on his way. He took out the trotter oil to rub down the barrel. The more he rubbed, the more the motion reminded him of his hand guiding Zoe's this afternoon as she stroked him to —

He broke off with a curse. Damn the wench. Thanks to her, he was getting hard just cleaning a gun.

But he couldn't help himself. Closing his eyes, he remembered her as she'd looked half-naked, her skirts pulled up, her bodice open . . . and him with his hands all over her. God, how beautifully she'd come apart at his touch. It had been the most erotic experience of his life. He would give anything to repeat it, to hear her soft, mewling cries, feel the sweet, wet silk of her —

The barrel clattered on the table, rousing him from his waking dream.

Scowling, he reached for the pistol lock so he could work trotter oil into it. Yes, she'd come apart . . . and moments later had accused him of using her. Of not doing his job.

Of destroying her hopes for a comfortable marriage to Keane.

So now I get to know what I'll be missing, and be even more miserable marrying the only choice of husband open to me.

Jaw clenched, he oiled the other pistol parts. All right, perhaps he *had* set out to prove that she deserved better, but he couldn't regret that.

I can't marry the man whom I do desire, can I? He doesn't want a wife — and even if he did, it wouldn't help my situation.

Tristan groaned. She'd meant *him.* And she was right.

The last thing he needed was some female sitting up waiting for him when he was late. Worrying about him. And caring about him and needing him and *wanting* him with that all-consuming hunger that made a man's breath catch in his throat and his body harden and his soul finally feel at home . . .

Damn her! Now she was getting inside his bloody thoughts and twisting them all around. This was madness. He hadn't meant for things to go this far with her. He hadn't meant to start caring about her or, for that matter, what she thought of him.

Yet he did. It bothered him how ready she was to believe he was a conscienceless thief. It annoyed him to have her accusing him of taking her case for ulterior motives.

He sighed. That shouldn't annoy him, since it was mostly true. He did wish to "hide the truth" and follow his "own plan." And he supposed he was somewhat guilty of ignoring her search for her Romany mother so he could focus on his own search for Milosh.

But bloody hell, he'd had good reason! Not that he would ever say that to *her.* There was no telling how she would react if he confirmed her suspicions that he'd actually stolen that horse. She, who grew outraged whenever he suggested that her father might have had a mistress!

He was probably right to have told her he'd give her case to Dom. Dom wouldn't try to seduce her. Dom would be methodical and careful.

Dom didn't speak Romany.

Gritting his teeth, he reassembled his pistol and filled his powder flask. It didn't matter. After talking to Milosh tonight, Tristan would speak to every Northern Romany he could find. The least he could do for Zoe was track down Drina. If he had no success, then he and Dom would work together until her mother was found.

He just wouldn't go anywhere near Zoe in the meantime.

A knock came at the front door.

"Shaw!" he shouted, then remembered the man had left for the theater.

Grumbling, he laid down his pistol and headed for the door. It was 7:00 P.M., late for someone to be appearing on their doorstep but not entirely unheard of.

He swung the door open, then gave a start to find a hooded figure in an all-enveloping cloak. Beyond the fellow, Tristan could see a tethered mare with what looked like a sidesaddle on her back.

A *sidesaddle*? His gaze shot back to the "fellow," who lifted his . . . *her* head just enough for him to see her face. God, it was Zoe. Here. And without Lisette or even that pup Ralph for company.

Jerking her inside, he shut the door. "Have you gone utterly mad? This neighborhood is no place for a lady alone."

She pushed the hood off her head, and he saw her reddened eyes and nose.

His heart dropped into his belly. "What's happened?" He grabbed her shoulders. "Is it Keane? Is it your father?"

"No! Why do you ask?"

"You've been crying!"

"Oh. That." She wouldn't look at him. "That's only because . . . well . . . I feel dreadful about this afternoon. I shouldn't have said what I did. It was wrong of me."

She'd come all this way for that? "Not a bit. You were mostly right. I shouldn't have pushed you, and I certainly shouldn't have taken advantage of the situation to pursue my own purposes."

"But now that I understand why you did, I feel awful about the things I said to you. I had no right to accuse you without knowing all the facts."

His pulse stopped. "What facts?"

"About *why* you stole the horse." Her gaze met his. "Lisette told me who Milosh is to you. And what your half brother did to you. All of it."

He gaped at her. Then he exploded. "Bloody, bloody *hell.*" Releasing her, he turned to pace the foyer. "I swear I will take my sister over my knee next time I see her!"

She eyed him warily. "Do you make a habit of such nonsense?"

"Of course not," he grudgingly admitted. "But I'm sorely tempted to try it. Perhaps then she wouldn't betray my confidences to clients."

"Clients. I see." She hugged herself. "Is that all I am to you then? A client?"

God in heaven, how was he to answer that? He scrubbed one hand over his face. "It's not that simple."

"Isn't it?" Her tone grew arch. "I know I'm unfamiliar with general business practices, but I don't imagine they include kissing and fondling one's clients."

"Especially since most of my clients are men," he quipped.

"Don't joke," she said in an aching voice. "Not about that."

He closed his eyes to blot out the hurt in her face. Damn. Clearly, he'd made a real hash of things this afternoon. He'd made her think he wanted more, and he couldn't even regret it. He could still feel her convulsing around his finger, hear her wonderful gasps of pleasure . . .

Ruthlessly he fought to regain control over his foolish lust for her, which was rapidly becoming an equally foolish yearning. "Why are you here, Zoe?" he asked sharply. "*How* are you here? Does your family know where you've gone?"

A blush stained her cheeks. "Not exactly. They went to Suffolk Street for the premier viewing of my cousin's work. I convinced them I felt ill from a long day of shopping in damp weather, so they left me at home with my maid."

"And you sneaked out of the house."

Zoe shrugged. "It wasn't hard. She thought I was asleep. She was downstairs with the other servants, having supper. I'd already told her I didn't wish to be disturbed, so she won't go in my room, I assure you."

He snorted, skeptical that any servant would leave her ill mistress entirely alone.

"So I slipped out," she went on, "saddled my horse while the grooms were eating, and came here."

"You rode here. Alone. Halfway across town. With only your cloak for protection from every damned cutthroat who roams the roads." The image of her being assaulted by some low villain fairly strangled his breath in his throat.

She tipped up her chin. "They're not roaming at this time of night, not while everyone's out and about, going to the theater and balls and dinners. I merely joined the rest of the crowd on the streets. I daresay they took me for some servant headed home."

"Servants do not wear kid gloves." He bore down on her. "Servants do not ride first-quality mares on fine sidesaddles. Hell, they don't ride at all. They walk." When she paled, he bit back an oath. "What was so bloody important that you would risk being murdered for it? And don't tell me it's any damned apology, because —"

"I came to stop you from talking to Milosh."

That was *not* what he'd expected. When he saw that she was serious, he stiffened. "Not a chance in hell."

She seized his arm. "Please, Tristan, I don't want to see you hanged just because you want . . . Well, I don't know what you want with him, but whatever it is, it isn't worth putting yourself into Lord Rathmoor's clutches again!"

"Don't call him that. Lord Rathmoor was my father. George is just the arse who came after him." Then her words registered fully. "And what in God's name do you mean about not wanting to see me hanged?"

"Lisette says that Lord Rathmoor's — George's — man of affairs, some fellow named Hucker, has been lurking about of late to report everything to his employer. That if you meet up with Milosh and your half brother finds out, he might go after Milosh just to force you into revealing your part in the theft, so you can save your friend."

"Hell and thunder," he drawled, "you and Lisette must have had quite the little conversation this afternoon."

"She's worried about you!" Two pink spots appeared on her cheeks. "*I'm* worried

268

about you."

And she'd come all this way because of it. He didn't want that to sway him. He didn't want that to thaw his heart — but it did. How could it not?

He forced a smile. "First of all, Hucker is no longer lurking about. Dom sent him packing days ago."

"But —"

"Second of all, George has no idea that Milosh was involved."

"You can't be sure of that!"

"No, but even if Hucker were here, and even if he tried to follow me, I would know it and I'd get him off my trail. I've been eluding men like him for years, sweetheart. And Hucker himself for the past few months. The man is *not* that careful."

He covered her hand where it still gripped his arm. "Besides, he's not here, so your worrying is for naught."

"Tristan, please —"

"I swear I'm not just seeking out Milosh for my own reasons. I mean to find out about Drina, too. You want that, don't you?"

"Not at the risk to you."

"I'll be fine." He chucked her under the chin. "I have plenty of experience in this. So let me take you home, or as near it as I dare go, and then I'll head on to Lambeth.

Tomorrow, if you can shake off your cousin, I will meet you at Rotten Row and let you know what I learned."

Her gaze, still clearly anxious, warmed him. "Let me go with you tonight."

"So you can protect me from the big bad Hucker if he emerges from out of the mist?"

She didn't smile. "You told me earlier that I couldn't go because you couldn't sneak me out of the house. But I already did that. So why *not* take me?"

"Because it will require a few hours, and you're liable not to arrive home in time to be there before your family returns."

"Trust me, sneaking into my house is far easier than sneaking out, and no one will know I've been gone, anyway. So even if they do come home, they won't bother me."

He shook his head. "I'm not sure I would count on that. But even so, Lambeth isn't the sort of place for a woman at night."

"Really? You said the Romany were there to sell items to theatergoers. Are none of those theatergoers women?"

"Probably, but —"

"And aren't you perfectly capable of protecting me?"

God, she was as adept at twisting a man about her finger as his meddlesome sister. "I'm not taking you."

Her gaze turned calculating. "I see. Then I suppose I'd better go home."

"Give me a moment to get my coat and my pistol. Then we'll head down to the livery where my horse is stabled."

"No, I'm riding out now." She headed for the door. "Perhaps I'll take the long way, see a bit of Covent Garden first."

"The hell you will!"

Covent Garden was a teeming mass of whores and pickpockets and devils just waiting for a tender piece like her to come along. It was all right at this spot of Bow Street, across from the theater, but wandering farther afield could be decidedly dangerous.

When she kept on toward the door, he growled, "Stop right there, damn you! You will wait for me to accompany you. You will —"

"You cannot command me, Mr. Bonnaud." When she lifted her hand to unlatch the front door, her cloak fell open to reveal the same redingote she'd worn earlier, the one he'd had his hands beneath . . .

He groaned. He couldn't command her, but she sure as hell knew how to command *him*.

As if sublimely unaware of what she did to him, she cast him a coy smile and opened

271

the door. "I am Lady Zoe, and I will do as I please. Good night."

"Damn it, Zoe." He rushed over to catch her by the arm before she could dart outside.

She stared pointedly at his hand. "I suspect it will be difficult for you to fetch your horse while holding me prisoner, but you're welcome to attempt it."

He let loose a colorful string of French curses that didn't seem to faze her one bit. If anything, her lips were tightly pursed as if she fought a smile.

That little show of humor utterly disarmed him. "All right, princess. I'll almost certainly regret this, but I *suppose* you may go with me to Lambeth."

"Wonderful!" She tugged free of him and smoothed her skirts. "Then I shall wait while you fetch your horse and whatever else you need for our expedition."

She was so bloody pleased with herself that it rankled. "Has anyone ever told you that you are a royal pain in the . . . er . . . derriere?"

"Derriere?" she said, eyes gleaming. "Why, Mr. Bonnaud, that's a much politer word than you generally use. I don't believe I've ever been insulted with such a milksop word. It's a bit like the opposite of 'damn-

ing with faint praise,' only you're praising with faint damnation."

Leave it to Zoe to throw his own words up in his face. "Fine. A pain in the arse. Happy now?"

"Delirious."

Her brilliant smile set his blood racing. She was a piece of work, and he wanted to kiss her senseless. And more. But he couldn't — shouldn't — which made him want to howl his frustration.

Instead, he bent close to murmur, "Be grateful we're in something of a hurry, princess. Otherwise, with no one around to remind me I'm a gentleman, I would do my utmost to get you into my bed. I would take my sweet time kissing and fondling and arousing you, until I had you begging me to seduce you. I can promise you would not leave here a maiden."

Her smile vanished, and her eyes went wide.

Content that he'd had the last word, he stalked out to fetch his horse.

14

The moon hung low in the sky as they headed for Lambeth, but there were plenty of gas lamps to light the way. Unfortunately, the streets were still crowded, so they couldn't talk much as they rode for Westminster Bridge.

Zoe hadn't intended this when she'd come to Manton's Investigations, but she didn't regret it, either. It gave her another chance to find the woman who'd borne her, the father who'd abandoned her.

And another chance to be with Tristan.

With no one around to remind me I'm a gentleman, I would do my utmost to get you into my bed.

Oh, and she might just let him, too. Because a part of her — a desperate, insane part of her — wanted to see firsthand what it was like to have the scoundrel seduce her.

Would it be like this afternoon, thrilling and daring and a little rough? Or would he be gentle with her because she was a virgin? He'd said he'd take his time, and despite the brutal cold of the night, the thought of that made her hot in places she should *not* feel hot.

They were finally headed into a less trafficked area, for few people were out and about near Westminster at this time of night. Tristan edged a little closer. She assumed it was a subtly protective measure until he spoke.

"So, exactly how much *did* my chatty sister tell you about me and George?"

"Everything, I think." She cast him a sidelong glance. "About his burning the codicil, about your stealing the horse, about your family fleeing to France so you could escape being hanged."

"Ah. I suppose that's why you sneaked out of your house and rushed right over to warn me." Bitterness crept into his voice. "To keep me from making another foolish mistake like the one I made in my youth."

"I gather it wasn't so much a mistake as a desperate attempt to save your mother and sister," she said softly. "I don't blame you for it."

"How good of you. But you've missed the point entirely, you and Lisette and Dom." He turned a stony countenance to her. "Yes,

I did it partly to gain funds for my family, but if that had been the only reason, I could have asked Dom to help me figure out a solution. Or gone looking for work in York."

His gaze locked with hers. "The truth is, I honestly thought I would get away with it. My plan was that George would know without a doubt — yet be unable to prove — that I'd stolen Blue Blazes from him. I wanted him to seethe over it and not be able to do a damned thing about it."

Jerking his gaze back to the road, he prodded the horse into a faster gait. "But as usual, fate was on George's side. It always is. Some blasted servant saw me take the Thoroughbred. I don't even know who it was." His voice hardened. "I don't care, either. Because I still blame George for the whole fiasco. And I still refuse to let him get away with what he did."

As they rode on, a terrible realization gripped her. "So *that's* what this is about. You're going to see Milosh because you want revenge." When he just stared grimly ahead, she asked, "How on earth can a Romany wanderer help you avenge yourself on George?"

Would he answer her? Or keep stoically heading off on his self-appointed mission?

After a moment, he released a drawn-out

breath. "The night that I sold Milosh the horse, he mentioned something about George's past. I got the impression he might know secrets about my half brother. I didn't press him at the time, because I needed him to buy Blue Blazes and I didn't want to spook him. But now I have nothing to lose by pursuing it."

"You have nothing to gain, either. Except a hollow revenge."

"And a future without fear." His eyes glimmered at her in the night. "He won't stop until he has me in a noose. So I must stop him somehow before he succeeds."

The conviction in his face gave her pause. Was he right?

She chose her words carefully. "I can understand why you hate George, but why does he hate you so very much?"

"God only knows."

"Surely you have *some* inkling of the reason."

"You think I provoked him into it. Is that it?"

She bristled. "I'm just trying to understand."

"Good luck. I don't understand it entirely myself." He shrugged. "Dom thinks it's because Father always seemed to like me best, and George resented that."

"But Mr. Manton doesn't resent you for it."

"No." He steadied his hat on his head. "Dom was never like Father, so they didn't quite . . . get on. Dom is cautious, he prefers stability to wandering the world, and he lives like a monk, none of which qualities Papa ever had."

"Or you," she said lightly.

That made him stiffen in the saddle. "Yes, I'm just a feckless rogue, hopping from bed to bed in an endless quest for pleasure."

"I didn't say that." She'd unwittingly insulted him again. "And you can't be that feckless a rogue, or you would have stayed out with my cousin till dawn last night. You wouldn't have worked all those jobs in Toulon and Paris to support your family." She gazed over at his rigid features. "And you wouldn't be heading off to find out about my parents for me."

"Ah, but you said it yourself — I was only using your case as an excuse to hunt for Milosh."

"Then why spend nearly three days traveling to Liverpool and back? Why cart me around a Romany camp?" She ventured a smile. "Twice, counting tonight."

"So I can get you into my bed, of course," he said in a hard tone. "Why else?"

Lisette's words echoed in her ears: *But don't let my big brother's blustering fool you. There's more to Tristan than he lets on.*

"If that's all you wanted, you would have done so back at Manton's Investigations the minute you had me alone."

He didn't seem to have anything to say to that.

"Tell me, Tristan, what are your plans for *after* you take your revenge against George?"

"I haven't thought that far ahead."

"Not at all?" she asked. "Have you no secret ambition? Perhaps an urge to run Manton's Investigations by yourself one day?"

"Hardly. I own a half interest in it, and that's as much as I want."

"So, you don't hope to start a similar business concern of your own."

"No."

"You're just going to keep working with your half brother for the rest of your life?"

"God, no." The answer seemed to surprise him as much as it did her.

They'd reached the bridge and had just started across when Tristan spoke again. "Once, a long time ago, I had hoped to be a land agent."

She schooled her features to nonchalance, though her heart had just given a wild leap.

279

It wasn't unusual for a man to give his natural children a position of some kind at his estate, but the fact that Tristan had longed for it gave her hope. "At Rathmoor Park, you mean?"

He nodded tightly. "My father kept promising to apprentice me to Mr. Fowler, our land agent at the time." An acid note edged his tone. "But somehow he never got around to setting it up. He was too busy enjoying himself — traveling the world, sharing my mother's bed, and racing his horses. He tried to make up for it in the codicil, but you know what happened there."

Yes. And now she knew what had happened to Tristan, too. *That* was why he'd been so testy about the English aristocracy when he'd spoken to Jeremy. Not because he was a bastard, but because his brother, the viscount, had cut him off from the path he'd expected to take. From the life he'd hoped to lead before everything had tumbled into disaster.

"Of course," he went on, "I probably would have been terrible at it, anyway. The only formal education I ever had was a few years in the dame school at Ashcroft. I don't know nearly enough about planting crops, I have only a rudimentary knowledge of accounting, and I've been away from England so long that I've forgotten the ins and outs of the game laws."

The wistfulness in his voice that he fought so hard to disguise nearly broke her heart. "You could learn all those things," she said softly. "I learned them."

His jaw went taut. "Are you offering to teach me, princess? After you marry Keane and are comfortably settled at your estate in Yorkshire? What an intriguing proposition. You could install me as your land agent and sneak out to come to my bed whenever you're bored with —"

"Don't," she said irritably. "You always do that."

"What?"

"Say provoking things to cover up the fact that you inadvertently allowed me a glimpse of the real you."

Silence stretched between them, punctuated only by the lapping waves of the Thames and the chugging of the steam packets beneath the bridge.

"There *is* no 'real' me," he said at last. "In my profession it is best to be a chameleon, and I have perfected the art of it, I assure you." He quickened his mount's pace, leaving her trailing behind.

As she tried to catch up, despair washed over her. Every time she danced closer to him, he threw up a barricade against her. Was it just her? Or was he this secretive with everyone?

They came off the bridge, and she heard a low rumble. Within moments, she saw lights and a massive field full of booths up ahead. Like a fair, the market drew all sorts of people, from rich to poor. A sort of make-shift stable stood on one end, where people could have their horses watched for a few pence.

"It may take us a while to find the Corrie family booth in this crowd, even with that sketch the boy gave us." He edged up closer to her as they approached. "Follow my lead and let me do the talking, all right? And pull that hood farther forward to cover your face."

"Why?"

"Because it's one thing for you to be roaming a Gypsy encampment during the day alone with me, but quite another to do so at night. If any of the fair folk making purchases recognizes you, your reputation will be ruined."

"That seems unlikely, since —"

"Just do as I say for once in your life, damn you!" He spurred his horse toward where the other mounts were being held.

"And he thinks he couldn't make a good

land agent," she grumbled.

As proud and domineering as the aristocrats he mocked, he would probably get along rather well with Papa, if the two of them could just get past their prejudices to see it. They both thought that she needed a keeper; that alone would bond them for life.

That was one good thing about Jeremy. He didn't try ordering her about. They were friends and equals, thank goodness, which would make him a good husband.

Well, except for his eagerness to seek out brothels and gaming hells. And his lack of enthusiasm about running the estate. And his condescending attitude toward the English.

She gritted her teeth. *Men.* They were the most exasperating creatures on God's green earth. And they thought *women* were a nuisance? Nothing beat the sheer arrogance of a man.

Tristan was grateful there was little opportunity to converse as they wandered the booths. He'd said enough already, damn it. What had he been thinking, blathering on about wanting to be a land agent? Now she'd think he was angling for a position at her estate. Because, of course, he'd managed to put that thought in her head, too, along with everything else.

You always do that . . . Say provoking things to cover up the fact that you inadvertently allowed me a glimpse of the real you.

She sounded just like Dom. Neither of them seemed to realize that the "real" him, if there was such a thing, was a man with no real home, no real country, no real place in the world. He had family and friends, yes. But one by one, they were finding spouses and feathering their nests and reminding him that his future was to be spent alone — always alone.

Once, he'd thought that was what he wanted. Now . . .

Zoe grabbed his arm. "That's the symbol for the Corrie family, isn't it?"

He followed the direction of her gaze. It was indeed. He strolled up to the booth but didn't recognize the man running it. Fortunately, a few moments' conversation in Romany gained him the direction of Milosh's booth.

As they neared it, he murmured, "That's him there, the man arranging those stirrups and horseshoes on a table. Milosh was always good at blacksmithing."

Milosh seemed to have changed very little. He might be a bit thicker in the waist than before, but he seemed to be as energetic as he'd always been, rearranging his stock to best advantage, pacing his booth, and scanning the crowd.

Ah, he'd spotted them.

"Good evening, sir, madam!" Milosh crooned. "We have every sort of useful thing for a horse, if you care to take a look, and we . . ." He trailed off as the light from his lamp fell full on Tristan's face.

"Good to see you, Milosh," Tristan said softly.

"Tristan?" Milosh said. *"Tristan Bonnaud?"*

"In the flesh."

Bursting into laughter, Milosh grabbed him in a hug and practically squeezed the life out of him before drawing back to hold him at arm's length and look him over. "You look well for a man who fell off the face of the earth," he said in Romany.

"So do you," Tristan said in English.

Taking his cue, Milosh shifted to English, too. "How many years has it been? Eleven?"

"Thirteen."

"Ah, yes. I had only been married a year the last time I saw you." He jerked his thumb to the back of the booth, where a woman and a strapping lad were unpacking some bundles. "My son is almost thirteen now. And I have three more like him. They're the ones watching the horses at the entrance."

"Damn," Tristan said. "I wish I'd known."

A crafty smile crossed Milosh's face. "I will tell them to watch out for you, given your fondness for . . . liberating horses from their evil owners, shall we say?"

"No, we shall not. I am free of that charge now, and I would thank you not to remind people of it."

Milosh nodded toward where Zoe stood back, with her hood half hiding her face, and switched to Romany. "People like *her,* you mean?"

"She knows everything," Tristan said in English.

"Ah, then she must be your wife." As Tristan hesitated, wondering if he should lie, Milosh strode up to Zoe and held out his hand. "Milosh Corrie at your service, madam. I am very pleased to make your acquaintance."

Zoe shook his hand. "I've heard a great deal about you from Tristan."

"None of it good, I expect." Milosh gestured to the back of the booth. "Come, you must meet my wife and son."

With a hesitant smile, Zoe pushed the hood off her head. "I would be honored."

Milosh stiffened. Before Tristan could even wonder at that, the horse trader spoke in a voice of wonder and shock.

"Drina?" he said to Zoe. "Drina!" Then he turned to Tristan. "How on earth did you find my sister?"

15

Zoe's head spun. His sister! Drina was Milosh's *sister*?

No, how could that be? She scanned the man furtively, looking for some signs of resemblance to herself, but could find nothing in his leathery skin and bearded face that gave her any certainty.

Unlike most of the Gypsies she'd seen that day, he was huge — not just tall, like Tristan, but barrel-chested and thick-waisted. He wore a heavily embroidered waistcoat beneath his threadbare black coat, and around his neck was tied a red and yellow neckerchief.

Well, he did dress with dash. But so did Jeremy, and he might not be of her blood at all.

Still, there'd been no mistaking the recognition in Milosh's eyes when he'd seen her face. And Rathmoor Park wasn't but two hours' ride from Winborough. Also, Tristan *had* said that the Corries were wont to winter in York.

Corrie. She swallowed hard. Her real name was Corrie, assuming this was all true. "So . . . so Drina was your *sister*?"

At the sound of her voice, Milosh blinked. Then dismay paled his swarthy cheeks. "No . . . I mean, yes, my sister. But you can't be her. You're too young. She'd be nearly forty by now. So who . . . how . . ."

Tristan stepped in. "Zoe is my client. She hired me to find her mother, whom she says was named Drina."

Zoe couldn't help noticing that Tristan refrained from giving her full name and title. Thank goodness he was thinking on his feet. She couldn't think at all. She had an uncle. An *uncle.*

Placing a steadying hand on her arm, Tristan stared at Milosh. "I take it you don't know where your sister is?"

"No, I haven't seen her in over twenty years." Milosh scanned Zoe hungrily, as if trying to parse every feature, the way she'd just done with him. "How old are you, girl?"

"Twenty-one."

A light sparked in his eyes. "You're my niece, then? Drina's daughter?"

"If it's the same Drina . . ."

"You're the very image of her, *chai.* The

likeness is uncanny, and the age is right. You have to be her daughter!"

Scowling, Milosh's wife approached him, and they began to argue in Romany. Zoe kept hearing the word *marhime* over and over.

With her heart in her throat, Zoe turned to Tristan. "What are they saying?"

"Apparently Drina was banished from the Corrie clan because she consorted with a *gadjo.*"

"Papa?" she asked shakily.

"I don't know. I suppose so. I can't grasp everything they're saying, but it appears that Milosh's wife is protesting that Drina was declared to be *marhime,* or 'unclean,' for reasons of promiscuity with a *gadjo.* She says that means *you* are *marhime* as well. That Milosh should send you packing."

Unclean. Zoe's belly roiled. That sounded almost worse than *bastard.*

He cast her a concerned glance. "Are you all right?"

She wrapped her arms about her waist. "Oh, certainly, I'm fine. Wonderful. Couldn't be better." She heard the rising note of hysteria in her voice, but couldn't help it. "Not only is it possible that Papa forsook his vows to Mama to be with the woman who is my mother, but now I hear

290

that my mother was banished for it." She fought for breath, fought to gain her bearings in this new world. "No wonder she sold me."

Tears stung her eyes. Had the beating her natural mother received been connected to her banishment? Was that why she'd abandoned her own child? Or had Drina simply felt incapable of raising the baby who'd brought her so much grief?

As tears spilled down her cheeks, Tristan slung one arm about her shoulders. "I'm sorry, princess."

She shook her head. "I wanted to know the truth. And you did . . . warn me that it might be painful."

The Corries' argument ended as abruptly as it had begun when Milosh growled something that sent his wife marching mutinously to the back of the booth.

As he faced them and caught sight of Tristan's arm about Zoe's shoulders, he scowled.

Tristan instantly dropped his arm. "I don't understand, Milosh. I didn't even know you had a sister."

Milosh kept sneaking glances at her, as if to confirm the evidence of his eyes. "By the time you and I became friends, Drina had already been banished for a couple of years.

291

She was only with my family that first summer we camped at Rathmoor Park, when you and I were mere lads. She was eighteen and promised in marriage to another Rom, so she was kept away from boys, especially *gadjo* boys."

"But you never mentioned her, never even spoke her name," Tristan said incredulously.

"I wasn't allowed. She was *marhime*! When one is banished, one no longer exists. Did you not learn that in all your years as my friend?"

Tristan shook his head. "I didn't realize it was so . . . final."

"Well, it is." Milosh glanced back at his sulking wife, then lowered his voice. "But I could never entirely accept the decision of the *kris*. I always hoped she might return to us one day, that I might have the chance to fight for an end to her banishment."

He looked at Zoe. "You said you have been looking for her. When did she vanish? Did she raise you alone? Or did she find another protector, or even a husband, after she left Hucker?"

"H-Hucker?" The ground dropped from beneath Zoe's feet. "George's Hucker?"

Tristan had gone rigid beside her. "What does John Hucker have to do with this?"

Milosh turned instantly wary. "You didn't know."

"Know what?" Tristan clipped out.

"I thought that's why you came here to find me — because you'd learned something about Hucker." Worry spread over Milosh's face as he saw their reaction to his comment. "Hucker is the one who seduced my sister. And given Zoe's age, he had to be the one who got Drina with child."

Got . . . Drina . . . with . . . child. Hucker, the horrible man who'd helped to rip everything from Tristan and Lisette and Dom. The horrible man who bullied women and children.

The horrible man who was her *father.* Her monstrous, abominable . . .

Her vision swam, narrowing to a tunnel filled with Milosh's startled expression. As her blood roared in her ears, she pitched forward, and someone caught her. Through a fog she heard voices calling and making demands. Then everything went black.

When she came to, she was half reclining on a pile of cushions and Tristan was holding a cup of strong spirits to her lips and urging her to drink. She took a swallow, gasped at the fierce burn, then took another.

"Better?" Tristan asked.

With a nod, she struggled to sit up.

293

"Perhaps you should lie there a moment longer," he said uneasily.

"I'm fine. Really, I am." But she remained seated, not sure she could trust her legs yet.

Wordlessly, he pressed the cup of liquor into her hands. She was grateful for it, if only to keep her hands from trembling.

She glanced around and realized she was in the back of the booth. It was warmer, probably because someone had pulled a flap down at the front to close the booth up. Milosh's wife had disappeared with their son, and now it was just the three of them.

Milosh — her uncle, for pity's sake! — sat cross-legged on the frozen ground and Tristan on a stool beside the cushions. Both of them regarded her with a concern that would have warmed her heart under other circumstances. Ones where she was *not* the daughter of a villain.

Her head spun again, and she took another sip of what she suspected was brandy. It warmed her, settled her a little. Only a little.

Milosh gazed warily at Tristan. "If you did not come here because you heard about Hucker, then why *did* you come?"

Tristan shrugged. "You were my friend and a Yorkshire Rom. Zoe hired me to find her parents, and it made sense that I should start with you."

294

That wasn't the whole truth, but she figured the whole truth was rather pointless now.

"So my sister has gone missing, then?" Milosh asked Zoe.

"She's been missing since my birth," Zoe whispered. "I was adopted by . . . an English couple. My adoptive mother, who's dead now, told her sister that Papa bought me from a woman named Drina."

Milosh spat an oath. "That's a lie. Drina would never have been so unconscionable as to *sell* a child of her blood. She might have behaved foolishly by sharing Hucker's bed, but that . . ." He shook his head.

Tristan stared balefully at his friend. "And you're sure it was Hucker and not some other fellow who got Drina with child? Because we considered the possibility that the culprit was actually Zoe's adoptive father, who might have made Drina his mistress."

Hope sprang in her heart. She would vastly prefer that Papa be her true father, infidelity or no, rather than that . . . that awful beast Hucker. Especially after hearing what he'd done to Lisette and Tristan and Dom. "Yes, perhaps your sister took up with my father, whom she met . . ."

Where could they have met? As she had

told Tristan, it was unlikely that Drina and Papa would have crossed paths in Highthorpe, given the villagers' dislike of Gypsies.

"I'm sorry, *chai,*" Milosh said matter-of-factly, "but Hucker is definitely your father. Your grandfather caught Drina in the arse's bed. And after she was cast out, she went to live in an abandoned hunting cottage at Rathmoor Park, where she and Hucker would meet. I did not know she was with child when we left the estate to winter in York, but I'm not surprised to hear that she was."

"And I never knew anything about this?" Tristan exclaimed.

"They kept their union secret because of George."

"George!" Tristan said in a hollow voice. "When was this again?"

"Do you remember the summer when George finished Eton and your father wanted to travel to Italy, so he put George in charge of the estate?"

Tristan's face grew gray. "I remember. George was a petty tyrant, stalking around giving orders."

Milosh nodded. "He would have cast my people off the land if your father had not given explicit instructions that we were to be allowed to stay. Even so, the situation with Drina and Hucker put a bad taste in our *rom baro*'s mouth, so he made the decision for us to go on to York. The last time I saw Drina, she said that Hucker meant to marry her."

His voice hardened. "But the next summer when we camped there again and I went looking for her, Hucker said she had left him." Milosh scowled. "I knew that was a lie. She was in love with him. And if I'd realized that she'd borne a child by him, I would have known for certain she hadn't left him by choice."

Tristan got a faraway look in his eyes. "So that's why, when I stole the horse, you warned me about Hucker's lies. It had nothing to do with George at all. It was Hucker you didn't trust."

"I don't trust either of them, and I daresay you don't, either," Milosh said. "But yes, it was mostly Hucker I was thinking of. I knew Drina would never have left the man unless he forced her to."

"That's why she was found beaten on the road my parents traveled!" Zoe blurted out. "Once she bore me, Hucker must have made her leave, and she was heading to York in hopes that your family would take her back."

A thunderous expression spread over

297

Milosh's features. "Beaten? That arse *beat* my sister?" He rose from the ground, his eyes gone dreadfully cold. "I will murder him. I will string him up by his cowardly neck, and I will —"

"You'll do no such thing." Tristan jumped to his feet. "If you go accusing Hucker after twenty-one years gone, he'll want to know how you learned about what happened to Drina. He'll be suspicious of why you're only coming after him now, when you already knew that she left."

"I'll tell him that Drina told me," Milosh said sullenly.

"Then he'll expect you to produce her. He'll want to know where she's been. He'll start asking questions about his child, damn it, and when you can't answer, he'll start trying to find out who you've been talking to."

Tristan's eyes blazed at Milosh. "I've been asking all over the Romany camps about Drina, with Zoe at my side. All it would take is one person connecting Drina and Zoe to me . . . No, he mustn't know about Zoe. He can't. He would go right to George with it, and you know what that would mean for her."

Zoe's heart thundered in her ears. Oh, Lord, a man like Hucker . . . If he *ever* learned who she was, that she wasn't the true heir to the title and the estate, he would blackmail Papa, blackmail *her* . . .

"Tristan's right — you can't tell him about me." She struggled to her feet. "You mustn't."

Milosh crossed his arms over his chest. "I can't ignore my sister's beating, either! Where is she? What happened to her?"

"We don't know, damn it!" Tristan cried. "And that's precisely why you can't rush off half-cocked. Zoe heard secondhand, from her adoptive mother's sister, the tale of how she ended up with her adoptive parents. Her adoptive father has so far refused to even confirm that any of it happened. For all we know, one of them invented the part about the beating."

"For all we know," Milosh countered, "Hucker could have *forced* Drina to sell her babe to a *gadjo* couple. Or sold the babe himself. Only Hucker knows what really happened." He balled his hands into fists. "And I mean to make him tell me, if I have to thrash it out of him!"

"Look here," Tristan said, his tone coaxing, "twenty-one years have already passed, so it won't hurt you to wait a bit longer for your answers. Now that we have some facts, we can confront Zoe's adoptive father and find out the truth from his perspective. No point in going to Hucker until we learn more from the man."

"Fine." Milosh clapped a hat on his head. "Let's go talk to him."

Panic seized Zoe, and she cast a pleading glance at Tristan.

But he was already shaking his head. "Not yet. We have to break it to him gently. He doesn't even know his daughter has been looking for her parents. This will take finesse —"

"Something *you've* never possessed," Milosh snapped.

Tristan stiffened. "I'm not the boy you once knew. Give me credit for having learned a few things in the years since we ran about Rathmoor Park." When Milosh continued to scowl at him, Tristan added, "If you go blundering into this, my friend, you might destroy several lives in the process. Not just Zoe's, but her father's and her aunt's . . ."

"And Tristan's, too." Zoe laid her hand on her uncle's arm. "Please, don't be hasty. Tristan and Mr. Manton run an investigative concern now, and its reputation will be ruined if this situation becomes public and damages me or my family. Indeed, if I'd had any inkling that my natural father might

300

be . . ." She choked back tears. "Please let Tristan guide you in this. I beg you, Uncle Milosh."

Only after Milosh caught his breath did she realize she'd called him "uncle" for the first time.

His eyes softened, and he covered her hand with his. "You don't understand, dearie. You are my family now. I must look out for you."

"I *have* a family, uncle. They've taken very good care of me."

"Then why are you out looking for your Romany mother?"

Excellent question. Tristan had been right about that, too. She should have left well enough alone and hoped that Drina never rose from the past to harm her.

Yet she couldn't regret it. At least now she knew what sort of life Papa and Mama had saved her from — one where she was the daughter of a man like Hucker. She shuddered.

When she realized Milosh was still awaiting his answer, she said, "It's hard to explain why I'm looking for her. I . . . er . . ."

"She's about to be married," Tristan put in smoothly, "and you know these *gadjos* — even the lowest gentleman won't want his precious line of inheritance besmirched by

Romany blood. So she needed to know if her natural mother would come back to ruin her marriage."

"Yes, exactly," Zoe said.

It had sort of been true . . . once. But marrying Jeremy was out of the question now. And not because Hucker was lurking about, ready to destroy her family if he ever learned the truth. That wasn't the problem.

She cast Tristan a furtive glance. The problem was that the only man she wanted to marry stood next to her.

Never mind that he wouldn't even consider a marriage to the daughter of his enemy. Or that he had no desire to marry anyone, anyway. Never mind that it was impossible, that it wouldn't help her situation, that she still had Winborough to worry about.

The thought of marrying another man while she felt *this* for Tristan seemed horribly wrong. She couldn't do that to Jeremy. Or to herself.

"So you see," Tristan said to Milosh, "you can't go after Hucker just yet. We need some time."

"How much?" Milosh demanded.

"A few days to get everything in order. Can't you give us that, for the sake of your niece and her family?"

"You mean the family who stole her from her people?"

"The family who took her in when her natural parents abandoned her," Tristan said in a hard voice.

Though Milosh flushed, he didn't protest the assertion. He rubbed his beard, then glanced to her. "Fine. A few days. But if I haven't heard from you by then, I will go after Hucker."

"I understand," Tristan said.

"Thank you, Uncle Milosh." Zoe stood on tiptoe to kiss his cheek. "You have no idea how that relieves me."

He nodded curtly. Apparently, pride was as important to the Romany as to English lords.

She slid a glance at Tristan, who stood stiffly by. And to those lords' illegitimate children, as well.

"We must go," Tristan told Milosh, "but we'll return as soon as we can. Tell me where you're staying during the day, in case I need to reach you."

Milosh rattled off something in Romany, then nodded at Zoe and switched to English. "Take good care of my niece."

Tristan squared his shoulders. "I always take good care of my clients."

The words made her despair. She would

always be merely a client to him, especially after this.

And there wasn't a thing she could do to change that.

16

As they walked back to the horses, they said nothing, mostly to avoid having people overhear them. That was Zoe's reason, anyway. She wasn't sure about Tristan's. She wasn't sure about anything regarding Tristan now. Finding out that her father was a man Tristan reviled had to have shaken him up.

Once they were back on the road riding toward Berkeley Square and the crowd thinned out, he finally spoke. "Are you certain you're all right?"

The unexpectedly solicitous remark made tears burn her eyes once more. "As right as I can be, under the circumstances."

He nodded, but said nothing more.

They went a long distance in utter silence. It made her want to scream. She ached for his sharp and cynical remarks, his liberal use of "princess" when referring to her. Being relegated to a mere client hurt after they'd been so intimate this afternoon.

Before long, she couldn't stand it anymore. "I don't know how we're going to approach Papa."

"*We* are not." He stared ahead at the road, his face set in harsh lines. "It's time I step out of this. You can speak to your father on your own this evening or wait until tomorrow so that I can report our findings to Dom. Then he and you can approach your father together."

"No!" It worried her that he wouldn't look at her. Probably couldn't *bear* to look at her. "I want *you* to do it."

"That's not an option." His voice held an awful, icy finality. "My brother is used to dealing with men like your father. Dom should handle this."

"I don't want Dom!" *I want you.* She caught herself before she could say it.

Because she didn't want him just for this. She wanted him for everything. But it didn't matter what she wanted. Aside from the fact that he wouldn't give her what she wanted, this wasn't about her and Tristan any longer. It was about finding out the truth of what had happened to her natural mother without setting off her testy uncle. It was about settling her future without ruining anyone's life.

Or risking pulling George into the matter.

Because if that happened, Tristan would almost certainly be hurt. Again. And she couldn't allow that.

But that didn't mean she was going to let him run off without finishing this.

She forced herself to sound normal, practical. "*You* are the one who knows the most about Milosh and his family and Hucker. It has to be you — you have to be there! If not for your wanting to find Milosh, we would never have discovered who I am."

"You might have preferred that," he said acidly.

Her throat tightened. Did he mean that *he* would have preferred it? Probably.

Then again, perhaps he was happy to have matters turn out like this. It gave him an excuse to do what he'd wanted to do all along — push her away before she got too close. He wasn't looking for a wife, a fact he'd made perfectly clear every time he'd disparaged marriage.

And now that she knew him better, she knew he wouldn't try to seduce her just for the fun of the thing. More was the pity.

"This has to be handled delicately," he said, the words clipped and impersonal. "I'm not . . . good at that, something which Milosh was only too eager to point out."

"Uncle Milosh was wrong! You've handled

my case admirably so far. I trust you to be careful with my father."

"And what about your cousin?"

"What has *he* got to do with anything?"

Tristan snorted. "He's the reason for all of this, remember? According to the plan you yourself laid out, you have to marry him. If I spook Keane by paying calls on you, when he already knows that your father doesn't approve of me, it won't help your situation. Keane will start asking questions, as he always does, and it will make it harder for you and your father to keep the truth from him."

"We can't keep it from him anyway, now that Uncle Milosh is involved," she said dolefully.

"Not necessarily. If we get your father to provide Milosh with the missing facts that could lead him to Drina, Milosh can go throttle Hucker on her behalf without anyone tracing it back to your family. Then you can marry your cousin."

"This afternoon you didn't want me to marry my cousin," she said hoarsely. "What has changed?"

"Everything, damn it!" Then he seemed to catch himself, to even out his tone. "You have to marry Keane. It's the only way for you to keep the title and the estate. As you said before, he's the one man who won't care if the truth gets out. Because then *he* would inherit. You'd still be safe."

The fact that he was now pushing her at her cousin made her despair. "He doesn't want me."

"I doubt that. But even if it's true, you can make him want you." He dragged in a long breath. "You have a talent for that."

"What's that supposed to mean?"

"Nothing. I'm merely pointing out that you were right. Marrying your cousin is sensible. Which makes it essential that I play a less visible role in the investigation."

"I don't want —"

"I don't care what you want!"

She must have made some shocked sound, for he muttered a curse under his breath and added in a coldly measured voice, "This is how it must be. You'll see the wisdom of it once you've had time to think."

Ooh, she absolutely *hated* when men started ordering her about without taking her feelings into consideration. She hadn't expected that from him, though perhaps she should have. He did have a tendency to think his way was always best.

Just like Papa.

Who wasn't even her papa.

That sent her over the edge. "Fine. Behave

like an arse then. See if I care." When that insult got no reaction from him, she saw red. "If you don't want to be there when I speak to the Major, don't come. Send your brother instead. Or your sister or whomever you wish. Just leave me be!"

Sick to death of worrying over it, over *him,* she spurred her mare into a gallop and headed for home.

That got a reaction at last. "Damn it, Zoe!" he cried, and galloped after her.

It was a mad ride through London streets. From previous stays in London, she knew the route with the least traffic this time of night, and she took it, determined to reach home without letting him see how her heart was breaking.

Her heart? No, certainly not. She would never be so foolish as to give her heart to that . . . that officious, pigheaded, surly scoundrel!

She reached Berkeley Square but was forced to halt at the end of the mews when something dawned on her. Since she'd sneaked the horse out of their stables earlier, she now had to sneak it back in. Heaven save her.

And now she could hear Tristan riding up behind her, no doubt ready to make more icy pronouncements.

Curse the man to hell. That was the problem with dramatic shows of anger. One always ended up in the same place one had started, with the same arse who was giving one all the trouble.

The same arse who rode up next to her and hissed, "Are you out of your mind, riding neck-or-nothing through London when —"

"As if you care." She slipped off the horse and gazed down to her family's stable at the other end of the mews. "Go away. I have to figure out how to get my mare back into her stall without anyone hearing me. Otherwise, they'll know I've been gone." She shot him a sullen look. "And we wouldn't want my cousin to guess, or he might not make the supreme sacrifice and marry me."

Tristan tensed, then dismounted, too. "Stay here with my horse. I'll take care of yours."

And before she could even protest, he'd caught her reins and was striding down to the stables. She stood there, uncertain, her heart pounding as he disappeared into the stable and then emerged without the mare.

When he approached, she said, "How did you —"

"If you'll recall, getting in and out of places without being caught is my particular skill. Can you get into the house?"

"I left the kitchen door unlocked, so yes."

He frowned. "You're assuming that it *stayed* unlocked. We'd best check." He tethered his horse to a nearby fence post, then offered his arm. "Let's go."

She ignored his arm, stalking off down the mews toward their back garden. He followed her through it and to the kitchen door without a word. He was probably chafing to be rid of her. Lord knew she was chafing to be rid of *him*.

Unfortunately, when she reached the kitchen door, she found it locked.

"Botheration," she muttered. "I expected to be home before they locked up for the night." She glared at him. "I can't get in. How am I to get in?"

He gave a long sigh. "Give me one of your hairpins."

"Why?"

"Just give it to me, all right?"

She yanked one out and handed it to him. He crouched to work it in the lock. Within seconds, she heard a click.

He stood and opened the door. "There you go."

"No wonder you play a thief so well."

His lips twitched, and she thought she'd finally gotten a smile out of him when they heard a noise in the mews.

"Now then, what's this?" said a man's voice. "Are you lost, laddie? I don't remember seeing you hereabouts. You're a fine one, you are."

Tristan tensed. "Damn, someone has found my horse."

"It's our neighbor's groom," she breathed.

The groom made a *tsk*ing noise. "I daresay it's the master's son, getting drunk and taking someone else's mount again. Damned fool. We'd best get you inside, all right, laddie? Give you a nice rubdown and settle you in for the night until we can find out who's your master. Can't leave you out here to be stolen."

When Tristan turned toward the mews, she whispered, "You can't go out there yet."

"I *know* that. The bloody groom will want to know who I am and why I'm lurking about in your garden."

"And it will get back to Papa that you were here." She tugged on his arm. "Just come inside for a bit and wait until he goes to bed. Then you can get your horse out of their stable the same way you got mine into ours."

He hesitated, still staring in the direction of the mews. But they could hear the clatter of hooves on cobblestones as the horse was

313

led into the stable next door. "You'd better hope it doesn't take that groom long to fall asleep," he hissed as they entered.

She closed the door softly and locked it. "It'll be fine. We'll just slip up the back stairs to —"

"Is that you, Polly?" came their housekeeper's voice from down the hall to the kitchen. "You'd better not be out in the garden with that footman, or I swear I'll box your ears."

"Hell and thunder," Tristan muttered under his breath.

"Come on!" She pulled him toward the back stairs.

They glided up as noiselessly as they could manage, and she half dragged, half shoved him down the hall and into her room just as they heard the housekeeper on the stairs below.

Swiftly she locked the door and put her finger to her lips. She listened for the housekeeper in the hall, but apparently the woman had continued on up to the maids' rooms in the attic. All the same, they both kept quiet until they heard the housekeeper retreat down the stairs, muttering to herself about ghosts.

"Do you do this sort of thing often, my lady?" he drawled.

Not *sweetheart* or even *princess,* but *my lady.*

"Oh, of course." She removed her cloak and hung it on her bedpost. "I'm the daughter of a villain, after all, so I'm always sneaking about, evading capture, lying, cheating —"

"That's *not* what I meant." His eyes glittered in the light of the fire now burning low.

"Really?" She took off her gloves and tossed them on the bed. "Then why are you champing to be free of me all of a sudden? Why are you so desperately eager to be rid of me and this case?"

"If you had any sense, you'd be 'desperately eager' to be free of *me.*"

She blinked. "Why?"

"Oh, for God's sake . . ." Stalking over to the fire, he stoked it with sharp thrusts of the poker. "Did you not pay attention to what my sister told you? George *hates me.* He'll strike at me by any means possible. So if Hucker learns that I . . . desire you, and George hears of it, the man will make it his mission to destroy you. And your family. Just for the pleasure of seeing me hurt."

"Surely that situation was the same before this evening," she murmured, all at sea.

"But he had no means to hurt you then.

315

He had no inkling of why you hired us. And, to be honest, I desire plenty of women. He knows it means nothing." Avoiding her gaze, he set the poker back on the stand. "*Meant* nothing, before. But you're the first woman I've even considered —"

She held her breath, hardly daring to hope.

"The point is," he said tersely, "the minute Hucker figures out that you're his daughter, he will tell George, and any hope of your secret being kept will end. And the longer I'm around you, the more likely it is that Hucker will figure out what you mean to me."

And what is that? No, she dared not ask. What if she didn't like the answer? "Yes, but how can Hucker even learn the truth? You said yourself that if Papa's information leads Milosh to Drina, then Hucker won't ever need to know of our involvement."

"He's been sniffing around. And all it will take is one look at you . . ." Striding back to her, Tristan lowered his voice. "Milosh recognized that you were Drina's daughter the moment he laid eyes on you. Don't you think Hucker will do the same?"

"Oh, Lord." That hadn't occurred to her.

He searched her face. "If I stay anywhere near you, and Hucker sees you when he's following me, he could very well guess who you really are — without Milosh saying a word. And even if the sight of you only rouses his curiosity enough for him to start digging into your past —" He swore under his breath. "You're better off without me around to ruin things."

He spun away from her, but she caught him by the arm. "So let me clarify one thing." She circled to stand before him, still holding him in her grip. "The fact that I'm Hucker's daughter doesn't repulse you?"

His gaze locked briefly with hers before drifting down to fix on her mouth. "You could be the daughter of Attila the Hun, and I would still desire you. Not that it matters. If you take up with me, you might as well throw Winborough to the wolves. Because George will make sure you never inherit. He'll drag you and your family through a scandal just to torment me. And if I were mad enough to make you my wife —"

"You . . . you've considered making me your *wife*?"

Her fingers dug into his arm now, but she couldn't seem to loosen her grip. Not when he was looking at her as if she dangled hope before him like a fisherman dangling bait before a trout.

"Zoe . . ." Letting out a shuddering

breath, he glanced away. "What I considered is inconsequential. I can't have what I want, and neither can you."

So that meant he *wanted* her as his wife? Truly?

But even if that were the case, he would never act on it. She now knew how protective he was of those he cared for. The only way to get him to consider it was to seduce him into it.

Did she dare?

In that moment, she made her decision. It was time to leap for the impossible dream, regardless of the consequences. Her world was already crashing down about her ears. Even if she followed her former plan, it might not prevent her family from plunging into scandal.

It wasn't as if following her initial plan was a viable choice anyway. She could no longer think of marrying Jeremy. And a life spent running Winborough on her own — assuming it was even conceivable anymore — was too lonely to contemplate.

Why not seize her heart's desire while she could? Right now, it was the only path that made sense. "This afternoon you said that princesses can have whatever — *whomever* — they damned well please."

Ignoring how he tensed and how her heart

clamored in her chest, she added, "Well, as it turns out, all this princess wants . . . is *you.*"

17

Bloody hell.

Tristan was in over his head and heading right for the rocks. Because he'd never yearned for anything as much as this woman. He'd given up on figuring out why. All he knew was that when he looked at her, he saw a creature like himself, neither fish nor fowl, living everywhere and belonging nowhere.

Except that she at least had a *chance* of belonging somewhere. She could have the estate she craved, the position she protected so fiercely. All she had to do was marry her cousin. A man who wouldn't appreciate her, who couldn't fathom the glory of her, who . . .

He gritted his teeth. It didn't matter. The only way to keep her safe from George and Hucker was for Tristan to get out of her life. Or, better yet, to make her *push* him out of her life so she could marry Keane with no regrets.

And he knew exactly how to do that. "To have me as what?" He forced a sneer into the words she'd thrown at him earlier. "Your paramour?"

He waited for her face to fall. For her to explode and rail at him. To shove him from her room and banish him from her ocean once and for all. It was her only prudent choice.

So he was shocked when she stretched up on tiptoe to whisper in his ear, "If that's all you will allow me . . . then yes."

His pulse quickened. She wanted him at the risk of her future, her estate, her family's reputation? *No* woman had ever wanted him like that, and especially not a woman like her. It was intoxicating.

It was dangerous. If a man weren't careful, he could begin to crave that whirlpool of wanting. If a man weren't careful, it could drown him in disappointment.

He'd learned long ago to be very careful.

"Do you even know what a paramour does?" he bit out, still not touching her. Afraid to trust himself to touch her.

She kissed his cheek, then had the audacity to lick his ear. "Many of the same things you did to me earlier, I hope."

In a flash, he remembered the feel of her slick flesh beneath his fingers, the taste of her breast in his mouth . . . the intoxicating look of her half-undressed, with her exotic eyes glazed and her lush lips parted in ecstasy.

His cock reared up. Hell and thunder, he saw it all so clearly. He closed his eyes to shut it out, but that only enhanced the image. Then she shoved his coat off his shoulders, and his eyes shot open.

God help him, his Gypsy princess was actually trying to seduce him.

He would never survive that. Nor would she. She would hate herself after it was done. And he'd still be unable to offer for her . . . because of Hucker, the bloody wretch who'd sired her and then abandoned her mother.

Damn it, hadn't he lost enough at that arse's hands? Must he lose a chance at her, too?

She pulled off his gloves, then worked loose his waistcoat buttons. "So tell me, what else does a paramour do?"

He tried to think of something, anything other than how badly he wanted to lose himself in Zoe. "I'll tell you what he doesn't do. If he has any sense, he doesn't deflower a woman when her father, aunt, and fiancé are due home any moment."

"Aunt Flo and Papa were invited to a ball after the showing, so they won't be home until very late. Even so, their rooms are downstairs; they won't know we're up here. They wouldn't bother me anyway, since they'll assume I'm sleeping." She opened his waistcoat. "And as for Jeremy, you know as well as I do that he probably won't even come home with them. Besides, he isn't my fiancé."

When she pushed his waistcoat off, he let her, partly because he wondered how far she would take this, and partly because he'd never had an innocent seduce him before. It was intriguing, enticing . . . tempting.

He scowled. Damn, he was already drowning. "Ah, but he *will* be your fiancé soon enough," he said, to remind himself as much as her.

"No." She untied his cravat. "You were right. I can't marry a man whom I don't desire. And I don't desire Jeremy."

That caught him off guard. "So you mean to seduce the man you do desire? Is that it?"

Sliding his cravat off, she threw it over the chair with his coat. "Why not?"

The fact that she avoided his gaze was too telling to let this continue. He caught her hand as she reached for his shirt buttons. "Because I won't marry you when it's done."

She flinched. Then her jaw stiffened, and she brushed his hands aside so she could unbutton his shirt. "I wouldn't want you to, anyway."

That hit him like a punch to the gut. "Because of your bloody Winborough? Because you have to protect your family?"

"Because paramours don't marry, do they?"

"Zoe, be honest," he said sharply. "You don't really want this."

She met his gaze with a defiant one. "You know what I don't really want? To go the rest of my life not knowing what it's like to share your bed. To throw away any chance of being with you because of a slim possibility that it might — only *might* — keep me from losing everything." Her voice hardened. "I refuse to let that dreadful Hucker win. And so should you."

That fairly knocked him off his feet.

Then she dropped her hands from him and turned away. "Of course, if you have no interest in bedding me because you think it would be disgusting to lie with the daughter of the man you loathe —"

"You are *not* Hucker's daughter," he said

324

fiercely, "no matter what your blood. You are Lady Zoe Keane. To me, you will always *be* Lady Zoe Keane, my Gypsy princess and the most wonderful woman I've ever known."

When she faced him warily, he added, "That's precisely why I don't wish to ruin your life."

"You know something, Tristan?" An arch look crossed her face as she began to unbutton her redingote. "For a scoundrel, you're awfully high in the instep."

As he followed the slow progress of her hands hungrily, his breaths grew heavy, labored. But when she pushed the redingote off her shoulders to reveal her shift, corset, and petticoats, his breathing shuddered to a halt entirely. "I'm just . . . giving you fair warning," he somehow eked out through a tight throat.

A coy smile tipped up her lovely lips as she glided toward him. "And now that we have that out of the way, why don't we move on to more important matters?" Seizing his hand, she placed it squarely on her breast. "Like showing me exactly how the scoundrel seduces."

And just like that, he went under the waves.

With a strangled oath, he yanked her into

his arms and covered her mouth with his. She would belong to *him* now — not to Keane or anyone else. He would keep her for however long he could have her without risking her harm.

She flung her arms about his neck and gave herself up to his kisses and caresses with the same heedless abandon she'd shown that afternoon, dragging him right down into the maelstrom with her.

Hell and thunder, she had such a delicious mouth, and her nipple instantly beaded up beneath his kneading palm. Frantic to know more of her, he used his other hand to work her hair free of its pins until the coil loosened and dropped to her waist, frothing against his arms like the relentless waves of the sea.

Then, still kissing her, he moved on to her laces, tearing at them until her corset was loose enough to pull off over her head. Her eyes shone emerald-bright as he undid her shift ties and lowered her chemise to expose her breasts to his gaze. She blushed, giving a glow to her creamy skin that he could see even in firelight.

"God, they're perfect." This was his first time seeing them fully bared, watching the nut-brown nipples harden into sweet little buds he wanted desperately to taste.

He drew her to the bed and sat down, then pulled her to stand between his legs so he could have her lovelies right where he wanted them. Then he sucked and teased them with tongue and teeth until he had her gasping and clutching his head to keep him close.

"You like that, do you, princess?" he murmured against her.

"Oh, *yes*. I never guessed that breasts could be so . . . so sensitive . . ."

He brushed a lock of her hair over one nipple, enjoying the gasp that escaped her lips. "If a man knows what he's doing, many parts of a woman's body can be a source of pleasure."

"Show me."

"Certainly, sweetheart. Whatever you wish." He pressed a kiss into the bend of her elbow, and she gave a low moan. He tongued it and then scattered open-mouthed kisses down her inner arm.

She was trembling now. God, she was so wonderfully responsive for an innocent. It stiffened his cock painfully. But then, Zoe never behaved according to expectation. That was what he loved about her.

Loved?

He tensed. A figure of speech, that's all. He might be mad enough to bed her, but he was *not* mad enough to hand her the means to drown him.

He licked the pulse at her wrist, exulting in its quickening beat. "The body is like a pianoforte, sweetheart. A good paramour must know just how to strike every note so that you hear and feel the symphony."

"A-are there places I could . . . strike your notes?"

His blood did a mad stampede. He pulled her hand to rest on the side of his neck. "Stroke me there and I am yours."

She lifted an eyebrow. "You don't want me to . . . stroke your . . . well . . . you know? What I did before?"

"Perhaps you remember what happened when you did that before." When she frowned, he added, "This time I mean to be inside you when I come. And if you stroke me there I won't last until then, I assure you."

He bent forward to tug her earlobe with his teeth. "Besides, there is so much more I want to do to you first. As I told you before — I mean to take my sweet time with you."

Her breathing came in endearing little gasps that got him even more hot and bothered. With a minxish smile, she not only stroked his neck but bent to kiss it just at the pulse, where it drove him mad.

"You are . . . far too good at this for a man's sanity," he rasped.

In a frenzy he undid her petticoats and shoved them off, then dispensed with her shift so he could get a good look at her — at all of her, from the hollow of her throat to the beautiful curls between her legs.

Until that moment, he'd half believed he could stop this if he could just see her naked, have that image to cling to once he left. What a foolish notion. Because seeing his pretty princess bared made him crave her as a sailor craved the sea.

"When do I get to see *you* naked?" she whispered.

"Whenever you like."

She cast him a sultry glance, then lifted his leg to work his boot off.

No one had ever done that for him. His swiving had mostly taken place in dressing rooms or quarters the women shared with others. He'd always tried to take his time with the lovemaking, but undressing fully hadn't been practical. He'd never known when they might be interrupted. So being undressed by a woman was a unique experience.

And ah, what he'd been missing! Having a bare-bosomed goddess kneel at his feet to remove his boots was at once painfully domestic . . . and highly erotic.

He filled his hands with her luscious hair, her luscious breasts, whatever he could reach. What would it be like to do this every night with her? The thought aroused him so keenly that when she rose with a smile to reach for his trouser buttons, he knew he'd never get through that without embarrassing himself. Just the reminder of her hands on him this afternoon had him close to it already.

Brushing her hands away, he ripped off his shirt, then his trousers and drawers, until he stood before her as naked as she.

Her eyes ate him up, though they shied away from his erection.

"Look at it," he growled.

Perhaps if she did, she would balk. He was desperate to come up for breath, to stop his mad plunge into her ocean before it was too late. But when she did as he asked, and her eyes went wide at the sight of him — though not, apparently, in fear — he realized there was no returning to shore.

Still, he had to be sure she understood what she was in for. He laid her hand on his jutting cock. "This beast is what I want to put inside you, princess. It will hurt you, I fear, and you'll never be the same."

She ran a finger along the length of him,

then smiled softly. "I should hope not. How good can a seduction possibly be if one ends up the same afterward?"

He groaned. Only she would look at it like that. "Then God help us both." And he dragged her into his arms for a long, hot kiss that sealed both their fates.

18

Zoe had won Tristan in her bed at last. It wasn't enough, but it was a start. Tomorrow she would think about the consequences and what she must do to secure her future, but for tonight, she had Tristan.

His "beast" pressed at her thighs like, well, a wild beast, and she rubbed against it. Would that feel as good for him as stroking it with her hand had?

Apparently so, for with a rough curse, he tumbled her onto the bed and covered her body with his. "God, Zoe, you steal the very breath from me." He nudged her legs apart so he could kneel between them, then braced his hands on either side of her shoulders.

The position was incredibly intimate, especially when she could feel the length of his arousal against her belly . . . and lower. But although his powerful body hovered over her, the muscles of his shoulders and thighs flexing as if to prove their strength, she felt utterly safe with him.

Desperate to touch him, she ran her hands over his chest and shoulders, marveling at the thickly hewn sinews. He remained still as she caressed him, though his eyes glittered hotly at her the whole while.

Then he dipped down to brush a soft kiss to her lips. "I've never been with a virgin, sweetheart. Show me how to please you. Where you want me to touch you."

"Everywhere." She was already aroused by the feel of his member rubbing between her legs. "Anywhere."

"All right then," he said in a husky drawl. "Whatever my princess desires."

Then he began a determined assault on her senses. He slid down enough to suck her breasts and then her belly, tonguing and kissing and nibbling her in places she'd never guessed could be so sensitive — her underarms, her ribs . . . her navel.

He seduced like a musician. Or an artist, painting her skin with lips and tongue and teeth, bringing her to life one hot caress at a time. Then his hand slid stealthily between her legs and delved into her tenderly, and she nearly exploded at that touch. Lord, he certainly knew how to play a woman, how to tease her until she went half-mad with wanting him.

When she squirmed beneath his deft strokes, needing more, he uttered a soft laugh. "You're such a wonder, princess. I've never seen a woman take such unabashed pleasure in the physical."

"Is that . . . bad?"

"God, no. Every man wants to know that his . . . efforts achieve the desired effect."

He thumbed the little button down below that was so sensitive, and she jumped beneath him.

When that brought his old smug smile to his lips, she muttered, "You simply enjoy . . . having a woman in your thrall."

"Not just any woman. You. I enjoy having *you* in my thrall." He fondled her again, his gaze now a molten blue. "You've had me in your thrall for so long that I deserve a turn."

"Have I?" Her blood roared in her ears. "For how long?"

He straightened until his upper torso towered above her and his thickened flesh stuck out over her lower belly. He used it to caress her damp flesh. "*This* is what I've felt for you since you ran from me in the woods the first day we met."

Her eyes widened. "Even . . . then?"

"Oh, yes."

He bent over her again, and a wildness

gleamed in his eyes as he undulated against her down there in slow, maddening strokes that made her ache and yearn.

His breathing sounded as ragged as hers. "I knew you were a pleasant armful the moment I tugged you onto my horse, but when you faced us all down and demanded we help you, I wanted nothing more than to drag you off into those woods and take you. I remember thinking it was a shame that you were an innocent and I couldn't touch you."

It was her turn to be smug. "You're touching me now." She thrust up against him.

"And I'm liable to regret it, especially if your father gets wind of it." He bent to whisper, "But it will be worth whatever punishment he demands."

That brought tears to her eyes. "Take me, Tristan. Now. Please. Make me yours."

An unholy light shone in his eyes. He searched her face, as if to be sure she meant what she said. But when her response was to try to pull him down to her, he seized her mouth in a kiss so deep and wanton that at first she didn't notice that something other than his finger was pressing inside her.

She tore her mouth from his. "Oh!" No wonder the mares bucked against the stallions taking them. It wasn't exactly . . .

comfortable.

"Relax, princess," he murmured against her cheek. "Let me in."

She willed herself to stop tensing up.

"Yes, like that," he said with a drawn-out sigh of pleasure. "You feel . . . so good."

"You feel . . . interesting."

He chuckled. When she glared at him, he said, "Sorry, sweetheart, but that was your oddest choice of words yet."

"Fine," she snapped. "You feel too big."

"No doubt." He inched in. "Do you trust me?"

She didn't even have to think about it. "Yes."

"Then trust me not to hurt you more than is absolutely necessary." He thrust deep and pain seared her, making her cry out and buck against him. He froze, a look of stark terror crossing his face. "My God, Zoe —"

"I'm . . . fine." She breathed hard a moment. The pain was already subsiding. "Truly . . . it's not bad."

He looked skeptical. "Then why are you grimacing?"

She gave a weak laugh. "I always grimace when . . . I'm being deflowered."

Lifting an eyebrow, he murmured, "Hang on, sweetheart, and we'll brave the maelstrom together. I'll get you safely home, and make it well worth your while in the process."

"You promise?" She looped her arms about his neck and tipped her chin up in challenge.

Hunger leapt in his face. "I swear it." Never taking his eyes off her, he slid out with a slow, deliberate motion. And in. And out again.

While kissing her neck, he slipped one hand between them to find her aching flesh. He teased it as before, but with his "beast" now sliding in and out of her, going deeper each time, the effect was intensified.

"That feels . . . good . . ." she said, surprised.

"I should hope so. I do have a reputation to uphold."

A laugh sputtered out of her. Everything instantly got easier, and she realized he'd made her laugh to relax her.

That touched her deeply, and she let go and gave herself into his hands. "Well, then, sir, show me your mettle."

His eyes darkened, and he fell into a rhythm that warmed her below. Then roused her. Then made her clutch his shoulders and arch up into his thrusts.

"Ah, princess, I was wrong."

"A-about what?" That interesting tingling

had begun between her legs again, and she thrust up to meet him, seeking more of the feeling.

"We aren't braving a maelstrom." His jaw went taut and his eyes blazed down at her. "You . . . sweetheart . . . *are* the maelstrom."

How could that be? She was the one drowning . . . in his musky scent, his now urgent kisses and caresses, in the rocking of his body that swept her up on wave after wave, higher and farther until she lost herself in the rising. Until she went up and up and up . . .

And crashed on his shore.

She cried out. Or perhaps he did. She didn't know which, because where he ended, she began. And as he spilled himself inside her and they clung together, their bodies quaking in the aftermath, she knew for certain that she'd found where she belonged.

He had indeed got her safely home.

Tristan stretched out beside her, his heart still racing like a skiff before a strong wind. He should leave. It was well past midnight; surely the damned groom who'd taken his horse was asleep by now.

But he couldn't seem to drag himself from Zoe, who was curled up next to him, her body gleaming in the firelight and her hand resting on his chest with a possessiveness that seared his heart.

What the bloody hell was wrong with him? By now, he was usually chafing to be gone from his bed partner, eager to escape whichever female clung to him after an hour or two of mutual pleasure.

But this was Zoe. She didn't cling. And he didn't want to be gone from her. Not now, not ever.

"Damn."

He hadn't realized he'd said the word aloud until she lifted her head to cast him a heavy-lidded glance. "Is something wrong?"

Yes. Everything. Nothing. He didn't know. He hated not knowing. "I should go."

With a nod, she took her hand from his chest. Which perversely made him want to stay all the more.

Stalling for time, he glanced around her room. It was pure Zoe — a riot of stripes and flowers in reds and greens and golds. "You really do like bold colors, don't you, princess?"

"I like having a bit of dash around me, yes. What of it?"

"I'm merely making an observation." He chucked her under the chin. "Don't get defensive about it."

That softened her. "Papa doesn't approve of my taste in furnishings." She made a face. "My entire room would be drowning in virginal white if he had his choice."

Tristan chuckled. "He's your father. He would rather keep you five years old for the rest of your life. And since he can't, he's trying to keep you on a pedestal with the other debutantes."

"Too late for that." She cast a glance to where blood smeared her thighs.

He sobered. "How well I know. I ought to apologize for taking your innocence. But I can't. I don't regret it."

She pulled a sheet up to cover the evidence of her deflowering, then cast him a small smile. "Neither do I."

He'd told her he couldn't marry her, but of course he must. He couldn't leave her ruined. Even he wasn't that much a scoundrel. Still, he must figure out how to do it so that she was protected.

She might not even *wish* to marry him. She was still an heiress, when all was said and done. To marry him would be to risk losing everything, if her cousin ever found out about her true lineage. And if Milosh had his way, that might happen sooner rather than later.

But surely she realized that. After all,

when he'd said he wouldn't marry her, she'd claimed she didn't want him to. Had she been telling the truth? He must determine that before they could go on.

He sighed. "We should probably discuss —"

A knock came at her bedroom door, startling them both. He froze.

"Zoe Marie Keane!" said the voice of doom through the door. "Open up this minute!"

Lord Olivier. Hell and thunder.

Leaping from the bed, Tristan scrambled to put on his clothes. Zoe started to do the same, then apparently remembered that she was supposed to have been in bed sick, because she grabbed a night rail hanging over a chair and slid it on.

"What is it, Papa?" she squeaked, her voice sounding unnatural even to his ears.

Tristan struggled to button up his trousers. Damn, damn, damn. This was not what he'd wanted — to force her into a marriage.

The banging on the door made them both jump.

"Open this door now, young lady, or I'm coming in!" Clearly, someone had alerted his lordship to the possibility that his daughter wasn't alone. Tristan didn't know how or who, but he'd had to flee jealous gentlemen friends of actresses often enough to recognize the signs of an irate protector.

With panic in her face, Zoe moved close to hiss at Tristan, "Go out onto the balcony."

"No." He wasn't going to run and hide like some ne'er-do-well. He'd taken her innocence, and now he would pay the price.

There was no time and no point to running, anyway. Her father was no fool — the first place he'd look was on the balcony, and Tristan didn't fancy dropping three stories and breaking his neck. They had a few minutes at most.

He seized her hand. "Tell me one thing, Zoe. Do you *want* to marry me?"

Her eyes went wide. "We don't have time for this!"

There was muttering from beyond the door, and the sound of a key in the lock. In a few seconds, it would all be moot. "Answer the question, damn it! Do you even *want* to marry me?"

"Yes!" She uttered a defeated sigh, then clutched his hand to her heart. "Yes. Of course I do."

"Thank God."

And at that moment, the Major burst through the door.

19

Zoe glanced to the bed. The bloodstain was covered up by the sheet, thank heaven. Not that it would probably matter. Papa looked fit to be tied. And of course, Tristan was standing there naked from the waist up, which was enough to let Papa know what they'd been doing.

Papa took in the scene with a grim frown. "I didn't want to believe it, even after the stableboy told me your mare had been missing earlier, only to reappear miraculously in the stables."

She groaned. So much for hoping that no one would check the stalls after the horses were settled in for the night.

"But after that fellow next door asked about a gelding wandering in the mews bearing a saddle stamped with the words *Manton's Investigations* . . ." He fixed a hard gaze on Tristan. "Choose your seconds, Bonnaud. We meet on the field at dawn tomorrow morning."

The Major's tone presaged war and terror and mayhem. He'd probably used that tone with his soldiers in battle but she'd never heard it before, and it sent a chill to her soul.

"You cannot fight him, Papa." Releasing Tristan's hand, she flew to her father. "He and I are going to be married!"

That only softened his stance infinitesimally. "Over my dead body, girl." He wouldn't look at her, and that hurt more than anything.

"I will gladly meet you on the field of honor if that's what you require," Tristan said, his voice nearly as solemn as Papa's. "But I don't fancy killing the father of my future wife. I daresay she'd have trouble forgiving me for that."

"*I* won't be the one to die, you damned blackguard!"

When Papa started forward with murder in his eyes, she threw her full weight against him. "Please, Papa! I don't want either of you dead! And I won't forgive *you,* either, if you kill the man I mean to marry."

That halted him. At last he looked at her, but to her surprise, there wasn't disappointment shining in his eyes. It was guilt. "I should have warned you better about Bonnaud last night. If I'd had any idea that he and your cousin were friends, that Mr. Keane would have the audacity to bring Bonnaud here —"

"I've known Tristan for months now," she confessed. "Don't blame Jeremy for this."

"Months?" Papa gaped at her. "But your cousin said you'd met Bonnaud recently. How . . . when . . ."

"It doesn't matter." The last thing they needed was the Major going off half-cocked to destroy Manton's Investigations. "The point is, we will wed, and that will set everything to rights."

"Only if I allow it. And I won't. I swear I will cut you off, girl, if you marry this . . . this fortune-hunting thief. He won't get a penny."

"I don't want her fortune." Tristan drew his shirt on. "Write up the settlement however you wish. I will not take your money."

"If there even *is* any money left once my cousin gets through with us," she muttered.

Her father looked decidedly ill. "What the devil do you mean, girl?"

"Oh, Papa," she said, her heart aching. "For once, be honest with me. I know that I'm not your blood. That I'm not a true heir to Winborough or the title."

Avoiding her gaze, he scowled at Tristan. "Is this *your* doing? Have you been filling my daughter's head with nonsense?"

"I hired him to find out the truth!" Zoe cried.

When her father's face paled to ash, she wished to God she hadn't been so blunt. Or so hasty as to tempt Tristan into her bed. Tristan had been right — this should have been handled with finesse, not by rubbing Papa's face in the faults of his adoptive daughter.

"You . . . you *hired* him?" Papa said. "You told our business to strangers?"

"It's not as bad as you think," she said hastily. "I had good reason to believe he'd be discreet. Besides, you left me no choice! You wouldn't tell me yourself."

Just then, Aunt Flo came in. "I trust, Roderick, that you got a suitable explanation for why —" She broke off as she caught sight of Tristan, who'd managed to get his cravat tied and was now donning his waistcoat. "Oh."

"Yes, *oh!*" Papa whirled on her. "This is all *your* fault, blathering to her about her mother and such. Thanks to you, she hired this fellow to find out about Drina! And now he's gone and ruined her!"

"Oh, Zoe," her aunt said in that tone of

346

disappointment that so grated on Zoe. "I thought you had better sense than to let some man's by-blow seduce you."

"Don't call him that!" Zoe took a menacing step toward her aunt. "Don't you ever call him that again, unless you're prepared to call me the same!"

When her aunt blinked and backed away, Tristan caught Zoe by the arm. "It's all right, princess. I'm used to it." He shifted his gaze to Aunt Flo. "And Zoe isn't ruined." He slid his hand down to take hers. "We plan to be married as soon as it can be arranged."

Her aunt gaped at them, then at the Major. "You're going to allow this?"

"He has no choice." Zoe steadied her shoulders. "I'm of age. I can marry whom I please."

"She's right about that," her father said wearily. He nodded at Tristan. "Now that this fellow knows our secrets, he will use them to get what he wants."

Tristan stiffened. "Keep your secrets, sir. They're of no use to me. As I said, I don't want your daughter's fortune. I just want her."

The way he said it, with a fierceness that showed he meant it, warmed her beyond words. It wasn't exactly a profession of love,

347

but then, he didn't believe in love, did he? For now, being desired by him was plenty.

"I want him, too, Papa. I'm sorry that I . . . destroyed all your plans, but I never wished to marry Jeremy. Being around Tristan has only made that more clear."

Apparently that had an impact on Papa, for some of the color returned to his face as he looked from her to Tristan. "I see."

"But I'm afraid, sir," Tristan ventured, "that in searching for Drina, we have inadvertently . . . well . . ."

"Opened a Pandora's box," Zoe finished.

"Oh, Lord," her aunt muttered.

"And that is solely my fault," Zoe went on. "So we should probably discuss what Tristan and I have discovered about my natural mother. I fear it may create . . . complications."

"Complications?" Papa's jaw went rigid. "What sort of complications?"

Zoe swallowed. "Well, for one thing, we found Drina's brother. And he's eager to find her now, too."

Papa's eyes widened. "Drina had a brother?"

"You didn't know?" Tristan said.

Papa was breathing heavily, his shoulders shaking. "No. We thought she might have a . . . a husband, but . . . we . . ." He staggered a bit.

"Papa!" Zoe hurried to his side. "Are you all right?"

He let her take his arm. "Just need . . . water . . ."

Looking alarmed, Aunt Flo rushed over to the washstand and poured some water into a cup, then brought it to him. "He should sit down," she told Zoe, taking his other arm and helping Zoe guide him to a chair. "This is very hard on your father's heart."

Papa fell heavily into the chair and gulped the water as they hovered over him.

"You look awful." Zoe knelt at his feet. "I'm so sorry. I didn't mean to —"

"No, no, don't worry, dear girl." Her father laid a shaky hand on her shoulder. "I always feared this day would come eventually. That one day Drina's family would come looking for her. And you."

"But she sold me to you," Zoe said. "Why would she want me back?"

"She didn't sell you." He frowned at Aunt Flo. "I don't know why Agnes told Floria such a thing, but it was nonsense."

"I know why," Tristan said harshly. "Because your late wife wanted to assuage her guilt over having stolen Zoe."

Papa glared at him. "We didn't steal her!

Drina gave Zoe to us."

"G-gave me to you?" Zoe said. "Like handing off an unwanted pet?"

"Not exactly." Papa uttered a sigh. "The poor woman didn't really have a choice."

Tristan was staring at her father with a hard look in his eyes. "Oh?"

Papa ignored him to focus on Zoe. "You see, my dear, when we found Drina, she was stumbling along the road toward York. We were headed in the opposite direction, but your mother . . . I mean, Agnes . . . felt sorry for her out in the snow, especially once she noticed that Drina was pregnant. So she begged me to stop and help the girl, Gypsy or no."

He drank more water, his eyes misting over. "I could never deny Agnes anything, you know."

"I — I know." Zoe was still reeling from the knowledge that she hadn't even been born when her adoptive parents met her mother. Until now, she'd assumed she'd been a babe in arms.

"We took Drina into the carriage," Papa went on, "but we couldn't get enough information from her to find out exactly where she was headed." His voice held an edge. "She was in a bad way, poor woman. She'd been beaten about the head and shoulders. It must have sent her into labor, for she bore you in our carriage a short while later."

"And then she . . . she just gave me to you? On impulse?" Zoe was trying to understand.

"No." He clenched the cup in his fists as if bracing himself for something. "It all happened very quickly. One minute we were birthing the baby, and the next she was bleeding to death, and there wasn't a thing we could do about it." When Zoe caught her breath, he cast her a guilt-ridden look. "I'm sorry to tell you, dear girl, but Drina has been dead since a few moments after your birth."

Dead. All this time. Her natural mother had died giving birth to her.

Zoe's head swam. Drina hadn't abandoned her. She'd died with Zoe in her arms.

Tears burned Zoe's eyes, both for the mother she'd never known and for the one she had. Two mothers now lost to her, both loving her.

The tears fell freely, and she let them fall. She let herself mourn the mothers who'd shown their love for her in their own ways.

"Oh, my darling girl, I'm so sorry," her father said.

"It's all right, Papa," she choked out,

351

though it was far from all right.

"You still have me," he said softly.

"And me, sweetheart." Though Papa tensed, Tristan ignored him and handed her a handkerchief. "Are you all right?"

"I — I will be." She dabbed at her eyes and her nose, trying to get control of her tears. "At least I kn-know that she wanted me."

Her father laid his free hand on her shoulder. "She did want you, indeed. She spoke very little at the end, but it was all about you. She kept saying, *'Mi babbi, mi babbi . . .'* and clutching Agnes's hand. We asked if she had a husband and she shook her head no, but we didn't know if she was saying she had no husband or she didn't want her husband to have the baby."

Zoe froze. Oh, Lord, she would have to tell Papa about Hucker. How was she going to tell him about Hucker?

"She said the phrase *'milosh corrie'* over and over in her language," Papa went on, "but we didn't know what she was saying and —"

Tristan stiffened. "Milosh Corrie is . . . was . . . her brother. Drina wanted you to bring the baby to him to raise, no doubt."

When a look of panic crossed Papa's face, a chill swept Zoe. "You knew," she said

352

hoarsely. "You *knew* it was the name of someone in her family."

"Not at first, I swear! A . . . A few years after you were born, I came across a Gypsy and asked him what the words meant. He said they might be a name. *Might,* mind you. I didn't want to believe it."

He cupped her cheek, and his gaze turned fierce. "Because by then you were ours. *Our* daughter, damn it! If this Milosh was your father, he'd beaten your poor mother to death. We weren't giving you up to some bastard who might hurt you."

Zoe swallowed. She could understand that.

But there was one thing she didn't. "Why didn't you just tell me all of this?"

"Zoe —" he began in that placating tone.

"I understand why you kept it secret when I was a girl. You didn't want to risk my blurting it out. There was a great deal at stake, after all. I do realize that — it's why I took great pains to hire investigators I could trust."

As Tristan began to rub her back, she couldn't keep the hurt from her voice. "But I asked you about it after Aunt Flo let it slip, and you *lied* to me. Surely I could have been trusted with the story by then."

The weight of what she'd done by opening the investigation hit her, making her heart catch painfully in her chest. "If I'd known Drina was dead, and there would never be any danger of her returning to make trouble for us, I . . . I wouldn't have gone off to hire the Duke's Men. I wouldn't have risked the title and the estate!"

When her father cradled his head in his hands with a groan, Tristan said in a cold voice, "Ah, but your father didn't dare let the truth get out to anyone. With one slip, you would risk more than your estate and title. Because essentially he and your mother stole you, breaking a number of laws in the process. He lied in registering your birth, he bribed a government official to record you as entering the country as his child, he probably tossed your mother's corpse into the woods to rot —"

"No!" Papa's head shot up. With a dark frown, he jabbed his empty cup at Tristan as if it were a weapon. "We buried her, I'll have you know. We even said a few words over her grave. There is no law against that."

"You made no attempt to look for her family."

"They abandoned her!" He glowered at Tristan. "Drina was alone on that road. So no, we did not go looking for the arses who'd abused the poor woman." He stared off into space. "You can't possibly understand what it's like to want a child so badly —"

"An heir, you mean," Tristan said bitterly. "That's all that your kind cares about."

"My *kind*? You, sir, have become cynical because of your father's ways." Papa's breath came in quick gasps. "Taking in Zoe had nothing to do with wanting an heir. But we could not . . . That is . . . ."

"It's all right, Papa." Zoe covered his hands with hers as she shot Tristan a warning glance. "You don't have to talk about it."

"But I do. Bonnaud thinks he knows everything about our 'kind.' But he doesn't know a damned thing about people. Or the meaning of sacrifice."

He rose from the chair to face Tristan. "I was injured in the war, sir. I cannot have children. Agnes knew that, yet she married me anyway. Because she loved me. Because some things are more important to a woman than . . ." He swept his hand to encompass the bed. "Than that."

As the color drained from Tristan's face, Zoe realized exactly what Papa was saying. He was injured *there* in the war, badly enough to prevent children. And perhaps lovemaking, too?

355

Lord, she didn't want to think about her parents doing *that*. Still, now that she'd experienced the joy of it . . . It would be horrible to be denied that union with the one she loved. And Mama had really loved Papa. There was no mistaking that.

"But Agnes wanted a baby," Papa went on. "She never spoke of it, not once. Never uttered a word of reproof. On our return from America, however, I saw the yearning in her eyes when she was helping with a fellow passenger's babe. So by the time we encountered Drina, I had already been pondering the possibility of our taking in a foundling."

He ruffled Zoe's hair. "So when Zoe appeared, we marked it as a sign. God in His mercy had dropped a child into our hands, and we intended to hold on to her, regardless of what doing so required." He stared fiercely at Tristan. "I'd do it again if I had the chance."

"Oh, Papa," she said, sniffling as she rose to put her arms around him. "I'm glad that you did it, too. I've had a wonderful life with you and Mama." She smiled at her aunt, who looked shattered by Papa's revelations. "And Aunt Floria."

Papa held her close, burying his face in her hair. "I'm so sorry I kept it from you, dear girl. Agnes wanted me to tell you years ago, but I was too afraid. And not because I didn't trust you."

Holding her away, he fixed her with an aching look. "In my eyes, you were my own daughter. I didn't want you ever to think otherwise. I didn't want to weigh you down with the truth. And . . . well . . . I wanted you to choose your husband without your illegitimacy hanging over your head to worry you."

She eyed him skeptically. "You wanted me to marry Jeremy."

"I'll admit I thought it would keep you safest. And perhaps I . . . I pushed you in that direction. But not if you didn't want him."

"So you're not disappointed in me for putting my own desires above those of the estate and the family?" she asked in a small voice.

"Disappointed!" He looked genuinely shocked. "I could never be disappointed in you, my girl. I may chide you and grouse about your clothes or your manners, but that's only the fretting of an old man concerned about his daughter's future."

His hands gripped her shoulders. "I don't say the words as often as I should, but I love you. Haven't you figured it out yet? You

357

are my whole life!" When tears stung her eyes again, he continued in a choked voice, "And I never intended to lay such a heavy burden on you, I swear. I'll admit that your marrying Mr. Keane would have solved a number of problems, but —"

"Well, well," came a voice from the open door, "so the truth comes out at last."

When Zoe looked up to find her cousin standing in the door taking in the entire family tableau, she groaned. "Oh, no."

"Oh, yes, coz," Jeremy said in a cynical tone. "You didn't think you could keep the secret from me forever, did you?"

He strode into the room. "So, which problem exactly will marrying me solve? Your family's need for money?" His gaze flicked over her in her night rail and Tristan without a coat. "Or your need for a father to claim Bonnaud's by-blow?"

20

Tristan, already on edge from Lord Olivier's accusations, was enraged at Keane's. But before he could vault across the room and put his fist in the man's jaw, Zoe's father said, "By-blow?" He glared at Tristan. "You got my girl with child, you damned arse?"

"Of course not, Papa." Zoe laid a cautioning hand on both Tristan and her father, then stared her cousin down. "As usual, Jeremy is being overly dramatic."

"Am I?" Keane said.

"I'd be careful if I were you, Keane," Tristan growled. "If you continue to besmirch the character of my future wife —"

"Ah." Keane's gaze grew calculating. "So Lord Olivier is the one trying to force Zoe to marry me. Not you."

"Jeremy!" Zoe snapped when her father swore and looked as if *he* might vault across the room. "Would you please stop inciting these two? They've had enough excitement for one night as it is."

When Keane merely lifted an eyebrow, Lord Olivier marched toward the man. "And why would I want my daughter to wed a whoremonger like you? Yes, I know what you were about last night, you and this . . . this . . ."

He waved back at Tristan, and Tristan winced. His sins were tumbling onto his head like an avalanche. He only prayed they didn't bury him.

"Bonnaud did not accompany me into the brothel," Keane drawled, to Tristan's surprise. "I expect he came here instead."

When Lord Olivier bristled, Zoe released a decidedly unladylike oath. "Would you please stop that, Jeremy? Do you *want* to die?"

"Better than being tricked into marrying a woman who doesn't want me," Keane said.

"No one has been trying to trick you into anything," Zoe said. "Papa and Aunt Floria were hopeful that we might consider marriage to each other, but I never wanted it. And I seriously doubt you ever did, either. My father and aunt are the only people who got that notion into their heads, and I have just been disabusing them of it."

"So you've convinced your father that he doesn't need my money, after all?" Keane asked snidely.

Lord Olivier stared Keane down. "I don't need money from *you,* sir. Your pictures may earn well now, but they are nothing to the wealth provided by the land. It is the land that brings fortune; it is the land that —"

"You sound like my late father," Keane said. "You may not realize this, sir, but even though you dislike my work, I'm not some pauper daubing paint onto canvas in a garret. Besides, as heir to half of my father's wealth —"

"Half?" Zoe put in.

"My sister inherits the other half," Keane said coldly. "We Americans divide our spoils equally, unlike you hidebound English. But as your father knows perfectly well, my half is substantial enough to support a wife and more."

With a flush rising in his cheeks, Keane bore down on Papa. "I assumed that a need for money was the impetus for his inviting me to London several times. You don't mean to tell me that this show of wealth hasn't all been an elaborate scheme to hide the fact that you need my money desperately?"

Zoe let out a breath. "*That's* why you kept asking about our funds? And how we could afford everything?"

"Of course." For the first time, Keane looked uncertain of his position. "I thought that your father was hoping to persuade me into giving him a loan. But now that I think about it, your family *has* been throwing you at me. So a marriage makes sense, too. It would certainly plump up the family coffers."

"You do realize that my brother-in-law is quite wealthy, don't you?" Zoe's aunt chimed in.

Keane crossed his arms over his chest. "Lord Olivier was just saying that marriage to Zoe would solve a number of problems. If not money problems, then what?"

That laid a pall over the room. If they told Keane the circumstances, they might as well hand the title and the estate over to him themselves.

Tristan sighed. Then again, it would be impossible to hide it much longer, now that Milosh meant to go after Hucker.

Of course, the earl didn't know that yet.

"It doesn't matter," Lord Olivier said loftily. "The point is moot, now that she's marrying Bonnaud."

Zoe let out a breath, then flashed Tristan a smile that took him off guard. She truly wanted to marry him, even given the difficulties it meant for her future. And her father was willing to let her, too. It boggled his mind.

Bonnaud thinks he knows everything about our "kind." But he doesn't know a damned thing about people.

He winced. Having lived with his biases so long, he was dismayed to realize how firmly they'd been based on his own experience with George and Father . . . and not on anything — or anyone — beyond that.

"But," Zoe said, "the point is not moot, Papa. We have to tell Jeremy what's going on."

Alarm lit his lordship's face. "The hell we do! It's a private matter. It doesn't concern him." To Tristan's shock, the earl turned to *him.* "You must explain this to my daughter, Bonnaud."

"I'm afraid I can't," Tristan said. "She's right."

"Not in this, she isn't!" Lord Olivier stared meaningfully at him. "You, of all people, should understand what is at risk. Are you really going to take the chance of losing . . . everything?"

"It was never mine in the first place," Tristan said softly. "All I want is Zoe, and I will take her any way I can get her."

Speaking the words made them real. And

true. Perhaps they'd been true for a while. All he knew was he wanted to snatch only one thing out of all the chaos: her. As his wife. None of the rest of it mattered.

Her father's eyes narrowed on him. "You mean that."

"Of course." He gave a faint smile. "Do you think I'm generally so careless as to leave my horse lying about a mews for some strange groom to find?"

"Tristan," Zoe said, "do not try to convince me that you planned this."

"No." His gaze locked with hers. "But I didn't fight very hard to keep it from happening. Did I?"

As the truth of that hit her, a brilliant smile spread over her face. It was the most beautiful sight of his life.

Then she gazed at her father, and her smile faded. "I'm sorry, Papa, but we have to tell my cousin about Drina. He's going to find out anyway." She slid a furtive glance at Keane. "Milosh is determined to exact vengeance from my . . . from Drina's lover for the beating the man administered. He only agreed to wait long enough for us to tell you the situation."

That gave Lord Olivier pause. "Drina's *lover*? You found out who he is?"

"I'm afraid so, my lord," Tristan put in.

"We . . . er . . . haven't had the chance yet to give you our report on that particular situation."

Keane was watching them all now like a hawk watches the prey he's waiting to pounce upon.

Unfortunately, there wasn't a damned thing they could do to stop that. Even if they kept everything quiet, once Milosh got to Hucker, the tale was bound to get out. Hucker would tell George, and George would try to make Tristan's life miserable by stripping his future wife of everything she ought to own. All George would have to do was tell Keane the truth.

So it would be best if they told him first, and all the interested parties could work together to solve the issue, because they might be able to negotiate a settlement of some sort with Keane. Surely he wouldn't want his family mired in scandal, even his English family. And if the family closed ranks, that would take the wind out of George's sails.

Besides, the earldom still belonged to Lord Olivier, and it might be some years before it was passed on. It was never good for the present holder of the title and property to be at odds with the heir. Even Keane must realize that.

"So," Keane said, "does someone want to explain to me what's going on?"

"Of course." Zoe steadied her shoulders. "But only under one condition."

Keane tensed. "And what is that?"

"Could we *please* continue this discussion fully clothed? Preferably somewhere else than in my bedchamber?"

To Zoe's immense relief, she got her wish, and a half hour later they were all assembled in the dining room. Aunt Flo had suggested that perhaps they needed some refreshment, and Zoe was grateful. She hadn't eaten in hours, and even her dinner had been scant since she'd been pretending to be too sick to attend the premiere.

So despite the tension of the situation, she fell on the food with a ravenous greed that went beyond hunger. In the midst of wolfing down a slice of ham, she glanced up to find Tristan, who sat next to her but at the end of the table, staring at her in amusement.

"A bit hungry, are you, princess?" he teased.

"I daresay *you* got to eat before we went to meet with Milosh."

"Actually, I did." He smirked at her, but for some reason it no longer bothered her.

His smirk was part of who he was. "And it's not my fault you came racing over to Manton's Investigations to apologize."

"Next time I run off half-cocked, sir," she said lightly, "I will make sure you feed me." Deliberately, she shoved a hunk of bread in her mouth.

Tristan laughed, and she nearly choked on the bread trying not to laugh herself. But she sobered when she caught Papa watching them.

"I still can't believe you have been sneaking about all this time with Bonnaud," he said sullenly.

Guilt gripped her. "I'm sorry, Papa. But I had to know the truth. I knew you wanted me to marry Jeremy, and I had to be sure it was necessary before I acquiesced."

Jeremy snorted. "It pains me how all of you assumed I would just up and marry the woman you chose for me because you wished it."

"They didn't realize you were a blind fool," Tristan said dryly. "It was reasonable to assume that any man of sense would want to marry her. Aside from the fact that she's beautiful and fascinating and —" He halted when he realized they were all staring at him. "Well, aside from all that," he continued gruffly, "she's an heiress. A very important heiress."

"Is that why *you* want her?" Jeremy asked.

When Tristan bristled, Zoe sighed. "I do wish you men would stop baiting each other." She set down her fork. "The fact is, by marrying me Tristan is making it materially difficult for me to continue as an heiress. So no, that is definitely not why he wants me."

Jeremy said, "Perhaps it's time you explained all that."

For the next hour, they attempted to lay out the situation for Jeremy, an endeavor that required quite a bit of explanation about the differences between English law and American law. Fortunately, Papa knew them very well. He *had,* after all, been considering the vagaries of her future since the day he and Mama had taken her in.

Jeremy was oddly silent until they were finished, asking only a question here and there. But once everything was elucidated to his satisfaction, he rose to pace the room. "So this has all been about Winborough and the earldom."

"Exactly," Papa said.

"And you're telling me that Zoe cannot legally inherit a damned thing."

Papa gritted his teeth. "If the truth comes out, no."

"So you hoped to coax me into marrying Zoe so she could still inherit the land and all that came with it, no matter what turned up in the future about her natural parents, since I am also your heir."

"That about sums it up, yes," Tristan said.

"And you kept this secret from me because . . ."

"That should be obvious," Zoe said. "Now that you know about it, you can challenge me for the inheritance once Papa dies. And you will win."

"Why the dickens would I do that?"

Utter silence reigned as they all gaped at him. Had he not understood what they were saying?

Zoe was the first to speak. "Because . . . because you would gain an estate and a title and a fortune, of course."

"I already have a fortune. And I intend to use it to see the wonders of the world, and paint every one of them." Jeremy scowled. "If I had your estate, I'd have to manage the damned thing. Either I would have to stay rooted in England, or I'd have to hire managers I trust not to cheat me at every turn — which we all know is virtually impossible when the owner doesn't live there."

"Well, I wouldn't say that you can't trust

anyone —" Papa began.

"Really? So why do *you* live in Yorkshire most of the year, my lord? For your health?"

"It's my home!"

"Precisely. But I am not looking for a home. So let's assume that I did hire a manager to care for my estate. I would still have an obligation, as a lord of the realm, to come to London to sit in Parliament for the months that it is in session. Am I correct?"

"That's mostly right," Tristan said coolly. "Though I believe you'd have to relinquish your American citizenship to claim the right to sit in Parliament."

"But you wouldn't *have* to claim that right," Aunt Flo said hastily. "You could still hold the title alone. And if you married Zoe, she would take care of all your duties to the estate, and you could just enjoy yourself."

Good Lord. Her aunt would do anything to avoid having Zoe marry a man Aunt Flo considered too low. "It doesn't matter, Aunt Flo," Zoe said to preclude Tristan from protesting, "because Jeremy and I are *not* marrying. Even if he wanted to do so, which I gather he does not."

"No offense, coz," Jeremy said, "but I have no desire to sacrifice myself for the English idea of heaven on earth. Which is not *my* idea."

Papa eyed him warily. "So what are you saying?"

"That I don't give a damn about saving Winborough for future generations or becoming an almighty English earl. I have worlds to paint, places to see. You can keep your title and your lands. I'm perfectly happy to stay mum about Zoe's natural parents if you four are."

"You don't want the title," Papa said incredulously.

Jeremy uttered a drawn-out sigh. "Did I not just say that?"

"Or the *estate*?" Aunt Flo said, disbelief in her face.

"Oh, for God's sake," Jeremy said, clearly flustered. "Has it not occurred to you English that not everyone wants what you revere?"

"No," Tristan said bluntly. "It hasn't."

"Well, it should. I'm free-living — I don't even know what to do with the property I already own. So, for the last time, I don't need Winborough, and I don't want an earldom." He flashed Zoe a rueful smile. "And I most assuredly do not want to marry a woman who has her eye on another man."

Zoe's heart had begun to pound. "But . . . but you would keep our secret? Let the world continue to believe that I am Papa's legitimate child?"

"Why not? It's no skin off my nose."

As the ramifications of that hit her, she beamed at Tristan. "I could still inherit. And have Winborough. And *you*!" Something perfectly delicious occurred to her. "You'd be my representative in the House of Lords. You'd take a seat there alongside George!"

"That does have a certain appeal." Tristan broke into a grin. "And it might possibly be the first time a bastard ever served in the House of Lords."

"They've been serving in the House of Commons for years," Papa mumbled. "I don't see why we can't have one in the House of Lords."

Zoe and Tristan both gaped at him, then burst into laughter.

"There is one more thing," Jeremy said.

Her elation vanished. "Oh?"

"I will freely relinquish all claim to the title and the estate . . . but only so long as my sister and I are always welcome in your homes."

"Of course!" Zoe said.

When Tristan said nothing, Zoe nudged him.

"Oh, all right," Tristan muttered. "Assuming you leave my wife alone. I mean to be the only rogue in her life."

"She's not your wife yet," Jeremy said, then laughed at Tristan's foul glance. "Very well, my friend. I will be as a brother to Zoe, no more."

Tristan rose and held out his hand solemnly. "Then you will always be welcome."

They shook on it.

"There's only one problem with all this." Papa shot Zoe a worried look. "Your cousin may have no choice but to inherit. You said something about Drina's brother wanting to go after her lover, your natural father. Who is he? Is he someone we could buy off or silence somehow?"

"Not if Zoe marries me," Tristan said with a sigh. "It's my half brother George's man of affairs, John Hucker. If Milosh attacks Hucker and it gets back to George, my half brother will come after Zoe just to punish me."

"I see." Papa mused a moment. "Does Milosh know what's at stake, how much his niece stands to lose if the matter becomes public?"

"Not yet," Tristan said. "I didn't want to reveal everything until I could consult with you about the matter."

"Good thinking." Papa rose from the table. "If the man cares about his niece, then surely he will care about her future. So we shall just have to impress upon him the direness of the situation, eh?"

"Exactly," Tristan said.

"Failing that, perhaps we could buy him off."

Tristan looked as if he was about to make some hot retort, but when Zoe laid a hand on his arm, he checked himself. "Actually, knowing the truth about Drina might be enough to quiet Milosh. That's all he wants — to know what happened to her."

"Not quite all," Zoe amended. "He does want vengeance over the beating, and is liable to want it all the more once he learns that she died from it. There's also the problem that Hucker might recognize me —"

"We'll cross those bridges when we come to them," Papa said soothingly. "Let's not borrow trouble just yet, dear girl."

"I did buy us a little time," Tristan said, "by insisting that Milosh keep quiet until I could meet with you."

"All the same, we should go talk to him right away. I don't like leaving these things hanging."

"Not tonight, Papa. It's nearly three A.M., and you look exhausted." Zoe skirted the table to take his arm. "Truly, you ought to sleep awhile first."

With a scowl, he shrugged her off. "I fought many a battle on little more than an hour's sleep. I think I can handle some Gypsy fellow."

"But Papa —"

"I'm fine — just leave me be!" When she winced at the reemergence of the Major, he muttered a curse. Then he cupped her cheek. "I'm sorry, dear girl. I don't mean to be short with you. But I can't sleep with this weighing on me anyway." He glanced at Tristan. "Can you take me to see this Milosh?"

"Absolutely, sir. Though we'll have to rouse him from his bed, I expect."

"Then let's get on with it. I want this matter settled."

"Yes, sir."

As they started to walk out together, Zoe said, "Tristan!"

He halted to look at her, one eyebrow raised.

"Thank you."

"For what?"

"For bringing all this trouble down on your head on my behalf."

A faint smile crossed his lips before he scanned her with a heated glance. "You're well worth the trouble, princess. Trust me on that."

Then they were gone. Aunt Flo said something about retiring and headed for the stairway. Zoe was still staring after her when Jeremy spoke.

"I have one more favor to ask of you, coz."

She glanced over at him. "What's that?"

"When everything is settled, you must introduce me to your uncle. I've never painted a Gypsy before." He grinned. "I understand they, too, like to dress with a bit of dash, and that always makes for an interesting image. Besides, their women are rumored to be quite beautiful."

Coming on the heels of everything he'd heard about her natural parents, she could hardly believe him. First he wanted brothels, and now he was hunting for beautiful Gypsy women to seduce? "You are utterly incorrigible! I begin to think it's a good thing you don't want to be an English lord. You would probably break hearts in every drawing room in London."

"No, indeed." He gave her a sly wink. "I would never limit myself to the drawing rooms of London."

And as she burst into laughter, he strode jauntily out the door.

21

Tristan rode in his lordship's carriage with growing apprehension. The man was quiet. Too quiet.

Not that Tristan could blame him. Lord Olivier couldn't be happy that his daughter had been seduced by a man he neither liked nor entirely trusted. In his place, Tristan would probably be silently plotting that fellow's murder.

In his *place?*

Oh, God, what a thought. Might he actually one day find himself with a daughter or daughters to protect from men like him? The very idea squeezed a vise around his heart.

He must be out of his mind to be thinking of marrying anyone. What did he know about being a husband? Or, for that matter, a father?

"Tell me something, Bonnaud," Lord Olivier said into the stillness. "Did you really steal a horse from your half brother?"

Wonderful. Now he had to deal with *that* again. "Yes. On his deathbed, my father willed it to me in a codicil, and as soon as Father drew his last breath George burned the codicil in front of me. So although the horse was *mine,* I stole it, legally speaking. I sold it to Milosh."

"Ah." His lordship stared out the window at a practically deserted London, his leathery cheeks washed silver by the weak light of the gas lamps. "How old were you?"

"Seventeen."

"Well, that at least explains why you did something so foolish."

Tristan flexed his hands on his knees. "I did what I had to in order to provide for my family. If not for my actions, my family would have starved." Sarcasm crept into his tone. "To quote a certain earl, 'I'd do it again if I had the chance.' "

To his surprise, Lord Olivier chuckled. "You're an impudent devil, aren't you?"

"Your daughter says I like to provoke her."

"And do you?"

"Yes. I confess I enjoy seeing her throw herself into it when she's got her dander up." He stared steadily at the man who would soon be his father-in-law. "But I would never hurt her. And I swear to you that I will take good care of her and try to make her happy."

"Do you love her?"

That flummoxed him — not only because he hadn't thought about it, but also because the question hadn't come from *her*. After all her talk about wishing to marry for love, what did it mean that she hadn't asked him if he loved her?

Nor had she professed any love for him herself. She'd said she wanted to marry him. But only after she'd found herself ruined. Had she really only wanted him in her bed, then been forced to accept a proposal once they were discovered together?

That was a disturbing thought. Especially given that he'd once told her that desire was the only real connection between a man and a woman. Perhaps she'd taken his words to heart, pursued him solely because she desired him.

No, that didn't seem like her. But then, he hadn't known her that long; perhaps he was seeing what he wanted to see.

God, he hoped not. He didn't want to be only a man she desired. Which was rather hypocritical of him, given his philosophy, but it was how he felt all the same.

"Well?" Lord Olivier fixed an unreadable

379

gaze on him. "Do you love her or not?"

He debated what to answer, but after all the truths that had been laid bare this evening, it seemed despicable to lie to her father now. "I don't know. I'm not sure I fully understand the concept of romantic love."

"Don't you? You persisted in offering marriage even when I threatened to cut you off. Even when you knew she wasn't really my heir and might lose everything if that news got out." His voice hardened. "Even after you'd had what you wanted from her."

Tristan hadn't even begun to have what he wanted from Zoe. But somehow, he doubted her father would like hearing that. "Yes. What of it?"

"Sounds like love to me."

"Or wishful thinking on your part. Forgive me for saying this, sir, but a man will do many things to quench his desire for a woman."

"True. But marry her? When he's already quenched his desire?"

His lordship was right. Tristan had desired many a woman, but never once had he proposed marriage.

Then again, he'd never compromised a virgin, either. Or been caught by her father in her bed. Perhaps this was how he behaved in that situation.

And perhaps he was just lying to himself about what he wanted, because the thought of loving Zoe, of desperately needing *her* love, incited panic in his breast. Mother had loved Father deeply, and it had cost her everything.

Love was the most dangerous drug on earth. He didn't want to be its latest acolyte. That way lay madness.

The carriage raced along for a while, the only sound inside it being the creak of the springs and the muted thuds of the horses' hooves.

At last his lordship broke the silence again. "Tell me about this John Hucker."

Tristan seized eagerly on the change of topic. "John Hucker does all the dirty work for my half brother. If George told him to cover himself in paint, he would ask what color."

"So he's a toady."

Tristan thought a moment. "I suppose you could say that." Apart from what Hucker seemed to have done to Drina, he'd never set out to commit any villainy on his own, to the best of Tristan's knowledge. It had always been at George's behest. Odd how Tristan had never thought of it that way.

"Regardless," Tristan went on, "he's a

nasty piece of work."

"Would he beat a woman bearing his child, though? That's the question."

"Perhaps. Honestly, I'm not sure. He was a decent fellow once, before George molded him in his own image."

"Ah."

Tristan spent the rest of the trip telling Lord Olivier everything he could remember about Hucker. And the more he talked, the more he realized how firmly George had put his stamp on the man. That didn't bode well for any chance of talking Hucker into keeping silent. They would *have* to convince Milosh to do so.

They'd nearly reached the winter lodgings in Battersea that Milosh had taken for his family when his lordship asked, "Given your dire history with Hucker, does it bother you that Zoe is probably his daughter?"

Zoe had seemed to think that it should. How odd that it didn't.

"No." He smiled at the earl. "Zoe may have Hucker's blood, but she's *your* daughter in character. And that's all that matters."

When his lordship's face lit up he was glad he'd said it, not only because it was true, but because the earl so clearly wanted it to be true.

A few moments later, Tristan was climbing down from the coach to knock on the door to the Corries' temporary residence. It took some time to roust anyone, but when he did, it wasn't Milosh who opened the door, but Milosh's wife.

"You!" she spat as soon as she saw him.

She tried to close the door, but Tristan blocked it with his foot. "I beg your pardon for disturbing you, Mrs. Corrie," Tristan said in English, for his lordship's benefit, "but I wish to speak to your husband."

Her gaze flicked to the well-appointed coach-and-four and her agitation became more palpable as his lordship stepped down to stand behind Tristan. The Romany did not have a good history with fine lords.

Tristan moved to block her sight of Lord Olivier. "Mrs. Corrie? Your husband?"

At last she returned her attention to Tristan. "He's not here," she said in Romany. "Thanks to you, he's gone."

"Gone!" Tristan exclaimed. "At this hour?"

"Gone where?" Lord Olivier demanded.

Tensing, she switched to a heavily accented English. "To the north."

Tristan's heart dropped into his stomach. "He went after Hucker anyway."

"Aye. He said he had to 'avenge' his sister. That he would beat the *beng* until Hucker

383

tells the truth."

"Hell and thunder." Tristan sympathized with Milosh, but beating the "devil" would only make matters worse. "He promised he wouldn't."

"Aye." She crossed her arms over her ample bosom. "He promised me the same. For a short while. But the idea of his sister being hurt by that man preyed and preyed on his mind until he could not bear it."

Lord Olivier released a breath. "How long has he been gone?"

"Since midnight," she said. "He took our best horse and rode off in a temper."

"We have to stop him," his lordship murmured. "If he goes blundering into this, who knows what will happen?"

"I agree." Pasting a smile on his face for Mrs. Corrie, Tristan dug one of Dom's calling cards out of his coat pocket. "If he should happen to return soon, please ask him to come to this address." He handed it to her, along with a gold sovereign. "For your trouble."

Her eyes widened, and her stance became a trifle less defensive. "He took the Great North Road."

"That doesn't surprise me. *Parrakro.*"

She nodded in response to his thanks. *"Latcho drom. Baksheesh!"*

After she disappeared into the house, his lordship climbed back into the coach. "What did she say?"

"She wished us good fortune and a safe journey." Tristan leapt in and ordered the coachman to drive on. "I daresay she wants us to catch her husband as much as we want to. She has to know what Hucker is capable of."

They headed back toward Mayfair.

"So, you'll be going on a trip up north, I assume," his lordship said.

Tristan nodded. "If I take Dom's carriage, I shouldn't have any trouble catching up to Milosh. He'll assume we won't know of his absence, so he won't be traveling at breakneck speed. And the Romany don't go by post; they don't trust their horses to innkeepers. So he'll have to travel more slowly, thank God."

"Take my carriage and my rig," Lord Olivier said. "They've got to be faster than anything your brother owns."

"I can certainly attest to that."

"And you'll pass near Winborough on your way, so you can stop in there to change horses. I'll write a letter for you to give to my estate manager."

"Thank you." Tristan hesitated before broaching a delicate subject. "But there won't be a need for the letter. Because I mean to have Zoe with me."

"Why?" The sharp word bit into the darkness.

"Milosh will listen to her, if he won't listen to me. He only initially promised to keep quiet because she begged him. He has a soft spot for her — he says she's the very picture of his sister. Assuming we catch up to him before he reaches Rathmoor Park, she will be most able to sway him."

His lordship pondered that in silence, then thrust out his hoary chin. "Then I will be going with you as well."

"My lord, this will be a long, hard journey." When Lord Olivier glared at him, Tristan added hastily, "And if you're worried about a chaperone, I also mean to take Dom. His status as Father's younger son still has weight up there. Besides, he knows those roads better than I, having spent more years traveling them. Surely you will feel safe having both of us with her."

"An excellent idea, but that doesn't change my decision. You are not taking my daughter off with you unless I go, too." He set his shoulders. "You're not married to her yet, lad."

Lad? He nearly laughed. No one had called him "lad" in some years. But given his lordship's advanced age, it wasn't that surprising. And much as Tristan disliked the idea of dragging both Keanes along, he also understood the man's reasoning. This past hour or two wouldn't have undone the years of rumor and innuendo that had probably biased Lord Olivier against him.

"Very well, the four of us will go together." Tristan shot the man a warning glance. "But there's no time to waste."

"I agree. You should go on to your brother's once we reach home, while I prepare for the trip. As soon as you return with him, we'll set off."

"Sounds like an excellent plan."

This time their silence was less fraught with tension. They reached Mayfair, and his lordship said, "I have one more question for you. We will speak of it once and never again."

Tristan suppressed a groan. What could the man possibly want to know now? "All right."

"Was tonight your first . . . that is . . . have you and my daughter been . . ." He uttered a pained sigh. "Is there any reason I should rush the wedding?"

God, what a question. "It was our first . . . encounter of that kind." He could feel the heat rising in his face. He'd never thought he'd need to have such a conversation with a woman's father. "So I should think we could wait, say, a month or so for the wedding."

Her father's stiff demeanor softened a fraction. "Good, that's good. I hadn't really given the matter of her actual wedding any thought before. She's never shown much interest in marrying anyone."

"Yes, I'm well aware of that."

Indeed, it was the one thing that worried him. What was the real reason she was willing to marry him?

22

It was barely dawn and Zoe had joined her father in his study only twenty minutes ago. But it felt as if she'd been waiting for Tristan and Mr. Manton *forever,* and she couldn't keep still.

Thank heaven Aunt Flo and Jeremy were abed and had no inkling of what was going on. At the moment, she couldn't deal with the questions and concerns they were bound to have, or with parrying her cousin's quips. She'd left a long note for both of them. That should suffice.

She paced to the window to look out yet again. "You don't think Mr. Manton and Tristan went on without us, do you?"

"I doubt it." Papa packed some papers into a satchel. "After all, it was your fiancé who insisted that you go along."

Her fiancé. What a lovely word. She'd never expected to like it quite so well.

"You've packed everything you need?"

Papa asked.

"Yes." She strained to see through the morning fog. Were there two men on horseback over there?

No. Only a dustman with a cart. She sighed.

"Tell me something, girl," Papa said. "Are you absolutely certain you want to do this?"

"Of course! Uncle Milosh is —" She winced. "I mean, Mr. Corrie —"

"It's all right," Papa said in a surprisingly calm voice. "He *is* your uncle."

"Whom I can never acknowledge as such publicly."

"Not if you want to continue as my heir." Papa came over to her. "But the quest for Mr. Corrie was not what I was referring to." He laid a hand on her shoulder. "Are you sure you want to marry Bonnaud?"

She eyed him askance. "It's not as if I have a choice."

"You always have a choice. I meant it earlier when I said I wanted you to choose your husband free of worry. I don't wish to see you forced into marriage to a man you don't love."

Sudden tears stung her eyes. She turned her head to keep him from seeing them. "I *want* to marry Tristan. Truly, I do."

"But do you love him?" he asked softly.

"Yes." After Tristan and Papa had ridden off to visit Milosh, she'd had plenty of time to think about it. And she knew now without question that she loved Tristan.

She loved his flirting . . . and his taunting. She loved how he called her "princess." She loved that he had dreams of a future beyond his expectation. Most of all, she loved that he understood her — from her ambivalence about being a bastard to her love of the land.

How could she not love him?

She wasn't sure when it had begun, but her feelings had solidified when he'd stood with her against her family, trying to calm Papa's anger, demanding answers on her behalf, behaving exactly how she'd always hoped her husband might.

Now her feelings were as firm as the cobblestones of the street below.

"Have you told him?" Papa asked.

She wrapped her arms about her waist. "No. And I don't intend to anytime soon."

"Why not?"

"Because . . . I don't know if he loves *me*. He once said love was an impossible dream, and if he still believes that, I don't think I can bear to hear it. I'd rather just go on praying that he will come around someday."

"It's not like you to be a coward."

She ventured a smile. "It's not like me to

sneak around behind my father's back, either, but I did."

For a second, she saw a flash of the Major, all stiff upper lip and bristly manner. Then he sighed, and his gaze transformed to that of a worried parent. "My dear girl, can you bear marrying the man without knowing if he loves you?"

"I can bear that better than living without him," she said truthfully.

Papa looked as if he might say something more, but then a pair of horses came into view, being ridden neck-or-nothing down Berkeley Street, and they realized Tristan and Mr. Manton were approaching.

Quickly, Papa turned from the window, strode back to his desk, and pulled out some sort of case, which he shoved into his satchel.

"What's that?" she asked.

"My pistols. We may need them."

"Lord, I hope not," she muttered as she followed him out of the room. Shooting people could get even an earl into serious trouble.

A short while later, the four of them headed off in Papa's spacious traveling coach, which wasn't quite so spacious with three tall and sturdily built men taking up all the room. This was going to be a very long trip indeed. Especially with what hung over them.

Determined to take her mind off what might happen if they didn't get to Milosh in time, she dragged the latest copy of the *Gardener's Magazine* out of her bag and tried to read.

"You might like the article about using goats to keep down weeds," Tristan said.

Having already dog-eared that page, she could only gape at him. She wasn't the only one — his brother and Papa both eyed him with amazement.

"What?" With a scowl, he crossed his arms over his chest. "I occasionally like a bit of light reading."

"About agriculture?" Mr. Manton said.

"That and treatises on weapons are the only sorts of literature you keep around Manton's Investigations." Clearly peeved, Tristan stared out at the sunrise. "Sometimes I get bored."

Coupled with what he'd told her last night, it broke her heart. "I'm not surprised you would find goats fascinating. They're critical to land management in Yorkshire. And as a former resident of Rathmoor Park, you would have to be aware of that. Did you read what he said about which poisonous plants they devour?"

Tristan swung his gaze to her and something flickered deep in his eyes that made her mouth go dry. Then he settled back against the squabs with a smile. "Hard to believe that they will ingest hemlock with no ill effects."

"I know! Isn't it astonishing? Then there's the . . ."

For the next few hours, the four of them discussed gardening. And animal husbandry. And enclosures. She was shocked to realize that her future husband was by no means unaware of the problems facing an estate manager. Granted, some of his ideas were outmoded, probably based on things his father had told him over a decade ago, but he had sound judgment. Even Papa looked impressed.

When the conversation stalled, however, they could no longer avoid the subject uppermost in their minds.

"Are you sure that Mr. Corrie is traveling the same road we are?" Papa asked Tristan.

"Yes. It's his speed I'm unsure of." Tristan's gaze met hers. "If he relies on his Romany friends for horses, he might not have to stop to rest his own as often as I assumed at first."

"But you said the Gypsies winter in cities," Mr. Manton put in, "so there shouldn't be many of them in rural encampments to help him."

"They don't all winter in cities. And he'll know which ones don't."

That sobered them. They were silent a long time, so silent that after a while Zoe dozed off. When she awoke, it was to Papa shaking her. "We've stopped for dinner, dear girl."

"Dinner?" Had she slept so long? Apparently so, for the sun was low in the sky now.

And she mustn't have been the only one who'd fallen asleep, for Papa was blearily combing his hair, which stuck out every which way. Mr. Manton looked more alert, probably because he hadn't been up half the night as they had, but Tristan —

She sat up straight. "Where's Tristan?"

Mr. Manton climbed out and turned to help her down. "While we're at dinner he's going to talk to the local Romany clan, find out if they've seen Milosh. We're ordering food for him to eat in the carriage."

"But Mr. Manton, surely Tristan should —"

He smiled. "Call me Dom." He eyed her closely as her father got out behind her. "The way I understand it, we're soon to be brother and sister."

It dawned on her that Tristan must have

told him about their plans to marry. "Yes, we will, indeed . . . Dom."

Dom broke into a grin. "Lisette will be delighted to see Tristan settled at last."

"I don't know how settled he'll be," she grumbled. "Even now he's running off to take care of things when he ought to be sleeping. He's been running hard ever since yesterday, riding here and there, squiring me about . . ." Making love to her. "He needs rest."

"Don't worry about my brother." The three of them headed for the inn door. "He's used to going for days, sleeping only in snatches when he's on a mission. It was one reason Vidocq used him as an agent so frequently."

She kept forgetting about that part of his life.

"Bonnaud was an agent for Eugène Vidocq?" Papa said incredulously.

"You've heard of him, Papa?"

"I've met him. Scary fellow."

Dom chuckled. "I agree. But effective."

"That's what my friend who introduced me to the man said. But how did Bonnaud get mixed up with Vidocq?"

While they ate, Dom filled Papa in on Tristan's many exploits as an agent of La Sûreté Nationale. Since she hadn't heard much about them herself, she was fascinated. And worried. She and Tristan hadn't talked about what he would do after he married her. Would he truly be content on an estate in Yorkshire? Wouldn't a man used to such an adventurous life get restless after a while?

Tristan was waiting for them in the carriage when they came out, and Zoe noticed that Papa seemed to eye him in a new light. At least this trip was affording her father a chance to become better acquainted with her future husband.

As soon as they set off, Tristan gave them his report. They'd missed Milosh by three hours, and he *had* changed horses at the local Romany camp. They were on the right road, but still too far behind.

Unfortunately, night was falling, so that would slow them down. But Tristan and Dom consulted and decided it would probably slow Milosh down as well. Still, they didn't dare halt their march north to take a room at an inn.

"He won't stop," Tristan said grimly. "I know him. He sees this as his family honor being at stake. Besides, it probably never sat well with him that Hucker seduced Drina, but now that he knows it resulted in a child . . . Thanks to me, he's got a bee in his bonnet, and he won't rest until he can let it loose to sting Hucker."

"It's *not* 'thanks to you,' " Zoe protested. "I'm the one who mentioned the beating to him. I'm the one who stirred everything up." She stared out the window. "I never should have pursued this. I should have left well enough alone and just refused to marry my cousin."

"Really?" Papa surprised her by saying. "Truly, girl, do you think you could have gone your whole life without knowing what happened?"

"No," Tristan answered for her, amusement in his voice. "Zoe always has to get to the bottom of things. It's in her nature. It's what makes her so interesting. Along with her fine —" He checked himself. "Wit."

She arched an eyebrow at him. "Very prudently put, sir."

"I'm nothing if not prudent," he teased. "Hadn't you noticed that about me?"

His brother snorted.

"If there is any blame to be placed," Papa said, "it belongs squarely on your aunt for telling you about the matter in the first place. But she was so determined to make sure you married well —"

He broke off with a scowl, as if realizing to whom he was speaking. "Anyway, what's done is done. No point in fretting over it now."

Perhaps not, but it was because of her that they were on this hard journey. And it *was* hard. They took turns watching out the window for signs of Milosh while the others attempted to sleep. By morning they were a day's journey from York, and while they broke their fast in an inn near a Romany camp, Tristan asked around about Milosh.

That set the pattern for the day. They would stop briefly to eat, and Tristan would head off to the nearest camp. Only once did he break the pattern. He returned more swiftly than in previous stops and ran into her coming out of the retiring room. Before she even knew what was happening, he'd whisked her back into it and swept her into his arms for a long, impassioned kiss, their first since being discovered together.

When they broke apart, he murmured, "Are you all right?"

"I've been better." She cupped his face in her hands. "But it's not me I'm worried about. It's you."

"I'm much better now, princess." He grinned, his gaze raking her with a familiar heat that had her blushing.

Then they heard her father's voice down the hall, speaking to the innkeeper, and their moment together was over. With a wink, Tristan slipped from the room. He must have evaded Papa, for when she emerged there was no sign of him, and her father and his brother were already returning to the carriage.

They reached York midafternoon. The last place they'd stopped, they'd missed Milosh by only a half an hour, so they hoped to catch up to him in York. While Tristan headed out to search encampments near the city, they had an early dinner.

This time when Tristan joined them, right before they finished eating, it was clear that the past two days had begun to take their toll. His skin had a grayish cast, and his eyes lacked their usual sparkle.

"We've got a problem," he said as he took a seat at their table. "York is too big to cover quickly. Some of the Romany are in encampments, but most took houses in different parts of the city. We'd need days to find them all. I did locate an area the Corrie family was known to frequent, but he wasn't there and the Romany who were there said they hadn't seen him this winter. Either he hasn't arrived yet, or he found somewhere else in the city to change horses."

"Beyond here, he may have trouble doing that," Papa pointed out. "The towns along the road from the city aren't friendly to Gypsies, so he would have to keep his own horse and rest it more often. He'll have to slow down."

"Then we're better off getting outside of York," Tristan said. "There's only the one road leading to the coast and Rathmoor Park. Once we're on it, we're sure to catch up to him. Your team will outstrip his horse easily. And if we reach the estate ahead of him, we can waylay him before he gets to Hucker."

Unfortunately, they hadn't gone far out of York when it began to snow. Before long the flakes were falling thick and fast, cloaking the rutted road and everything beyond it in white.

"We'd better take refuge, at least until the snow stops," Dom said. "Milosh won't be able to continue on horseback easily, either, so it's not as if we'll lose time."

"He may actually be behind us, too," Papa pointed out. "Depends on when he reached York and where he went. So halting might be a good idea. We're only a few miles from Winborough now. We can stay there until morning."

"We could all use a good night's sleep," Zoe said, with a furtive glance at Tristan. Truly, he looked as if someone had trampled

401

him beneath a plow.

"I don't like it," Tristan said. "What if Milosh *isn't* behind us? What if he presses on? If he reaches Hucker and George gets wind of it . . ."

"I'm the one with the most to lose," Zoe said softly, "and I think we should stop." When his gaze shot to her and he looked as if he might argue again, she added, "For Papa's sake. He can't keep going like this. And neither can I."

She knew Tristan would never halt for his own sake, but perhaps he'd do it for someone else's.

After glancing at her father, who looked quite the worse for wear, Tristan sighed. "Fine. But only until the snow stops."

"If it makes you feel better," Dom said, "while the rest of you sleep, I'll keep watch on the main road in case Milosh passes by."

"I should be the one to do that," Tristan said.

"Absolutely not," Zoe said. "Dom knows Milosh, too, and he can certainly recognize a lone Romany rider. You're exhausted. You need sleep more than the rest of us. I daresay you haven't slept an hour altogether in the past two days."

"But —"

"If you don't let Dom do it, I swear I'll

borrow one of Papa's pistols and shoot you. At least then you'd get some rest."

"Zoe Marie Keane!" Papa put in. "I can't believe you would even think —"

"She's merely paying tit for tat, sir," Tristan drawled, "since I threatened to shoot *her* the first time we met."

"Thrice, as I recall," Zoe said primly. "Don't make me do the same."

The corners of his mouth twitched. "Very well." His gaze fell tenderly upon her. "Dom can watch the road, and I'll sleep. Happy now, princess?"

"Delirious." She smoothed her skirts. "I'm always happy to get my way."

Dom gave a bark of laughter. "Be careful, old chap. That one will lead you a merry dance."

Tristan's eyes gleamed at her. "Fortunately, I like nothing better than a merry dance."

23

Winborough wasn't what Tristan had expected. He'd thought it would be much like Rathmoor Park, with a grand manor house and a few outbuildings and several tenant farms on the outskirts. He hadn't expected to ride for what felt like miles past farm after farm, then a full dairy, a deer park, and a tannery before they even reached the drive.

Around them, the extensive gardens with their snowy gazebos and follies, their expertly shaped hedges and elegantly carved paths, looked like a fairyland that had sprung from out of the English earth, especially with the moon shining full upon them.

In the midst of the circular drive ahead, a massive fountain stood like a sentinel guarding a mystical portal. And the house that loomed through the haze of snow was easily three times the size of Rathmoor Park.

When they'd stopped for dinner in York, the earl had sent an outrider ahead to alert the household staff of their impending arrival. So the windows were lit and huge torches cast an eerie glow upon the massive edifice of yorkstone and glass, with gilded finials and crenellated towers.

In a flash, Tristan understood why Zoe had been so determined to preserve it. She hadn't lied about the hundreds of people dependent on the estate. *This* was what she'd been fighting for — this sprawling network of farms . . . these beautiful gardens . . . this stately mansion. No wonder she'd been reluctant to let it fall to Keane, who knew nothing about managing a large estate.

Tristan's heart began to pound. He was only marginally more capable of handling something this significant. The thought that she expected him to aid her in preserving it for their children and their children's children struck him dumb with terror.

He felt her gaze on him, and her father's. They were waiting for him to say something, but what could he possibly say that would be adequate?

"Nice place you have here," he quipped. "A bit small for my tastes, but I suppose I could get used to it."

To his relief, his lordship laughed. "It does get a bit crowded," Lord Olivier said, "but we manage."

Tristan glanced at the man, carefully avoiding Zoe's gaze. "I can see how it would be difficult when you have only, what, fifty rooms to choose from? Seventy-five?"

"A hundred and three," Zoe said in a small voice.

He looked at her at last, his heart sinking to see the anxiousness on her face. For once, he must refrain from cowering behind a wall of wit. This was her whole world. And the damned fool woman meant to share it with *him,* God help her. So the least he could do was be honest.

"It's a lovely estate, sweetheart," he said. "Exactly right for a princess like you. And obviously very well managed."

She blinked. "Do you really think so? Papa and I work very hard at it."

"It shows."

Her smile blazed so bright that it tightened a fist about his heart. "Oh, but you simply must see it in full light in the autumn," she exclaimed, "when the fields are heavy with grain, the sheep are fat and saucy, and the leaves are turning. It's glorious."

The thickness in his throat grew painful. "I'm sure it is." Glorious . . . and too rich for his blood.

He scowled. Damn it, he had as much right to be here as any man. She'd chosen him, and he would make sure she didn't regret it.

He still wasn't sure *why* she'd chosen him, though. She hadn't mentioned love; was it just because he'd compromised her?

That possibility had nagged him ever since they'd been found together, especially because they'd had no more than a few minutes alone. He didn't want her to take him by default. Which was ludicrous. He ought to rejoice that an heiress wished to marry him. That he'd soon have a home, a place in the world.

Yet he couldn't, until he knew why. As he'd told Keane, he wanted to be the only rogue in her life. But he didn't want *only* to be the rogue in her life.

Having reached the entrance, they were greeted by a veritable regiment of servants. The male ones, especially, looked more like soldiers in livery than like actual servants. They behaved as if they were reporting to their commanding officer, and Lord Olivier certainly spoke to them in such a fashion.

Zoe leaned over to Tristan. "Papa hired most of our male staff from among the men who served under him during the war. He said it was a crime how soldiers were treated once they were no longer of any use."

"It is," Tristan agreed. But he'd never met an earl who cared.

And when Lord Olivier smoothly introduced him as Zoe's fiancé, Tristan was forced to revise his opinion of his lordship even further. Especially when the servants accepted the pronouncement without a murmur, and Tristan was instantly accorded a respect he wasn't used to from the servants of anyone but Max and Lisette.

Dom came inside only long enough to drink some brandy to warm him. Then, at his lordship's insistence, he headed back out in the earl's curricle, which could afford him some protection from the weather while he waited by the road.

Within moments, Tristan was shown to an elegantly appointed bedchamber with a roaring fire. A bath was swiftly provided, and he was more than happy to soak off the grime of the road. The warm water soon lulled him to sleep in the copper tub.

He awoke to the feel of cold water lapping against his chin. Shivering, he left the tub and dried off, then dressed in the spare set of clothes he'd packed for the trip. He wanted to be ready at a moment's notice to deal with whatever arose.

A glance at the clock showed that they'd barely been at Winborough an hour. Since his little nap would hardly make up for the past two sleepless nights, he ought to sleep.

But how could he, with what was hanging over his head? What if they'd missed Milosh? What if the man was even now demanding answers of Hucker and jeopardizing Zoe's future? Milosh might have the good sense to be discreet . . . or he might not.

Unable to keep still, he headed downstairs. Out of habit, he'd memorized the layout of the parts of the mansion he'd been through, and having done so stood him in good stead now. Within a few minutes he'd made his way to the impressive entrance hall.

There wasn't even a footman around at this hour, nearly 1:00 A.M. He paused to assess his choices. Should he ride out to relieve Dom at his post? No point in them both losing sleep. But that would mean summoning a footman to call for a horse. Perhaps he should just head out to the stables, explain the situation, and gain a mount.

As he hesitated, he heard a curse from down the hall that sounded decidedly feminine. Curious, he followed the faint sounds of someone moving about until he happened upon an open door and a light

409

showing through it.

He entered the room and instantly took in what appeared to be a very feminine drawing room, much like one Lisette had at the Lyons town house. There was a sewing table in one corner, a semicircle of richly upholstered chairs across from a long sofa, and —

Well, well, wasn't *that* a fetching sight. In the corner partially blocked from sight by the open door, Zoe, dressed only in her night rail and wrapper, stood atop a chair. She'd dragged it up to a massive eight-foot-tall japanned piece of furniture that looked like a bureau with a cabinet on top.

The bureau stuck out a few inches farther than the cabinet, so Zoe had one knee on the bureau, one foot on the chair, and the upper doors of the cabinet open as she stretched up, apparently trying to reach a box in one of the larger pigeonholes on top.

Careful not to disturb her, Tristan closed the drawing room door and locked it, then simply stood there enjoying the sight of her with her hair tumbling to her waist and every curve of her lush buttocks molded in fine linen as she strained for the box.

Suppressing a chuckle, he came as near as he dared and said, "Need help with that, princess?"

With a little squeal, she whirled and

410

teetered atop the chair. Laughing, he caught her by the waist to steady her.

She grabbed for his shoulder with one hand while she swatted his arm with the other. "You scared the tar out of me, Tristan Bonnaud!"

"Sorry," he said, utterly unrepentant. "I was too mesmerized by your exceedingly fine arse to think straight."

"You're supposed to be sleeping."

"Worried about me, princess?" He loved that she worried about him. Surely that meant she wanted him for more than just a bedfellow.

"Someone has to. You won't worry about yourself."

Her breasts were right before him, and he seized one in his mouth, tonguing the nipple through the linen.

With a heartfelt sigh, she dug her fingers into his shoulders. "We shouldn't. You need to sleep . . ."

"Can't," he muttered.

"Me neither." She buried her hands in his hair as he slid her night rail and wrapper slowly up her legs. "I . . . I . . . what are you doing?"

Taking his bride-to-be once again. Finding out how deeply her feelings ran. Assuring himself that she still wanted him, that two days in a carriage with him hadn't given her second thoughts.

"I'm getting a good look at you." Yes. That too.

Her calves gleamed golden in the firelight, rousing his cock.

"But . . . but someone might come in."

"Unlikely. I locked the door."

Her breath quickened as he slid the hem of her garments up past her knees, then her lovely thighs.

"It was locked last time . . ."

"Yes, but your father is undoubtedly passed out in his bedchamber tonight. And he expects us to be the same."

At last he unveiled her pretty little triangle of reddish-brown curls, and his mouth went dry. "No drawers. Aren't you the naughty girl?"

"There's nothing wrong with not wearing drawers to bed," she said primly.

"I wholeheartedly agree." He shoved the bunched-up night rail and wrapper into her hand. "Hold this."

A tiny frown formed between her eyebrows, though she did his bidding. "Why?"

He spread her curls open to expose the tender folds he yearned to taste. "Because, sweetheart, I want to make a meal of you." He crouched to lick her delicate flesh.

"Oh! You want . . . to . . . to . . ."

"Yes." He laved her with his tongue, relishing the musky woman smell of her. And the way she shivered beneath his strokes.

"Tristan, you really shouldn't . . ."

"Hush, sweetheart. Let me do what I do best."

"That's not . . ." she began.

But he was already sucking her swollen bud the way he knew most women enjoyed it. The way he hoped *she* would enjoy it.

"Ohhhh . . ." She clutched his head, anchoring him to her mons. "My darling . . . *Tristan* . . ."

The word *darling* reverberated in his brain. She'd never called him that. It sounded wonderful.

Desperate for her now, he set about making her desperate for him. He did have one advantage. She desired him. And he damned well meant to make the most of it.

He teased her with his tongue, reveling in her gasps, drinking in her scent, enjoying the way she began to shimmy and quiver beneath his intimate caresses. He loved the taste of her arousal; it drove him mad. He didn't know how much longer he could —

She came, crying out her pleasure so sweetly that his cock hardened to iron. As her knees buckled, he swept her off the chair and onto the bureau's projecting surface. Hastily opening his trousers and drawers, he parted her legs and leaned in, then hesitated there, giving her a chance to refuse him.

When she threw her arms about his neck, it was all the invitation he needed. Seconds later, he buried his aching cock inside her. Though she uttered a little cry of surprise, she tucked her feet behind his thighs to fit herself better to him.

He nearly came right then. She felt so good, so hot and welcoming. With any other woman, he would have pumped swift and hard until he spent himself. But he didn't want that with Zoe, especially now. Last time they'd been together, she'd felt pain; this time he wanted her to have only pleasure.

"Tristan . . ." she breathed against his ear as he began to move inside her. "I missed you."

"In your bed, you mean," he ground out to hide his disappointment.

Despite the raging need of his cock, he kept his strokes slow and easy. He dragged the neck of her night rail down so he could fondle her breast, making her squirm.

"Is that why you're . . . marrying me?" he asked, burning to know the truth. "Because you like *this*? Being seduced by a scoundrel?"

"No!" She drew back to stare at him in a daze. "And you're no scoundrel."

"Are you sure?"

"Yes." Her eyes shone warmly at him, full of an emotion he dared not trust.

He kissed her, afraid to hope, not even sure what he hoped for. No, he knew what he hoped for. Like his mother, he yearned for the impossible dream.

Damn her. He drew back so he could see her face as he thrust hard into her. "Are you marrying me only because I ruined you?"

"Of course not." Her body dragged him in, pulling him deeper.

"Then why?"

A sudden wariness leapt into her features, and she buried her face in his neck. "Because . . . because I want to."

"But *why* do you want to?" He could feel his release just there, yet it would not come. Ruthlessly, he increased his pace. "If not because of *this* . . . why?"

She met him thrust for thrust now, her hair a wild tangle upon his shoulders. "Because . . . you make me laugh."

"I made you laugh before. And you still planned to marry your cousin."

"I . . . I came to my senses."

A pity *he* couldn't come to his senses. Couldn't stop asking her for the impossible. "Yet you won't answer me. The truth, Zoe. Why. Marry. *Me?*"

He found her pleasure spot and fingered it deliberately, determined to bring her to bliss. If he could bring her there, perhaps he could go there, too, and stop this mad wishing and yearning for more.

She gasped. "Does it . . . matter?"

"*God,* yes." He drove into her over and over, seeking release and that something else he wanted, that something he didn't dare name. "Damn it, tell me why!"

"Because I love you!"

As the words reverberated in the room, she convulsed about him, milking his cock and making mewling noises that roused him somewhere other than his cock.

Then she clasped him close and murmured into his neck, "I love you . . . my darling."

That sent him over the edge. With a deep plunge, he found his release at last. Tangled up in her words, scarcely daring to believe them, he spilled himself inside her.

With his body falling into contentment and his mind still reeling, he heard her whisper, "Happy now?"

He could barely contain the giddy laugh that rose in his throat. "Delirious."

And the fact that he spoke the truth struck terror in his soul.

24

Her heart aching, Zoe cradled Tristan against her. She should have kept quiet. She shouldn't have told him how she felt. And yet, he didn't seem unhappy to hear it. Indeed, he was kissing her and nuzzling her and holding her so tenderly it made her want to cry.

The man certainly knew how to make a woman love him.

Let me do what I do best.

That, too, made her want to cry. Was that how he saw himself? "It's not true, you know."

He froze. "What isn't?"

Belatedly realizing what she'd last said to him, she added hastily, "That pleasuring a woman is what you do best."

"Ah. That." For a moment, he relaxed against her. Then he jerked back to stare at her. "Wait, are you saying that I didn't give you pleasure?"

His offended tone made her laugh. "No . . . I mean, yes. Oh, Lord, I am mangling this very badly." She caught his dear face in her hands and said, "I'm saying you have many wonderful talents. And while pleasuring a woman is certainly one, it's not the only one by far."

That seemed to satisfy him, for his expression turned smug. "So you *do* enjoy my lovemaking?"

She lifted an eyebrow. "If you can't tell that, sir, you are blind and deaf and probably stupid."

If he'd been a peacock, he would have been strutting about, displaying his feathers. Instead, a slow smile lifted the corners of his mouth. "And what are these other 'wonderful talents' of mine, sweetheart?"

"For one thing, you're a very good investigator. You found out things about my past that even Papa never did."

"That's because he wasn't looking," he said dryly.

"True." She ran her hands over the coat he filled out so very well. "But you do tend to ask the most important questions and cut right to the truth of matters. I'm not very good at that myself."

He chuckled. "That's because you don't stop to think before you speak your mind.

Which happens to be a quality I like."

She dropped her gaze to his expertly tied cravat. "Even when I blurt out things I shouldn't?" *Like utterly unwise declarations of love?*

"Even then," he said in a husky tone.

He had to know that she was referring to the words he'd practically dragged from her, but he kept silent, content just to thread his fingers through her hair and smooth it out over her shoulders.

At last he released a low breath. "And it's not that I don't . . . that I . . ."

"Shh." She pressed a finger to his lips. "I know what you think about love. And it's fine. You want me as your wife, and that's enough."

She ventured a look at him, shocked to find that he wasn't eyeing her with the relief she'd expected, just an unsettling intensity she didn't know how to read.

Lord, but she was tired of trying to figure him out.

Pasting a smile to her lips, she slid off the bureau and began arranging her clothes. "Anyway, before we got carried away, you offered to help get my box down."

"Right," he said, and there was definitely relief in his voice. Like Papa, he preferred having things to do over talking about how he felt.

Climbing atop the chair, he reached up for the box that was the size of a smallish pistol case. "This one here?"

"Yes, thank you."

He climbed down and handed it to her. "What's in it that you would risk breaking your neck for?"

"This." She opened the box to reveal a red and gold patterned scarf with a knotted fringe. "I haven't looked at it in years, but as I lay in my bed, the memory of it popped into my head and I had to come find it."

Her throat tightened as she stared at it. "When I was a little girl, Mama told me that one day she would explain all about the woman it belonged to. And that until she could, it was to stay in its special place up there in the cabinet. I think she put it up so high precisely so I wouldn't go trying to play with it."

Carefully, she removed the scarf. "From time to time, she would take it out and let me hold it and caress it and even play with it a little. But watching me with it always seemed to make her sad, so after a while, I didn't want to do that." She stroked it as she used to. "I stopped asking for it when I was eight or so."

He took the scarf from her. "You think it belonged to Drina."

"It must have. Mama was probably waiting for Papa to let her tell me about my natural mother." Her throat felt tight and raw. "As a girl, I loved this scarf. I couldn't wait until I was old enough to wear it. I can't believe I forgot about it."

"You didn't realize its significance, that's all. But you're old enough to wear it now." He tied it about her neck tenderly. "It suits you."

"I shall wear it in Drina's honor." She touched it, and tears welled in her eyes.

The sight seemed to disturb him. "We will find out what happened to her and who hurt her," he said fiercely. "I swear we'll avenge her."

She shook her head. "No need for vengeance. I don't want her sacrifice on my behalf to be in vain. Hucker mustn't win. Or George."

"Never," he vowed.

Brushing away her tears, she forced a smile for his benefit. "Now, you and I both need to sleep while we can. All right?"

He nodded.

But when she headed for the door and he didn't follow, she paused. "Are you coming?"

"In a few minutes. It wouldn't do for us to be seen coming up the stairs with you looking like *that,*" he drawled. "Your father might make good on his threat to call me out."

She laughed. "Yes, I daresay he might." She gazed at the face she was growing to love so well. "But don't be long."

"I won't."

The words *I love you* were on the tip of her tongue. But his expression had closed up again, and she couldn't bear another answering silence. Instead, she walked out of Mama's favorite drawing room, leaving him to his dark thoughts, whatever they might be.

Still, as she headed for the stairs, she prayed that one day he might say the words back.

The moment Zoe left, Tristan dropped into a chair and stared blindly into the fire. He'd finally got the words out of her that he'd only half realized he was waiting to hear. She loved him. Zoe *loved* him.

Was she daft?

Apparently so, given that she'd looked expectantly at him, waiting for him to confess the same. And he should have, if only to make her feel more settled about the marriage. But he didn't like to lie.

Would it be a lie? God, he wasn't even sure. What did he know of love?

All right, so he couldn't stop thinking about her or wanting her. And the prospect of a future in this house, managing the estate at her side, raising children, even serving in Parliament on her behalf, was so intoxicating he could hardly contain his eagerness to begin.

The problem was, what if it didn't last? What if he, like Father, couldn't be the man she needed? He'd spent half his days in and out of women's lives, never having to please one of them beyond the bedchamber . . . never *caring* enough to do so. What if that was all he knew how to do?

The thought terrified him. Give him a forger to arrest or a murderer to hunt down or a thief to follow any day, over a woman looking at him with love in her eyes and expectations for him that he wasn't sure he could meet.

Especially if this mess with Hucker meant she lost everything. The last time he'd been in a bind over how to support his family, he'd stolen a horse and gotten them banished from England. God only knew what would happen this time.

Scowling, he rose from the chair. He was

424

not going to muck her life up. No matter what it took, he would keep her out of this business with Hucker.

Which was why he'd best go check on Dom. He glanced at the clock. Surely he'd given her enough time to fall asleep. He headed out into the hall, but before he could even consider walking down to the stables to hunt up a horse, Dom entered.

He stopped short when he saw Tristan. "Thank God you're awake," Dom said, his face as pale as the snow he stamped off his boots. "We have to go now."

Tristan headed for the closet to hunt up his greatcoat. "I take it you have news of Milosh?"

Dom followed him. "Almost certainly. A man was riding along the road, headed back toward York. I hailed him and he stopped, said he was coming from the coast. So I asked if he'd happened to pass a Gypsy fellow on horseback. I fully expected him to say no."

Watching as Tristan donned his coat and hat, Dom frowned. "But he said that he *had* seen such a man about five miles back. I asked how that could be, since I'd been sitting there a while, so the Gypsy should have ridden past me before meeting him on the road."

The two of them hurried for the door.

"Turns out," Dom said, "there's an alternate road that runs from York to the next town up ahead, which the Gypsies like to take to bypass Highthorpe. No one saw fit to tell us that."

Tristan's heart began to pound. "No one may have known. What passes for a road with the Romany can be little more than a cart track. And if their purpose is to avoid confrontation with the ignorant townspeople of Highthorpe, then they would almost certainly keep it secret."

"Well, this fellow knew, and judging from what he said, Milosh now has an hour on us."

"At least he'll be struggling through the snow on a lone horse," Tristan said. "We'll have his lordship's curricle and a matched pair to plow through. It might gain us some time."

The brothers rushed out the front door and nearly bowled over a man in his thirties. Tristan recognized him from earlier. His name was Pipkin, and his lordship had mentioned that the man had served as a rifleman under him. Now he was the undercoachman.

"Sirs, do you wish the horses stabled for the night?" Pipkin asked.

"No," Tristan said, "but when my fiancée and his lordship awaken, tell them we've taken the curricle to Rathmoor Park."

"Very good, sir."

Pipkin didn't so much as question Tristan's right to order him about or run off with his master's equipage.

"And this is most important," Tristan added. "Tell his lordship and her ladyship *not* to follow, do you understand? They're to remain here until our return."

That gave Pipkin a moment's pause. "Yes, sir," he said at last.

As the two of them rushed down the steps to the waiting curricle, Dom asked Tristan, "Are you afraid we won't catch up to Milosh?"

"Exactly."

"Then perhaps we ought to rouse his lordship and take some of his soldier-servants with us."

"Absolutely not."

Dom caught Tristan by the arm before he could climb in. "But if you're right, and we're forced to go onto the estate, we don't know how many of George's men we'll end up facing."

"It doesn't matter." Shrugging off Dom's arm, Tristan leapt into the curricle. "I have to keep his lordship and Zoe out of it. I can't risk Hucker learning about her. You know damned well he'd use the knowledge that she's his daughter to blackmail her and Lord Olivier. Or worse yet, he'll tell George, and George will use that knowledge to destroy us both. It's how he works."

"True." Reluctantly, Dom joined him in the curricle.

As they headed off, Tristan's mind drifted back to the last time he'd made love to Zoe. To the sweetness of it, the tenderness of it. To the words that kept singing through his heart.

"Do you think your mother loved Father?"

Instantly he cursed whatever impulse had made him broach the subject. He and Dom had never spoken of Dom's mother, not in all their years together. It was a sore subject.

To Tristan's surprise, Dom took the question in stride. "Honestly? I have no idea. She died giving birth to me, remember?"

Tristan persisted, though he knew he shouldn't. "Yes, but surely you heard *something.* Surely you at least know whether they initially married for love, no matter what happened later."

"Marrying for love wasn't always the fashion back then. And considering that Father took a mistress only five years into their marriage . . ."

"Good point."

They rode a bit farther before Dom spoke again. "Still, George used to talk about it. Not that you can believe a damned thing he says most of the time, but he did claim that Mother loved Father rather desperately."

Tristan considered that. "Perhaps that's why George resents me and Lisette so much. Because our mother stole him from your mother."

"Perhaps." Dom stared ahead at the road. "But if so, he's a fool. Because I'm fairly certain that Father didn't love Mother."

"Why?"

"Our father was incapable of love, in case you hadn't noticed."

That caught Tristan off guard. Unable to be tactful, he said, "He told *my* mother that he loved her."

"Of course he did. It was what she wanted to hear. But at heart our father was a selfish being. He never cared to be inconvenienced, and telling your mother he loved her saved him from having to show it." Dom shot him a sidelong glance. "Think of it. Did he ever once do something for any of us at a sacrifice to himself?"

"The codicil."

Dom snorted. "He wrote it on his deathbed. When a man is staring the Grim Reaper

429

in the face, he sometimes makes a last-minute bid for Paradise by setting things right. It doesn't mean much when the weight of his life has been negligence."

That gave Tristan pause. He'd never thought of Father as selfish. He should have, for now that Dom said it, it was painfully evident. But Tristan had been so focused on trying to figure out why Father hadn't loved him and Lisette and Mother enough to provide for them that it hadn't occurred to him that perhaps Father had merely been incapable of love.

"And in case this conversation was provoked by your current situation," Dom added, "you're not like him in the least."

Startled by that astute perception, Tristan said, "How do *you* know? Perhaps I just said I'd marry Zoe to avoid the inconvenience of dealing with his lordship's wrath over my . . . er . . . association with her."

"Right. Because dealing with him day-to-day won't be the least bit inconvenient," Dom said sarcastically. "Not to mention dealing with *her* day-to-day, meeting her expectations, being the man she needs —"

"You're not helping," Tristan gritted out.

Dom laughed. "You're experiencing the same panic every bachelor feels as the day of his wedding looms. It doesn't mean you can't handle marriage. It just means you have the good sense to realize it's a weighty responsibility."

Tristan wanted to ask if that was what had happened with Dom and Jane, if his brother had panicked and somehow driven her to jilt him. But this conversation was too important to obscure matters by plucking at Dom's insecurities.

"Do you love her?" Dom asked.

Tristan groaned. "Why the bloody hell must everyone keep asking me that?"

"Because it's the only thing that makes marriage worthwhile. If you don't love her, then brave her father's ire and her own disappointment and cry off."

"I can't. I compromised her."

"Ah. You didn't tell me that part."

"Yes, well, I wasn't eager to tell you that I'd mucked everything up again."

"Again? It's been a long time since you mucked anything up, old chap. You've been a model citizen for some years."

"And something of a rogue."

"True." Dom shot Tristan a sidelong glance. "Which is why it's curious that you want to save Lady Zoe's reputation by marrying her."

Tristan bristled. "Only a blackguard would refuse to marry her after taking her innocence."

"Exactly." Dom smiled fondly at him. "And that reaction is precisely why you are nothing like Father. Because he was perfectly happy to give your mother child after child without the bond of marriage. Didn't bother him a whit."

"She was a French actress," Tristan pointed out.

"Yes. And your new lady, for all her trappings, is the illegitimate daughter of our sworn enemy and a Gypsy. Some would say she's nothing but trouble. Her own cousin didn't wish to marry her, yet you do. That doesn't sound like the choice of a man incapable of love, does it?"

No, it did not. And in the midst of his confusion over what he felt for Zoe, that was oddly reassuring.

25

Zoe tried to sleep, but it was hopeless. She was too on edge. Besides which, she was hungry. So, less than an hour after she'd left Tristan, she wandered downstairs in search of food. She'd barely reached the bottom of the staircase when their undercoachman leapt up from a chair where he'd apparently been awaiting her.

Her blood began to thunder in her veins. "What is it?"

"Your fiancé and his brother left half an hour ago in your father's curricle. They instructed me to tell you that they were heading for Rathmoor Park, and that you and his lordship are to remain here until their return."

"The devil we are! Go ready the traveling coach for us right this minute. I shall rouse Papa."

Pipkin looked panicked. "But . . . but, my lady, Mr. Bonnaud said —"

"I don't care what he said," she snapped. "You do as I tell you, or there will be hell to pay. Mr. Bonnaud isn't my husband yet, you know."

Nor would he ever be if he got into a brawl with his half brother. That devil would as soon shoot Tristan as look at him.

Her stomach roiling, she hurried for the stairs. She was not going to sit here and wait around for news that George had hauled Tristan off to gaol or knifed him in the back or shot at him because he was trespassing. There was still a chance that she could reach Tristan first. Papa's coach-and-four could outrun the curricle any day of the week, even with snow on the roads.

Tristan was *not* going to risk his life over *her* future. It had been one thing when he was trying to catch up to Uncle Milosh before the man got to Hucker. But if matters had progressed beyond that . . .

No, she wouldn't endure it. Let Uncle Milosh do as he pleased with Hucker. If it meant ruin for her, then so be it. But she was *not* going to sacrifice Tristan to stop Uncle Milosh.

When she reached Papa's room, she found her shouting had apparently roused him, for he was already dressing. After explaining the situation, she headed off to get her own clothes on. Twenty minutes later, they were climbing into Papa's coach-and-four. Two of their sturdiest grooms joined them on horseback as outriders.

While the equipage barreled down the drive at top speed, manned by Pipkin and drawn by a fresh team of horses, Papa watched her with a veiled expression. "You realize that if you go in there and expose yourself as Hucker's daughter, we may not be able to stop the man from spreading the tale far and wide. Bonnaud says he's a nasty piece of work."

She nodded. "But Uncle Milosh might expose me anyway. And while losing Winborough and the title wouldn't be my first choice, I vastly prefer it to having my fiancé jailed or murdered before I can even marry him."

"Very well. So long as you recognize what the consequences could be."

Oh, she did, only too well. The weight of it all lay on her chest, and not just because of what might happen to Winborough.

"Papa," she asked, "what Tristan said that night you found us together . . . about the things you did that were against the law. Is there a chance . . . have I put you in the position of . . . of . . ."

"Of course not, dear girl." He reached

435

over to pat her hand reassuringly. "Your fiancé vastly underestimates the power of an English earl. The burial in the woods isn't illegal. The bribery of an official is a minor offense. There's no legal requirement in England to register a birth, so the lie I told in the baptismal record is between me and God, and I daresay He will understand."

"And the stealing of a child from her family?"

He drew in a heavy breath. "Forgive me for saying this, but Drina was a Gypsy. I fear no one will make a fuss about that."

"Except Uncle Milosh."

"Whose complaints will be ignored because of who he is." When she winced, he added, "I am sorry, dear girl, but that is the way of the world."

"I don't have to like it, though," she said tersely. "Just as I don't have to like that by English law, my lack of a blood tie to you outweighs my being your child in every other way."

"Well, with any luck the world will never learn of that." He forced a smile. "And if it does, I may still live long enough to convince your cousin that he should take over Winborough. Or, failing that, convince his sister."

She blinked. "His *sister.*"

He nodded. "When the title goes to the heirs general, they choose from among all possibilities. As my direct descendant, you would be first choice, but if your true heritage is exposed, they would move on to Mr. Keane *and* Miss Keane."

"Of course!" She broke into a smile. "I was so focused on Jeremy's being the heir that I forgot about that. Since he doesn't want the title, his sister might actually be a better choice."

"I could marry her to solidify the claim," Papa said with a twinkle in his eye. "You are not the only one who can marry for the sake of the estate, you know. And she is only, what, thirty or more years my junior?"

"Papa!" she cried. "You wouldn't!"

He laughed. "No. But my point is that these things work themselves out. And you should have some faith in your Mr. Bonnaud, too. He might surprise you by settling this matter without bloodshed."

"I dearly hope so."

"Still, when we arrive, you must leave this matter to me." He patted the pistol case at his side. "Stay in the carriage. No point in letting them get a look at you if they don't need to." He smiled sadly. "According to Bonnaud, you are the very image of your poor mother, so it was probably only a matter of time before Lord Rathmoor or his lackey saw you in public and recognized Drina in you."

"Don't *you* think I look like her?"

He winced. "She'd been beaten, my dear girl. I couldn't tell what she looked like."

When Papa fell silent, she tried not to think of what her natural mother's final hours must have been like, but it plagued her. She could too easily imagine Drina stumbling through a snowy night like this one in search of help for her coming babe.

That painful thought reminded her of Tristan's wild promise to avenge her natural mother one day. Suddenly the long-ago prediction of that Romany fortune-teller leapt into her mind.

You are a woman born of secrets and sadness. It will either destroy your future or lead you to greatness. A handsome gentleman with eyes like the sky and hair like a raven's wing will come into your life. If you let him, he will become the hand of your vengeance. If you let him, he will shatter your heart.

She shivered. She dearly hoped that Tristan had been right when he said that fortune-telling was all "rot." Because with George and Hucker involved, becoming the hand of her vengeance could very well lead to his death.

And *that* would definitely shatter her heart.

The closer Tristan and Dom got to Rathmoor Park without encountering Milosh, the more they resigned themselves to having to deal with both him and Hucker. While Tristan tooled the horses, Dom loaded their respective pistols, which each stowed in his greatcoat pocket within easy reach. Tristan also had a blade in his boot, and he knew that Dom kept one somewhere as well.

When they reached the outskirts of the estate, they had to make a split-second decision. Hucker's house on the property? Or the manor? Which way would Milosh go?

"Hucker's house," they said as one.

At this hour, Hucker would have no reason to be in the manor, and he'd already been living as a tenant during the last summer Milosh's family camped at Rathmoor Park.

Their hunch proved good when they drew up in front of Hucker's cottage and heard shouting inside. Through the early light of dawn, they caught sight of a servant running down the road toward the manor, probably going to fetch help. He was already too far away to stop, and anyway, it would take both of them to deal with Hucker and Milosh.

Cursing, Tristan and Dom leapt from the curricle and rushed through the open door.

In the front room they found Hucker facing down Milosh with a fowling piece. Apparently Milosh, who held a nasty-looking knife, hadn't given Hucker time to load, for the older man brandished the gun like a club as the two men circled each other.

"Where is she, damn it?" Milosh demanded. "Where is my sister? If you don't tell me —"

"I don't know!" Hucker cried. "I swear on my mother's grave I don't know what happened to Drina after she left here."

When Milosh looked as if he would lunge for the man, Dom darted forward to grab the Romany man from behind. Milosh began to struggle, so Tristan hurried to place himself between Milosh and Hucker.

"I told you not to come here, damn it!" Tristan spat at Milosh.

Milosh jerked his head toward Hucker. "I couldn't let that beast there escape punishment for beating her!"

"*Beating* Drina?" Hucker's face turned thunderous. "If she told you that, she lied. I never laid a hand on Drina. I loved her!"

Tristan shot Hucker a contemptuous look. "Yes, we could tell by the fact that you got her with child, then sent her out in the cold to suffer alone to bear it."

Hucker was already shaking his head. "She wasn't alone, and she weren't out in the cold, neither. I sent her to her people! If anyone beat her, it was them."

"You know that's a lie!" Milosh shouted at Hucker. "I asked you about her the next summer. Why would I have done that if she'd made it to 'her people'?"

"The Corries ain't the only Gypsies in England," Hucker said. "You banished her, so I sent her with his lordship to —"

When Hucker's face lost all color, a chill swept Tristan. "His lordship?" he echoed. "My *father*?"

"It wouldn't have been Father," Dom said coolly. "He was out of the country then. He means George."

Hucker wore a look of panic.

Tristan marched up to him, fists clenched at his sides. "What did my damned half brother do?"

Hucker lowered the fowling piece, his eyes hollow in his face. "His lordship wouldn't have hurt her. She was bearing my child, for God's sake!"

"He must have done something or you

441

wouldn't have mentioned him." Tristan towered over him. "So what the bloody hell did George *do*?"

"He . . . he said he would take her to the next encampment of Gypsies."

Drina had left the estate with *George.* Oh, God. "And you believed him?" Tristan asked hoarsely. "You let her go off with that . . . that . . ."

"I had no choice!" With desperation on his face, Hucker glanced around at the three of them. When he saw their cold expressions, he slumped against the wall. "He gave me no choice. For months, I'd been . . . stealing from the stores of food, taking a bit here and there for me and Drina. I hadn't been steward very long, and the two of us could hardly live on my salary. With the babe on the way . . ."

His voice hardened. "I was always careful not to get caught, careful to keep him from knowing about her. But that day, I was worried. I thought she might be in labor, so I weren't as careful as I ought to have been."

"And George discovered what you'd been up to," Dom said.

The life went out of Hucker's eyes. "He spotted me leaving with a game hen under my coat that I was hoping to sell, and he followed me to the cottage. He was so angry, he was. Kept raging about 'whores' on the estate corrupting his servants and his —"

When Hucker broke off, Tristan groaned. George hadn't been able to stop Father from having his mistress at Rathmoor Park, so he'd taken his anger out on Drina and Hucker instead.

Hucker's breathing grew heavy. "He threatened to have me hanged for theft, he did. Said if I didn't cast her out, he'd turn me over to the magistrate. And what good would I be to her and the babe if I was dead?"

"Yes, much better to become his man of affairs," Dom said dryly.

"More like his lackey," Hucker growled, "under his thumb for all eternity."

"And all you had to do was hand her over to him," Tristan said, his gut twisting at the thought.

"It wasn't like that," Hucker said defensively. "I begged him to be merciful, to let me escort her to her people. He said he'd do that himself."

Tristan snorted. "Why the hell would George be merciful to some Gypsy woman? Surely you didn't really *believe* he would take her to a place of safety."

Hucker swallowed. "He said . . . he didn't

want her returning, trying to worm her way back into my life. He said he would take her to her people and pay them to keep her away. Then I would be free of her."

"And you *wanted* to be free of her?"

"No! But he gave me no choice." Hucker shot Tristan an imploring glance. "I had to send her off with him. It was the only way to save us both!"

"It didn't save *her.*" Tristan glared at the man. "Drina was found beaten on the road to York. She *died* on the road to York." He heard Milosh's low cry of pain behind him and prayed the man wouldn't mention that Drina had borne a child. "And that is how my wretch of a brother 'saved' Drina."

Hucker began to shake. "Dead? Drina is *dead*?"

"And good riddance, too," said a voice from beyond them.

Tristan froze. Slowly he turned to find George standing in the doorway, a pair of dueling pistols in his hands and murder in his eyes.

"Well, well, look who has come back to spread lies about me," George said.

Bloody hell.

Tristan slid his hand casually into his coat and closed it around his own pistol, but he didn't dare shoot — not when George had them in his sights. The minute Tristan showed his pistol, George would fire, and he would be in the right. Tristan was trespassing, and George would claim it was self-defense.

"Lies?" Tristan said. "Are you denying that you beat poor Drina to death?"

George cast a furtive glance at Hucker. "I never touched her."

"I happen to know for a fact that you did," Tristan said. "I have a very reputable witness who says he found her wandering the road, half-frozen and badly beaten."

"Do you? And he believed the claims of some damned Gypsy woman who probably spread her legs for every —"

With a roar of rage, Milosh lunged forward, but Dom managed to restrain him. For the first time since his arrival, George turned his attention to Milosh.

"Ah, if it isn't the good Mr. Corrie." George aimed a pistol at him. "The man who probably helped my father's bastard steal and dispose of my horse thirteen years ago. I daresay if I were to exert myself, I could find out exactly who bought Blue Blazes — and from whom. That would certainly cook *your* goose, wouldn't it, Corrie?"

"If you'd ever been able to determine such

a thing," Dom put in, "you would have done it years ago. You had no evidence then, and you certainly have none now."

"Leave it to the barrister to speak of legalities," George said snidely. "Wait, *not* a barrister, eh? Just an aspiring one."

Though a muscle worked in Dom's jaw, he showed no other sign of agitation. "I have a thriving business, brother. Didn't you know?" His tone turned taunting. "Meanwhile, the estate you were willing to lie and cheat for is crumbling down about your ears."

"Shut up!" George shifted his aim from Milosh to Dom. "Or you'll end up in the grave with Tristan and his friend."

"Oh," Tristan said smoothly, "so you plan to kill us? Not very sporting of you. And not even feasible. There are three of us, and you've only got two pistols."

"Hucker!" George said in a commanding tone. "For God's sake, use that gun."

Hucker lifted the fowling piece. "It ain't loaded."

"Well, go load it then!"

When Hucker hesitated, George tensed. It was obviously starting to dawn on him that this might prove trickier than he thought. He aimed at Tristan's heart. "I only need one shot to kill *you,* don't I? I found three

446

men trespassing, one of them clearly a thieving Gypsy. They were struggling with my man of affairs, and I had to protect him. Little did I know that two of them were my brothers."

Tristan laughed coldly. "Really? You plan to convince a magistrate that you accidentally shot the brother you've been trying to ruin all your adult life?"

"Hucker will support my story."

Hucker stiffened and glared at George, but remained silent. He was clearly an unknown quantity in this equation.

Apparently George thought so, too, for he said, a bit uneasily, "And no one will heed a damned thing Corrie says."

Milosh came toward him. "Which is why after you shoot them, there's nothing to stop me from throttling you. From watching the life drain from you, the way you watched the life drain from Drina."

"I didn't kill her, damn it!" George's pistol wavered between Milosh and Tristan. "She wasn't dead when I left her."

"No, just nearly dead," Tristan drawled with one eye on Hucker. "Your beating and the cold finished her off."

"Shut up, damn you!" George cried, steadying the pistol on Tristan.

But before Tristan could pull his own

447

weapon, another voice said from just behind George, "Pull that trigger, Rathmoor, and you are a dead man."

Tristan groaned. The Major had come. He had a gun to George's head and would clearly use it if he had to. Pray God Lord Olivier had possessed the good sense to leave Zoe behind.

"Who the devil are you?" George asked.

"Remember that reputable witness I told you about?" Tristan said. "That's him."

"Major Roderick Keane, at your service," Lord Olivier said.

"How did you find us?" Dom asked.

"Followed the tracks in the snow, of course. It's not for nothing I was in the army."

George seemed to have finally identified his lordship's other self. "Lord Olivier? How did my brothers convince *you* to join their ridiculous charade?"

Though George sounded surprised, he appeared oddly unconcerned, which gave Tristan pause.

"Never mind that," his lordship said. "They've done nothing to you. So put your pistols down and let them go."

"The hell I will." George lifted his head, and a grin of triumph spread over his face. "Hear that? It's the sound of my men coming to aid their master."

As Dom let out a curse, Tristan's heart dropped into his stomach. Bloody, bloody hell.

"I can't believe you two continue to underestimate me," George said gleefully. "I'm not stupid. Don't you think I sent for my men before I headed here?"

They heard other sounds outside now, not only of men tramping about but of Lord Olivier's oaths as he was relieved of his weapons.

"I'm sorry, milord," came a lad's voice. "It took a while to get the fellows out of bed, but we're here now."

"Excellent," George said. "We have a nest of knaves to root out." George nodded to Hucker. "Take that pistol the French whore's bastard has been fondling all this while, will you?"

Hucker hesitated a moment before coming up to remove the weapon from Tristan's hand inside his coat pocket. The familiar dead look in Hucker's eyes had returned.

"You're going to let him do this?" Tristan muttered. "After what he did to Drina —"

"Hucker!" George said. "Bring them here. Now!"

Hucker wavered and his hackles rose, but like a dog in training he came to heel, using

449

Tristan's pistol to prod the three of them out the door.

Dom exchanged a glance with Tristan and very subtly touched his own coat pocket. No one had thought to check him yet, but they would soon.

Once they were outside, Tristan made a quick assessment. Things were bad, but not as bad as he'd feared. George's lackeys had dwindled in number since Tristan's youth, but they still outnumbered Dom, Tristan, the Major, and Milosh by far. And they were armed with scythes and swords and a rifle or two. The odds weren't overwhelming, but the battle would be a bloody one if it came to that.

There was no sign of Zoe or even of Lord Olivier's carriage. He ought to have been relieved, but despair swept over him. Though he didn't want her caught up in this, neither could he bear the thought of dying without telling her that he loved her.

Loved her?

Oh, yes. He'd been such a fool. With George's cruel face before him, all he could think was how he'd been wrong about so many things. About Father, about his own character, and yes, about the possibility of falling in love.

The thought of her rose in his mind with

a painful sweetness that staggered him. He couldn't live without her. Nor did he want to die without telling her.

He steadied his shoulders. He was *not* going to die, damn it, nor were the rest of them. George hadn't had the last word — and if Tristan had anything to say about it, he never would.

26

Zoe heard the commotion a short distance away from where Papa had pulled the coach off the road that led through the woods. That alarmed her so much that she leapt out.

"My lady," one of the outriders said sharply, "his lordship's orders were clear. We are to stay out of sight."

She shook her head. "Something's wrong. I feel it. And those horses we heard riding up from the estate a few moments ago can't be good."

Pipkin stepped down from the perch. "What do you want us to do, my lady?"

She surveyed the three stalwart fellows, who bore no resemblance to the sweet, easy-to-manipulate Ralph. "Have you any weapons with you?"

They laughed. Apparently Papa had warned them to come armed, for they pulled out pistols, knives, and a couple of flintlock rifles.

"We should reconnoiter first," said Pipkin.

The others agreed. They didn't want her to come along, but she told them flatly that they were not leaving her behind. Not with her father, her fiancé, her uncle, and her fiancé's brother possibly in danger.

When they reached the edge of the woods and could see the house of the tenant farm in the dawning light, her heart sank. The four men she cared about were facing down ten fellows armed with weapons of varying sorts. Two men stood apart from the others — she could only assume they were George and Hucker.

"Shall we drive to Ashcroft for help?" one of the outriders asked.

She shook her head. "No time."

The other outrider pointed to the side of the woods near the house. "If the three of us can take positions in the woods around them, we may fool them into thinking there are more of us, especially if we tether our two horses at intervals, too. Those chaps aren't hardened soldiers — just servants and farmers with weapons. A few shots from many directions, the sounds of horses responding to the shots, and we'd scatter them. They'll think there's an army."

"Do it," Zoe said.

The men melted into the woods and she edged as close as she dared, trying to hear what was being said in the clearing.

"What do you mean to do with us, Rathmoor?" Papa asked, his voice ringing loudly in the morning air.

"I can't let you leave here."

The man who'd answered held two pistols. One of them was aimed at Tristan. Her stomach clenched painfully.

Especially when Tristan advanced a step toward his half brother. "Let the rest of them go. It's me you want. And you're not going to murder four men in cold blood. Even you can't cover up that crime."

"It's not as hard as you think," George said, a hint of desperation in his voice. "We saw men running away, we thought they were thieves, and we shot them."

"But m' lord —" the other man said in a low voice.

"Shut up, Hucker. You'll be well compensated for your help, don't worry."

Hucker. The sight of the man who'd sired her pierced her through. Could he really be such a villain?

Perhaps not, but George certainly was, and he was unpredictable. She needed to stop this before he did as he threatened. And that would give Papa's men enough time to get into place.

She walked into the clearing. "If you kill them, Lord Rathmoor, you'll have to kill me," she called out as she approached. "And I don't think you'll have an easy time explaining how a lady got mistaken for a thief."

When sixteen men whirled in her direction, she swallowed hard. She was somewhat reassured when she saw that her presence seemed to make George's men decidedly uneasy, murmuring among themselves.

"Oh, for God's sake, who the hell are you?" George asked.

But Hucker had seen her, and the color drained from his face. "Drina?"

"No." She took a shuddering breath. "Drina's daughter."

Hucker whirled on Tristan. "You said Drina died on the road!"

"She did. But only after giving birth to your child."

"Yes. I'm *your* daughter, too, Mr. Hucker," she reminded him.

She had to buy Papa's men more time. She could dimly see Pipkin edging through the woods. Hucker might be willing to shoot Tristan, but surely he wouldn't allow his own daughter to be hurt.

"My daughter," Hucker repeated in a

wondering voice. He shot Tristan a glance. "You found her?"

Tristan nodded, but his eyes were only for her. The look he gave her was so sweet, so precious, that it made her pulse quicken. Was it love she read in his eyes? Or was that just wishful thinking?

"Lord Olivier and his wife took me in," Zoe said, careful not to mention that they'd made her their daughter. "That was after they buried my mother — the woman you beat so badly."

"I wasn't the one who beat her!" Hucker scowled at George. "It was him."

"You know they're just lying to rattle you," George said nervously.

"Telling the same lie? All of them?" Hucker advanced on him. "For twenty-one years, I prayed that one day she would show up here; that doing your bidding would prove worth it because she returned." He lifted the pistol in his hand. "That's how I know she's dead. Because if she were alive, she would have come back to me by now."

"Don't be a fool, Hucker!" George cried. "Put that gun down."

"You killed her," Hucker said. "You killed the only woman I ever loved!"

"I didn't kill her, damn it!" George swung his pistol around to aim it at Zoe. "But I'll

456

bloody well kill your daughter if you don't put that gun down."

Zoe's heart dropped into her stomach — she had to stop this right now. Beyond George, she could already see Tristan and her father heading for him, and that would surely mean a bloodbath.

She said hastily, "I wouldn't advise aiming guns at me, my lord. Lord Olivier's men have you surrounded. If you so much as nick my arm, you and your men here will all die together."

George's pistol hand wavered. "You're lying."

She raised her voice. "All right, lads! Fire at any of these fools who moves!"

One of the farmers turned to peer at the woods, and got the scythe shot out of his hand for his trouble. He and his fellows started to glance nervously about them. Another shot came from a different side of the woods, and that really spooked them.

Papa took over. "Tell your men to go, Rathmoor, and we'll leave them be. It's over."

When George hesitated, Hucker approached the men. "If you want to see another dawn, boys, you'd best return to your homes. This here is Major Keane. Served in the army. He'd as soon mow you

457

down as look at you."

That was all it took to have them retreating, grumbling among themselves.

"Come back here, you cowards!" George shot into the air, but that only sent them fleeing faster. While he was still glaring after them, Papa lunged forward to wrench the loaded pistol from his other hand.

"Damn you all!" George tossed down the empty one. "You are on *my* land."

His face a vengeful mask, Hucker headed for George. "You killed her. You beat my Drina to death."

"I didn't kill her!" George cried, backing away.

"But you beat her, admit it!" Hucker aimed his pistol at the viscount once more.

"All right, all right!" George said. "But she gave me no choice. She wouldn't get out of the damned carriage!" When a shocked silence fell in the clearing, he thrust out his chin. "She just kept going on and on about her love for you, and how I should give you another chance. How the two of you were meant to be together, if I would just allow you to marry. I couldn't get her to shut up!"

Hucker's face turned thunderous. "So you beat her for it?"

"No! Not for that. The bitch told me there

458

were no other Gypsies between here and York, and I damned well wasn't driving her all the way to York. So I stopped near High-thorpe, and when she wouldn't get out, when she started begging me on the life of her babe not to leave her in a place that hated Gypsies —"

"You beat her," Tristan said coldly. "To get her out of your carriage. A woman with child."

"A Gypsy whore bearing a bastard!" George spat. "Is it right that whores like her and your mother can spawn their by-blows right and left, while my own mother, the sweetest woman in the world, died bearing my traitor of a brother?"

"George," Dom said tersely, "dying is one of the risks of childbearing."

"No," George snapped. "Bearing you was certain death for Mother, and she knew it. But she ignored the doctors who said she shouldn't have any more children." His face filled with hatred as he glared at Tristan. "She couldn't stand that *your* damned mother was stealing Father away from her bit by bit, because Mother wasn't supposed to share his bed."

The color drained from Dom's features. "What are you talking about?"

George scowled at him. "I used to hear

them arguing about it. He told Mother he wouldn't be the cause of her death. That's why he brought that whore back from France."

Dom looked stricken. "George, I'm sorry . . . I had no idea."

George shook with anger now. "Whenever Father was around, Mother was brighter, sweeter. She would sing to me, and things would be normal, and then . . ." He stiffened. "He'd head off to his whore, and the light would go out of her."

The light seemed to go out of George, too. "She must have found some way to get him into her bed, because next thing I knew, she was telling me I was to have a brother. She was so bloody happy that I was sure everything would be good again." His voice hardened. "Until she died *having* my brother."

"Good God," Dom said.

Zoe could only stare at him and Tristan, feeling as stunned as they looked. A look of sympathy flashed briefly across Tristan's face.

Very briefly. Because then he was marching toward George. "You're forgetting that it was *Father* who made the choice to share my mother's bed, *Father* who brought Mother back from France to be his mistress.

And Zoe's mother had nothing to do with any of that — yet you murdered her!"

"Zoe?" George glanced at her. "Your name is Zoe?"

With a curse, Tristan halted.

"You're *Lady* Zoe Keane." George's eyes lit up like those of a shark scenting blood in the water. "Lord Olivier's daughter. And a countess in her own right. At least, until I tell the House of Lords that you're really some Gypsy whore's daughter."

In a flash, Tristan drew a knife from his boot, which he brandished at George. "You say a word to anyone about that," he hissed, "and I will find you and cut you into so many pieces that they'll never know what happened to you."

George, the fool, taunted him. "I take it you have a soft spot for her ladyship. Isn't that sweet? Two by-blows in love. It will make it all the more pleasurable when I expose her as a Gypsy's bastard."

"Then again," Tristan said in a chilling voice, "why wait?" And he was on George, with the knife to his throat.

For the first time that day, George showed fear.

"Tristan, no!" She rushed over to catch his arm. It shook with the force of his fury. "Listen to me. I know how much you hate him, but murdering him solves nothing."

"It solves a great deal for me!"

"You say that in the heat of your anger." She clung desperately to his arm. "But once you've killed an unarmed man, the stain of it will haunt your soul for the rest of your life. He's still your brother."

"Only in blood."

"Yes, but much as I wish it didn't, blood still counts for something in this world." She held on to his arm for all she was worth. "Not to mention that you'll be hanged for it. Is he worth that?"

The pulse throbbed in Tristan's neck, and his arm was so very rigid that she feared he wouldn't heed her.

"Please, my love," she added, "I don't want to see you hang."

It must have been the "my love" that did it, for Tristan's arm went slack. Then he drew the blade away from George's neck. "You're right," he said to Zoe. "He's definitely not worth hanging for."

With a shove, he sent George sprawling on the ground and sheathed his knife.

She threw herself into his arms with a little cry. "Oh, my love, are you all right? He didn't hurt you, did he?"

"No," he said softly, then kissed her with a fierceness that left her gasping.

"That's enough," Papa grumbled. "You're not married yet."

"Listen to the man," Milosh said. "None of that, now."

She and Tristan broke away, laughing.

"Marry!" George picked himself up off the ground. "You think to marry her, bastard? And sit in the House of Lords with your betters? That will never happen. I will —"

"You'll do nothing," Papa said firmly. "A number of witnesses here heard you confess to beating a woman with child nearly to death. Your own men heard you threaten to kill a lord of the realm and your brothers. You lift one hand against me and mine, and I will have you arrested and charged and see you hang. I'll only keep your secrets if you keep mine."

George was quivering, his hands fisted at his sides and a vein throbbing in his forehead.

"It's over, brother," Dom said softly. "Have the good sense to recognize when you've been bested."

"Come, lads," Papa called out as his men emerged from the woods, "let's go home."

Tristan offered her his arm. "Shall we, princess?"

"Yes." She beamed up at him. "Oh, yes,

my love."

Tristan looked as if he was about to say something, but before he could speak, they heard George growl behind them, "You thieving bastard. You are *not* getting away with this!"

The next part happened in a blur. Somehow George wrested the pistol from Hucker and was swinging it toward them, for she heard Hucker cry, "Tristan, watch out! He's got your gun!"

Shoving her aside, Tristan whirled and bent to draw his knife from his boot in one smooth motion. As George steadied his aim, Tristan let the blade fly.

It caught George in the throat.

He dropped the pistol to grab for the knife and wrench it free, sending blood spurting out, coursing down the front of him. He was dead before anyone even reached him.

Tristan stood frozen beside her. Then he said, in a hollow voice, "*Now* it's over."

Several hours later, they were all gathered in Hucker's house. The local authorities had just left. Tristan stood near the window, watching them leave, his face still a rigid mask. Dom sat next to her at a table, and Papa was talking to Hucker.

Zoe was so grateful Papa had been with

them. The minute George had perished, Papa had sprung into action, his military training taking over. It was Papa who'd marshaled them all inside, Papa who'd had the local magistrate summoned, Papa who'd explained to the authorities what had happened.

Papa had persuaded the magistrate that Tristan had acted in self-defense. When his testimony was supported by Hucker, the lord's own man of affairs, the authorities could only accept it. There would still be an inquest, of course, but there was no doubt about the outcome.

And that was partly thanks to Hucker. He must have had a talk with George's men, for not a one of them said anything to gainsay Papa's version of events. No doubt they'd figured out that it wouldn't sit well if it was learned they'd nearly been part of a plot to murder an earl and his daughter, not to mention Lord Rathmoor's heir and his other hated half brother.

At Papa's suggestion, Milosh had left before the magistrate was summoned. A Gypsy at the scene would be blamed even if he hadn't done anything, and no one wanted that. Besides, anything that tied her to her natural parents was to be eradicated.

Because apparently Hucker and Papa had

come to an agreement of sorts, before the authorities arrived. Zoe was to continue as Papa's heir, as Papa's child. The world would never know her as Hucker's daughter. Hucker had assured Papa that he could keep the secret — and ensure that George's men kept the secret as well, to the extent that they knew it — as long as the men all kept their positions under Dom, who was now the new viscount.

Dom had agreed to that readily. As always, Tristan was the brother of his heart; he would do anything for Tristan. Even if it meant keeping Hucker in his employ.

Though Dom didn't seem to mind that possibility too much. As Hucker walked up to them, Dom rose to offer the man his hand. "Thank you for what you did for us. If you hadn't stepped in to help his lordship send those men away, who knows how much blood would have been shed? You saw how few supporters we really had."

Hucker shook his hand. "Didn't matter. His lordship used fear like a club. Fear don't gain you loyalty. It just gets people going along with you to stay safe. Once his lordship asked them to risk their lives, they wasn't going to stick around."

"Fear doesn't gain you loyalty — interesting philosophy," Dom said. "I will keep it in mind now that I am master of Rathmoor Park."

"About that, m'lord." Hucker rubbed the back of his neck. "I was thinking, well . . . you're not going to be wanting me around, what with my connection to George and all that's gone between us."

"You'll always have a place with me," Dom said, an edge to his voice, "if you want it."

"Thank you, sir." Hucker shot Zoe a furtive glance. "But Lord Olivier has offered me a position as his gamekeeper. And I'd like to take it. On account of . . . well . . ."

"I understand."

Zoe caught her breath. She understood why Papa had done it — he wanted Hucker where he could keep an eye on him. But what did Hucker want?

He turned to her next, his hat in his hand. "Don't let Lord Rathmoor's nasty words sit on your mind, m'lady — your mother weren't no whore. She was a fine woman. We wanted to marry, and we would have, too, if not for my stealing. I was just so eager on account of your birth coming on, that I took chances I shouldn't have."

She gave him an encouraging smile through the tears stinging her eyes.

"I know I have no right to you as a father.

467

You've got a fine one right there already, a good man who knows what's what. Not a bully of a lord, like Lord Rathmoor was. And I swear I won't bother you none, or let any of your people know who you are to me. I just want the chance to see you from time to time, you know? But if you don't want me to take the position his lordship has offered —"

"It's fine." She rose and offered him her hand. "You saved the life of my love. You will always have my thanks for that."

Hucker took her hand in a hard grip, his eyes misting over. "And you will always have me. However much you'll take of me."

For a moment she glimpsed what Drina must have seen, a man who hadn't yet been warped into a hard, cynical creature by the manipulations of his master. A man capable of choosing the right path, given another chance.

Then he drew his hand from hers and bobbed his head. "Guess I'd best go tell the viscountess about her husband's death."

As he clapped his hat on his head and headed for the door, Tristan roused from his trance enough to call out, "Hucker!"

Hucker halted to look warily at him.

"Thank you for doing what was right. I will never forget it."

468

Hucker nodded. Then he left.

Tristan faced Zoe, his eyes intent on her, then spoke to Papa and Dom. "Could the two of you give me a moment alone with Zoe?"

"Of course," Dom said. As he passed Tristan, he paused. "You had no choice with George, you know. He would have killed you. Or her ladyship."

"I know."

Papa headed for the door with a glance at her. "Don't be long."

"We won't, Papa."

As Tristan approached her, a wave of dread struck her. Until now, his only words since George's death had been to the magistrate, a clipped recitation of the events, leaving out only the parts about her connection to Hucker.

He looked terribly solemn as he took her hands in his. "It has occurred to me that you are finally free. I'm fairly certain that Hucker will never speak of your past. George can no longer hurt anyone, and Milosh has no reason to stir up trouble. If Keane proves true to his word, then you can marry whomever you please. Your secret is safe. So if you don't wish to marry me —"

She could hardly breathe. "Do you not

469

wish to marry *me* anymore?"

He looked stricken. "Oh, God, no. I mean, yes, of *course* I want to marry you." His gaze was filled with such yearning that it reassured her. "But I will always be a bastard, a former thief, and a man who killed his brother. You deserve better."

She clutched his hands to her chest. "I will always be a bastard and the natural daughter of a rather questionable character. I will always be living a lie, and if you marry me, so will you. So perhaps *you* are the one who deserves better."

"There can be no one better than you," he said with such intensity, it warmed her soul. "I love you, Zoe."

"You . . . you do?"

A smile broke over his face. "How can I not? You're the sun and the moon, the flame to my candle, the bread I need to live. I cannot survive without you."

Her heart felt as if it might burst from her chest. With joy ripping through her, she cupped his head in her hands. "Then we *have* to marry. Because I wouldn't want you to die for lack of me."

With a low moan, he dragged her into his arms and kissed her deeply, sweetly, a promise of many kisses to come.

When he drew back, she whispered, "Do

you realize that if Hucker and Drina had been allowed to marry, you and I would have grown up here together?"

"I hadn't thought of that, but you're right. Clearly we were meant to be together from the beginning." A grin crossed his face. "Though it was probably just as well we *didn't* grow up together. Because somehow, I don't think Hucker would have refrained from killing me if he'd found you in my bed."

His eyes gleamed at her. "And he would have found you there, you know. Because I would have seduced you the moment I saw you turn into a fetching Gypsy princess of eighteen or so."

"Always so sure of yourself," she said archly. Taking his hand, she headed for the door. "But I suspect if I had grown up with a strapping fellow like you, *you* would not have been the one to do the seducing."

When he burst into laughter, she drew him out the door and into her life. Because, as he'd said: one way or another, a princess always got to have whatever she wanted.

EPILOGUE

Winborough, Yorkshire
May 1829

The musicians played beautifully, a smattering of people danced a Scotch reel most enthusiastically, and champagne flowed like a river from a miniature fountain on Winborough's lawn. But the group near the hedges were too absorbed in their argument to pay heed to Winborough's annual Whitsun festival, at which servants, tenants, and lords mingled in merry celebration.

Tristan was very decided in his opinion on the topic and fully expected his brother to agree. "Will you please tell my wife that elder is by far the most effective plant for hedges?"

Zoe, who looked most fetching in a dark blue evening gown, scowled at Dom and Tristan. "I don't care what you think. I wish to try holly. I've heard good reports of its success."

472

Lord Olivier jumped in. "But dear girl, every time we planted holly in the past, it didn't take. It's our cursed Yorkshire soil."

"Nonsense," Dom surprised Tristan by saying. "It's the season you choose for transplanting the seedlings that affects how it grows. Everyone tries to do it in winter, but holly must be transplanted in summer."

Zoe beamed her triumph. "Exactly! I have been trying to tell these two obstinate fellows that very thing, but they're stuck in their ways and will not listen to me."

"I would listen to you more often, princess," Tristan said, "if you didn't always raise the subject when you're dressed in something with dash, like that gown, which shows your fine . . . er . . . figure to full advantage."

Though she self-consciously adjusted her mother's scarlet scarf, which she wore as a fichu, she still scowled at him. "Don't try to distract me with compliments, sir. You just always agree with Papa."

"Not always," Tristan said. "I hate his preference for port over Madeira."

But it was true that the two men agreed more often than not. It was a bit disconcerting. Every time Tristan chafed at the Major's overbearing aristocratic manner, the man went and did something sensible that destroyed another of Tristan's biases.

"I must admit, however, that I have deferred to him on the subject of hedge planting," Tristan went on as Jeremy Keane approached them, "but only because your father showed me his records of his lack of success with it."

"Good God," Keane said, having overheard Tristan, "are you four discussing hedge planting *again*? I swear, you have to be the most boring aristocrats in England." He glanced at Lord Olivier. "Excepting his lordship, who occasionally tells stories about the war."

Dom laughed. "What would *you* have us talk about, Keane?"

"Art? Racing? Women?"

"I'm too old for talk of women," Lord Olivier said.

Tristan slid his arm about his wife's waist. "And I'm too married."

"You most certainly are," Zoe said with a sniff. "And don't you forget it."

Keane turned to Dom. "You're a bachelor, sir. Don't you have any salacious tales of opera dancers with which to entertain me?"

"Dom with an opera dancer?" Tristan chuckled. "That's rich."

Zoe got a gleam in her eye. "Jeremy, ask Dom to tell you about his former fiancée.

The very pretty one who's presently visiting her cousin, his brother's widow, at the dower house on his estate. And who's engaged to another man, yet hasn't married him yet."

"That's not amusing, Zoe," Dom growled.

"I suspect it wasn't meant to be," Tristan said. "Zoe's been spending a bit too much time with our sister, and they're both bent on marrying you off to Jane."

"Run, Manton," Keane drawled. "Run fast and far. There's nothing more dangerous than female matchmakers. I've been dodging them for years."

"Thank God," Tristan said with a heated glance at his wife. "Otherwise, I wouldn't have this fetching armful to warm my bed."

Keane laughed, her father cleared his throat, and Dom rolled his eyes, but Zoe stretched up to kiss him on the cheek — exactly the reaction he'd been looking for.

Aunt Flo approached, clucking her tongue. "What are all you young people standing about for?" She shooed them. "Go dance! For heaven's sake, how are we to get the hoi polloi dancing if you do not?"

With a laugh, Zoe told Tristan, "Perhaps we *should* take advantage of the fact that they are now playing a waltz."

"Absolutely." Tristan squeezed her waist.

"Dance with me, princess."

"That's all?" she teased. "Just a dance?"

"For now," he murmured, delighted that she'd caught his reference to their very first dance.

As soon as he'd drawn her off, he added in an undertone, "You were hoping for more, were you?"

Her smile turned coy. "Absolutely. But later."

He gave a mock sigh. "Oh, very well." Though they hadn't quite reached the other dancers, he took her in his arms and began to waltz there, so he and she could talk more freely.

It was a glorious night. The stars glittered their approval, and the moon hung high in the cloudless sky. It accentuated Tristan's impression that he was living a dream.

Because, in truth, he was. His entire family was together again in England after all these years. Indeed, they were all here tonight — Lisette and Max taking their first few days away from the baby, and Dom enjoying a short respite from his responsibilities as viscount.

More important, Tristan finally had a real home, a place in the world. He had Zoe to tease him, teach him about estate management, warm his bed . . . to love him. And in some months he would have a child to dote on and worry about and love, too. What more could a man ask for?

"Did you notice Hucker dancing with your lady's maid?" Tristan asked Zoe.

"I did, indeed."

"Do you mind?"

"No. She's a lovely woman, and he deserves a bit of happiness after all these years without Drina, don't you think?"

"I suppose. I still have trouble thinking of him as anything other than George's lackey. Even though he has proven to be a model gamekeeper."

They always referred to Hucker and Drina by their names. For her, "Papa" and "Mama" would forever be the Keanes. But sometimes Tristan caught her in conversation with the gamekeeper and knew that they were speaking of the life that might have been.

Hucker had been true to his word. Not a breath of the truth about Zoe had risen anywhere in the county or beyond. It helped that none of George's men had really been able to make out the conversation that night.

It also helped that Dom now paid their salaries and had given them a generous raise, one he could ill afford. George had left the estate in dire straits, and Dom had his hands full trying to keep it going.

Especially since he was still involved with Manton's Investigations. Victor had taken over most of it and was hiring replacements for Tristan and Dom, though the brothers still helped from time to time when needed. But Tristan found himself less interested in that by the day. His home and his work were here now, and he couldn't be more content.

Fortunately, Keane was still adamant that he had no desire whatsoever to be Lord Olivier's heir, so they had nothing to worry about on that score.

Which reminded him . . . "When the hell is Keane returning to America?"

"Actually, I'm not sure." She glanced over to where Keane was deep in conversation with the duke, who'd gone from being an admirer of Keane's art to being a friend and advisor. "Does it seem to you that perhaps he's running from something at home?"

"I don't know, and I don't care. His exhibition ended a month ago."

Zoe laughed. "He's only at Winborough for a week this time, so why do you care if he stays in England longer? Does he annoy you that much?"

"He certainly did when he visited in April to paint Milosh. Those two did *not* get on. Milosh thought Keane was a pompous oaf, and Keane found Milosh 'too ordinary.' I spent half my time playing mediator before Keane happened upon a more apt subject for his depressing paintings — some village ratcatcher with an interesting face and a bloody net."

She laughed. "I had no idea! Why didn't you tell me?"

Tristan scowled. "You'd just learned you might be bearing my son. I didn't want to upset you."

"Your daughter, you mean," she said with a grin. "And it wouldn't have upset me. Jeremy would get on anyone's nerves after a while, and Uncle Milosh is cranky on the best of days." She glanced about. "Speaking of him, is he here?"

"Somewhere." The Whitsun celebration was traditionally held for everyone involved with the spring planting, even Romany workers. "He said they're breaking camp in the morning. Now that the planting is done, they're going north to attend one of the larger horse fairs."

Her face fell. "I was hoping they'd spend the whole summer. And then winter in York after the harvest."

"You know they prefer to winter in London," he said softly. "Besides, it's one thing to have them camp here and help with the planting or the harvest. Though some villagers grumbled, no one found it suspicious. But if you go hieing off to a Gypsy encampment in York —"

"I know, I know," she grumbled. "Besides, I can see him once or twice when we go to London for the season."

"For the *season*? But you're having a baby!"

"I'll have had her by then. And I'll want to show her off."

"Him," he corrected her.

It was a running joke between them that she wanted a female heir and he wanted a male, but in truth he just wanted a healthy child. And for his wife to survive the birth.

He'd never forgotten George's terrible tale of Lady Rathmoor choosing to share their father's bed, despite knowing that having another child could kill her. It hadn't negated the horrible things George had done, but it had helped to explain what had warped him beyond redemption.

It also explained why he'd hated Tristan so. And why he'd found it so hard to love Dom unreservedly, the way Tristan did.

"You need to stop tormenting Dom over Jane," Tristan told Zoe. "He has a great deal to handle right now."

"Well, so does Jane," Zoe said with a sniff,

having instantly taken up Lisette's cause once she'd met Dom's former fiancée. "George's widow, for one."

"Yes, I heard that she is having a difficult time with her husband's death. Hard enough to hear that George was killed while trying to murder his half brother, but then to have some of his unsavory deeds exposed afterward . . ."

Zoe stared earnestly at him. "Did George really force those tenants from their homes and break their leases, as they claim?"

"It appears so. George threw his weight around with a lot of people. And now those people are all coming out of the woodwork, trying to get a piece of the estate. They know that Dom won't blackmail them into silence, the way George did."

"What a legal nightmare," she said dolefully.

"Dom will sort it all out, don't you worry. Not for nothing did he train as a barrister."

They danced a moment in silence, intimately entwined, swept up in the music and their thoughts.

"Do you realize how very lucky we've been?" he said softly.

"Very lucky," she agreed. "Or perhaps just fated to be together, as that Romany fortune-teller said."

He eyed her skeptically. "The one who said you were born of secrets and sadness?"

"Yes. And I was, you know. She also said that it would either destroy my future or lead me to greatness."

He snorted. "She gave you two opposite possibilities, so one of them was likely to prove true. And that has nothing to do with us being fated to be together, anyway."

"Ah, but I never told you all of it." Zoe positively smirked at him, a bad habit she'd picked up from God only knew where. "She said that a handsome gentleman with eyes like the sky and hair like a raven's wing would come into my life."

Though that gave him pause, he wasn't about to let *her* know it. "That describes probably a third of the men in England," he said dryly. When she frowned, he softened his tone. "Much as I like the idea of our being fated to be together, my love, I wouldn't base it on some fortune-teller's spurious predictions."

"There's more." She gazed up at him, her eyes soft and warm in the moonlight. "The woman also said, 'If you let him, he will become the hand of your vengeance.' What do you say to that?"

A chill passed down his spine. "That was just a lucky guess."

"I suppose you're right. She also said, 'If you let him, he will shatter your heart.' And you certainly haven't done that." She cast him an arch glance. "Though you very nearly did, before I convinced you to give yours to me, instead."

"I would never have shattered your heart," he said. "Because when a man is entrusted with the most precious thing on earth, he knows it. And he treats it with the love and respect it deserves."

He bent to brush his lips over hers. "Besides," he said in his best seductive manner, "if I'd shattered your heart, you would never have let me back into your bed — and I'm not fool enough to risk that."

A laugh sputtered out of her. "You, sir, are a scoundrel in married man's clothing."

He grinned. "The better to seduce you with, my lady." He lowered his mouth to hers. "The better to seduce you with."

AUTHOR'S NOTE

Whenever you read about Lady Somewhere (the Countess of Somewhere), you're reading about a woman with a courtesy title given to her because she married Lord Somewhere (the Earl of Somewhere). But, once in a great while, titles were handed down to women (according to the rules governing the title when it was first established), and that meant that the daughter could inherit the title. That's why poor Zoe is in a pickle. Because *she* will be the one inheriting the title. Her problems would be similar if she were a son who was not the legitimate blood relation of the noble father. One had to be both a blood relation and legitimate to inherit a title and an entailed estate.

So adoption wasn't an option. Until the early twentieth century, there was no such legal construct in English law. A couple could certainly take in a little boy, give him their name, leave him their unentailed property, and in every way treat the boy like a son. But he could not inherit the father's title or entailed estate. There was no legal way to accomplish that . . . except by lying to everyone, as the Keanes do in my book.

As for the Romany, it is difficult to research them in our period because many of the sources from that time are biased against them. But I did find a few that seemed evenhanded, and there is some recent material on the Web written by the Romany themselves. The term "Gypsy," while used a great deal during the Regency, wasn't what the Rom called themselves, even then. It's misleading, because it tries to encompass the Romany, Scottish Travelers, Irish Travelers, tinkers, and a number of other British nomadic groups, all of which are culturally and ethnically different. And yes, the Romany often did take houses for the winter. Given the vagaries of English winters, that's no surprise!